Identity Crisis

by Scott Bicheno

One man's search for meaning in a world that's losing its mind.

To Katty, Jack and Izzy.

Thanks to all those who generously provided their support and encouragement, especially Liz and Hugh for their sensitive and insightful feedback.

The ego is not master in its own house – Sigmund Freud

The most basic question is not what is best, but who shall decide what is best – Thomas Sowell

You're so vain, you probably think this song is about you – Carly Simon

Chapter 1 – Insurrection

The sheer scale of losses astounded even the most jaded financiers. For a short time the UK government had been completely committed to the bailout of Clark's Bank. The 153-year-old institution, together with its nightmarish portfolio of ludicrous loans, idiotic investments and heinous hedges, had become public property. Its feted CEO, Sir Raymond Payshus, had gone into hiding, so when he accepted an invitation to a radio interview it came as a considerable surprise, not least to the show's producers.

"...but we need speculate no longer because Sir Raymond Payshus is sitting in front of me right now," said Iain Tegritie, presenter of the morning current affairs radio programme. "Sir Ray, can you please explain what happened at Clark's?"

"I think you've already summarised it quite well Iain," said Payshus. "Clark's invested heavily in the US subprime mortgage market and, following its collapse, was hours from insolvency. Rather than accept the loss of control and shareholder value that would have resulted from a government bailout we came to a mutually beneficial arrangement with Mr Kleptov, which enabled him to move substantial funds to a location more convenient for him, and in the process resolve our extraordinary cash-flow challenges. We, in turn, took the opportunity to try to recoup our losses by investing the majority of our fresh funds in areas we considered to have the best risk/reward profile at the time: Irish commercial property, Greek government bonds and Dutch tulip bulbs. The rest we kept on deposit in a basket of Icelandic banks as they were offering the best interest rates at the time."

"And how did that all pan out?" asked Tegritie.

"We lost the lot," said Payshus, causing a yelp of incredulous laughter to erupt from somewhere in the back of the studio.

"So then you came crawling, cap-in-hand, to the government, looking for a bailout," said Tegritie, as the source of the noise was led, still whimpering, away. "I can't believe they didn't laugh you out of the room."

"Why would they do that? It was the Chancellor who introduced me to Mr Kleptov in the first place, on his yacht, lovely vessel, have you ever been on her? No, I don't suppose you have. Anyway, Chancellor Leech effectively brokered the original deal and – this is a funny story – as he was finalising the bailout, he joked that if my bonus had been based on losing, rather than making money, I would now be the richest man in the world!"

The anecdote was met with stony silence.

"I guess you had to be there," said Tegritie, eventually. "But since you mention bonuses, is it safe to assume you won't be getting one this year?"

"Far from it old chap. I'm contractually entitled to a bonus based on turnover, not profit, and I can see no reason not to accept the full award of just under two hundred million pounds."

"You fucking what!?"

"Earned every penny of it. Tricky business, banking; pay peanuts and you get monkeys."

"You surely can't expect to get away with that."

"Already have, I'm afraid. Rather more zeros on my bank balance this morning than there were yesterday, I'm delighted to say. I wonder how much Manchester United costs these days, can't have Johnny Foreigner having everything his own way in the football, now can we?"

"But even if the government isn't willing to do anything, the people won't stand for this."

"And what, precisely, do you think they can do about it? The people have no influence, no power, nothing significant players like me don't choose to give them, and I'm tired of pretending it's otherwise. Those few remaining members of the public who still think their vote counts for anything get to choose between candidates with the collective IQ of a boiled potato. A group of people so incapable of higher thought that we barely have to bribe them anymore."

"We?"

"The individuals who run things of course, us: the board members, the oligarchs as you doubtless call us, the money. We can pull the plug on any career, political or otherwise, whenever we want. That's the real power Iain, patronage. Those people you think are in charge were put there by us and they know it. They do what we tell them, and we let them keep their positions. Everyone's a winner."

"Everyone?"

"Oh, are you still bleating about *the people* Iain? For God's sake grow up. They're too lobotomised by cheap alcohol, reality TV and internet porn to even notice. Somewhere in the murk of their plebeian subconscious they know the world is far too complicated for them to even begin to understand and they're more than happy to leave the running of it to their betters. For far too long we've tried to maintain the illusion of fairness, equality and democracy but, quite frankly, we can't be bothered anymore. We run things, you do what you're told, that's just the way it is and it's time people started looking facts in the face. Now, if there's nothing else, I'm due for a meeting with someone of infinitely greater consequence than you or any of your audience so I must bid you good day."

As Payshus stood up and left the studio Tegritie was left, possibly for the first time in his life, speechless. Only after his producer shouted, "For fuck's sake say something!" into his earpiece did he recover some composure.

"Well there you have it ladies and gentlemen: the unvarnished truth," said Tegritie. "A global network of oligarchs is apparently running everything and is no longer inclined to even pretend otherwise. The question is what, if anything, can the rest of us do about it?"

Before the interview even concluded Twitter was seething, unified under the hashtag #doingsomething, and calling for militant action. Even satirical tangents such as #Payshuspoints, in which Twitter users awarded points to the most amoral, self-serving suggestions, often involving cruelty to young domestic animals, served only to fuel the livid consensus. A Facebook group called 'Doing something' emerged soon after and topped a million members by the end of the day. A video recording of the interview was released on YouTube and briefly supplanted a clip of a cat being made to look like it was singing a Taylor Swift song at the top of the trending list.

Fanned by messages of support from across the world, the flames of indignation spread rapidly as people of all perspectives united in revulsion, not so much at their own impotence, but at having their noses rubbed in it so cruelly. If his aim had been to crush the last vestiges of defiance from the general population, Payshus had achieved the exact opposite. By spelling out to people just how docile they had become, he spurred them into action. The first 'Doing Something' mass demonstration took place in central London within a week and was followed by daily iterations across the country. Being told they were powerless gave people the motivation they needed to assert whatever power they *could* muster. Within a week of the interview a wave of demonstrations, civil disobedience and criminality spread across the country. Branches of major banks were vandalised, the City of London was ablaze and otherwise law-abiding people stopped paying their bills. Civil society was being brought to its knees in what was soon labelled the 'Payshus Insurrection' by the British press which, shockingly, declined to use the '-gate' suffix to label a major scandal for the first time since 1972.

At first the UK government attempted to placate its citizens by rushing through platitudinous pieces of legislation such as a penny off the cost of a pint, a new subsidy for open-air music festivals, and the commencement of an inquiry into whether or not Sir Payshus should have his knighthood revoked. But these were rightly interpreted as further evidence of elite contempt for the population and only served to make things worse. One of the gestures, however, had consequences far greater than any of the politicians who commissioned it could possibly have conceived.

The 'Destructive Greed' inquiry was originally intended to channel public ire more narrowly towards the financial sector, but the inquisitor broke with tradition and actually did some real inquiring. In their desperation to sell the report as truly independent, the government made the mistake of appointing someone who actually was. Luther Martin was given just two weeks to produce the report, partly due to the urgent need for something to appease the baying mobs and partly because it had been made explicitly clear what was expected. The inquiry was supposed to conclude, essentially, that shit happens, especially when bankers get too greedy, and to recommend measures to be put in place to mitigate the negative effects of such shit happening in future.

Martin may have got the memo, but if so he ignored it, recognising it as a once-in-a-lifetime opportunity to actually do something. He identified an insatiable desire for ever-greater revenue and profit as one of the key factors in bringing about the collapse of the Western free-market economies, but he wasn't distracted by talk of capitalism versus socialism. He observed it was individuals, not systems that created the kind of imbalances responsible for the current crisis, and insisted it was no more constructive to punish a banker for seeking profit than it was to punish an athlete for trying to win, or a celebrity for showing off. It was in their nature and it was that very nature which, to a large extent, compelled them to choose their career path in the first place.

Just as some bankers seek to bend the rules to increase their profits, so athletes sometimes use drugs to gain a competitive advantage and many celebrities exploit their fame while bemoaning intrusions into their privacy. Greed isn't necessarily good, deduced Martin, but it is natural and, as countless failed social experiments had proven, it is the main driver of individual productivity and, therefore, of collective wealth. What fascinated him was not regular greed, but the mega-greed practiced by the elite. What drove people who already had more wealth than they and their extended families could ever count, let alone spend, to seek yet more? Martin was convinced the root of the problem lay there.

He concluded the cause of all kinds of socially destructive behaviour was an underlying need to compete, to dominate, and above all to win on the part of those concerned. In short, the nature of their personalities meant they were never at peace, never satisfied, and were compelled perpetually to strive for more. If, Martin proposed, people of this type could be identified and kept away from positions that channelled this flaw into socially destructive outcomes, it should be possible to ensure there would never be a repeat of the current crisis.

The Destructive Greed Report concluded with a recommendation that amounted to the greatest social engineering experiment in living memory, which the desperate government rushed through Parliament into law as the Simpson-Oxford Act. Every UK citizen would have their psyche screened through a combination of brain scans, interviews, questionnaires and observation, with the results quantified. The resulting psychological profile would then be delivered to every UK citizen in the form of an 'Id Card,' which they would be legally obliged to carry with them at all times. By making every individual's psychological profile available for all to see, informed judgments could be made regarding their suitability for a given role. Not only would this prevent pathologically competitive people from damaging wider society, so the theory went, it would also create the opportunity to redirect their insatiable drives in a more socially benign direction.

Chapter 2 – Id

As he rested his head on the top of the office water cooler, Dave Dalston regretted the necessity of getting drunk whenever the football was on. Thursday hangovers were not unfamiliar to him and, while being far from ideal, they were at least an improvement on Monday, Tuesday or Wednesday ones. The positives ended there, however, as this one was especially punishing, brought on by an aggressively zealous approach to drinking unjustified by, or perhaps as a consequence of, the uneventful game.

While performing the all-too-familiar drinking session post-mortem, in which he tried first to recall, then mitigate, his more odious drunken acts, Dalston remembered the main reason he had taken a run-up at the beers the previous night: the letter. It read: "You have been processed and will receive your Id Card shortly." but there was a cold, officious tone to it that made him feel especially uneasy. So he did what he usually did when stressed, or jubilant, or bored, or awake, and went to the pub. A quick survey of his mates and regulars when he arrived revealed a lightness of spirit he could only long for, so he made a calculated decision to get shit-faced and, once more, his problems magically disappeared.

But the next day they were back and had brought their siblings paranoia, nausea and self-loathing with them to join the fun. There was also their distant cousin: the email from the boss marked 'High Importance' and requesting 'A quick word.' Since there was no precedent for this quick word to consist of anything along the lines of: "Hi Dave, just wanted to say top effort. Your work, appearance, office banter and all-round contribution are of the highest order, so well played mate, keep it up. In fact, here's fifty quid to go and get off your tits at lunchtime," Dalston braced himself for the prospect of his day degenerating from crap to apocalyptic.

"Hi MJ, what can I help you with?" he said, in the jaunty, wide-eyed, overcompensating way of the self-consciously hungover, as he entered his boss's office.

"Sit down Dave," said Mike Johnson, head of trading at Gold & Mackenzie, without looking up. "You are, I hope, aware of the need for Gold & Mackenzie to respond vigorously to the changes brought about by the Simpson-Oxford Act?"

"Too fucking right, mate. What's that all about, eh?"

This was apparently not the response Johnson was hoping for. He sighed heavily, placed the palms of his hands gently together and bowed his head until the tips of his index fingers touched the end of his nose, as if praying for divine intervention. "Well, it's all about changing the direction society is heading in, as a matter of fact," said Johnson.

Dalston belatedly realised this was not the time for flippant rhetorical questions, so he did his best to reflect Johnson's earnest body language.

"Don't cup your chin like that Dave, you're not a bloody philosopher – quite the opposite in fact," said Johnson. "Just try to listen to what I'm saying. The Simpson-Oxford Act is very important. Things keep getting arsed up and this is an opportunity to prevent it happening again, but it requires everyone to commit, even – actually, especially – you."

Dalston quickly removed what he mistakenly believed to be a pensively arranged cluster of fingers from his chin. Now acutely aware of the offending hand, he tried to find a use for it that wouldn't antagonise his boss.

"Have you lost something? No? Well stop groping yourself man, it's disturbing," remonstrated Johnson. "Now, where was I? Oh yes, changing the world. Let me fill you in on some of the finer points of the Act that may have escaped your otherwise exhaustive research. It has been conclusively proven that most irrational decisions are made as a result of base impulses such as pride, competitiveness, vanity, and so on. 'No shit,' you may be thinking, perhaps closely followed by 'so what?' Well throughout history nobody really had a problem with all this willy-waving, figuring it was just what being a human was all about.

"But the thing is, we actually have been suppressing those urges for thousands of years, which, along with an inability to lick our own genitalia, is what separates us from the animals. So if we can wear clothes, use tools and resolve minor disputes without clubbing each other over the head, then why can't we conquer this final obstacle to man's enduring, uninterrupted happiness, the unshackled ego? That question was largely left to academics and other self-appointed moral guardians to mull over until the Payshus Insurrection brought things to a head."

The lecture continued for several more minutes, with Johnson choosing to interpret Dalston's hungover cold sweats and dry-mouthed unease as evidence of his message getting through. In spite of himself, and partly in a bid to moderate the pain Johnson's increasingly animated diatribe was causing his dehydrated brain, Dalston reflected on the infamous Payshus radio interview with a fresh perspective. This might actually be a big deal, he mused, but was nonetheless relieved when Johnson seemed to be coming to his conclusion.

"The good news for you and me, Dave, is they're not going to try some infantile shit like 'banning greed,' far from it, in fact," said Johnson. "It looks like the people in charge of thinking about things like this have accepted that the key to a compliant, productive population is to at least let people feel they're pursuing their ambitions, which usually focus on the accumulation of cash. The damage was done by people who already had loads but were nonetheless insatiable in their quest to acquire yet more. That, Dave, is pure ego – the ultimate pissing contest – and it's ruining things for the rest of us, who ask nothing more than a Ferrari or two, perhaps a yacht, maybe even a minor sporting franchise, to keep us happy.

"Now, the reason I've taken the time to explain this is that a lot of us, even geniuses like you, are going to lose our jobs over this. It's no good going to all the trouble of giving people Id Cards unless you're going to use them, and priority number one is to make an example of 'greedy bankers.' Which means we've seriously got to keep our heads down and pretend to be good citizens for a while, capiche?"

"I hear you boss, you've got nothing to worry about with me," said Dalston.

"If only that were true Dave, if only," sighed Johnson. "Your idea of keeping your head down is doing two lines in a row. Do you even remember what you got up to last night?"

"Erm, yeah. Me and the lads had a few cheeky ones and ended up at a club. Nothing special."

"So you don't remember stopping a policewoman on Tottenham Court Road and offering her a hundred quid to get her kit off?"

Dalston winced as he was finally confronted with the source of his lurking paranoia and started to get flashbacks of the incident in question.

"If you're going to try to stuff a handful of coke-laced twenties down the top of a female copper, Dave, it's probably best not to chuck her your business card too in case, and I quote: 'you get bored of being a rug-muncher,' don't you think?"

"Oh shit, I didn't, did I? Bollocks, I'm really sorry boss."

"So you fucking will be if that sort of thing ever happens again. The copper in question wanted us to sack you, but that's exactly the kind of publicity we don't need right now. So the police chief persuaded her to let it go and his re-election fund is looking a lot healthier as a consequence. But it's the last time we'll bail you out Dave. I suggest you stay well out of trouble for a while, is that clear?"

"Crystal, boss."

"Now go home and pull yourself together. You're no use in your current state anyway; I'm getting pissed just being in the same room as you."

***

Another brown envelope awaited Dalston on his doormat, addressed to 'Mr D. Canine-Dalston,' which he concluded was clearly a piss-take by a government not content with merely sucking the joy out of life. Wincing, he decided to get it over and done with and find out what horrors lay therein straight away.

Dear Mr Canine-Dalston,

Please find enclosed your Id Card. As a result of recent screening your psyche has been measured according to four primary categories, the score for each of which is the average of four secondary categories. Your new surname suffix is the zoomorphic adjective associated with the primary category you scored highest in. Please carry your Id Card with you at all times, as failure to do so is a criminal offense. You will be contacted shortly regarding any adjustments required.

Appetite – Canine: 8

- *Ambition: 8*
- *Libido: 8*
- *Greed: 7*
- *Hedonism: 9*

Aggression – Simian: 5.5

- *Competitiveness: 8*
- *Anger: 3*
- *Assertiveness: 5*
- *Control: 6*

Anxiety – Feline: 6.5

- *Fear: 7*

- *Conscience: 4*

- *Pessimism: 6*

- *Vanity: 9*

Affection – Delphine: 6

- *Optimism: 7*

- *Sensuality: 7*

- *Empathy: 4*

- *Honesty: 6*

You can find the answers to any further questions you may have at the following website: idformation.gov.uk/faq.

Sincerely,

Susan Percilious

Permanent Undersecretary for Personality Monitoring

Ministry of Optimisation

HM Government

"Canine? So I'm officially a fucking dog now?" Dalston said to himself and continued muttering what bollocks it all was as he made a cup of tea and switched on the radio. Tegritie was on again and he liked him, not because he gave much of a toss about current affairs, but because the sound of some poor sap getting humiliated live, for his entertainment, tended to cheer him up.

"...and that's just the sort of right-wing attitude you'd expect from the Minister," said a politician Dalston had never heard of.

"Define 'right wing'," said Tegritie.

"Excuse me?"

"You just described the minister's attitude as 'right wing'; I'd like you to define that term, if you will."

"With all due respect Iain, you've been a political journalist for 30 years, I'd kind of assumed you knew what it meant."

"I know what it means to me, but I'd like to know what you mean by it."

"OK, well, the term 'right wing' covers a lot of issues, of course, and is, essentially, defined, as it were, as the set of political views and positions to the right of the political spectrum."

"So your definition of 'right wing' is… 'right wing.' That doesn't really help; can you try to expand the definition so it's not entirely circular?"

"Erm, OK then, right wing views are defined as those in opposition to left wing ones."

"I see, so maybe you can define left wing for us then?"

"To be frank Iain, when I accepted your invitation to come on this programme I didn't expect to be subjected to some kind of semantical Spanish Inquisition."

"Nobody does, but you did expect to be asked questions, surely, and that's my question. But maybe I wrong-footed you, so let me try another angle: Is the Labour Party left wing?"

"Of course, yes"

"And are you a member of the Labour Party?"

"You're on fire Iain – spot on again!"

"So, therefore, you would describe yourself as left wing?"

"Yes, as you well know."

"Since that is how you define yourself, politically at least, you must surely have a pretty clear idea what the term at least implies. So, I will ask you once more, please define left wing for us."

"Fine: to be left wing is to believe in fairness."

"Ah. OK. Great. Well, time constraints and my own flagging morale make me disinclined to ask you to define 'fairness.' You'd probably say it means 'left wing.' But can I therefore assume, from your earlier answer, that you think being right wing is to believe in unfairness?"

"Yes."

"So, then, your definition of right wing is 'unfair'?"

"I, ah, suppose so, yes."

"We got there eventually didn't we? And by revealing that your political development peaked at pre-adolescent and has regressed since, you've spared me the ordeal of having to interview you any further on the grounds that I'm more likely to get a sensible response from a pot plant. Thank you and good day."

"Hold on a minute, you can't talk to me like that."

"I just did. Now I'm sure you've got all sorts of important business to arse up, so please don't let me delay you any longer."

"You haven't heard the last of this Tegritie; I'm going to make you regret the day you ever met me."

"Sir, you can consider that ambition already achieved."

Chapter 3 – Issues

Reinvigorated by tea, schadenfreude and a feverish snooze on the sofa, Dave Dalston decided to celebrate the departure of his hangover with a return to the pub to meet his three closest friends. After reflecting, with his customary surprise, on how well the first pint was going down, he steered the conversation straight to the Id Card.

"So it turns out I'm Dave Canine-Dalston now – a dog! What about you guys?"

"No way, I'm a dog too," said Jack Morrison. "I don't mind it though; kind of makes me sound posh, having a double-barrelled name."

"Everyone's got a double-barrelled name now Jack, so how does that make you posh?"

"I'm not saying I'm posh, I just like the sound of it. Is that alright?"

"I'm Simian, and that's blatantly fucking racist," said Albert Blake.

"You think everything's racist Al," said Morrison. "Remember when they announced a black-out during the Insurrection and you thought they were deporting people of a tanned persuasion?"

"I never said that Jack, I just don't see why they've got to bring black into it."

"It was to protect people, you tool – telling them to turn out the lights so their houses wouldn't get attacked. That's just the colour things go when there's no light. What do you want them to say: 'ethnic-out'?"

"Fuck off, I'm just saying, that's all. Anyway, if they're not racist how come they're calling me a monkey? Answer that Stephen Hawking."

"Because you're a cheeky cunt."

"I can explain," interrupted Nick Georgiou, "which I wouldn't have to if you'd read the shit that came with your Id Card."

"Here we go," said Blake, rolling his eyes and slumping in his chair.

"Your id is the most basic, fundamental part of your psyche – the bit you're born with – and those tests we all had to do were so the Department of Optimisation could work out what makes us tick and give us marks out of ten. The reason you're now called Simian-Blake is because the one of the 'Four As' – appetite, aggression, anxiety and affection – you scored most highly on was aggression, and that's the animal label they've given to the category that represents your most feral inclinations, not because they're in any physical way comparing you to a monkey."

"Although, now that you mention it..." said Dalston.

"Yeah, very funny Scooby," said Blake. "But I reckon those tests were just for show – they decided to call me Simian as soon as I walked through the door, and with my new surname people don't even need to look at me to know I'm black."

"Your surname already said that Al, you just pronounced it wrong," sniggered Morrison.

"Oh great, Scrappy's getting involved too, how about I change your name to Jack No-Teeth-Morrison?" said Blake.

"There's a simple test Al," sighed Georgiou, "are all black people now called Simian? No. Are there some white people called Simian? Yes. So stop being such a paranoid, attention-seeking dick and chill the fuck out."

"So what's your new name then, Nick Doner-Kebab?" said Blake.

"Nice to see your anti-racism campaign is still going strong Al. No, I'm now known as Nick Delphine-Georgiou, if you must know, because I'm so sensitive, innit."

"Sounds like a bird's name if you ask me, so fair enough," said Blake.

"OK, if you ladies have finished, what I want to know is: what's the point of all this?" said Dalston. "I know they've got to do something after the Insurrection, but I don't see how calling us all dogs, monkeys and dolphins is going to change anything."

"What worries me even more than that, Dave, is what has already changed," said Georgiou. "They would never have dared try shit like this even a year ago. Governments love using things like wars and disasters to increase their power over the rest of us. They always call them 'emergency powers,' but they never let go of them once the supposed emergency is over. This is a whole new level though. Nobody's going to use these moronic new surnames, but the fact that the government is even giving it a go is seriously fucked up."

"What are you saying Nick?" said Blake.

"I'm saying now the government has a database with a psychological profile of everyone and, what's more, they're forcing us to carry that profile around with us. Never mind racism, mate, this could be the start of discrimination on a whole new level. I can see it now: it was greedy bankers who got us into this mess, so just make sure bankers aren't greedy anymore by banning all Canines from senior roles at banks. And while you're at it stop Simians from being teachers or coppers in case they go around battering people."

"Or, on the flip side, stop Delphines from being coppers in case they go around giving criminals the benefit of the doubt the whole time."

"Maybe, although that would actually be quite handy for me. But it's beside the point. Who's to judge which kind of psyche is best suited to what kind of job? Is that any better than discriminating between people over race, or sex, or looks, or anything?"

"That's a good point," said Morrison, "how come they don't measure other stuff on this Id Card?"

"Because they're not interested in that stuff now," said Georgiou. "Egotyping is the 'in' thing and all that currently matters to the 'we know best' types are your basic drivers – the psychological make-up you were born with. The Four As are supposed to represent our four key primal urges and they should really be called The Four Fs: Fight, Flight, Feed and Fuck. At best these egotypes are crude caricatures: I'm some kind of touchy-feely poof, you're a nutcase Al, and those two are selfish cunts. OK, there might be some truth in all of that, but we're also other things. We all know what I do for a living – that's not generally viewed as very honest is it? And yet they've given me nine-out-of-ten for honesty."

"I don't know mate, that gear certainly did what it said on the tin last night," said Dalston.

"Have I ever let you down? So I guess it depends on how you view honesty, but I'm pretty sure 'doesn't rip his mates off in drug deals' is not the official government definition. Anyway, at worst this new way of classifying people is going to get factional and nasty, I reckon."

"Alright, sorry to steal your thunder Nick, I can see you're on a roll here, but do you think you could tell us sometime before last orders what 'You will be contacted shortly regarding any adjustments required,' is supposed to fucking mean?" Dalston replied.

"That's what I've been trying to tell you, man; it's all going to go Pete Tong. They clearly want to start mucking about with – or 'adjusting' – people and that only ever ends in tears. I don't know what they're going to do, but this Insurrection has given a few smart-arses the license to play God, and that scares the fuck out of me."

"Nick, man, you're never happy," said Morrison. "You're always moaning about how shit everything is, that it's not what you know but who you know and all that. Now we finally get the chance to put things right and you've got a face like a slapped arse. Cheer up for fuck's sake."

"Point taken Jack, but for me the answer is less control, not more. Now, instead of people getting top jobs because of where they went to school, they'll get them because some self-appointed expert has decided their Id Card is a good match. I refuse to be happy just because we're 'doing something'."

"Well, we've got to try some shit, mate, because things are fucked as they are. What happened to the idealistic bloke I used to know? Your answer seems to be to do nothing – very fucking radical."

"Hitler was idealistic Jack, so were Stalin, Mao, Pol Pot and countless other genocidal nutters. I've grown up and now realise that power concentrated in the wrong hands is worse than doing nothing. If I believe in anything, it's the market."

"Yeah, I'm sure you do a great trade there, ripping off teenagers and tourists Nick, but I fail to see how shopping for bongs, beads and Che Guevara t-shirts is going to solve anything."

"Not Camden Market you muppet, *the* market, the *free* market, the only place real change happens, and the only place real democracy happens."

"Real democracy? What are you talking about?" said Blake. "Real democracy is when you vote for who you want running the country, not when you go down the shops. The 'market' you're suddenly so fond of is run by exactly the kind of people everyone suddenly thinks we should get rid of. Right now the market is not the solution Nick, it's the fucking problem."

"Your real democracy means we're forced to pick between two equally useless sets of twats once every five years and you call that choice? Politicians are no different to the fat-cats everyone is demonising. They're in it for themselves, but rather than selling us actual stuff, they sell us promises none of them have any intention of honouring. They spend most of their time in power worrying about the next election and they know that if they bribe enough people with handouts they'll get voted back in, but they also know the one thing they can't be seen to do is increase taxes."

"I think I know where this is headed," said Morrison, "so how do they get hold of all this extra cash then Nick?"

"I'm pleased you asked," smiled Georgiou. "They borrow from the banks and have to keep borrowing ever more from them to pay the interest on previous loans and to keep bribing voters. Just like I'm suddenly all nice and respectful to Jack when I want a few quid from him, the government is hardly going to risk pissing-off the banks it has made itself so dependent on, so it lets them do what they want."

"Hold on," said Blake. "So you're saying the banks only got us into this mess because the politicians let them, and the reason they let them is they want to keep borrowing money from the banks? That sounds like bollocks to me mate; the government can just take money from the banks if it wants, or at least print as much as it needs."

"What do you think money is Al? It's nothing by itself – just a token, an IOU you get in return for your labour. With money you get to exchange your labour for someone else's, but as soon as you sever that connection it loses value. That's why places like Zimbabwe and Venezuela have crazy inflation. Indiscriminately printing money just serves to devalue it because it's not attached to anything concrete."

"Alright Adam Smith, thanks for the lecture, but it would be nice if you got to the point while my pint has still got some bubbles in it, and I'm not talking about your relatives."

"Wealth itself is not so much the possession of money, but the spending of it. There's not much point in being a millionaire if you just sit on the cash, live in a shit-hole and eat beans on toast every day. You need to spend the cash on cool stuff and then earn some more. Wealth is the flow, rather than just possession of money, and governments are at the mercy of markets whether they like it or not, because they drive the flow."

"It still looks like your precious market is the problem Nick. It's capitalism mate – you just said it yourself – stop everyone chasing the money."

"But you're still left with a similar problem. What's the alternative to 'capitalism,' as you put it – socialism? If you get the same reward regardless of how hard you work, or even whether you work at all, where's your incentive to get out of bed in the morning? Productivity goes down the toilet under socialism and, while money is theoretically taken out of the equation and everything is equal, everyone is equally much worse off."

"So if you reckon socialism's not an option, but also money is the root of all evil, then where does that leave us?"

"Listen to what I've been saying Al, money's not the problem – it's just the mechanism we use to exchange our labour for someone else's. Maybe debt is the root of all evil; it was the repackaging of toxic debt that kicked-off this crisis after all. But you can no more stop people lending to each other than you can stop them buying stuff. Also, a lot of wealth is founded on perfectly wholesome debt, otherwise known as investment, which in turn provides jobs, which pay taxes, and everyone's a winner."

"You're not wrong Nick," said Morrison. "And the thing is, thousands of people in the City are going to get paid a shit-load in bonuses this year based on the amount they lend. The mental part is that it doesn't matter whether those debts go bad in future, the bonuses get paid regardless, so long as it doesn't go tits-up before the end of the year."

"I don't see you complaining on the way to the Lambo showroom every February Jack," said Blake.

"I won't apologise for taking money that's put on a plate in front of me, and I don't see Dave wringing his hands with guilt when he's stuffing a ton down some stripper's pants either. As long as banks are set up the way they are, people like me are going to coin it. It's like the whole system exists just to keep me in sports cars and pricey watches."

"The problem is the way big companies are run," said Georgiou. "A public company is owned by its shareholders, but they hardly ever get involved in making any decisions. In fact public companies are run in a pretty similar way to democratic governments: a small, self-selecting pool of candidates, an under-motivated, ill-informed electorate, and overwhelmingly short-term incentives."

"The thing is Nick," said Dalston, "you said socialism doesn't work because it goes against human nature by removing the profit motive – agreed – and you said it's in the nature of bankers to be short-termist and self-serving, so that tendency needs to be moderated – and even Jack seems to agree with that. So it looks like the way forward is to take account of people's nature and, unless I'm missing something, isn't that exactly what they're doing with these Id Cards?"

"Fair point, mate, but it's one thing to acknowledge and take account of human nature, it's quite another to crush it. The more you try to take people away from what's natural to them, the more force you have to use. That's what happened with the commies; people didn't want to work hard and then get fuck all in return, so they had to have secret police, state brainwashing, and all that other fun stuff to make them do it. That's the direction we're headed in."

"Oh calm down Nick, they're just trying to improve things, to have less selfish pricks in important jobs," said Blake. "You're trying to make it sound like Emperor Ming has taken over."

"Just watch what happens, Al. One day you'll wake up and find you've no longer got any say in how you run your life. That might be a smoother transition for a squaddy, but this will make marching up and down the square seem like fucking Woodstock, mate."

***

Dalston's brain was still hurting from trying to process the conversation when he got home from the pub with the customary midnight kebab, so he craved something nice and superficial to mong at on TV. He flicked onto Last Roll of the Dice, a reality TV programme in which a mixed group of faded or fleeting celebrities were forced to admit, live on air, that the show was the last chance they had to resurrect their showbiz careers.

The presenter, having to support herself on crutches after winning the previous week's episode of LROTD, mercilessly probed the current contestant about the personal implications of failing to maintain/establish a showbiz career. "You've bet your whole life on being famous, haven't you? Can you actually do anything else? How do you think your three young children will cope with the crushing disappointment of your humiliating public failure?" This sadistic preliminary almost always concluded with the sobbing breakdown of the celebrity, an eventuality made inevitable by the live, real-time voting system in which the public used a mobile app to submit unlimited votes (only 99p each) either in favour or against the celebrity over the course of their appearance.

Dignity, stoicism and courage were invariably punished by an electorate impatient for its hit of cheap emotional voyeurism, so savvy contestants were quick to turn on the waterworks. Any time the number of negative votes exceeded the positive ones they were disqualified and the winner, who would host the next show, was the person to last the longest before being voted off.

Another, more immediate cause of the celebrities' misery was that they were about to step inside a giant, hollow, clear plastic cube – The Dice – positioned at the top of Pen y Fan in the Brecon Beacons. Wearing only elbow pads, knee pads and a crash helmet (to prevent excessive bleeding, which might obscure the footage), the enclosed contestants were then flung from the highest peak in southern Britain, with an array of external, internal and body-mounted video cameras live-streaming their ordeal. History had shown there was a direct relationship between the extent of a celebrity's suffering and their audience approval. If the celebrity blacked-out they were soon voted off by a public frustrated at having their entertainment cut short.

The latest contestant's on-air nervous breakdown was interrupted by an ad break, which gave the show's producers the opportunity to coerce the quivering wannabe-starlet into The Dice. The first ad was for noneedtothink.com, a shopping service with the motto 'Freedom from decisions,' which offered to remove the risk of spending money on the wrong things by taking control of your bank account and, based on a sophisticated algorithm, making the best buying decisions for you. The only interaction required was the one-click approval of a weekly basket of goods, which would range from groceries to financial services. The latest ad was announcing a special on cars, with a free, branded teddy-bear for every car of a certain make purchased through the site. It was followed by a trailer for the latest episode of Pub, Curry, Yoga! a TV programme concerned solely with the manufacture, documentation and discussion of extreme flatulence.

That was enough for Dalston, who flicked channels until he settled on another, slightly less harrowing, reality TV show called Britain's Got Issues. It soon became clear this episode of the pioneering talent show, which received many plaudits for giving the 'cerebrally underprivileged' the same opportunities at establishing a showbiz career as the rest of the population, was not going well.

It was Autism Week and, while there had been no shortage of people on the spectrum applying to the show, getting them to publicly audition was quite another matter. Less than half of the contestants even made it onto the stage, having decided against it at the last minute. Several of those who did get that far froze under the gaze of the spotlights or, when asked why they wanted to be famous, said they didn't anymore and walked off.

One young girl ignored the panel entirely and instead used her smartphone to live-stream herself breathlessly describing the experience of being on the show over social media. She eventually announced her Instagram ID to the world and then just stood on the stage, staring at her phone, immersed in the consequent frenzied exchange. After several minutes of this, the silence punctuated only by increasingly exasperated pleas from the producers, she was escorted from the stage, not before taking several photos of the bemused judging panel and publishing them, to the delight of her exponentially growing social media following.

Dalston always felt conflicted when watching BGI, finding the often bizarre performances highly entertaining, but also harbouring a lingering anxiety about the extent to which the contestants were exploited rather than empowered by the experience. The sheer self-reliance of this set of contestants, however, and their apparent indifference to the panel, made them seem anything but victims. When the next contestant was asked his name he just stared at his feet and asked, "How much does it cost to be in the audience?" After monotonously repeating the question several times, in spite of considerable wrong-footed gibbering from the panel, he finally got his answer. There was a pause, during which he briefly looked up, slowly scanned the entire auditorium, then looked down again, before asking: "How many votes do you get per episode?" and once more remorselessly repeated the question until the panel capitulated.

"So, at fifty pounds per ticket you bring in around a hundred grand per episode from the gate," he announced, without looking up. "That's about the same as the cost of a one-minute slot of TV advertising, of which there are around sixteen per episode, including those immediately before and after the show – I've counted. You probably trouser half of that revenue, and you get around 70p of the one pound it costs to vote on the show. Adding on the registration fees you make contestants pay, the eighty percent of royalties you keep from any contestant's commercial success, your share of revenues from the Further Issues follow-up programme, and the countless other endorsements, merchandising, and assorted commercial opportunities you so thoroughly exploit, I reckon you bring in around two-point-three million quid per episode. Even if we allow a generous three hundred grand in costs to produce an episode, there are still two big ones unaccounted-for. Can you please tell me where that money goes?"

Three of the panel immediately looked at the fourth, the creator and owner of the show, Sven Garlic, with genuine curiosity now tempering their bemusement. Eventually Garlic answered it was none of the contestant's business, to which the contestant calmly replied "Yeah, I figured you'd say that," and walked off.

During the period of subsequent on-air panic, Dalston reflected on how much more pleasure he got from the discomfort of the show's panel than he ever had from the humiliation of the contestants. He realised he was on the edge of his seat awaiting the next spanner in the works, which came in the form of Davina Jones, a tall, striking young woman with short, peroxided hair and dark makeup, who reminded Dalston of the Darryl Hannah character in Blade Runner. To his disappointment, but to the evident relief of the panel, Davina answered the panel's fatuous questions promptly and politely, albeit in a way reminiscent of the generic answers you would expect from a beauty pageant contestant.

"Are you nervous?" asked one of the judges.

"Yes, a bit, does it show?" she simpered.

"Why do you want to be famous?"

"It's been my dream to be a singer since I was a little girl."

"What will you do if you win Britain's Got Issues?"

"I'll give some money to my Mum, some to autism charities, and maybe keep just a bit to treat myself."

And so the interview continued, with frequent, generous helpings of syrupy sentiment throughout. By the end the entranced panel was tempted to crown her the winner of the entire series there and then, but there was still the small matter of her performance to be addressed. Davina announced it would be 'Weak' by Skunk Anansie and launched into a rendition Skin would have been proud of.

As the rapturous applause concluded, Davina was asked to comment on her performance. "Thank you everyone for your kind encouragement," she said. "I'm so grateful for the opportunity to perform in front of you and if the public votes for me to come back I promise my next performance will blow their minds."

Chapter 4 – Image

Next day Dave Dalston was shopping on Hampstead High Street. He bought some distressed jeans at a shop so exclusive it didn't even have a name, just a pure white facade with no clothes in the window and a solitary small black circle above the door. Underneath the Dot, as it was generally known, a security team vetted potential shoppers according to their suitability. Anyone not making the grade was politely refused entry and no amount of pleading, threats or histrionics could change the team's hive mind. The often dramatic spectacle of pampered Hampstead youths reacting badly to being refused entry had become a tourist attraction in its own right and there was often a crowd of jeering onlookers present, eager to compound the humiliation of the rejected.

Shopping at Dot complemented Dalston's self-image perfectly; exclusive, expensive and scrotum-shrinkingly self-conscious. He was dimly aware there was a limit to the value you can add to a pair of jeans. Even if you were to hand-stitch the jeans from Madagascan silk harvested by endangered pygmies and imbue the garment with a GPS chip, go-faster stripes and a rear-mounted fart-filter, you would struggle to justify the £1,100 he just parted with for his premium pants. But that wasn't the point; if you were fortunate enough to be let into Dot it was inconceivable you wouldn't buy anything, and since even a plastic bracelet embossed with a dot cost £50, you might as well go the whole hog and buy an actual piece of clothing.

Besides, how else would people know you're the kind of person who gets let into Dot and can afford to blow over a thousand pounds on a pair of trousers? Wearing a pair of Dot jeans confirmed his superiority. Even better, on the rare occasions he encountered someone else wearing Dot, he had the special pleasure of exchanging a brief, understated flash of recognition that managed to express both mutual regard and contempt for everyone else. A grand well spent, all things considered.

Criminally close to Dot was Fonez!, a mobile phone shop aimed at the youth market and the very last place Dalston would normally find himself, with its open-doors, mass-market strategy and garish, bling-encrusted handsets. He just couldn't understand why even teenagers would spend their not-very-hard-earned cash on such superficial tat. Anyone displaying a Fonez! phone while trying to gain entry to Dot would be lucky if the bouncers didn't beat them to death, there and then. If only to confirm things were as bad as they'd ever been, upon leaving Dot Dalston found himself staring uncomprehendingly at the latest Baby Princess pink handset with a pulsating LED love-heart on the back. Having shaken his head in disgust he was about to move on when something inside caught his eye that shocked him so much he felt like he'd been punched in the stomach.

Dalston nearly knocked a couple of people over as he sprinted into the store, his gaze darting around as he tried to catch a second glimpse of what had got him so worked up. He started pacing around the store opening cabinets, looking around counters and even behind the displayed handsets, but to no avail. The alarmed staff were on the verge of calling the police when one of them bravely approached him, at that moment resembling nothing more than an electronics fetishist desperately seeking gratification.

"Can I help you sir?" said the sales assistant.

"A girl!" shouted Dalston, confirming the assistant's suspicion that he was dealing with a rabid pervert.

"Look bruv, this ain't that kind of place, you get me. We sell phones here, yeah, there's a clue on the front of the shop, innit."

"What? Look, there was a young girl in here a minute ago, where did she go?"

"We get loads of birds coming through here, man, what does she look like?"

"Pre-teen, shoulder-length brown hair, brown eyes."

"Sorry bruv, I ain't seen no one that age in here for a bit. You sure it was her?"

"I was looking at the window display and I could have sworn I saw Amy – my daughter – here in the shop."

"Oh right," said the relieved assistant. "So what, you were out shopping with her and she's gone AWOL is it?"

"No, I haven't seen her since I split up from her Mum, and they don't even live nearby, but I would've bet my life I just saw her in here. I guess not, though."

"You know what would cheer you up? A new phone. What have you got right now, bruv? Let me guess, you shop at Dot so it can only be a iPhone yeah? I knew it. What did you get?"

"I'm sorry?"

"At Dot, blad, what gear did you buy?"

"Oh, some jeans."

"Nice, those new ones yeah? I was gonna get some of them too, but the dickheads at the door have got a shit attitude. I was looking to lay down some proper wedge and the fucking idiots looked at me like I was something they just stepped in, know what I mean. How's a bloke supposed to look the part if he can't even get into the shop in the first place, for fuck's sake? No offense, fam, but how come you got past them bouncers?"

"Beats me, mate. Sorry, I didn't catch your name."

"Dev Sharma at your service. So did you get that iPhone as soon as it came out? That was six months ago, bruv! You can't be seen wearing your Dot jeans carrying a antique like that around, that's just disrespecting the Dot, innit. Check this out, it's called Cosmic Phone and it does literally everything."

"Erm, literally? Are you sure?"

"That's what I'm trying to tell you, man; there's nothing this phone can't do."

"Can it help me pull?"

"Are you having a laugh? If you walk down Hampstead High Street chatting on Cosmic Phone you're going to need to wear a sign around your neck saying you're not available for sex, because the bitches are going to be throwing themselves at you, innit. They'll be trying to rugby-tackle you to the ground just so they can get a shot at your cock, you get me."

Dalston couldn't resist a chuckle at Dev's sheer nerve. "Love it. You've cheered my right up, my friend," he said. "Do you know what, I might just have one of those Cosmic Phones after all. I'm Dave Dalston, what's the damage?"

"It's quite a coincidence you ask that, Mr Dalston, because we happen to be doing a deal on Cosmic Phone right now, but it's only for people who shop at Dot, you hear what I'm saying. For you, my friend, I can reluctantly let go of one of these epoch-defining pieces of kit on a bargain ton-a-month contract. And while it pains me to virtually give away such premium kit, I don't want a discerning punter like you to be inconvenienced by needless obstacles before living the Cosmic Phone dream."

"Jesus Christ Dev you do talk an awful lot of shit, just put me down for one."

Enriched with a new phone, Dev's business card and the promise to call him if he ever needed literally anything, Dalston decided to try out his Cosmic Phone straight away by calling the lads, who were all up for a cheeky one. However, he couldn't help noting the complete absence of screaming, pantiethrowing groupies and concluded this was probably due to the fact that half the other people walking down Hampstead High Street were also using a Cosmic Phone. Before long he dismissed the suspected sighting of his daughter as a hallucination, but resolved to have another try at seeing her soon.

Having established his mates were just up the road at the Holly Bush, he was looking forward to showing off his shiny new gear, but not everyone was impressed.

"So you've basically blown two and a half grand on a phone and a pair of jeans," said Al Blake. "Don't you feel like a bit of a twat?"

"Why would I? This is quality gear. Primark's not for everyone," countered Dalston, rolling his eyes.

"But you can get a perfectly good pair of jeans and a decent phone for a fraction of what you spent, what a waste!"

"No, it's my money and I spent it on stuff I fancied, how can that possibly be a waste? If I'd thrown the gear in the bin, or if I'd set fire to my wallet, that would be a waste, but what the fuck else do I earn money for if not to buy shit I want with it?"

"No argument there, mate, but there are so many people worse off than you for whom the two k you could have saved by not being such a posing wanker could have made a real difference, that's all."

"Look, I pay an absolute shit-load in taxes, most of which gets doshed-out to people worse off than me. Maybe some of them really are in the shit due to circumstances beyond their control, but I bet most of them have just decided it's easier to live off hand-outs than roll their sleeves up and earn their own wedge. So forgive me if I choose to enjoy what little money I have left over after the tax-man and countless other fucking parasites have had their pound of flesh."

"But Al, you're missing the point," said Nick Georgiou. "If Dave doesn't keep buying ostentatious status-symbols then he might have to confront the fact that he's just another regular punter. All these poncey clothes and gadgets buy Dave the delusion he's elevated above the hoi polloi, and part of an elite the rest of us can only dream of joining."

"You know what? Fuck off, the pair of you," said Dalston.

"What makes you think it's a delusion though, Nick?" said Jack Morrison. "People judge you by how you look and the stuff you have. Our business is all about snap judgments and if you don't look the part you might as well not bother. Yes, it's superficial, but nobody's got time to look under the skin of things. If everyone went around wondering what the point of everything is the whole time, nothing would ever get done."

"Well said Jack," Dalston agreed. "So if Mother Theresa has finished today's sermon, does anyone fancy a bit of poker? I just bought some new chips too."

Poker at the pub was a well-established tradition between the four friends. The game was Texas Hold 'em and it soon developed along familiar lines. The city boys – Dalston and Morrison – were accustomed to gambling for big stakes and played accordingly. Morrison was an especially instinctive, aggressive poker player, frequently betting big with nothing in his hand, purely due to what he perceived in his opponents' body language.

The rest of the players were all fully aware of Morrison's playing style and each had their own ways of dealing with it. Dalston was cut from the same cloth but a bit more circumspect, so he would often wait for Morrison to make his move and then, if he detected a bluff, would raise him back. Blake, who earned the least out of the group, was quite the opposite – very cautious – and if he bet, the chances were he had something, which often scared everyone else out of the pot. Georgiou liked to keep everyone on their toes by mixing it up – sometimes aggressive, sometimes conservative. He seemed to derive more pleasure from toying with his opponents than from any financial gain.

After an hour or so Blake was chip-leader. In the key hand to that point Morrison for once failed to read Blake and went in big on a bluff. After a series of raises and re-raises he belatedly realised he'd made a mistake and threw in his cards without even seeing the Flop. But the status of stack-leader had gone to Blake's head, and he started playing hands he would normally throw away. In one subsequent hand Blake's Queen/Jack unsuited was upgraded to a pair when the Flop yielded another Jack, leading him to bet heavily. Georgiou, however, had been dealt a pair of Kings, which was enough to win after the Turn and the River yielded nothing of further use to either of them.

The session was effectively concluded in one hand when all four players paid to see the Flop. Their hands were as follows:

Morrison – King and 9 of Diamonds

Blake – a pair of 10s

Georgiou – Ace, King, unsuited

Dalston – a pair of 6s

The Flop was: King of Spades, 8 of Diamonds, 2 of Diamonds.

Blake opened the betting after the Flop but was raised by Georgiou, re-raised by Dalston, and re-raised once more by Morrison, who had a strong pair and an eye on the Flush. That was too rich for Blake's blood, but Georgiou called and so did Dalston, despite his pair of 6s looking highly vulnerable to the higher pairs implied by his opponents' aggressive betting. The Turn yielded an Ace of Hearts, which strengthened Georgiou's position, who consequently bet heavily. Morrison decided to call him, as did Dalston. A 6 of Clubs duly arrived on the River, causing Dalston to raise Georgiou's opening bet, and Morrison to throw in his busted Flush. After another couple of raises Georgiou called and the remaining two players showed their hands. Dalston cleaned-up, his three 6s beating Georgiou's two-pair – Ace, King.

"Jesus H Fucking Christ Dave, what the fuck were you doing staying in such a big pot with a pair of 6s," said a disgusted Georgiou.

"I think you just answered your own question Nick – you've got to be in it to win it," said Dalston.

"If he's stupid enough to stay in with fuck-all then he deserves the rewards I guess," said Blake.

"Yeah, stop crying Nick, I don't see you complaining when you call one of his bluffs and take him to the cleaners," said Morrison.

"It's just like with the pricey gear mate – I spend my money how I want, and right now I want to buy a round. Anyone got a fucking problem with that?" asked Dalston.

***

Dalston's unlikely victory apparently spoiled the taste of the beer for the other three, who called it a day after his round. Back home he was flicking through the channels when he was pleasantly surprised to see Davina Jones was once more on Britain's Got Issues. Her initial appearance on the show had attracted a fair bit of media attention as she was beautiful, talented, and one of the few participants in Autism Week to deliver a performance at all.

In subsequent interviews Davina found herself positioned as spokeswoman for all people with Autism Spectrum Disorder. While she appeared to be pleased there was suddenly such mainstream interest in ASD, she stressed that everyone with ASD was different and she could not possibly claim to represent any other, let alone all of them. Davina's radio exchange with Iain Tegritie was typical.

"Thank you for coming on to talk to us Ms Jones – it must have been a rather strange few weeks for you," said Tegritie.

"You can say that again Iain, I've really been blown away by the public's response to my performance."

"What do you think has caused such a strong reaction?"

"Apart from the quality of my performance you mean?"

"Forgive me, of course it was an excellent rendition of, erm..."

"Weak."

"Yes, of course, but no other performances have been met with this level of public response. Do you get any sense of what has set yours apart?"

"I think it was a combination of my choice of song, the performance itself, and my subsequent willingness to do interviews like this."

"Right. And how have those other interviews gone?"

"Great!"

"What did you speak about?"

"This sort of thing."

"Right, erm, well, yes, of course," dithered Tegritie, agitated by his inability to get to the story he wanted. "And the show itself, can we presume by your participation that you approve of the concept?"

"Talent shows? What's not to like?"

"Well, indeed, but this is a specific type of talent show isn't it?"

"It certainly is Iain."

"And you're comfortable with that?"

Davina's patience was wearing thin. "Look, I don't know what the problem is here," she said. "You've been pussy-footing around what you want to know for ages now and I'm not going to do your job for you, so either ask me what's on your mind or let's call it a day, because this is getting painful."

"OK then," huffed Tegritie. "What additional challenges did your autism present when appearing in Britain's Got Issues?"

"I can't believe you chose to define me by my disorder, that's so offensive, is that all you see? I am a person in my own right as well you know!"

"Yes, of course, I apologise if I spoke out of turn, as it were, of course you are far more than just your, erm, disorder as you put it, I just..."

"Chill, Iain, I was just messing with you. I'm actually delighted to bring attention to ASD, in large part to educate people like you. What you really wanted to ask is: what's it like to have autism – right?"

"I suppose so, yes," sulked Tegritie.

"That's an impossible question to answer because each manifestation is unique. It's not like having a missing limb, or whatever, each person with ASD differs from what is considered 'normal' in a different way. And, incidentally, that's another major problem when trying to discuss ASD and its symptoms: defining 'normal'."

"What do you mean?"

"What is normal? Can anything really be described as normal? Are you normal?"

"As normal as anyone I suppose."

"You can't say that. Even if you try to claim you're a normal middle-aged, British, white man, does that mean all other such people are abnormal, since none of them are identical to you?"

"OK, point taken, and I'm the first to stress the importance of semantics, but ASD stands for Autism Spectrum Disorder, surely a disorder is, in effect, an abnormality?"

"Yes, but what I'm trying to do is destigmatise terms like 'abnormal' and 'disorder.' Everybody is abnormal, but one of my abnormalities happens to have a name, it's just a matter of degree. That's why it's a spectrum – you could argue everyone's on the spectrum, it's just most people are so slightly affected they're not labelled."

"So are you saying everyone is autistic?"

"Firstly, I prefer to say people *have autism*, rather than are *autistic*, because autism doesn't define them, it's just a set of characteristics some people have to a greater or lesser degree. Calling someone with autism autistic is like calling a disabled person a cripple. While it's technically accurate, it runs the risk of focusing all attention on one specific condition and ignoring their many other qualities.

"But yes, many of the characteristics people associate with autism are essentially exaggerations of things most supposedly normal people have. Many of the challenges we face are social – how to relate to other people, how to *fit in*, how to help other people relate to us. But which normal person doesn't experience those sorts of challenges from time to time? How many people really get you? Part of being a human being is basically to think everyone else is barking mad, that they're wrong, because if they're not wrong then you must be.

"So to answer your original question, I can't say what unique challenges I faced as a person with autism performing live in front of millions because I only know what it's like to be me, so how can I compare my experiences to anyone else's? Speaking for myself I have worked all my life to understand the rules of social engagement and I think I've succeeded. In fact it's possible I understand them better than many who are not diagnosed as being on the spectrum, because most people don't really think about these things, they just rely on intuition. I've studied how people interact, what they expect of each other, what is considered normal, so very little surprises me. And I have the added advantage, in common with a lot of other people on the spectrum, of genuinely not caring what most other people think of me."

"Really? I find that hard to believe."

"I don't care."

That conversation stopper served its purpose and effectively ended the interview. Davina's confident performance boosted her burgeoning public profile further. The other media were delighted to see Tegritie handled with such skilful disdain and ensured his public humiliation was prolonged. As a result Davina's next BGI appearance was eagerly anticipated, not least by Dalston.

The BGI semi-finals took place just two weeks later and, after the winner of the Bipolar Week finished sobbing his way through Radiohead's 'Creep,' it was Davina's turn. Following a few more minutes of anodyne chit-chat with the panel, her performance began. Expected to perform Christina Aguilera's 'Beautiful,' it soon became clear there had been a change of plan.

"Some of those that work forces, are the same that burn bridges," Davina whispered.

"Some of those that work forces, are the same that burn bridges," she repeated, over a pulsating electric guitar riff.

After a few more repetitions the guitar tempo increased slightly, with a cluster of three short chords setting up the next vocals.

"And we do what they tell us," Davina chanted several times, causing the BGI panel to exchange increasingly bemused glances and shrugs as they tried to fathom what she was playing at.

The guitar reached a crescendo. "Those who judge, feel justified, they hold all the cards, they're the chosen ones," sang Davina, now in full voice. "They justify, those they use, by pretending to care, they're the chosen ones."

Two things simultaneously began to dawn on Garlic and the rest of the judging panel: first that the song being performed was 'Killing in the Name' by Rage Against the Machine, and secondly the lyrics had been altered. There was also a sneaking suspicion the new lyrics were referring to them, and not in a good way. Garlic attempted to intervene.

"Davina, we're a bit confused up here, what are you singing?"

"...they hold all the cards, they're the chosen ones," she persisted, ignoring the interruption.

"I have to warn you Davina, if you don't start singing what was agreed I will be forced to ask you to vacate the stage."

Garlic's warning coincided with a pause in the singing as the guitar began a slow progression of chords, inching higher and louder towards a fresh crescendo. Davina stared intensely at Garlic and a wry smile spread across her face. She saw no reason to alter the lyrics to the song's infamous conclusion and launched into them with indignant fury.

"Fuck you I won't do what you tell me!" she screamed, "Fuck you I won't do what you tell me!"

Garlic was now in a state of total panic, eventually managing to compose himself sufficiently to order the plug pulled on the performance. The order was taken literally, leaving the entire massive auditorium not only silent, but completely dark.

In his living room Dalston fell back in his chair, stunned. As a generic information screen appeared on the TV, apologising for some unspecified technical problem, he reflected on what Davina had done. Her first compliant, obliging appearance had been a ruse, designed to lull the producers of the programme into complacency. All her subsequent publicity-seeking was designed to maximise the audience for this performance. Davina not only saw BGI for the cynical exploitation of naive, vulnerable people it was, she also wanted the world to see it that way too. In a brilliant judo move Davina used the power of the show against it and Dalston was enchanted. He had to meet her.

Chapter 5 – Initiation

The societal consequences of the Id Card scheme were making themselves apparent. There was little point in measuring the composition of everyone's psyche unless you were going to use that information. More importantly, it was vital for the UK government to be seen to be doing something or potentially face another insurrection.

The pathologically self-serving and short-termist behaviour of the bankers (who were mainly of Canine egotype) in catalysing the economic crisis had led to the conclusion that the kind of people naturally drawn to banking were most likely to produce destructive outcomes. So it was decided most senior bankers should be barred from working in finance, or any similar profession, and instead be compelled to work in sectors that might benefit from their brand of single-minded pragmatism.

Education and healthcare, while initially seeming unlikely destinations for such types, were a constant thorn in the side of all governments, as reform had proven impossible. It took little time for the government to see what a golden opportunity this was to get those ruthless corporate chest-beaters to do their dirty work for them. Conversely, while many incumbent senior teachers and nurses (typically Feline or Delphine) were insufficiently assertive for their wild classrooms and chaotic wards, their softer skills were deemed ideal for professions such as banking, which would benefit from a more subdued, nurturing approach.

Thus began a social engineering experiment of unprecedented extent and ambition. The Ministry of Optimisation sent out another round of letters telling people which professions their egotypes prohibited them from occupying and which were deemed 'appropriate.' A system of taxes and subsidies was applied to both employers and employees, making it prohibitively expensive not to follow the recommendations. There was a six-month deadline imposed for individuals and companies to ensure their appropriateness.

Sir Raymond Payshus had faced a wave of public condemnation following his infamous radio interview. So, under intense pressure, he publicly volunteered to be a pioneer of the new system by taking the role of headmaster and maths teacher at Hill Street Comprehensive School in North London. The supplanted maths teacher had become a recruitment consultant, which was the one profession booming on the back of the forced reallocation of thousands of jobs and was already busy alienating every candidate he encountered by berating them for their inadequate qualifications, sloppy appearance and bad attitudes.

Payshus reasoned that he had risen to the top of one of the most brutal and competitive professions of all, so whipping a few urchins into shape should be a walk in the park. The role of headmaster was well within his comfort zone as a former CEO, and he was confident of getting the staff onside swiftly. However, his first maths lesson was a step into the unknown. After introducing himself to class 9B, Payshus commenced teaching the topic of probability. Initially the class was quite subdued, which he interpreted as deference to his manifest authority. Before long, however, it became apparent the kids were just biding their time.

"So, can anyone think of a real-life example of probability?" Payshus asked the class. "Yes, Jason."

"How about this," said a boy with a suspiciously deep voice, apparently attempting a West Indian accent. "What is the probability that a banker wouldn't sell his Gran's gold teeth if he had half the chance? Answer: zero percent." Laughter exploded around the classroom at this quip, and Jason was soon exchanging hand-slaps with the children around him. The topical significance of the jibe was not lost on Payshus and he realized the matter needed addressing before they could move on.

"I see you follow the news, Jason, very good," said Payshus. "OK, let's do this; does anyone have any questions about me and how I've come to be your teacher?"

"Yeah sir, is it true you used to be a banker?" said a girl with a slightly less exotic accent.

"That's right, Freya, I was the head of a bank called Clark's."

"Why did you rip-off all those people, though?"

"I didn't rip anyone off; the bank made a number of poor investment decisions, for which I must take my share of responsibility, and was left with too little reserve capital to cope with the wider problems created by the sub-prime lending scandal in the US."

"So you took loads of people's money, blew it on some dodgy bets, then just went 'sorry man, shit happens' and everyone's supposed to just take it?" said Freya, incensed.

"And then he goes on the radio and laughs in our faces," said Jason, kissing his teeth in disgust.

"When people buy financial products they're always advised of the possibility they could lose as well as gain money," said Payshus. "There's no such thing as a sure bet, or everyone would be doing it, but yes, we screwed up. I hold my hands up, and now we're trying to make sure that sort of thing never happens again."

"By becoming a teacher?" said Jason. "So is that what happens – people who turn out to be shit at their old jobs get to be teachers instead? Great!"

"That's not the case at all Jason, and mind your language if you don't want to get in trouble."

"Oh, I'm shitting myself now. If you ask me you're still a bit of a banker, sir."

This comment was met with a roar of laughter Payshus couldn't understand, but before long he was besieged by questions from all directions, all followed by more laughter and approving hand-slaps.

"How come you're such a banker, sir?"

"Are all your mates bankers too?"

"How many times do you bank a day?"

Later in the staff room Payshus recounted his experience to some of his new colleagues and was rewarded with sidelong glances and smirks. After enquiring what was so funny, he was eventually advised the solution to the mystery lay in identifying a word that rhymed with banker. When he commented on the immaturity of the joke, he was reminded the kids in question were thirteen years old.

This sort of thing was happening in parallel all over the country. In Cambridge a leading corporate lawyer had been allotted the role of ward sister at Addenbrookes Hospital. Once more the imposition of private-sector rigour on a public-sector organisation initially improved efficiency, morale and results, but before long cracks started to appear. Patients began complaining of being asked to sign blanket waivers indemnifying the hospital and its staff from pretty much everything before they were even allowed to enter the building. Once under the care of the ward being run by the former lawyer, patients found their every request or claim of discomfort greeted by torrid cross-examination.

"Nurse, my leg hurts," began a typical exchange.

"Are you sure?"

"Yes, I can feel it. Hurting."

"Could it have been the way you were sitting?"

"Possibly, but I think it's more likely to be the compound fracture I got when that car ran me over."

"Allegedly."

"What?"

"When the car allegedly ran you over – it has yet to be conclusively proven that was how you sustained the alleged injury."

"Alleged injury? You mean you don't even believe I was injured? Take a look!"

"Now, if I were to take a look at your alleged injury, that could be used as proof in a court of law that I was aware of an injury and yet failed to take any remedial action. You surely can't expect me to put myself in such a precarious position."

"To be honest I don't know what the hell you're talking about, but wouldn't all this be irrelevant if you just helped me get better, starting with some of your strongest pain-killers."

"Nice try, but if I were to give you some pain-killers I would effectively be admitting knowledge of your discomfort, and it could be proven..." And so on.

One exception to this vocational chaos was Payshus' replacement. In a straight swap Poppy Syndrome – the former Head of Hill Street – was put in charge of Clark's Bank, which was now majority-owned by the state following its bail-out. She placed the culpability for the current mess squarely at the feet of the financial sector and already had a lot of ideas about how things should be done differently.

Syndrome's assertion was that the economic crisis was a product of elitism and inequality, of a cabal of privileged fat-cats making decisions designed entirely to enrich themselves at the expense of everyone else. Furthermore, while they were able to benefit fully from the profits of their actions, they were rendered immune from the consequences of failure by an unlimited government safety-net.

The thing Syndrome found most galling was the inevitability of that failure. Successive governments for half a century had attempted to reconcile the conflicting public desire for both lower taxes and better public services, while at the same time seeking to bribe the electorate directly with spurious public sector jobs and near-universal benefits. The only way to pay for this electoral sleight-of-hand was to borrow the money from the banks, thus creating such a dependence that any government treating the banks with anything other than benign indulgence would soon collapse. This included the complete compliance of the supposedly independent financial regulator, whose executive board was appointed by the government anyway.

Combined with the conflicted credit-rating agencies and auditors, who derived the majority of their revenue from the financial sector they were supposed to be assessing impartially, this state of affairs effectively invited bankers to dream-up ever more exotic and opaque financial products to justify their obscene bonuses and satisfy insatiable shareholder demand for growth. Even the concept of shareholder control was itself a mirage as most shares were owned by other financial organisations with a strong vested interest in maintaining the status quo.

Armed with a tax-payer safety-net, obsequious regulation, and complicit shareholders, banks had been free to sell collateralised debt obligations, credit default swaps, and all manner of other arcane financial derivatives to each other with impunity. Both the buyers and the sellers knew there were deeply flawed products, but a commission was paid every time one was sold, so the game of bad debt pass-the-parcel grew ever more frenzied as the bonuses mounted, until the music stopped. Then, as effectively prearranged, the protagonists simply handed over the resulting toxic ordure to the tax-payer and slunk off to their tax-havens to reflect on what fun it had all been.

In a presentation to senior executives Poppy Syndrome shared her vision, entitled 'Inclusive Banking for a Better Society.' In essence, Clark's bank was to make public service its primary purpose, with Key Performance Indicators adjusted accordingly. Bonuses, while reduced, would still be paid according to KPIs being met or ideally exceeded. Employees were now incentivised to improve lending to small businesses and first-time house-buyers, to invest ethically and sustainably, and to ensure the bank's deposit-to-loan ratio never fell below 50% by offering generous interest rates to depositors.

IBBS became universally lauded as the way forward for financial services. Before long, with savings account interest at double the rate of any of its competitors, Clark's was awash with lovely, clean, safe depositor cash. This was lent-on to small businesses and first-time house buyers at favourable rates, ensuring a massive share of the UK retail lending market. The investment banking division, which had been separated from the retail division in order to insulate depositors from poor investment decisions, operated on a strictly ethical basis. The cost of vetting every investment for ethical failings, and the meagre returns offered by ethical companies, meant profitability was relatively low. However Clark's Nice and Ethical Fund soon became a key component of pension and hedge funds looking to tick the corporate and social responsibility box, thus ensuring its popularity.

Start-ups were soon proliferating, as anyone with half an idea was able to secure funding for its attempted commercialization. The epitome of this new wave of entrepreneurialism was catshit.com, a website that stripped social networking down to its one core function – the sharing of pictures and videos of cats being cute, falling off things and jumping out of their skins when surprised by cucumbers. As traffic to the site increased exponentially, investors jostled for the opportunity to buy a piece of the action, and by the time it went public catshit.com had a market value of £5.4 billion, despite only reporting revenues of £48.57p.

Politicians were quick to recognise the electoral benefits of the economic boom caused by this speculative exuberance, so the government offered further support by underwriting Clark's small business loans. But the real uptick in opinion polls coincided with a surge in the housing market, which the government greedily stoked by also underwriting first-time-buyer mortgages from Clark's. Since performance was now measured according to socially (and thus electorally) desirable lending, the bonus sums at Clark's soon rivalled those paid during the pre-Id Card boom.

Syndrome, as CEO of Clark's, was a major beneficiary of this bloated bonus pool, but felt conflicted about extracting such large sums of money from what she considered to be a largely philanthropic venture. She was also frustrated by having to put the needs of state shareholders before what she considered to be greater societal needs. Both dilemmas eventually yielded a single, common solution – the Syndrome Philanthropic Investment Vehicle – into which she channelled her new-found wealth. SPIV enabled her to help out those people she felt were in the greatest need, unconstrained by shareholders, committees and countless other conflicting interests.

Clark's had been transformed from a national liability into the poster-child for post-financial crisis corporate responsibility. Fuelled by cheap loans to entrepreneurs and house-buyers, the economy was booming once more. The government was making daily statements on the matter in a bid to associate itself as closely as possible with this reversal of national fortunes and behind the scenes urged Syndrome to keep the credit taps flowing. In order to do so it became necessary to relax the bank's obligation to cover at least half of the total value of its loans with liquid deposits, but that seemed a small price to pay for getting the country back on its feet. As the loans flowed, so did the bonuses and Syndrome faced no shareholder opposition when she suggested her own bonus rate be increased. She found her sudden wealth enormously empowering and was enraptured by the difference she was able to make to so many lives. Syndrome was increasingly of the view that she had single-handedly got the country back on its feet.

Chapter 6 – Inertia

At Gold & Mackenzie entire departments had been created to ensure it was seen to be adhering to the letter of the Simpson-Oxford Act. Legions of thought police were now roaming its corridors, clamping down on the slightest symptoms of ego-driven behaviour which, Dalston lamented, covered pretty much everything he did. Among the newly outlawed activities were: high-fives, discussions about sport, any reference to the attractiveness of women or any part of their anatomy, the 'double-pistol' finger-pointing gesture and peeing with one or both hands against the toilet wall.

His colleagues seemed to be adapting to this better than he was. The office default expression was now one of alternating earnest graft and evangelical zeal, such that most co-workers now reminded him of Animal from the Muppets. All of this could possibly have been tolerable were it not for the transformation of his friend, Jack Morrison.

Dalston and Morrison met soon after the latter joined Gold & Mackenzie as an intern. He recognised a kindred spirit immediately and the feeling was mutual. Although they were roughly the same age, Morrison had gone to business school while Dalston worked his way up the old-fashioned way. He had taken it upon himself to show the cocky newcomer the ropes, a process that began at 7pm on the first Friday after Morrison joined the company and ended at a strip-club many hours later.

Deep down Dalston always felt like a bit of a fraud. He had fallen into the hedge-fund game through a mate of a mate who insisted "If you've got a brain, a gob and some balls then you'll be just fine." A cursory self-examination confirmed he had the requisite qualifications, so he thought 'fuck it' and said "I'm in." What his mate had failed to mention was that the opportunity on offer was junior executive or, as his new boss preferred to call it: "VP of Doing What You're Fucking Told." Duties included trips to the dry cleaners, scoring coke and fielding obnoxious rhetorical questions with good humour. Dalston assumed people who worked in the city all communicated exclusively in this way, but through sheer bemusement and desperation he occasionally made the mistake of taking them literally.

"Do we pay you to stare at the fucking wall?" began a typical exchange.

"Erm, no."

"So then, have you just been promoted to Chief Wanking Officer? Don't answer, you berk. Because if not, why aren't you fucking doing some fucking work?"

"Nobody's given me anything to do."

"Jesus fucking Christ, would you even be able to find your own arse without a map?"

"Yes?"

"Well halle-fucking-luja, let's see if we can give you talent number two. Do. You. Know. How. To. Make. Coffee?"

"I certainly do."

"Then what are you still doing here? Strong, milk, one, and make it snappy. Chop, chop!"

Throughout the ordeal his antagonist would periodically look around the office, soaking up the approval liberally supplied by a collection of leering sycophants and underlings, all simultaneously grateful it wasn't their turn to be victimised and experiencing a degree of schadenfreude bordering on sexual arousal. While unpleasant, Dalston rightly assumed this ritual humiliation was standard issue for junior executives and was merely the adult continuation of school-ground bullying. He just had to keep his head down and before long it would be someone else's turn.

Thanks to his business school background Morrison skipped the junior phase and joined as a full executive at around the same time Dalston was judged to have been sufficiently humiliated to earn a promotion to the same rank. But while he still carried the instinct to avoid eye-contact and minimise human contact, Morrison had no such psychological scar-tissue, and thus took a different approach to white-collar browbeating.

"Think you're something special just because you've been to *bizznizz* school do you, newbie?" Morrison was asked by a senior trader, not long after joining the company.

"Seems as good a reason as any for being an obnoxious wank-stain. What's your excuse, Granddad?" he replied, calmly, maintaining eye contact throughout.

"You've got off to a very bad start my friend, you really don't want to be going to war with me."

"I don't want to go anywhere with you, unless it's Switzerland to have you put out of my misery. So why don't you go and find someone even more retarded than you to bore to death, unlikely though it is that such a cabbage exists."

"Fine, you want to play it that way do you? Well just watch your back from now on."

"Good God, you mean you've been flirting with me all this time? Sorry mate, totally misread your signals there, but flattered though I am, even if I was gay, I'd still have some pride, so I urge you to direct your depraved attentions elsewhere."

By that stage even some of the other wannabe alpha males started laughing in spite of themselves and the antagonist's humiliation was complete. He walked off vowing vengeance but ultimately, bully that he was, sought easier prey elsewhere.

Displays such as this encouraged Dalston to rediscover his former cockiness and a fine bromance with Morrison ensued. They both fully embraced the 'work hard, play hard' ethos and challenged each other to earn ever-greater sums of money, while finding increasingly frivolous, ostentatious and self-destructive ways to spend it. It was not unusual for people to arrive at work having been out the entire previous night. Lockers in the office gym usually contained at least one complete change of clothes, as well as a discreetly hidden wrap of cocaine to ensure a bright start to the day despite the previous night's debauchery.

That was before the Payshus Insurrection, however, and the society-wide puritanical spasm that followed it. Previously the company had turned a blind eye to, and even tacitly encouraged, hedonistic behaviour on the part of its employees. This was ostensibly in the name of morale, but really to ensure salaries were spent as rapidly as possible. An employee with a big mortgage, expensive car and an escalating coke habit was obliged to make the company ever greater sums of cash in order to earn commission and maintain their lifestyle. But the prospect of being forced to retrain as psychiatric nurses made believers of the senior management and they concluded the best way to keep the Ministry of Optimisation at bay was for their workforce to be the model of austere humility.

Such a cultural U-turn was no simple undertaking, with staff often falling off the wagon in humiliating outbursts of shallow self-absorption. On one occasion a star trader cracked and started prancing around the office waving a handful of cash and shouting "Shut your mouth and look at my wad!" repeatedly, in an exaggerated cockney accent. Only once he was cornered in accounts, where he was apparently offering to rent a startled bean-counter's girlfriend for the night, was he able to be coaxed over to HR for further retraining.

But to Dalston's surprise Morrison had not been called into HR once. In fact he had improbably become the very model of post Simpson-Oxford piety. His face was so set into a mask of evangelical zeal that Dalston wondered if he'd been snorting Botox instead of coke. Morrison used to be the king of the high-five and the double-pistol, but now he downplayed his every professional achievement, insisting he was "nothing without the world-class team behind him." He also become teetotal overnight and preferred to get an early night to ensure he could "give 110 percent" the next day at work.

Confused by his friend's seismic lifestyle shift and frustrated by the loss of his wing-man, the change hit Dalston hard. He wanted to grab Morrison by the shoulders, shake him and tell him to snap out of it, but with the pub-lunch now taken out of the equation, the open-plan office offered few opportunities for such encounters. He had to abandon the tactic of loitering around the toilets in the hope of pissing next to Morrison when complaints resulted in a mandatory visit to the company psychiatrist.

If he had been even slightly less self-absorbed it would have been obvious to him that Morrison's change was simply a matter of pragmatism. Because they regularly partied together and had similar jobs, he had come to the erroneous conclusion that they were two peas in a pod. But in one important area they were diametric opposites: Dalston was primarily a hedonist – he worked to live; while Morrison's main motivation was ambition – he lived to work. So, when it became clear the new way to accumulate corporate brownie-points was puritanical zeal and conspicuous self-sacrifice, Morrison switched absolutely and without hesitation. He would no sooner harm his career prospects by carrying on as before, than he would come to work dressed as a middle-aged woman. Any confusion this caused his friends was their problem.

Morrison's Damascene conversion had the side-effect of making Dalston's regular M.O. incongruous and conspicuous, resulting in regular appointments with HR, which now existed almost entirely to root-out the kind of behaviour that would attract the attention of the Ministry of Optimisation. It also seemed to be the only part of the company still allowed to use rhetorical questions, albeit of an especially sinister and passive-aggressive variety. Dalston's favourite sport when faced with such provocation, perhaps as a result of his early career humiliations, was to answer them literally.

"Do you know why you're here?" one of the rapidly growing brigade of retraining managers asked him following his latest indiscretion.

"Yes."

"And?"

"Sorry – yes I do know why I'm here, yes."

"Would you care to elaborate?"

"No, I'm fine thanks."

"Please, Mr Dalston, would you tell me why you've been asked to meet me," persisted the retraining manager, apparently impervious to Dalston's flippancy but making copious notes nonetheless.

"Because I've been naughty?" he replied, unable to restrain himself.

"Because. I've. Been. Naughty," noted the manager in a sombre drawl. "Yes, and no, Mr Dalston. I wouldn't use such puerile terms, but I think we can agree some of your recent behaviour has been decidedly inappropriate, don't you?"

""Don't I what?"

"Agree your behaviour has been inappropriate."

"Inappropriate for what?"

"Excuse me?"

"Well, 'inappropriate' is a relative term. By itself it means nothing, it has to be used in context. For example: 'that haircut is inappropriate for a woman of your age'."

"What's wrong with my hair?"

"Nothing."

"But you said... Anyway, we're straying somewhat from the point don't you think?"

"No."

By now Dalston's strategy was starting to have the desired effect and the manager was slowly coming to the conclusion rhetorical questions were not going to pay their usual dividends.

"I'll get straight to the point then shall I?"

"Unlikely, on recent evidence."

Kicking herself for her inability to make a nuance-free statement, the manager soldiered on. "Despite numerous attempts to help you, Mr Dalston, you continue to behave in a manner detrimental to Gold & Mackenzie."

"Really? How?"

"I have a list of some of your most inappropriate transgressions, which I'm happy to read out if it would help."

"Help who?"

"You, to see the error of your ways."

"So there are degrees of inappropriateness, are there?"

"Excuse me?"

"You said '*most inappropriate*,' which implies things can be more or less *inappropriate*. It would help if you could make it clearer just how *inappropriate* each transgression was," said Dalston, thrice employing the curly-fingered quotation marks gesture.

The manager, now desperate to regain the initiative, lunged into the comforting arms of corporate-speak.

"I don't think it's optimal to leverage the bandwidth required to transition such granularity, going forward," she blurted.

"What?"

The manager re-blurted the same statement.

"Do you mean you don't want to go into that much detail?" said Dalston.

"Yes."

"You should've said. Well I do, and you said you wanted to help, so what's the first item on the rap-sheet?"

"You had the top three of your shirt buttons undone and your tie loosened to such an extent that you gave the impression of cockiness, arrogance, and indifference to the sensibilities of others."

"How inappropriate is that?"

"I'm pleased you agree."

"No, tell me how inappropriate that behaviour is, out of ten."

"I'm sorry?"

"If zero is: 'not in any way inappropriate,' and ten is: 'so inappropriate it made you shit yourself,' then, out of ten, how inappropriate is an unbuttoned shirt and a loose tie?"

"Erm, five."

"And is that the most inappropriate thing I stand accused of?"

"Hardly. You boasted loudly about a recent sexual conquest."

"How inappropriate was that?"

"By itself, four."

"Not bad, I'm getting better. At this rate I'll soon be totally appropriate."

"Unfortunately there were several complicating factors."

"Ah."

"You felt the need to share the precise details of your liaison, including positions attempted, sounds made by your partner and the final resting place of your (*ahem*) emissions. At least another couple of points there. And then, when challenged on the appropriateness of your comments by a female colleague you announced, within earshot of the rest of the office, and I quote: 'The dirty slag's just jealous she didn't get a taste of my gentleman's relish. There's plenty more to go round sugar tits, don't you worry your pretty little head.' All in all at least a nine, don't you think?"

"Seems fair."

"And then there is your regular intoxication at work, your offers to 'buy' interns for use as your 'personal slaves' and your repeated, indiscriminate use of phrases such as 'it's a dog-eat-dog world;' 'money talks, bullshit walks' and 'second place is the first loser' to justify your odious and selfish behaviour. Do you need any more examples?"

"I think I get the picture."

"Oh good."

The manager, sensing a decisive shift in momentum, decided some silent treatment was in order, and just looked sternly at Dalston, who realised a show of contrition was required.

"Listen, sorry if we got off on the wrong foot," he said, dialling up what he judged to be the optimal level of unctuous smarm to placate the newly-emboldened manager. "I can see the error of my ways now and I promise to do everything I can to become a better person."

His abrupt change of tone might just have worked had he not got carried away with his faux humility and actually grabbed and kissed the manager's hand.

"Such solemn vows would be far more convincing if you had not made and broken them so many times before, don't you think?" said the manager. "You clearly need a more robust wake-up call to help you see the correct way to behave, so I'm going to recommend a month's unpaid suspension. Perhaps this public shaming and loss of earnings will jolt you into a sincere change in attitude and a month of contemplation will give it time to sink-in, I'm sure you'll agree."

"No I fucking won't, bitch! Who the fuck do you think you are? No jumped-up little HR stuffed shirt tells me what to do. Wait until Johnson hears about this."

"Shall we call his office now? We can let him know about your two-month suspension straight away."

"Two months? But you said one month a minute ago."

"That was before you so kindly reminded me just how far from rehabilitation you truly are."

The manager offered him the phone.

Dalston's eyes spoke of loathing and bitter resentment, but his mouth remained closed. He remembered his previous meeting with Johnson, concluded he was unlikely to be any kind of ally and meekly declined the unused phone. Utterly defeated, he walked out of the meeting room and the building, taking only a few personal possessions and what remained of his dignity with him.

Chapter 7 – Introductions

A forty-eight-hour bender ensued and Dalston eventually found himself in Camden Lock on a Sunday afternoon nursing a world-class hangover. It combined with his work-related depression to rob him of the pleasure he usually derived from watching the bizarre melting pot of hipster youths, tourists and traders of exotica that inhabited this unique corner of North West London.

In the stables market one stall announcing itself as The Hidden Agenda didn't seem to be selling anything but was nonetheless inundated. Intrigued, he approached to see what all the fuss was about and was stunned to see none other than Davina Jones holding court to a gaggle of starstruck teenagers, desperate to be associated with the person who so skilfully sabotaged Britain's Got Issues.

"Shows like that just wind me up," she explained to her audience. "They claim to be giving the average person a chance to achieve their dreams, but they're actually the most shamelessly exploitative set-ups – dangling the carrot of fame in front of the most desperate and gullible of people. Once they lure them in, they publicly humiliate them in the name of ratings and then squeeze the maximum profit for themselves out of whoever survives the ordeal. If they were giving away heroin outside schools they would be put away forever, but because they claim to be offering a chance at stardom the system gives them the green light to do whatever they want. The fact that the psychologically different are considered equally fair game just makes the whole thing even more disgusting."

"But how did you get the guts to stand up there on TV and diss them like that?" asked one admirer.

"I was pissed-off. If someone messes with you, you mess with them back twice as hard. That's the only way they know not to do it again. I'm not kidding myself though, the show will continue just fine in spite of my efforts, but maybe they'll take the piss a bit less from now on."

"Man, when you shouted 'Fuck you I won't do what you tell me' at them I was, like, screaming my tits off – I just wanted to get over there and fuck them up myself. You're my hero Davina."

"Don't idolise me, I'm just another person like you. I stood up to these manipulative pricks, but any of you could too. All you need to remember is that if you don't want anything they have to offer, they can't hurt you. Once you know someone can't hurt you it's a lot easier to stand up to them."

"But weren't you worried about looking bad on prime-time TV, like if they chucked you off or called you an idiot or whatever?"

"Why? Who are they to hurt my feelings? If a dog pisses on your foot you don't take it personally – you just boot the little shit and tell its owners to keep a better eye on it. But you don't reckon the dog did it to upset you, do you? You don't take it personally – the dog just felt like pissing on something and you were there. These pricks don't give a damn about you one way or the other, you're just a piece of meat to chew up and spit out when they've extracted what they want. So if they don't care about me, why should I give even a fraction of a fuck what they say or do? They're parasites, like bacteria. It's what they do – it's all they do. To be honest, as individuals I'm indifferent to them, but I don't like the consequences of their actions. If you don't want what they're offering, and don't care what they think, then you're invulnerable. Indifference is strength, don't forget that."

While he was listening to all this from the back of the crowd Dalston found himself thinking back to his recent troubles at work. Gold & Mackenzie had loads of what he wanted, and he was deeply anxious about their current low opinion of him. In other words they had him by the balls, and they knew it. The only way he could be free of them would be to resign, but then what would he do? He had a massive mortgage, still owed loads on his Audi R8, and the maintenance of his myriad addictions and noisome habits required a turnover most small companies would kill for. It was all very well Davina saying indifference is freedom, but she didn't seem to have anything worth giving a shit *about*.

Even so, he hung around the stall, waiting for an opportunity to speak to her. Superficially this was because he thought it would be cool to see if he could get this militant skirt into the sack, but there was also a grudging admiration for a person who seemed immune to the many honey-traps he so willingly succumbed to. Eventually the groupies moved on and he introduced himself.

"Hi Davina, at risk of saying the same thing you seem to have heard a hundred times already today, I loved what you did on BGI."

"Thanks a lot – it was fun – and the hundred-and-first compliment is no less welcome than the first. If it's made people question the motives of those tossers a bit more then I'm delighted. To whom do I have the pleasure of speaking?"

"Sorry, Dave Dalston. So what are you selling then? I can't see any of the standard Camden tat."

"Freedom, and there's no charge."

"So you're giving away *'freedom'* for free?" he said, doing the wiggly double-finger quotation gesture in case his scepticism failed to register.

"Yes, would you like some?"

"Since it's free I'll have ten boxes please – gift-wrapped, with a big pink bow."

"Hard though you've tried to hide it, I sense you're not entirely convinced. Let me ask you this: what are you doing tomorrow?"

"Easy tiger, we've only just met. How about we get to know each other a little better before we take things to the next level, eh?"

"Don't flatter yourself Casanova, just answer the question."

"OK, well, I don't know to be honest."

"Why's that – don't you have a job or anything?"

"I do, but I've just been suspended from it for two months."

"What for?"

"Behaving '*inappropriately*'."

"You like that air quote gesture, don't you? Anything to do with the Simpson-Oxford Act?"

"Spot on! For some reason they think my behaviour is too ego-driven."

"Shame. If only they could see the humble, self-effacing person standing in front of me, they'd be sure to realise their mistake."

Dalston was taken aback. "Are you saying I come over as big-headed?"

"The initial evidence seems pretty conclusive."

"Amazing, I don't know what's going on, all of a sudden everyone thinks I'm an egomaniac when I'm the same ordinary bloke I've always been."

"Maybe they've always thought that."

"No way, I would have known."

"I'll let you be the judge of how sensitive you might have been to other's views in the past, but I suspect where people previously tolerated your behaviour, the Simpson-Oxford Act has made them feel empowered to speak up. This isn't a good time to be a big-head."

"Wow, why don't you say what you really think?"

"I just did."

"You have got to be one of the most utterly honest people I've ever met, and easy on the eyes, too. OK, you've convinced me, I will meet up with you again."

"And you've got to be one of the most delusional, but I concede you're not too bad either. Listen, I'm here to talk about The Hidden Agenda, not to pull, so if you're not interested can you go and letch at someone else please? Or better still go home and have an overdue wank."

"Alright, calm down, I was just having a bit of fun. So, where were we? I've been suspended from my job for not having a rod up my arse. What's it to you?"

"How do you feel about being suspended?"

"Gutted – I don't get paid!"

"So?"

"What do you mean 'so'?"

"Why is that a bad thing?"

"Erm, because money comes in quite handy for, like, buying things."

"So if you didn't need to buy things then getting suspended wouldn't be so bad?"

"Well, that's a big 'if.' I heard what you were saying earlier about indifference being freedom and all that, and I suppose that's what you were referring to when you said you were offering freedom. That's great if you're a crusty who doesn't have anything to lose, but I've got a ton of stuff and a penthouse lifestyle to maintain, all of which costs money."

Dalston couldn't disguise a look of casual contempt. Davina's good looks, rather than softening his sentiment towards her, antagonised him as he considered her a waste of quality talent. This attitude was not lost on her.

"My lifestyle wasn't imposed on me, mate, I chose it, as you did yours, and you can choose a different one anytime you want. You might consider asking yourself why you're so committed to your current one."

"Because it makes me happy, I guess."

"And are you happy now?"

"Definitely not."

"I rest my case," said Davina and, after giving him an arch look, turned to talk to another stall visitor. Dalston thought of grabbing her attention back to deliver a final, stinging riposte but realised he didn't have one, so he just walked away laughing to himself.

Further into the market he came across a stall manned by Dev Sharma, selling a variety of mobile phones and accessories, the latter of the most ostentatious and tacky variety.

"Dev, good to see you again, mate," said Dalston. "What are you doing here? I thought you worked at Fonez!."

"I do, bruv, but I don't want to be a fucking wage slave forever, know what I mean." said Dev.

"So what, you're setting up your own phone shop here in Camden Market?"

"Yeah, for starters, but one day I'll put Fonez! out of business. From little acorns, you get me."

"Do I dare ask where you get all this kit from?"

"Here and there, blad, here and there. Listen, there's loads of gear about, you just need to know where to look. I first got into this when I realised what a fucking skank the phones I was selling at the shop were. Sorry to break it to you, but you paid way over the odds for that Cosmic Phone I flogged you."

"Oh great! Thanks for that."

"No-one held a gun to your head, geezer. Anyway, dog-eat-dog and all that, we all got to make a living, innit. What do you do?"

"I work in the City."

"Ha! So you fuck over entire countries for a living, and you've got the nerve to give me dirty looks for talking you into buying a phone. At least you've got something to show for it, you hear what I'm saying."

"Calm down, mate, I was just admiring your gall for saying that shit to my face. As you say, I didn't have to buy the phone, so fair play to you. But some of this gear looks a lot like what I saw in the shop."

Dev stood up, came around to the front of his stall, and stood with his face an inch from Dalston's. Or at least it would have been if Dev had been half a foot taller, but the implied threat was clear nonetheless.

"I do hope you're not trying to say it's nicked, blad, because that would be a very serious accusation indeed, you get me." said Dev.

Dalston looked down at him and realised he would fight, without hesitation and to the death, to defend himself from this slur, regardless of how much truth it contained.

"Easy tiger, just making an observation. I don't for one second suspect any of your gear of being anything other than one hundred percent legit. Now how about taking a step back and taking a chill-pill, eh?"

Dev regarded him with suspicion before slowly walking backwards, thus demonstrating he was only standing down because he felt like it and had not in any way lessened his resolve to batter Dalston if the situation called for it.

"You got to be careful how you say things, bruv, a lot of blokes wouldn't be as understanding as me and would fuck your shit up for a comment like that, you feel me."

"OK, OK, how about you let me buy you a pint to make everything better?"

"Yeah, alright, Mo can keep an eye on things." Dev turned to what appeared to be a teenage boy. "Just tell people what shit costs and no trade-ins, alright. I'm having so much trouble trying to shift all those fucking out-of-date johnnies you scored I'm tempted to sell them as waterproof phone cases, know what I mean. So no more Jack-and-the-beanstalk bollocks, yeah."

After acknowledging the required degree of grovelling and forelock-tugging from his minion, Dev nominated the Lock Tavern for the promised pint and started walking there without waiting for Dalston's consent. "I do the little cunt a favour and he thinks he's Richard fucking Branson – trying to do deals with everyone instead of just flogging the gear like I told him. If he wasn't my cousin he'd be out on his arse."

"Maybe he was just trying to impress you."

"He wants to impress me he needs to shift those rubbers for a profit. Either that or fucking use some of them, but he'd need to be able to talk to a bird without shitting his pants first, know what I mean."

Once at the pub Dev, still apparently bearing the emotional scars from their earlier exchange, was keen to move the conversation on. "So what do you do in the City then, bruv?"

"I'm a trader, or at least I was until I got suspended the other day."

"Suspended? What the fuck could a City trader possibly do that his company would think is out of order? I guess you're not bringing in the readies, yeah?"

"There's nothing wrong with my work, the problem is this new law. My company has gone mad for it, to try and suck up to the ego police."

"You mean all that Id Card shit?"

"Yeah – the set of laws that come with it are called the Simpson-Oxford Act, and they threaten to punish companies if any of their employees behave inappropriately, which effectively means acting like you reckon yourself too much."

"You're joking, right? You can get nicked for showing off? I was almost jealous of you working in the City, but fuck that shit. Anyone who tries to tell me how to behave is getting slapped, you feel me."

"Totally mate, but the job pays a ton of wedge and, to be honest, I need the cash to maintain my rock 'n' roll lifestyle."

"I hear you, fam, you can't live the dream without a fat wad in your pocket. So what's the deal – they going to let you back?"

"I guess so, after two months, but then I'll have to report to this retraining bitch who'll try to suss out if I'm a reformed character."

"No problem, just tell her what she needs to hear and job done, innit."

"That's the plan, but she gets in my head and winds me up, and I end up telling her to suck my dick."

"I can see how that might be a problem. So you've got to find a way of talking to this bird without getting vexed, yeah?"

"Exactly."

"Has she got a decent rack?"

"What?"

"Her jugs, mate, has she got a proper pair?"

"Erm, average I guess, I didn't really check."

"Jesus Christ, bruv, I thought you was a pro. When you're talking to punani that's doing your head in, imagine you're having a go on her tits and you can put up with any amount of grief coming out of her gob, innit."

"You make it sound so simple."

"It is! That's what I'm saying, it's just people make it complicated by banging on about respecting women and that. Just keep your eyes on the prize and don't get distracted by all that background noise. It's scientifically impossible for a bloke to talk to any woman for longer than five minutes without getting the arsehole, unless he's focused on sealing the deal. Fact."

"You might be onto something there. Do you know who Davina Jones is?"

"That bird from BGI? Yeah, I think she's got a stall around here somewhere."

"That's right, I was chatting to her before I met you. She wound me up almost immediately, but I really wanted to keep talking to her because I want to get her in the sack."

"There you go, now just do the same thing when you talk to the company bird and Robert's your father's brother."

"The problem is my gob runs wild when I'm on the pull. I might be able to put up with her, but she'll probably make me public enemy number one if she sees me in full flow."

"Looks like if you can solve that problem, then everything's sorted. The tricky bit is looking all humble, even when you still totally rate yourself, you hear what I'm saying."

"Then you end up like my mate Jack. He's gone from being a total geezer to a corporate zombie overnight – it's doing my head in."

"I don't get you, bruv."

"It was always me and him kicking things off at work. We were the life and soul – he was my partner in crime – we used to tear the arse out of it. Then this Simpson-Oxford shit kicks-in and suddenly he's all 'yes sir, no sir, three bags full sir,' you know what I mean?"

"So he's decided to be a good boy, and you haven't, and you're the one in the shit, am I right?"

"That's the long-and-short of it, yeah."

"Looks like a simple choice to me, blad, your gob or your job, innit."

Dalston suddenly jumped out of his chair and started walking across the room.

"What? Chill, bruv, I'm just calling it like I see it," said Dev.

"Amy! My daughter. I just saw her again, over there."

With Dev in tow, startled drinkers assumed either Dalston was mentally ill or the two of them were about to attack someone. His frantic walk took him to the pub's small beer garden, where he further confirmed his apparent insanity by peering under tables, lifting chairs and opening parasols in a futile search for his estranged daughter.

"Mate, you've seriously got to get a grip," said Dev.

"I think I'm going fucking mad, Dev," said Dalston once he had completed his search. "I could've sworn I saw her walking across the pub into the beer garden, but now she's just disappeared."

"Have you lost something?" said Davina Jones, who was sitting alone at one of the tables.

After a double-take Dalston composed himself. "Davina, hello again, you didn't see a little girl walk in here just now did you?"

"Pretty sure there have been no children out here while I've been here, sorry. Have a seat, you look like you've seen a ghost."

"Cheers," he said, once more coming to the conclusion he was having some kind of hallucination. "This is a friend of mine, Dev Sharma. Dev, this is Davina Jones, who was..."

"On the telly dissing BGI – yeah, I saw that," interrupted Dev, casting a lecherous eye over Davina. "So you some kind of retard rights campaigner or something?"

Davina was not impressed. "I presume by 'retard' you mean people who are psychologically different. I didn't like the way the show was exploiting vulnerable people, so I decided to do something about it. If you think that makes me a 'campaigner' then so be it."

"Alright sweetheart, just saying, innit. No need to get your knickers in a twist."

Davina chose not to rise to the provocation, having concluded they weren't going to get on in the few seconds she had been exposed to Dev.

"So what's all this about your daughter, Casanova?" she said.

"Why she call you that, Dave?" said Dev.

"Because that's who he acts like. Now wait your turn, Ali G."

"You saying I act like Ali G? Fuck off bitch!"

"I rest my case. Now if you don't mind, you were saying Dave?"

Dalston found himself surprisingly unsettled by the instant antagonism between his two new friends. He assumed any two people he got on with would also get on with each other and felt somehow culpable when it failed to happen.

"It's a bit of a long story. When Amy's Mum – Mel – got pregnant I wasn't ready to have a kid. I said all the right things at the time about supporting her and the baby, but before long I started seeing other birds too. I was young and still had wild oats to sow, I suppose."

"Totally, bruv," said Dev, while Davina's expression revealed resigned disappointment.

"Eventually she found out and obviously wasn't happy. The thing is I did have a lot of time for her; we really got on. She wasn't just some bit on the side and I had been faithful to her for months, which is still a record for me. But she just wasn't up for it anymore after she got in the club and didn't drink or anything. She just started banging on about the baby and getting a flat with an extra bedroom for the nursery and all that domestic shit. I was starting to feel middle-aged, man. Like I said, it was just too much too soon. I promised her I'd be a good boy, but I couldn't keep it up, if you get what I'm saying, so she chucked me out.

"Mel still let me come and visit Amy after she was born and I tried my best, buying her stuff and chucking her some cash every now and then. After a couple of years Mel and I started seeing each other again and eventually I even moved in with them. It was pretty cool waking up every morning and hearing Amy talking and living the whole family dream. I started to see what the fuss was all about with kids and was determined not to fuck things up again.

"But I did. One night I got pissed and met some bird in a club. I went back to hers and did the business and then crashed out. The next morning I was gutted and couldn't believe what I'd done, but figured what Mel didn't know couldn't hurt her. However the bird had other ideas: she'd taken photos of me with my kit off while I was asleep and threatened to publish them online unless I chucked her some cash. She'd gone through my wallet too, so she knew who I was. I was so worried about Mel I went straight to a cashpoint, got out two hundred quid and gave it to her.

"But that wasn't the end of it, of course. She started texting me asking for more cash, or else, and at first I paid up. Eventually I realised it was never going to end and I had to call her bluff, so I confessed to Mel, saying it was a drunk one-off and begging her to forgive me. She was gutted, of course, but I thought I might just get away with it until that bitch posted the photos on Instagram, which Mel saw. I think the one of me wearing knickers and a bra was the straw that broke the camel's back, although I still don't remember putting them on. Mel not only chucked me out but said I couldn't see Amy either in case I corrupted her, or something like that, but probably also to punish me even more. So I've hardly had any contact with Amy for a few years now, apart from when I thought I saw her just now and the other day in Dev's shop."

"Do you miss her?" said Davina.

"Of course, man. But Mel's not having it. I even thought of getting lawyers involved, but in the end I just accepted it and got on with my life. I think about her every day though."

"So you've given up, innit," said Dev, exasperated by the tale. "I'd never let no-one keep my kid from me. You've got to grow a pair, you hear what I'm saying."

"Hold on Ali, maybe staying away is the best thing for Amy," said Davina. "It's not going to be good for her seeing her parents arguing and not knowing when her Dad's going to be around."

"I figured you was a rug-muncher. You remind me of that mad bird in 'The Girl With The Dragon Tattoo,' so seeing as we're playing nicknames I'm going to call you Lisbeth – no, even better, Lezbeth," laughed Dev, congratulating himself on his wit. "So what about his rights then, Lezbeth, that's his kid as much as hers. I reckon you should just tell your ex you're seeing your kid whenever you want and there's fuck-all she can do about it."

"I think I've just stayed away because it's easier," said Dalston. "You just go from day-to-day, week-to-week, month-to-month working, going out, doing your thing, and before you know it a couple of years have gone by."

"Maybe that's why you drink so much, so you don't have to think about it," ventured Davina.

"Or maybe he just likes having a laugh," said Dev. "You might want to try it sometime Lezbeth. Just say the word – I'll show you a good time, know what I mean."

Davina briefly regarded Dev as if he'd just shat himself before her attention returned to Dalston.

"You might have a point Davina," he said. "I do like a laugh but maybe I'm also deliberately distracting myself – I'd never really thought about it like that. Perhaps that's why I keep thinking I see Amy when she's actually not around; it's my head trying to tell me something."

"Yeah, it's saying have a fucking drink, you poof," said Dev. "Don't listen to this dyke, Dave, she's trying to get in your head and turn you into some dickless pussy. They're not happy until you do what you're told, then they accuse you of having no balls. You can't win, bruv, so best to just do what you want, innit."

"Well, Dave, it looks like you've got a straight choice," said Davina. "You can carry on as usual and not see your daughter, or you can compromise and maybe get to see her occasionally. I guess it comes down to what's most important to you."

Chapter 8 – Interventions

Sir Raymond Payshus had not been having an easy time of it in his new role as secondary school headmaster and maths teacher. Every method he had ever used to control and dominate other people in the corporate world was useless against teenagers who found him about as intimidating as Mickey Mouse. In the corporate world people cared only about jobs, promotions and bonuses, but in the school-kid world an entirely different system of incentives, fears and priorities applied. Payshus had taken to blogging about his experiences and, with so much time now on his hands, Dalston found himself surprisingly entertained by the accounts.

If anything, Payshus observed, the school social environment was even more political than the corporate one. Boys who were good at fighting and/or sports, and girls who were beautiful were generally the most popular, although some apparently tough boys were loners, and some pretty girls were ostracised. There was also a powerful system of patronage, with many of the most popular kids boasting an entourage of lieutenants, social-climbers and assorted sycophants. These social strata had direct equivalents among both boys and girls, and relationships between the sexes seemed only to happen between kids of equivalent social ranking. It began to dawn on Payshus that these were very similar to the social dynamics found in the adult world, just in a much more confined environment.

Alphas could boost their status by starting a relationship with each other, an occurrence that took on the seismic significance of a royal wedding when it happened, which was frequently. Such relationships were usually more political than romantic in nature, rather like a medieval aristocratic marriage. They were almost always initiated and controlled by the girl, with the boy usually pathetically grateful to be involved – at first. In keeping with tradition she was careful not to upstage or belittle her boyfriend, as she now derived part of her status from him, so she talked-up how big, tough and handsome he was and even allowed herself to be ordered around to a limited degree. But it was clear to Payshus that little the boy did was not endorsed by the girl.

The end of these often ephemeral liaisons was a dangerous period for the girl as, released from her spell, the boy could turn on her. Such an event was made more likely by the apparent need to mark the end of the relationship with a propaganda campaign of such focused ruthlessness Joseph Goebbels would have tipped his hat. All other relationships across the two groups of followers ended immediately, on pain of social annihilation, and all concerned set about character-assassinating their exes as widely as possible.

While mulling how to influence this complex dynamic to his advantage, Payshus figured the low-hanging fruit was likely to be found among the loners, misfits and geeks. However, he soon discovered they had their own agenda that was, if anything, even more counter-productive. Because social capital was so much harder for them to acquire they were prepared to do more to get it. Disruptive behaviour could happen at any time and take any form, because the only outcome of importance to the disruptor was the approval of the rest of the class. A suitably nihilistic act could even have the perpetrator branded 'a nutter' and elevated in the eyes of the other kids for a bit. But you were only as good as your last prank, and it had to rise above the many others being attempted, so an arms race existed in which otherwise bright, sensitive and well brought-up kids focused on committing the most heinous classroom crimes possible.

In spite of how alien this environment was to Payshus, he was still convinced the same underlying rules should apply. These were still people, after all, albeit partially formed ones. Both sets of people conformed to Maslow's Hierarchy of Needs by seeking security first, then social advancement, with status and ultimately self-esteem as the goal. The main difference was adults do so primarily through the accumulation of wealth, while his school-kids had, if anything, a more complex set of criteria for acquiring and displaying social capital. At the conclusion of his most recent blog post Payshus mused that the key to controlling the school might lie in converting teen social equity into a simpler, more liquid and commoditized form.

**

Susan Percilious, the civil servant charged with implementing the Id Card scheme, had also been busy publishing her views and experiences, but preferred the more sound bite-friendly medium of Twitter. Dalston knew to expect only the most unashamed self-promotion but followed her tweets regardless, if only to get a snapshot of how the great experiment was progressing.

@reallySuePercilious

Delighted to see the #IdCard scheme being embraced so enthusiastically by the entire country.

@reallySuePercilious

You should all be proud of yourselves! Already the changes brought about by the #IdCard are transforming society.

@reallySuePercilious

This is how to bring about change. When markets and human nature fail, a benign guiding hand is needed. We listened to you and we acted. #doingsomethinggood

Public opinion also seemed to be overwhelmingly positive:

@baizuo

Finally something's being done about the sickening social injustice that has been criminally blighting this country for too long. #IdCard #doingsomethinggood

@KateCares

Its about time those #wankers got knocked down a peg or two but how about taking there money away and giving it to people who really need it? #doingsomethinggood

Dissenting voices were soon dispatched:

@normie

Is it just me or is all this #IdCard stuff a little bit creepy?

@KateCares

yeah ur so right @normie everyones really creeped out by all this fairness and progress. What the fuck is ur problem?

@baizuo

@normie I suppose you long for a world in which the #wankers still get to do what they want and ruin the economy once a decade. I'm so sorry for being happy that we're finally #doingsomethinggood – I'll hand myself into the police immediately!

@RedPillTime

@KateCares @baizuo Get back in your box for fuck's sake! @normie was making a perfectly valid point that you're entitled to disagree with but there's no need to be a dick about it. What the fuck is UR problem?

@KateCares

@RedPillTime my problem is that there's no pleasing some people. The moment anyone tries to do some good hate-speakers like you have to shit on it just because its not about lining ur pockets #nazi

@baizuo

@RedPillTime If you can't be happy that society is improving then you should just keep quiet. I wonder what your boss would think if he/she knew what a #nazi you are.

Before long Percilious, emboldened by all this public support, began testing the boundaries of the scheme's remit:

@reallySuePercilious

So banks are becoming less greedy and schools more disciplined, but this just feels like the start of something much bigger. I wonder what else we can achieve. #IdCard #doingsomethinggood

@reallySuePercilious

I think we can all agree that replacing Canines and Delphines with Felines and Simians in many top jobs has made the country less greedy, oppressive and unfair. #IdCard #doingsomethinggood

@reallySuePercilious

But it's also fair to say that Canines and Delphines still have plenty to offer, so long as their more unhelpful tendencies are managed. #IdCard #rightaction

@reallySuePercilious

While there continues to be overwhelming public support for the #IdCard scheme, it has been brought to my attention that pockets of opposition remain, chiefly within the Canine community. I call upon them to embrace this once in a lifetime opportunity. #rightaction

@reallySuePercilious

Bigotry and prejudice are unacceptable ways of expressing any frustrations you may have with the #IdCard scheme. If Canine leaders are unable to control their more passionate constituents the government will be forced to intervene. #rightaction

***

During his suspension Dalston was able to follow the progress of the Id Card scheme closely. He hadn't previously paid much attention to current affairs because he believed very little of what was reported affected him directly. Foreign wars, natural disasters, some random crime, one twat being replaced by another twat in Parliament, who gave a fuck? Even the business reporting wound him up as he had far more comprehensive sources of information at work. He usually just flicked straight to the sport and even then only when the football season was on.

His social media use was confined mainly to Facebook, on which he was largely passive. He found it mildly diverting to see what his Facebook 'friends' were sharing and liked the viral posts featuring videos of people or animals suffering assorted indignities. He would occasionally comment on current affairs-related posts but often with a simple, unqualified, abusive comment. He was aware some people were more engaged, and he sometimes felt moved to antagonise other commenters if he found them especially strident. Typically he would try to throw the ball back in the court of the shrill, denouncing types by posting something like "OK then, what would you do?" then dismissing the response as "bollocks".

On Twitter he was even more passive, preferring to like and retweet rather than offer any comment of his own. He was dimly aware that the consequences of getting things wrong on Twitter were much more severe than on Facebook and didn't feel strongly enough about anything to risk it. As for the other major social media platforms, he felt they were mainly just for women banging on about makeup and teenagers sending each other photos of their genitalia.

The prevailing opinion on Dalston's Facebook feed was that the Id Card scheme was a good thing because it was an attempt to make sure things like the financial crisis never happened again. On the surface that seemed to be pretty hard to argue against, but nonetheless a sizable minority did. Most of them were people who felt negatively affected by the scheme, notably those who had been forced to move jobs and weren't happy about it. Then you had people with broader objections, usually along libertarian lines.

Nick Georgiou was a vocal member of the dissenting camp and Dalston was keen to test out some of the stuff he had picked up during his time off on his mates, so one evening they all met up at the Duke of Hamilton in Hampstead.

"So Nick, it looks like you're not the only one worried about this Id Card business, eh?" said Dalston.

"No Dave, but it fucking depresses me that I'm in the minority," said Georgiou.

"Why's that?" said Al Blake. "Firstly you're wrong – society has decided to do something positive for once and yet you've got a face like a slapped arse – and secondly it's fucking great that most people are right behind it. It's easy to just sit in the pub and moan Nick, but at the very least don't get in the way of people who are trying to do the right thing."

"I'm not getting in anyone's way Al, I just think the whole thing is fucked up that's all. Surely you don't think it's wrong for me to express my views."

"In this case I'm saying it is. Sometimes what's happening is bigger than any single person's opinion, and everyone needs to acknowledge that and work towards the greater good. If you can't say something positive then you should stay quiet."

"Says who?"

"Says me."

"Or what?"

"Or you might find things going very badly for you very quickly, mate."

"Is that a threat?"

"Just watch your mouth."

"Sounds like a threat to me. So Al, what you're saying is 'shut up or I'll hit you.' Nice chat, we must do this more often."

Blake just glowered at Georgiou and Dalston seized the opportunity created by the impasse to redirect the conversation in a more constructive direction.

"I'm torn, if I'm honest," he said. "On one hand this shit is what got me suspended and I'm with Nick that there's something properly dodgy about the government having this much power over us. On the other, even us City boys have to admit we blew it with the financial crisis, so I suppose we can't really moan when it gets thrown back in our faces."

"It's good to hear you being so positive about it Dave, because I was wondering if the penny would ever drop," said Jack Morrison. "It's just like investing; there are upsides and downsides. We rode the wave for a while and now it's broken so we've got to sit tight and take our licks. If you'd joined the dots on this a bit quicker, Dave, maybe you wouldn't have got suspended."

"Yeah thanks for that Jack, I guess not everyone finds capitulation as easy as you do."

"Dave, Dave, Dave. When will you ever learn? It's just a matter of looking facts in the face. We fucked up so we have to be punished. End of. If you view taking your punishment as capitulation then you still don't get it. You have to submit completely or they'll find you out. Look at those fuckers still snapping and losing their shit in the office – they probably think it's a capitulation too and eventually it catches up with them."

"Maybe, but who says we fucked up anyway? It was Payshus and cunts like him that did the damage; we're just the foot-soldiers doing our jobs, doing what we were told. Why should we be punished for that?"

"That's what the Nazis said after the Second World War, mate," said Blake. "Just following orders is not an excuse; you were part of the problem, even if it was only a small part, so you need to be part of the final solution."

"You might want to be a bit more careful with your historical references there, Al," said Georgiou. "But this does seem to be an issue of collective punishment. Jack and Al are arguing in favour of it, but Dave doesn't seem convinced and to be honest I'm with him on that. What are the limits of collective responsibility? Since you're so keen in bringing up the war, Al, do you think Germans today should be punished for the shit their ancestors got up to seventy-odd years ago? I know you don't hold white people today responsible for all the bad shit other white people got up to in the past, even though some of your ancestors were almost certainly slaves, so where's the line in the sand?"

"But this is happening now," said Blake. "Calling for collective responsibility now is very different from hassling you over some stuff that happened before you were born. Whether Dave likes it or not, everyone blames bankers for a lot of the shit we're in and, let's face it, if enough people believe something then it doesn't really matter how accurate it is, it effectively becomes true. You can moan about it all you want but that's not going to change the fact that most people think you broke it, so most people think you've got to fix it too."

"I totally concede that Al, but I'm just not sure how happy I am about it," said Dalston. "In theory you're right but in practice, when you're one of the people being collectively punished, it's harder to justify."

"In other words you're all for doing the right thing until it becomes a bit of a drag for you and then you're like 'fuck this, we're going too far.' Why don't you just buy yourself another Ferrari mate, that should sugar the pill."

"Jesus Christ Al, you're on form today. Why don't you go and shoot a foreigner to get it out of your system?"

Dalston's comment resulted in another sulky impasse.

"Alright, let's all take a deep breath, eh?" said Georgiou. "This is uncharted territory for all of us and it's no surprise feelings are strong, but I also reckon chats like this are a really good way of trying to get our heads around it all. For the sake of keeping the peace I'm willing to concede that if we're going to have this massive social experiment we might as well give it a go. OK Al? But I also think it's perfectly reasonable to analyse what's going on and express any concerns you might have."

There was a general nodding of heads and muttering of 'fair enough' around the table.

"So my core concern, which nearly got my head kicked in a minute ago, is about the unintended consequences of social engineering," he continued. "Yes, the crisis and insurrection were fuck ups. Yes, we needed to 'hashtag-do-something,' and yes, it's reasonable to focus a lot of that on the financial sector. But as I've said before: 'something' doesn't mean 'anything' – it needs to be qualified. I presume you don't think it would be cool to just kill all the bankers and start again, Al."

"Of course not. That's a fucking stupid thing to say," said Blake.

"Maybe, but I'm trying to make the point that ideally we don't just want to do something, we want to do the *best* thing, which isn't easy. For the sake of this argument let's say the two most extreme positions we could adopt on this are doing nothing at one end and killing all the bankers at the other end."

"For fuck's sake," Blake muttered, eliciting sniggers from Dalston and Morrison.

"We agree those two extremes are both undesirable, so what we're looking for is some point in between them – the ideal equilibrium – right?" persisted Georgiou. "To find it we need to work out what form it should take but also how far we should take it. The government has decided it should take the form of the Id Card scheme, which itself has pros and cons – don't forget how much you hated it at first when you thought it was racist Al – but it is what it is, and that's the path we've collectively chosen. Then it decided to use the information provided by the Id Cards to embark on a pretty radical social engineering experiment, with hardly any precedent to draw on and little research into potential outcomes. I'm saying this move is going too far towards the extreme action end, as opposed to the doing fuck-all end, that's all."

"OK Nick, I'm happy to run with this to see where it goes," said Morrison. "I agree the wrong kind of action is bad, but the flip side is that even with the right action, if you don't follow through on it then it's not going to work, is it? You could be, like 'we've got this magic wand that will sort everything out but let's not use it just in case it pisses a few people off.' What's the point of that?"

"Definitely, mate, I completely agree so long as we actually have a magic wand," said Georgiou. "But that's the thing: I just don't think we do. We've got a vague idea that maybe some personality types are destined to fuck things up if you put them in certain situations so let's take them out of there and everything will be cool. There are so many unknowns it's not even funny. What do we do with those people? Who do we replace them with? How do we know the fuckups were all down to them as individuals rather than some collective failure or even a completely different set of factors?"

"Alright," intervened Dalston. "We can all agree there's been an almighty fuckup and the City should take a lot of the blame. But, as ever, the solution is tricky. I'd like as much focus as possible to be on trying to find a constructive solution, which brings us back to the collective responsibility thing. Al seems to want to punish us for screwing things up but, even allowing for my natural bias, I still can't see how this will sort things out in the long term. You'll get people like Jack keeping their heads down until it blows over, then it will be business as usual again."

"So you think you should just be let off the hook?" said Blake. "You think there should be no consequences, no deterrents, no punishment?"

"No I don't – I accept there need to be repercussions," Dalston replied. "But just like Nick I reserve the right to question the nature of them."

"Sorry man, when you fuck up you lose the right to question your punishment. You don't get convicted murderers going up to the judge and going 'that's a bit harsh, man, don't you know how much prison sucks?' and then getting time off."

"Yeah but that's an individual crime, I'm talking about collective punishment. What about the wars we've been in? Loads of people think those were wrong, but nobody's saying squaddies like you should get punished because you were just doing what you were told. It was the politicians who made the decision to go to war and the army leaders who got their strategies and tactics wrong, not you."

"When you put it that way I can see your point, to be honest. There's a big difference between individual and collective punishment. So we can't just fuck over all the wankers without throwing the baby out with the bathwater. So where the fuck does that leave us?"

"That's the big question, man," said Georgiou. "And I think we're going to find out before long. I'm forced to concede Al's point that, no matter what I think, there's currently overwhelming momentum towards punishing bankers and turning society on its head. It's going to be fascinating to see how this plays out and I fear the worst, but it is what it is.

"Do me a favour though guys, no matter where you stand on all this, keep your eyes and your mind open. There will definitely be a shit-load of unintended consequences and the wrath of the mob might not stay limited to City boys. Al, just remember this: first they came for the bankers and I stayed quiet, because I wasn't one. Then they came for the dealers and I stayed quiet because I wasn't one. Then they came for me and there was no one left to speak for me."

Chapter 9 – Indignation

The collective punishment of the Canines was indeed having unintended consequences. While many of them chose to keep their heads down and ride it out, a significant minority were increasingly inclined to express their dissatisfaction with the new state of affairs. As the single figure most associated with destructive Canine behaviour Ray Payshus had wisely opted to stay out of the spotlight, but others were less reticent. Dalston was especially struck by a radio interview between Iain Tegritie and Steve Sybarite, the former head of a major management consultancy, who had undergone the now-familiar reciprocal job swap with the leader of an inner-London council.

"Mr Sybarite, you've gone on the record saying the Id Card scheme is, and I quote: 'a load of bollocks'," said Tegritie. "Can you tell us why you think that?"

"Well firstly I'd like to point out it was just one small part of a much longer conversation, which wasn't actually on the record. You presumably got that quote from the *Times* story headlined 'Sybarite in foul-mouthed anti-Id Card tirade' and it's important to note the story was based on one anonymous source, which is pretty far from me going on the record."

"I do apologise Mr Sybarite, so does that story not represent your position on the Id Card scheme then?"

"Actually I do think it's a load of bollocks, but until now I've never gone on the record to that effect."

"So you want us to know an article which accurately represents your views arrived at that position via a route you're not entirely happy with, is that right?"

"Yes."

"Great. Well if there's nothing else – does your seat need adjusting? Perhaps you'd like a quick massage to really get you in the mood? No? Then, if it's totally OK with you, I'll carry on with the interview, alright?"

Sybarite sighed audibly.

"So why is it a load of bollocks?"

"Because the government has panicked and rushed out a knee-jerk response to a very complicated matter. They quite rightly shat themselves during the insurrection and decided to look into it. So far so good, but then they got all carried away and decided, on the back of one report, to turn everything arse-over-tit. Now I've got to spend my days listening to lesbians moan about the lack of traditional Namibian cuisine at their world food workshops while some prick in a

Che Guevara T-shirt tells my clients they should be running their businesses along the lines of a Bolivian cocoa collective. If that's not bollocks then I don't know what is."

"Who are you to call Namibian cuisine or Bolivian cocoa bollocks? Have you even tried either?"

"No, and it wouldn't matter if the food was so good it made me shoot my load, that's not the point. I worked all my life to get to the top of the consulting business and I'm pretty bloody good at it, even if I say so myself. But now, just because the government wants to cover its arse, I'm removed from that position against my will and put in charge of the biggest collection of dickless blokes, moaning birds and general liabilities I've ever seen in my life. If it was happening to someone else I'd be pissing myself laughing!"

"We get that you're not happy about your personal arrangements, but this isn't about you, it's about the greater good."

"Hold on, you asked me why I wasn't happy about the Id Card scheme and I answered..."

"Yes, but I assumed your objections would amount to more than just sulking about a bit of personal inconvenience. Everyone else is managing to look at the bigger picture, why can't you?"

"Alright then, let's look at the big fucking picture, shall we? There is absolutely no proof that putting a local councillor in charge of a management consultancy firm will produce any kind of positive outcome for anyone involved or for society in general."

"Maybe not, but we do have proof that leaving you in charge of it will definitely produce a negative outcome, don't we?"

"No! I'm just being grouped in with banker types in general because I work in a high-value, white-collar industry too. I didn't cause the goddamn financial crisis and nor did my profession. The fact that a few blokes with gold cufflinks flushed loads of money down the toilet is now being used as proof anyone in a pricey suit must be a liability and needs to be put in professional quarantine, sharpish."

"Has your company ever advised banks?"

"Of course, but..."

"Then you can't say your hands are clean. You must have known something was going on; did you do anything to try to prevent the crisis?"

"If any of our clients had indicated they intended to follow a similar strategy to the one adopted by Clark's we would have strongly advised them against it."

"That's hardly the same. I'm afraid if you're not part of the solution then you're part of the problem. You should consider yourself lucky to be given a second chance to do the right thing. Rather than bitch and moan, try celebrating this opportunity for redemption."

"You act like I killed someone!"

"You did worse than that, you abused your privilege, you raped the country and you murdered hope. Your previous job was granted to you by society and you threw it back in its face, so now we're taking it back. You had your chance and you blew it."

"Society didn't grant me shit. I had to scratch and fight every step of the way to get where I did. I pay a shit-load more into the pot than I will ever take out, I employ a lot of people and I generate wealth by the ton. The government is just using the financial crisis as an excuse to rip off people like me and give jobs to leftie scroungers who've never done a proper day's work in their lives."

"If your idea of a proper day's work results in financial catastrophe and civil breakdown then maybe we need a few more 'leftie scroungers' in charge. But let me put this to you: why should your personal convenience trump the collective good?"

"Because this has fuck-all to do with the collective good and everything to do with petty vengefulness. One small lot of people cock things up and now all the nasty, bitter little rodents who've been lurking under the floorboards sense it's their moment. That's all this is: opportunism. Any whinge is now bound to receive a sympathetic hearing and be rewarded with someone else's job. Bollocks is too kind a description for this epic shit-show."

"That's a pretty contentious position to adopt in these febrile times, especially when there's nothing you can do to change it. The Id Card scheme is already way past the point at which we could stop it, even if we wanted to."

"Well, we'll see about that. I've spoken to a lot of other Canines who are furious about how things have turned out and aren't about to take it lying down. Just you wait and see, there will be consequences."

"Ominous words, Mr Sybarite."

While not on the scale of the Payshus interview, Sybarite's veiled threats ignited an outpouring of public indignation. Mainstream media went into a feeding frenzy of shocked editorials expressing dismay and revulsion at the lack of Canine collective spirit. Social media followed suit and, as ever, amplified what it cherry-picked from the media. Statements of support for Sybarite and his ilk, almost entirely from other Canines, were shouted down with increasing ferocity. It soon became apparent the greatest hostility came from Felines, although Simians were often quick to support their positions. Delphines were, on the whole, conspicuously absent from both sides of the dispute.

This dynamic was played out repeatedly to the point of cliché: defiant Canine rant leading to immediate Feline condemnation and fervent Simian cheerleading. Before long Canines found themselves pre-emptively attacked and singled out as Ray apologists, in reference to Payshus. Attempts to see things from both sides led to similar condemnation and many Canines felt unable to express their true feelings on the Id Card scheme or, indeed, anything else. The term 'Canine' itself became a pejorative liberally used to silence dissent online. Delphines, who were largely disinclined to pick a team in this snowballing factional conflict, often found their hands forced by Felines and Simians, who accused them of being Canine sympathisers if they failed to fully get in line with their agenda.

Consequently Delphines found themselves fragmented into sub-factions largely imposed on them by the nature of their treatment at the hands of the Felians, as the combined Feline/Simian super-faction soon became known. Those Delphines who quickly got onboard with the demonization of Canines were spared retribution, especially if they claimed to be Felianists. At the other end of the spectrum were perceived Canine sympathisers – branded 'Felophobes' –who publicly questioned the blanket demonization of the Canines or expressed general concern about the emerging faction-based sociological dynamic. They were often dealt with more harshly than actual Canines on the basis that they made a choice, while Canines couldn't help themselves.

The grey area in between these two extremes was fluid, with a given Delphine's position in the equilibrium determined by their most recent public act of devotion or heresy. An 'ally' could lose status immediately as the result of denunciation by a Felian. Conversely a Felophobe could redeem themselves in the Felian court of public opinion through acts of contrition and repentance judged sufficiently abject. Both fallen and repentant Delphines found themselves at the centre of a disproportionate amount of attention on mainstream and social media. Contrite Delphines were treated as hapless victims, once corrupted by the Canines but now redeemed and in need of Felian munificence.

Many fallen Delphines, however, concluded they could never do enough to placate the Felians and therefore doubled-down on their heresy, figuring they were already damned so they might as well enjoy it. This brought them to the attention of opportunistic Canines, who at the very least considered their enemy's enemy to be their friend and saw the chance to add some much-needed numbers to their faction group. As a result the Delphine faction was split, such that roughly a third of them were adopted by the Felians, a third by the Canines and a third remained in the hellish limbo of being continually denounced and claimed by everyone else.

The vast majority of Canines, having been branded heretical by default, also decided to make a virtue of necessity and surrender to their base inclinations. Most of the time this amounted to unbridled hedonism and there ensued a nationwide orgy of feasting and fornication that would have given Caligula pause for reflection. Initially this was fuelled by Canines blowing all their cash on the presumption their property was likely to be appropriated by Felians before long anyway, so they might as well enjoy it while they could. But such was the momentum of this mass bender that it soon escalated to criminality, as groups of Canines did a runner from massive bar tabs and obscene restaurant bills.

The judiciary was now dominated by Felians, who determined criminality should be viewed through an egotype filter that presumed malevolence on the part of Canines but offered limitless mitigation for errant Felines. Simian transgressors were required to be viewed as unwitting victims of their innate aggressiveness and were therefore to be rehabilitated rather than punished. The outcome of Delphine criminality was usually determined by an ad hoc blend of contrition from the offender and discretion from their accuser. Since the recruitment of Delphines was a cornerstone of Felian political strategy, they were threatened with draconian punishments, but at the same time offered lenience in exchange for factional compliance.

The most sought-after and richly rewarded gesture of contrition was to inform on a Canine. Initially this just took the form of reporting an established crime, but in time the reporting of 'precriminal' behaviour on the part of Canines or even Delphines became the preferred source of instant redemption. This otherwise efficient system hit a major obstacle at the point of enforcement, however, as the sizable Canine minority within rank-and-file police force were reluctant to implement a system so specifically designed to discriminate against their own kind. Since any refusal to do their jobs would, at the very least, result in them being reallocated to become, say, sewage engineers, such coppers tended to dissent by simply turning a blind eye. Once it became clear they could act with impunity, other Canines descended even further into unbridled debauchery. This in turn poured fuel onto the flames of Felian ire and before long some parts of the country were on the verge of civil war.

The political consequences of this were severe. The Id Card scheme had been sold to the public as the answer not only to the Payshus Insurrection, but to many of the social ills that contributed to it, so for many people this fresh unrest was proof of an incompetent government. A motion of no confidence was narrowly defeated in Parliament, but the incumbent administration remained weak and vulnerable. Partly to avoid stoking the flames further, the main opposition parties resisted jumping on the factionalism bandwagon and backed government pleas for calm and moderation. This left the field open for opportunistic new political movements to offer more radical solutions.

Among them was the Felian Liberal Authoritarian Party, which argued that since the greater Felian faction represented the majority of the UK population, it was only fitting they should run the country too. From a standing start FLAP rapidly gained momentum on social media, with endorsements from a number of celebrities and public figures. The veneer of conventional legitimacy offered by FLAP served to recruit many new Felines and Simians to the party. While they remained wary of entering into full-blown political combat, they assumed FLAP must be acting in their interests, so before long the nascent political movement was able to claim a significant proportion of the UK population as members.

Chapter 10 – Imitation

It was increasingly clear that being Dave Dalston was currently a losing proposition. Not only was he a superficial, narcissistic lout, he was also a Canine and thus a poster-boy for everything UK society had decided was wrong with itself. He was sorely tempted to join the Canine rampage, but since he preferred the more exclusive types of debauchery for which you have to pay top dollar, he felt compelled to keep his job at Gold & Mackenzie. It had been made abundantly clear the only circumstances under which his security pass would be reactivated would be when he showed himself to be so humble as to make the Dalai Lama look like Muhammad Ali. His lapse in front of Human Resources meant mere earnest vows and docile body language wouldn't be enough. He needed to provide conclusive proof that a new leaf had been not just turned over, but filled with prose so humble and contrite it brought a tear to the eye.

The most obvious way to acquire that kind of recognition, he concluded, would be to eschew his Canine nature openly and prostrate himself at the feet of the Felians. Unfortunately he knew very few members of either contributing faction. Al Blake was the only one of his inner circle who belonged to one and he was of limited use since he was a bit of a loner and considered social media to be a waste of time. While Dalston largely agreed, he thought social media represented his best chance to establish his repentant credentials publicly. His first faltering steps involved sharing news stories that denounced the more egregious acts of Canine bad behaviour on Facebook, usually accompanied by a brief commentary lamenting those few bad apples who were ruining everything for nice Canines like him. The only tangible result of this was to alienate a large proportion of his existing Facebook friends, as discussion prompted by his posts dissolved into acrimony with frightening speed and violence.

Dalston once shared an article published by the *Guardian*, entitled 'How Canines are violent even when they're not,' which examined the public utterances of a number of prominent Canines and explained why their words were tantamount to physical assaults inflicted upon anyone who read, heard or was even told about them. His accompanying commentary said, "This is a great piece showing how us Canines can often be our own worst enemies and what we can do to help make the world a better place." It got very few 'likes' and among the comments were:

"Mate, if you hate urself so much then fuckin do something about it instead of trying to bring everyone else down FFS."

"What happened to you Dave? You used to be a laugh and now you're just some kind of whinging bitch sucking up to Felians the whole time. Get a grip!"

"So if Canine words are violence, and you're a Canine, then surely the mere act of sharing this, with commentary, is violent, and thus makes the world a worse place. It strikes me, therefore, that the world would be most improved by you shutting the fuck up."

Dalston soon became a pariah among his old Facebook friends with very few new ones to show for it. It was baffling; plenty of other people seemed to be showered with likes and approving comments in response to the most mundane of posts. In fact he even tried precisely copying the Facebook activity of some of the most popular people but was greeted by a silence that was, in many ways, even more dispiriting than the abuse. Eventually a member of his dwindling Facebook entourage, Dev Sharma, felt sufficiently moved by his plight to send him a direct message.

What the fuck are you playin at bruv? You gone fuckin mental or summing? Why do you keep putting all that random shit up on FB – are you trying to pull?

Hey Dev, no I'm just trying to change my profile a bit – maybe get in with the Felians.

Why you bothering with those pussies man? They keep trying to get me to join their cult coz I'm a simian innit, but I told them to suck my monkey dick."

Because it's not a great time to be a Canine and I'm also in the shit at work for behaving like a prick. So I need to at least make it look like I've learnt my lesson.

Bit of a rebrand eh? OK I get where you're coming from now, bruv, and it's a bit of a relief to be honest. Right, well you clearly haven't got a scooby what ur doing so why don't I let you buy me a beer in return for showing you the ropes?

They met at the Steeles on Haverstock Hill and, after detailing his circumstances and the need to start earning again, Dalston urged Dev to share his bright ideas.

"The thing is, bruv, you've got to treat this shit like trying to get a bird in the sack, innit," said Dev, once the beers were dealt with. "You can't just steam in there and go 'yeah, yeah, you're really fucking beautiful and interesting and shit, now get your pants off.' Firstly they're not that stupid and secondly there's got to be something in it for them. You might think your cock is the eighth fucking wonder of the world, but you can't blame a bird for not just taking your word for it, know what I mean."

"Yeah Dev, and believe it or not I haven't tried the 'wonder cock' chat up line for ages."

"There's hope for you yet. So what d'you do when you want some fresh punani? How d'you talk a bird into it?"

"Well, I guess I take her out, treat her, try and have 'proper conversations' with her, that sort of thing. And I also try to get a sense of what she's into; some birds just need a few quid spent on them, other ones just need you to agree with all their shit and be all sensitive. It depends."

"Exactly! But that's not what you're doing online, blad. You're acting like some 15-year-old trying to cop a feel at the fucking school disco. You're being too direct, innit, you need to take a step back and get a strategy together. Those Felines aren't just going to roll over and let you tickle their tummies just because you said some blatant shit about them being right all the time, you get me. They'll smell a rat, just like you when you're in too much of a hurry to chat a bird up. You need to lull them into a false sense of security before you try and seal the deal, hear what I'm saying."

"But it's not at all like chatting a bird up – it's a different fucking language! For a start I never try to chat a bird up on Facebook; you've got to be there in front of them, using your body language and reading theirs so you can fine tune the patter. And also I'm not trying to get these fuckers into the sack, I just want to be accepted by them. It's a completely different thing."

"It's not, but I get your point. What we got to do is adapt your technique, innit. You're right to say social media is pretty different from face-to-face, but luckily there are loads of handy tools available to help you. Which bits of Vertoo are you using?"

"Vertoo?"

"Yeah, you know, the social media handbook."

"Never heard of it mate."

"Oh my God are you fucking serious, blad? That's classic that is – you've gone piling in to social media without even checking out Vertoo first? What the fuck is wrong with you, man? That's like bringing a set of nail clippers to a gunfight! Jesus Christ this is worse than I thought, we're seriously going to have to start from square one."

"What the big deal? I've been on Facebook for ages."

"Yeah but you've just been dicking about, innit. Now you want to get in with the pros and they don't fuck about. It's war out there, bruv, and if you don't tool up and get into training you're going to get chewed up and spat out so quick… well, as quick as you already have, for fuck's sake. How do you expect to compete when you don't even know the rules of the game, geezer? Vertoo is the place everyone goes to learn how to win online, but don't just take my word for it, fuck off home and check the site out. Then try some of that shit out online and see how it goes, you'll be fucking amazed, man."

Concluding his work was done for the time being, Dev soon went back to tend his stall. Dalston saw little reason to delay and Googled 'vertoo' on his phone while he had another pint in the pub. He was immediately greeted with a cartoon angel that invited him to click on its halo if he wanted to 'win at the internet.' He did and was presented with the Vertoo logo and the strapline 'Know your rights. Show you're right."

The site had a traditional layout, with a navigation bar offering the following options: Causes; Argument; Pick a Team; News; Certification; and Forum. 'Causes' revealed a drop-down menu with the following further options: Political; Social; Personal; Scientific; Economic; Philosophical; Charity; and Other. A quick look at Political revealed a mix of traditional political parties and causes together with contemporary ones, including the Felian Party. Having hit the jackpot so quickly he decided to first have a browse around the rest of Vertoo.

The 'Social' sub-section of 'Causes' covered the well-established array of gripes, issues and crises assumed to be afflicting society by the kind of people most drawn to social media debates. Inequality, prejudice, hate, and all the old - isms were all well represented in a wiki style, designed to guide the aspiring internet combatant through their respective pros and cons. One passage in particular startled him:

"Remember, in the UK it is a crime to cause offense by anything you say. Furthermore, the law states that something is deemed offensive if 'the recipient or any third party considers the words, perceived tone or presumed intention to be threatening, offensive or upsetting in any way.' Thanks to another law against 'victim blaming,' not only is there no requirement for the accuser to prove or even detail the nature of the offense they took, and it's actually a crime to ask them to do so. What this means for the competitive internet user is that the quickest way to silence opponents is simply to claim something they have said offended you. Such is the inclusiveness of this law that you can even make an accusation on behalf of someone else and are under no obligation to reveal their identity."

Dalston had to re-read the section several times to make sure he'd understood it correctly. Apparently if you don't like what anyone is saying online you merely have to tell the police they have offended either you or anyone else for them to be arrested and silenced. It seemed too easy, but at the same time he wondered how it worked in practice. One puzzle was what would happen if two people both accuse each other of being offensive – do they both get arrested?

Fortunately the Vertoo piece was extensively cross referenced and featured an FAQ section in which that very issue was raised. "It is impossible for a mutual accusation of offensiveness to result in a dead heat, there has to be a winner, which is usually determined by the victim equity of each protagonist." The words 'victim equity' were hyperlinked to another page titled 'Victimhood,' listed in the 'Personal' sub-section of 'Causes.' Dalston considered it the best summary of the current social whirlpool he had read:

"Establishing victimhood confers a number of benefits to the internet warrior. Most importantly it is the primary source of online status. Equally useful for both initiating and victoriously concluding confrontations, establishing your victimhood is the most efficient way to acquire ad hoc allies and secure the denunciation of your opponent. At any given moment there are literally millions of people on social media, especially Twitter, just waiting to run to the aid of anyone claiming victimhood. Of course their real aim is to unilaterally adopt the victim as a client, in order to champion them and denounce others on their behalf, but far from detracting from their utility as online allies, such a strong personal incentive makes them more dogged and dependable. It should be noted, however, that victimhood is heavily influenced by identity and is both hierarchical and fluid. Currently the hierarchy of victimhood stands as follows:

1. Transsexuality (male to female)

2. Race (Afro-Caribbean)

3. Sexuality (non-heterosexual)

4. Religion (non-Christian or Judaism)

5. Politics (collectivist)

6. Disability (physical)

7. Transsexuality (female to male)

8. Sex (female)

9. Race (other non-white)

10. Culture (non-Western)

11. Religion (Judaism)

12. Poverty

"*White, male, straight, Christian, healthy, wealthy individualists are afforded zero victim equity and the further you are from them in the hierarchy, the more of it you possess. To resolve matters of competing victimhood the Discretionary Intersectional Committee (DIC) developed the above ranking table, but it is regularly reassessed and can take on different characteristics in specific regions and at different times. For example the UK is currently undergoing a period of intense political upheaval founded on fresh dogma, stridently enforced by its adherents. As a consequence political affiliation is far further up the victimhood hierarchy there and anyone accused of opposing the dominant new political force – Felianism – is denounced as a Felophobe, which is currently considered a greater smear even than racist or transphobe.*"

Dalston tried to memorise the table. It was impossible to deny that public opinion was overwhelmingly in favour of the Felian movement, and people were sufficiently enthusiastic about their new cause to defend it furiously. But his failed attempts to join them showed him mere zeal wasn't sufficient for acceptance because there were distinct online 'tells' that separated true Felians from impersonators, and until he mastered them he would continue to be a political, social and professional pariah. To demonstrate true commitment he had to get his hands dirty in the arena of social media combat.

Navigating to the 'Argument' section revealed the following subsections: Fallacies; Accusations; Rabble Rousing; Trolling; Facts; Conspiracies; and Gaslighting. Dalston didn't even know what half of these words meant and was engulfed by a vertiginous sense of being hopelessly out of his depth. How could he possibly go up against people for whom these terms were familiar? 'Fallacies' sounded like something to do with oral sex, but he forlornly concluded that was unlikely to be the case. 'Trolling,' he presumed, was derived from computer games and 'Gaslighting' sounded decidedly sinister. But in the absence of any alternatives he gritted his teeth and pressed on, pausing only to get another pint.

'Fallacies' was at the top of the argument category for a reason. It referred to the many argumentative shortcuts, cheap shots and low blows people use to attack their enemies' online statements. The first was 'Strawman' which was the technique of responding to an argument by attacking a slightly different but much easier one. Even if that technique doesn't win you the argument immediately, your opponent will often feel compelled to address your Strawman and thus be in a weaker position. This technique, explained Vertoo, is especially useful against people who know what they're talking about, as it both negates their expertise and seizes the initiative.

Vertoo stressed once more that victimhood is the primary source of online authority and the first strategy, especially if immediate denunciation was not available, should be to establish a higher level of victimhood than your opponent by the most efficient means possible. For those low on the victimhood hierarchy a strong secondary strategy was to pursue proxy victimhood via 'client-seeking' from accredited victims. By unilaterally jumping to the defence of one, Dalston learnt, you can appropriate most of their moral capital without actually having to experience any victimhood yourself.

"Once a client group is established, it is just a matter of learning to recognise the situations that permitted you to issue denunciations on their behalf," explained Vertoo. *"Denunciation is an act of social violence no less profound and damaging than a cutting insult or a punch in the face. It establishes strength, dominance and authority. Defending a victim who hasn't even been attacked was a great way of using the Strawman fallacy for client-seeking, but a more direct route is the simple Ad Hominem attack."*

Assuming it was merely a posh way of calling someone a poof, Dalston pressed the 'Ad Hominem' hyperlink, only to find it was a bit more complicated. *"The key to getting the upper hand in most virtual confrontations is misdirection,"* he was told. *"Defending your actual argument is very dangerous as any successful attack on it, however minor, can damage your position and embolden third parties to join your opponent. The absolute worst-case scenario is for any part of your position to be proven wrong. This invariably becomes the thin end of the wedge (see 'Slippery Slope fallacy'), with the assumption that if you were wrong on one matter, no matter how trivial and superficial, your credibility on everything else should be called into question."*

Dalston concluded that unless you're very sure of your position the best tactic, when attacked, is to misdirect immediately. The first and most important misdirection technique any online warrior should learn, advised Vertoo, is the Ad Hominem (at the person) attack. This technique is closely related to the Strawman fallacy as they are both members of the 'Red Herring' family and shares its advantage of combining counter-attack with misdirection. In this case, however, rather than putting words in your opponent's mouth, you abandon any pretence at debate and simply attack them as an individual. An easy starting point for the Ad Hominem attack was the 'Fallacy of Composition,' through which you find the most contentious and unflattering thing a person has ever said or done and seek to define them by it. This was also a useful tool for stripping out nuance, the internet warrior's arch enemy, from the exchange, as it reduces your opponent to a one-dimensional caricature.

While it all seemed somewhat arcane and technical, a lot of it resonated with Dalston's own experiences online and he was fascinated to see what he had presumed to be visceral, instinctive argumentative techniques examined in such a scientific way. Victimhood is impossible without oppression, he learned. Where victimhood confers online equity, oppressiveness subtracts it, so the most effective ad hominem attacks are those that paint your opponent as an oppressor. While the two are in direct opposition, they're not mutually exclusive, so it is possible to be both a member of a victim group and still be accused of being an oppressor. These hybrid situations were usually resolved by referring to the DIC hierarchy, since each victimhood has its own equal and opposite oppression:

- *Trans – transphobe, TERF*

- *Race – racist*

- *Sexuality – homophobe*

- *Religion – islamophobe, anti-Semite*

- *Politics – fascist, nazi*

- *Disability – ableist*

- *Sex – sexist, misogynist*

- *Culture – cultural appropriator*

- *Poverty – capitalist*

Vertoo noted that, while DIC was the generally accepted authority on the relative status and importance of the main victimhood classifications, each one can also be sub-graded according to criteria put forward by the Panel of University Social Science Institutions. It was therefore possible for a member of a victim group to still be considered a net oppressor if their oppressive characteristics were considered to outweigh their victim status. There was also a subset of Ad Hominem allowing you to denounce a person as a traitor to their victim group if they deviated from the approved victim narrative. It yielded epithets such as 'Uncle Tom,' 'internalised misogynist' and 'self-hating gay,' but these were largely reserved for use within the victim group.

The ultimate purpose of an Ad Hominem attack was to burden your opponent with negative victim equity and thus render any arguments they tried to put forward null and void. Ultimately, if their equity was sufficiently low it became possible to use any argument they put forward as further evidence of their heresy and depravity, at which point they were entirely neutralised.

Dalston was fascinated to learn the tactical benefits of denunciation didn't even end there. Through the attribution of further layers of negative equity, you can make your opponent such an egregious oppressor that merely attacking them in a public context will, in turn, increase your own equity. The most fruitful time to do this was soon after they achieved pariah status but before their denunciation went viral, after which your own contribution would be lost in the pile-on. The ultimate combination of the Strawman, Ad Hominem and Slippery Slope fallacies was to find some way, however tenuous, to link your opponent to Adolf Hitler.

"Hitler has the most negative victim equity of any individual in history," said Vertoo. *"Even his name radiates such intense levels of social toxicity that its mere mention is usually sufficient to close down a conversation. The power of Hitler as an internet WMD lies not so much in his supreme oppressor status but in the total unanimity of that view. Invoking any other oppressors, however negative their equity, might possibly encounter some dissent or mitigation from people with good knowledge of them. There is absolutely no possibility of anyone challenging your positioning of Hitler, so using his name comes with zero risk attached."*

Dalston had to stop reading at that point, so overwhelmed by all the fresh information that he was no longer retaining any of it. He also felt empowered and excited, and wanted to put some of these techniques into practice immediately, so he clicked on the 'News' section. It offered a choice among 'Saints;' 'Sinners;' 'Conspiracies;' and 'Trending'. Sinners were the pariah figures he'd just read about and saints were their diametric opposites: victims of such exemplary status that merely praising them online conferred an immediate equity boost.

It was clearly possible to maintain an elevated level of online status merely through a sustained programme of publicly defending saints and denouncing sinners and heretics but, given the ephemeral nature of each boost, the technique required a level of commitment Dalston could not contemplate. He didn't fundamentally care about online equity in general, it was merely his most likely means of acquiring a degree of acceptance from the Felians and thus to demonstrate penitence to his employers. He was delighted to see 'Felian Correctness' listed as one of the topics in the Trending section and made a mental note to jump down that rabbit hole next.

Chapter 11 – Incentives

Iain Tegritie was interviewing Susan Percilious, Permanent Undersecretary for Personality Monitoring, on his radio show. The Id Card scheme was well underway and Tegritie wanted to know if it was achieving the desired results – as did Dalston when he tuned in.

"So, Ms Percilious, you've put everyone to an awful lot of trouble with this Id Card business," said Tegritie. "Wasn't it all just a complete waste of time and money?"

"As you know full well Iain, in the aftermath of the Payshus Insurrection there was overwhelming public desire to examine, once and for all, the causes of calamitous events like the collapse of Clark's Bank, which affect everyone, not just the companies involved," Percilious replied. "The subsequent public inquiry established conclusively that certain toxic personality types, when given positions of influence, bring about negative outcomes, so the clear course of action was to identify those types and remove them from such positions. That is exactly what we did."

"And how's it going?"

"We're very excited about the positive effects the scheme is having. Banks are no longer being run purely on the basis of greed and are prioritising positive social outcomes. Law firms now place social justice above merely winning for its own sake, which still results in a far higher conviction rate for hate crimes. And journalists, or at least some of the newer ones, are no longer peddling gossip, innuendo and tittle-tattle and are instead focusing on the important issues."

Tegritie took the bait. "The important issues eh? And just who decides what's important, you? I think you've just revealed your true colours Ms Percilious; this whole thing is just a massive ego trip for you isn't it? You get to sit there in your ivory tower playing God with the rest of the country; promoting someone here, removing someone there and generally mucking everyone around on the off-chance you occasionally get it right by pure fluke."

"I think it highly unlikely all the positive outcomes I just detailed came about by 'pure fluke' Iain. And I don't know what you're so upset about, you haven't been moved. Yet."

"Well, that tacit threat proves my point entirely. At the very least the Id Card scheme has concentrated power too much in one place. What if you didn't like the way I conducted this interview? Would I find myself flipping burgers tomorrow or, God help me, working for the civil service?"

"I've been very clear from the start that reallocations are decided by the Optimisation Committee, not just me."

"And who appoints the members of that committee?"

"I do, but the process is totally transparent and I fully encourage constructive debate within the committee."

"Right, so your defence against my claim that you have too much power is to say you're kept in check by a committee that you chair, meaning you're the sole arbiter of what conversation is acceptable within it, and the other members of which you personally appoint. Forgive me if I'm not totally reassured."

"Iain, you're chasing a red herring here. The entire Id Card process has been incredibly transparent and unanimously approved by Parliament every step of the way. Perhaps if people like you just got on board with it then the outcomes would be even better, but I guess some people are just never happy."

"If everything's going so well then let's have a look at a few other examples. What about that patient who was left to die in an accident and emergency department because he refused to sign a document indemnifying the hospital and its staff from, and I quote 'everything including negligence, misconduct and sexual predation'? Or what about that school where discipline has deteriorated so much they had to send in the police, who were driven back and are now on indefinite leave with goddamn post traumatic stress disorder? The list goes on!"

"It's easy to cherry-pick outliers, Iain, and those examples in no way undermine all the excellent work being done in the vast majority of cases. In fact, I have here the latest figures from the Institute of Data Investigation, Observation and Testing, which reveal that 97% of people who were asked what they thought about their reallocated position said they were either happy or very happy."

"Yes I saw that survey too. I also know it was made clear to respondents that if they expressed anything other than satisfaction with their new positions they would be reallocated once more, and I quote 'to a position more befitting their exceptional requirements.' And is it not also the case that the majority of the 3% who didn't express satisfaction have been given unspecified roles within your own ministry? Perhaps you could tell us what some of them are doing."

"Those people reallocated to the ministry have been honoured with the task of administering the Id Card scheme and, in effect, ensuring the future prosperity of our country. As the results I've already referred to show, they are clearly doing an excellent job, for which we should all be grateful."

"So you keep insisting. But even if you don't accept my own earlier examples as significant, you surely don't intend to try to sweep the growing factionalism under the carpet. Thanks to your Id Card system our society has split itself in four and two of the groups have organised together in an apparent bid to impose their will on everyone else. Can you give us your position on this and what you intend to do about it?"

"A social experiment on this scale is bound to have a small number of unintended consequences, but it's vital we don't allow those to distract us from the primary purpose, which is to ensure toxic personality types are no longer allowed to pollute positions of critical national importance. We can all agree that a repeat of the Clark's crisis and the consequent insurrection must be avoided at all costs."

"For the sake of argument I'm willing to concede some minor collateral damage is inevitable, but what about the Felian Party? This isn't just some minor anomaly, it's a national movement that claims the majority of the population as constituents and threatens to upset the current political order. Are you just going to stand by and let that happen?"

"Maybe the current political order needs upsetting. After all, this was the political system that allowed the crisis to happen in the first place. One of the most amazing things about the Id Card scheme has been the new opportunities created by replacing the old order. People have been given professional opportunities they could never have hoped for previously and have flourished. The same goes for the Felian Party; people aren't talking about left/right, black/white, rich/poor anymore, they're spontaneously grouping together on the basis of their personalities, not their appearances or backgrounds, and I think that's a fascinating development."

"So you're saying we've shaken things up, the dust is settling in a new way and it's not for us to question this process. Perhaps supporting the Id Card scheme does mean supporting the collateral phenomena that come with it. The Felian Party wouldn't exist without the Id Card and, it could be argued, the Id Card needs the Felian Party to function. While I still have a number of reservations, I'm willing to concede it may be better to reserve judgment for now and let the scheme evolve."

"That's very gracious of you Iain, and I hope your listeners can join you in acknowledging that the Id Card scheme exists for the greater good and its positive effects will be greater and arrive more quickly if we all unquestioningly support it."

Tegritie's interview of Percilious had a profound effect on FLAP and the broader UK political landscape. It served to legitimise the movement and rubber-stamp it as a viable political party. The government was, however, incensed by one of its own senior civil servants appearing to actively encourage this nascent political threat and Percilious was suspended from her position, pending an official enquiry into her behaviour. The enquiry was rendered redundant by her resignation, with the political establishment receiving a further blow when it was announced that Percilious, whose egotype was a rare double primary of Feline and Simian, had been appointed Chair of FLAP.

The interview also awoke in Dalston a high level of curiosity around the circumstances surrounding the demise of Clark's and the Payshus Insurrection. He reflected on the famous Tegritie/Payshus interview with a fresh perspective and marvelled at how such a relatively mundane event could have such a profound domino effect. He used the ample spare time at his disposal to read around the events leading up to the collapse of Clark's. One hyperlink led to another and he eventually found himself back at the blog Payshus was keeping to chronicle his time at Hill Street School.

Payshus had decided that since it was largely impossible to threaten school children with anything both effective and legal, his only hope of imposing order and exerting influence over the school would be through a system of incentives. His many years in the financial sector had taught him that people are simple, transactional creatures, so he set about designing a bespoke currency to be used solely within the confines of the school for the purpose of bribing the pupils into obedience.

A tariff system was devised around a currency called the Hill, which was pegged to the most basic unit of scholarly output: a completed piece of work given a grade of 'E'. 'D's were worth two Hills, 'C's three and so on. Additional Hills could be earned from commendations in non-academic disciplines such as sport, and teachers could award discretionary credits for good behaviour as well as fines for misbehaviour. Payshus commissioned the design of a smartphone app to keep a real-time tally of every student's Hill balance. The app synced with a website accessible by teachers, pupils and parents, and through which Hills could be spent on rewards. So pleased was Payshus with his innovation he decided it was also the perfect vehicle for teaching his pupils about real money and business, so he added a feature to the app allowing pupils to trade Hills among themselves.

The scheme was initially an unqualified success. Already hard-working kids redoubled their efforts but the effect on underachieving pupils was especially profound. They responded far more strongly to material incentives than the traditional threats and warnings of destitute adulthood. However, while the more disruptive kids initially went along with the scheme, they soon grew demoralised and resentful at the far greater quantities of Hills accumulated by the brighter, more studious kids. They soon concluded extortion, enabled by the trading system, was a far more efficient route to wealth. Attempts to mitigate this trend by increasing the rewards for the lowest grades and for participation in sports not only induced contempt from the intended beneficiaries but also from the high achievers.

Nothing worked and for a while the scheme looked destined to collapse, until one of those high achievers, a girl named Isabella, decided to pool the resources of a number of her contemporaries in order to bribe one of the alpha bullies responsible for much of the extortion. The number of Hills they could collectively offer was far greater than the bully could hope to acquire from even the most concerted mugging campaign, so he and his gang were employed to protect Isabella's collective from the predations of others. Isabella consequently attracted a lot of other bright, hard-working kids to her group, but soon rival groups emerged, equipped with their own hired thugs. An arms race followed that concluded with the establishment of seven groups each consisting of 40-60 kids with a roughly even demographic make-up. There were conflicts, but the size of each group meant they were rarely conclusive, and a kind of cold war stalemate settled over the school.

While Payshus was happy to have stumbled upon a mechanism for keeping the peace, he regretted that the bully types seemed to consider protection of their benefactors a full-time job and were consequently achieving less than ever academically. The solution to that problem, he decided, was to award Hills primarily on the basis of collective, rather than individual, attainment. While this did much to resolve the underachievement problem it also led to a wave of consolidation as kids defected to groups considered most likely to win awards. This process only stabilised once there were just three mega-cabals left, each led by the most politically talented kids.

Having seen that banking techniques could be applied to schools, Dalston wondered if the converse was true and sought out the blog of Poppy Syndrome, who was the other half of the straight swap with Payshus. If anything her approach had been even more successful. Not only did her Inclusive Banking for a Better Society strategy yield the kinds of social benefits the creators of the Id Card scheme could only have dreamt of, but Clark's was also making lots of money. Just as Payshus had introduced the free market into Hill Street School, so Clark's was benefitting from some public sector structure, inclusivity and focus on social outcomes.

Freed from the constraints of quarterly earnings season, Syndrome was able to implement longer-term strategies and give them sufficient time to play out. She was also in the right place at the right time. Due to the collapse of Clark's there was now great demand for companies to demonstrate positive social outcomes from their activities, as well as the usual financial achievements. Share prices were as likely to be boosted by corporate responsibility KPIs as they were by positive movements of the bottom line, so Clark's new policy of focusing on the most socially virtuous companies for its investments and support was, literally, paying dividends.

The other main transformation of Clark's under Syndrome's tenure concerned how its employees were incentivised. It was no good asking them to focus on non-commercial objectives in their approach to the job but still incentivising them in the traditional manner. So Syndrome introduced a special management layer to Clark's dedicated to a continual process of staff assessment based on a range of KPIs, only a minority of which concerned money. As well as their contribution to the corporate strategy, Clark's employees were judged on qualitative criteria such as perceived attitude and philanthropic outcomes. In addition a strict dress-code was imposed on all staff, to create a greater sense of equality within the company. Syndrome was acutely aware of the need to be following both the letter and the spirit of the Id Card scheme as closely as possible, and she considered such measures to be a great way to minimise the incidence of ego-led behaviour within Clark's.

Chapter 12 – Imposture

The time spent away from Gold & Mackenzie had left its mark on Dalston. He was now aware of a world beyond the echo chamber of strutting City peacocks and coked-up sociopaths but was nonetheless drawn back to it. The simple truth was his funds were dwindling rapidly so if he wished to maintain his high-flying lifestyle he had no choice but to get back on the financial treadmill. Thankfully the lessons learned from Vertoo served him well and he had a growing online reputation as an Id Justice Warrior. He hoped his acceptance into Felian groups, known for their intolerance of just the kind of behaviour that got him suspended in the first place, would serve as proof of his contrition.

At the end of his two-month suspension he was invited back to the Gold & Mackenzie offices to meet the very retraining manager who suspended him during their calamitous previous meeting. One of the most important things he learned from that, and his recent attempts to curry favour with the Felians, was that merely going through the motions and trying to tell people what you think they want to hear rarely worked. He now knew most people could smell bullshit a mile off and concluded the only way to appear sincere was to believe you actually were. He knew he was completely sincere about his desire to be reinstated in his old job and to do what it took to achieve it, but he also knew he was fundamentally unrepentant. He couldn't deny, however, that his arrogance had led him to underestimate his opponent last time, a mistake he was determined not to repeat.

"Ah, Mr Dalston, we meet again," said the retraining manager.

"Yes, and let me start by apologising for my behaviour the last time we met. I was under considerable stress at the time, but nothing can excuse how I acted."

"Well, we're delighted to hear it Mr Dalston. The aim of this meeting is to assess to what extent we have understood what is now expected of us and what remedial measures we have undertaken. We will ask you a series of questions and we want us to answer them honestly, do we understand?"

Dalston scanned the room for additional HR managers and even inspected the walls and ceiling for two-way mirrors and listening devices, but concluded it was just the two of them in there. He was confused.

"Yes?" he ventured.

"Yes what?"

"Erm, yes we understand?"

"Good. Now we've already indicated we know your behaviour was incorrect when we last met, so can we tell us precisely how you erred?"

"Yes we can, erm, I mean to say, everything about my behaviour was wrong. I came into the meeting with a cocky attitude, and when you challenged me on it I became defensive. Then, when you quite rightly suspended me, I was aggressive and rude."

"And have we thought about why your attitude may have been so counter-productive?"

"Yes I have. Shit, sorry we. Look, can I just say I when I'm referring to myself? I'm finding all this 'we' stuff confusing."

"We consider 'I' to be a problematic pronoun that reinforces selfish, egotistical mindsets. Every time we say 'I' we take one more step down the path towards self-absorption and away from working towards making the world a better place. After all, there is no 'I' in team!"

She actually said it. He could only sit and stare at her for several seconds afterwards, partly out of shock, partly to see if she was taking the piss, but mostly because it required all his self discipline to prevent himself from laughing out loud. Luckily the manager misinterpreted the hiatus.

"We can see our words have struck a chord, good. So, we were reflecting on your previous attitude."

"Yes, we were," said Dalston gravely, determined to make the most of this lucky break. "The real truth is we were a shallow, superficial man, motivated only by possessions, conquests and hedonism."

"You were."

"I were?"

"You can refer to yourself in the singular when referring to your prior, ego-driven self."

"Ah, right. Thank you for helping me understand the grammar of contrition," he said, wincing inwardly at the borderline sarcasm of his words. He decided to power-on regardless, as he felt he was getting the hang of this counter-intuitive language. "And you're so right – we don't even recognise that person anymore, so much have we changed since then."

"Why should we believe you?"

"We would like to bring your attention to our social media activities during the period of our suspension…"

Dalston went on to detail his embrace of Felianism, which not only demonstrated his acceptance by the types of people who would not have tolerated his former self, but also spoke of a kind of collectivist zeal not generally associated with your classic egomaniac. He almost brought a tear to his own eye recounting the friends he had lost in the process of reforming his personality, and crowned his routine with a denunciation of his fellow Canines that would not have looked out of place in Maoist China.

The retraining manager regularly interrupted with cross examinations aimed at testing the depth of his conversion and regarded him throughout with the kind of narrow-eyed suspicion associated with fathers upon first meeting their daughters' boyfriends. Fortunately the show of sincerity he was able to muster proved to be sufficient, as the manager grudgingly and with graphic explanations of the dire consequences that would accompany even the slightest relapse, ended his suspension.

The first person to welcome him back into the Gold & Mackenzie fold was Jack Morrison, who congratulated him on turning his life around with an avuncular tone Dalston found irritating. Inviting him to green tea in the office kitchen, Morrison explained his had been just one of many similar suspensions as the company strove to get on the right side of the ego police. The process had been an unqualified success, resulting in the eye of Sauron moving onto other city institutions slower to wake up and smell the coffee. This left Gold & Mackenzie free to refocus on its core competency of generating obscene amounts of revenue from moving other people's money around.

The latest innovation, Morrison explained, was the Securitised High Interest Tranche. This new financial derivative was created by combining AAA-rated paper, such as sovereign bonds, with the kind of debt that could only aspire to junk status. The latter consisted mostly of payday loans bought from the original lender at a discount, meaning typical SHIT yield piled up so long as the debtor kept paying. This was guaranteed by the growing enthusiasm of payday lenders to offer fresh debt, having used SHIT peddlers to wipe their balance sheets, thus creating a perfect credit Ponzi scheme. The consequent, unprecedented, zero default rate was all the rating agencies needed in order to extend the rating from the AAA component of the SHIT to the entire package, despite it being largely comprised of debt very unlikely ever to be repaid.

Hi yield AAA-rated debt was normally the kind of thing City types had erotic dreams about. But the market hadn't forgotten what happened last time bankers started dicking about with arcane derivatives and was hesitant to commit to this latest piece of financial sleight-of-hand. Necessity being the mother of invention, further artefacts were therefore magicked into existence by traders desperate for something new to flog. With corporate responsibility now the overriding priority for financial regulators worldwide, the Corporate Responsibility Attainment Paper was created as a crude way of commoditising this otherwise vague concept. A single CRAP was produced according to an intricate formula that took account of a company's size, its demonstrable compliance with the Simpson-Oxford Act, and various other CSR box-ticking exercises such as supporting charities, planting trees and employing people with questionable haircuts. When combined into a package these CRAPs served to detoxify SHITs by coating them with a veneer of corporate and social sanctimony.

There was still some hesitance to accept the legitimacy of CRAPs, however, as there had been little time to gauge market sentiment towards the commoditisation of corporate responsibility, so what was needed was a regulatory stamp of approval. This was secured via the traditional route characterised by corporate donations, expensive dinners and the promise of lucrative non-executive directorships for compliant regulators once they retired. Before long the UK's financial regulatory body was convinced Gold & Mackenzie represented the very pinnacle of banking ethics and was delighted to rubber-stamp the Tremendously Underwritten Regulatory Document. When bundled with a SHIT and a CRAP, the TURD provided the final polish needed to reassure the market enough for trading of the resulting financial product, the Aggregated Regulatory Securities Endorsement, to commence with unrestrained ardour.

ARSE-fuelled optimism soon spread to the rest of the financial sector and, as a consequence, the City of London was soon in the middle of a bull run. On top of that, the massive increase in unsecured personal loans enabled by ARSE trading stoked equivalent exuberance in the consumer credit market. The government was predictably quick to claim credit for the economic boom caused by such a massive increase in liquidity. Behind the scenes, politicians made it clear to regulators that everything should be done to perpetuate this boom, while companies like Gold & Mackenzie switched their focus almost entirely to this dream derivative.

Dalston was delighted to find himself in such a benign business environment upon his return to work, especially since he had racked up a fair amount of debt of his own during his suspension. That was soon a distant memory as the unbridled joy of finding so many suckers falling over themselves to buy ARSEs among his clients provided the perfect distraction. It did feel fundamentally odd to be making so much money while sober, however. A boom like this in the past would have resulted in there being as many dealers as traders at Gold & Mackenzie, but these days Morrison didn't even keep a bottle of JD in his desk drawer and lunch had been reduced to a sandwich on the go. Of course Dalston was delighted to be back in the groove, but his reprieve felt a bit empty.

Another niggle was the sheer ease of making money in the ARSE era. There was barely any selling involved and it was effectively a license to print money. For the first time in his life Dalston started thinking about the ethics of what he did for a living. All the traders knew this was just a Ponzi scheme destined to collapse sooner or later, but nobody seemed to care. In fact he could detect from the conspiratorial smirks around the office that the sheer, naked gall of the enterprise was a big part of the fun for many of his colleagues. Most of his clients would probably suffer massive losses eventually and another speculative bubble was being inflated, which would result in another financial crisis when it popped.

His unease crystalised further one evening when he was drinking with some of his colleagues at one of their favourite City clubs. Sharp suits had largely been replaced by Dot casual clothes and it was clear many of the people buying champagne and expensive cocktails were not typical City types. It dawned on him they were more like the kind of people he would normally expect to see in his local pub, and he wondered where they found the cash to fund such an opulent upgrade in their social habits. The answer was obvious: they were spending borrowed, SHIT, money.

Switching on his TV after a hard day at the money printers, he decided to watch the news for a change. The Felian Liberal Authoritarian Party was dominating the news agenda, having rapidly evolved into a significant political movement. Powered by expert use of social media, FLAP's rapid ascent had been driven by a grass-roots organisation known as Imperium. It had few core members and was run by just three permanent activists known as the Triumvirate, but it was extraordinarily efficient at recruiting, organising and channelling an exponentially growing social media following.

Imperium's political strategy focused on the principle that Canines were violent, amoral predators, from whom Felines, Simians and even Delphines needed protection. The majority of its activity was geared towards the identification and denunciation of 'problematic' Canine behaviour, of which there was initially too much to keep track of, even for its network of unpaid spies, snitches and zealots. In time, however, the Canine rampage abated, thanks partly to the impossibility of keeping hangovers in abeyance indefinitely, but also to the capitulation of the Canine-dominated police.

Sensing the change in the political climate, the upper echelons of the UK police imposed an ascetic regime on their employees eerily similar to the one Dalston had recently fallen foul of. Police across the country began regularly hosting 'atonement sessions,' in which Canine police officers were encouraged to unburden themselves of their original sin. A typical scene would involve several people sat in a circle, with one standing up and confessing to being a Canine. The confessor would be met with stony silence until such a time as their subsequent self-flagellation was considered to be sufficiently abject by any Felians present – it was compulsory to have at least one – who then initiated a measured round of applause.

This was just the start of the redemptive journey for your average Canine copper, however, with far more profound absolution available to those demonstrating sufficient vigour in their apprehension of Canine criminals. Police forces around the country started openly appealing to the public for information on Canine misbehaviour, however slight. This approach got the political seal of approval via a series of hastily drafted, barely debated and summarily passed laws focused on the word 'hate,' collectively referred to as the Rebalancing Act.

Their effect was to render previously innocuous acts criminal if they were deemed to have been committed under the influence of 'hatethink.' The official definition of hatethink was: 'Any activity which is perceived by the victim or any other person, to be motivated by oppression based on a person's faction or perceived faction.' As the historical victims of factional oppression, Felines and Simians were deemed incapable of hatethink, so the enforcement of these new laws focused entirely on Canines and, to a lesser extent, Delphines. For police of all ranks, responding to hatethink reports not only enabled them to demonstrate their rejection of Canine ideology, it was also a much easier way for them to hit their other performance targets. As a result, the investigation of traditional crimes such as theft, arson or murder was deprioritised, unless they were also reported as hatethink incidents.

Had the members of Imperium presented Parliament with a wish list of legislation to further their interests, they couldn't have done better than the Rebalancing Act, which effectively gave all Felians the power to criminalise any Canine or Delphine whenever they pleased. Furthermore, the consequent retreat of nearly all Canines and Delphines from the public domain was interpreted as public consensus in favour of the Felians. Imperium exploited this opportunity to further manipulate the public discussion such that even those few remaining sceptics were driven to self-censor for fear of repercussions.

FLAP was still marginalised from mainstream politics, however, due to having no MPs, and Parliament was inclined to restrict its electoral opportunities as much as possible, in the hope the movement would lose momentum. Thick-skinned incumbent politicians were some of the few people Imperium had been unable to dominate on social media, so the Triumvirate adopted a strategy of pressuring them indirectly through private companies. Corporations were both terrified of the potential for reputational catastrophe presented by social media and totally clueless about how to defend themselves from it. As a result their reactions to being accused of hatethink, or even of tolerating it, were entirely Pavlovian and if they could identify any individuals to scapegoat they were fired without hesitation. Companies would then signal their corporate contrition through grovelling public apologies and generous donations to Imperium's nominated charity: the think tank Safety Not Freedom.

It soon occurred to all organisations that the most efficient way to stay on the right side of the social media mob was to ingratiate themselves to FLAP. That, in turn presented the party with a backdoor into Parliament as the majority of MPs relied on the private sector for both contributions to their election funds and lucrative non-executive directorships when they retired, so they were keen to stay on the right side of them. Thus FLAP was able to indirectly exert significant influence over the UK government without having a single MP of its own.

FLAP was able to bring about even more substantial political change through the introduction of a form of direct democracy via social media. Converting its sudden popular support into members of Parliament through the traditional electoral process would have taken years, so FLAP decided to play to its strengths. It designated a distinct hashtag to every significant political event in the UK and instructed its followers to make social media posts commenting on it. Before long some MPs were bringing attention to its campaigns in Parliament and the news media started running stories with headlines like 'Why is the government ignoring will of the people?'

This continual pressuring of business, politicians and the media eventually led Parliament to introduce a monthly review of social media activity around these hashtags and thus the thin end of the wedge was established. Soon the cadence of these reviews became weekly and then daily, and before long MPs were conducting their parliamentary business mainly over social media. By the time Dalston switched on his TV, FLAP's followers were in the middle of lobbying for another vote of no confidence in the Prime Minister. Earlier that day Parliament had reviewed the progress of this campaign and the result was still in the balance.

To Dalston this seemed like a clear opportunity. Not only could he further absolve himself of Canine original sin by publicly supporting this Felian cause, but if FLAP came into power it was vital he be seen to back the winning team. So he took to Twitter.

@DalstonDave

I can't believe this is even close! This is the best opportunity this country has had for real change in living memory and too many people are bottling it! Put your money where your mouth is and support #noconfidence2 now!

Thus far his social media activities had garnered him a following of a few thousand, meaning he was usually rewarded with some kind of interaction each time he posted. His quest for social credit forced him to persevere in the face of largely negative responses from a small number of accounts. That was when he recalled the core principle stated by Vertoo: victimhood is power. By abusing him these trolls were also giving him exactly the kind of victimhood he needed to counteract his intrinsic Canine oppressiveness. This emboldened him and he was increasingly inclined to phrase his tweets in a way he thought would be most likely to provoke the trolls. With his new allies and the belief he was on the right side of the debate, he quickly grew in confidence.

@DalstonDave

Q: What's the difference between a Canine and a Nazi? A: Nazi's have better dress sense

@k9andproud

@DalstonDave so your saying you want to dress up like a nazi?

@woke_a_f

@k9andproud That is such a fucking typical Canine reaction. Why can't you see that @DalstonDave isn't saying anything about clothes you bigoted prick? He's saying you're basically a Nazi and, it turns out, a thick one at that.

@k9andproud

@woke_a_f Wow, you call me thick. Can't you see I was trolling? What's the difference between a Felian turncoat and a thick cunt? Nothing!

@DalstonDave

@k9andproud the fact that you keep doubling down on your Canine bullshit just goes to show what a literal Nazi you are. It's quite simple: try to be less of a cock. Go away, educate yourself and do better.

@k9andproud

@DalstonDave @woke_a_f You guys are fucking obsessed with nazis man. You know who else was? Hitler! Go away and think about that you pair of brainwashed fucknuggets.

@woke_a_f

@k9andproud @DalstonDave reported to Twitter. I'm exhausted from trying to re-educate Canines and you're clearly never going to learn so people should be protected from your hateful hatethink.

Dalston was amazed to discover he and his allies were able to get their opponents permanently banned from Twitter so easily, while the opposite clearly wasn't the case. This led him to conclude the entire administrative process of the platform was based on weight of public pressure. In that sense Twitter had become its own form of direct democracy, but unlike the nascent UK system this one offered far more targeted power.

Chapter 13 – Interrogation

During yet another bout of online combat days later, Dalston was interrupted by a message on his phone.

Hello daddy

He hadn't spoken to his daughter Amy for months, ever since his last bust-up with her mother, after which he had been completely excluded from both of their lives. He had put his recent mistaken sightings of her down to missing her so much, but here she was, messaging him.

Amy?

Yes how are you?

Delighted to hear from you baby, is everything OK?

It is with me but im worried about you

What, why?

All this stuff ur doing online isnt like you

Well that's sort of the point Amy. I got in trouble for being 'like me' before so I'm trying to turn over a new leaf.

By starting fights on twitter?

No, it just turns out supporting the Felian movement brings out the worst in some people and I'm just sticking up for myself.

That's not always how it goes tho daddy ive heard you sometimes join in on other peoples comments and say some really horrid things

Yes, that's true, but we have to stick up for each other or the other people will win.

Is that what its all about winning?

Not ultimately but that's what the world is like. Unfortunately some people just don't see the world the same way we do and they can get nasty. It's important to stand up to bullies and not let them win.

How do you know there wrong?

What do you mean?

You said its important to beat them because they dont see the world the same way you do. But how do you know ur way of seeing the world is right and theres is wrong?

Well it's a bit complicated to explain here. Maybe we could get together sometime soon and talk about this stuff.

I think mummy is still quite cross

What makes you say that?

I heard her talking to her friends about you and she says youll never change. I also heard her talking about what ur like on twitter and thats why I decided to message you. Im still not allowed on twitter

Do you think I'll never change?

No I just think you need to understand what the problem is before you can do anything about it

That's a very grown-up comment Amy, and I think that's exactly what I'm doing. I realised the reason I made some bad decisions in the past is my Canine nature and by spending as much time as possible with Felians I'm trying to correct that. Do you see?

Sort of but i dont think you change just by hanging around with different people

Surely it can't hurt to try though.

That depends to me it looks like ur just swapping one set of bad decisions for another

I promise you it's more complicated than that.

I hope so anyway I have to go now please think about what I said. I love you daddy

I love you too baby.

As soon as their exchange was over Dalston cried openly for the first time he could remember. Suddenly all this stuff – Twitter, Felians, Gold & Mackenzie, the Id Card – just seemed utterly trivial. What good were passing fluctuations in online status when you're unable to share them with the people you love most in the world? As he sobbed into his hands it occurred to him this wasn't just about Amy. He was forced to confront the fact that the events following the introduction of the Id Card had been hugely stressful for him. He had essentially been told his identity was deficient and wrong and needed to be corrected, but he wasn't sure how to do it. The effort of trying to find out was taking a profound mental toll and more than anything he felt completely alone. He was estranged from his daughter, he had been told to change his personality for reasons he still didn't understand

and he now spent most of his time with people he hadn't even met, picking fights over things he didn't really give a shit about.

More than anything at that moment he craved some honest interaction and thought immediately of Davina Jones. While he couldn't consider her a friend, she seemed like just the kind of level-headed person he needed to speak to, who furthermore didn't come with any historical baggage. He messaged her and was relieved to find she was online.

Hi Davina.

Hello Dave, long time no speak. How's life?

OK but I've had a fair bit of hassle since we met at the market.

Like what?

I did a lot of thinking while I was suspended, including what you and I spoke about, and I decided to turn over a new leaf.

Doesn't sound so terrible to me.

Yeah well I'm still not sure what to make of it all. I managed to convince my work to take me back but I'm definitely on my third strike and can't afford to fuck up again, so I'm having to be on my best behaviour.

I bet that hurts.

LOL yeah. And on top of that, to show everyone what a reformed character I am, I've been getting involved with the Felians and campaigning for FLAP, especially online.

You're a Canine aren't you?

Yup, but that's the point isn't it? Canines aren't exactly flavour of the month right now so I figured I should join a better team.

By better you mean the team that's on top right now?

I suppose so, yes.

So what's the problem?

For a start it's fucking hard work. I spend all day walking on eggshells, acting like a pussy just in case I get grassed up for reckoning myself too much. Then I get home and I'm steaming into these Twitter fights without a clue what's going on. At the end of it all I'm knackered!

It sounds to me like the problem is you're being forced to be someone other than you really are the whole time. That would stress me out too.

Funny, that's more or less what Amy said.

Your daughter? You spoke to her?

Yeah I didn't see her but she messaged me just before I spoke to you.

Wow, I'm really happy for you. How did it go?

She was concerned about all this fucking about I'm doing on Twitter and implied it's not helping me get back in her Mum's good books.

Ah

Anyway I was really emotional after we finished and I needed someone to talk to. For some reason you were the first person that sprang to mind.

I'm touched.

Listen, do you fancy grabbing a drink? I'm buying.

Sure, I'm at the stall so why don't you bring some tins along?

It was early evening by the time Dalston got to Camden Market and he was pleased to find Davina alone on The Hidden Agenda stall, listening to some bafflingly violent heavy metal. He handed her a Beavertown Neck Oil and cracked one open for himself.

"Thanks a lot for meeting me at such short notice Davina."

"No problem Dave, you sounded like you needed a chat."

"Yeah, bit of a head-fuck, all this stuff."

"I had a quick look at your Twitter account just now, you certainly have been a busy boy. Look, I barely know you, but all this Id Justice Warrior stuff just isn't sitting right. With all due respect, my first impression of you was pretty much the exact opposite: a standard cocksure wannabe alpha-male who thinks just because he's got a few quid in his pocket that makes him something special. Luckily you do have some charm and just enough of it manages to penetrate the oafish facade to make it worth finding out if there's more to you, or we wouldn't be speaking now."

"To be honest Davina, you're probably not a million miles off, but the problem is cocksure wannabe alpha-males are seriously out of fashion at the moment."

"Right, so you decided to pretend to be the opposite and now you're realising that strategy probably isn't sustainable. Look, I've been there Dave; I tried being a girly girl when I was at school and I even pulled it off for a bit, but I always knew I was going through the motions and as I got older I found the gossiping, hair braiding and unicorn posters too much to bear. The same always happens when I try to hold down a proper job. I can just about handle the repetition and mind-numbing banality, but as soon as some jumped up prick tries to push me around I end up telling them to fuck off and it's game over."

"So you've ended up here, which is fine for you I guess, but as I said when we met before, it's not for everyone."

"I'm not telling you to start a stall in Camden, Dave, but I'm also telling you the dicking about you're doing is going to end in tears."

"So what the fuck should I do then?"

"Well that's the million-dollar question isn't it? Look, the only place you're going to find the answer is inside your own head. The fascinating thing about you, my friend, is that you're potentially at the start of the most important journey any person could ever take – the quest to know yourself."

"Oh God, are you really going to try to exploit my current tricky situation to shove some mystical mumbo jumbo down my throat? Because that's the last fucking thing I need right now."

"Listen, Casanova, it doesn't matter to me what you do. You're just some bloke who called me up asking for help and, for some reason, I decided to indulge you. But just as soon as think you don't need it or you've better options elsewhere, just say the word and I can get on with the million other things I could be doing that will almost certainly be more rewarding than wiping the dribble off your dopey chin."

"OK, I apologise, but you need to give a bloke a bit of warning before you start banging on about journeys of discovery and that kind of shit."

"No I don't. Listen or don't, it's your choice. Which is it?"

"Listen."

"Good. You just took the first step to an open mind: open ears. If you can't truly hear what is being said then how can you learn anything?"

"I hear you," he said with a knowing smirk.

"Thank God for that," she replied, returning the smirk. "The point of all the stuff I said earlier about getting to know yourself is that hardly anyone does. Most people go through their lives putting on an act. Part of it is trying to fit in, not get into trouble, etc, but the more significant part is they've never taken the trouble to examine themselves, so they have to put on an act because they've got no alternative. How can you be true to yourself when you don't even know who you are?"

"That all sounds very clever but it's a bit abstract for me to get my head around. Of course I know who I am – I'm Dave Dalston, innit. I like nice clothes and getting off my tits and I don't like being skint or celibate."

"I'm going to assume you're at least partially aware of how utterly superficial that summary is, but let me ask you this: do you ever surprise yourself?"

"What do you mean?"

"Like, do you ever have unexpected feelings or do things and then wonder why you did them?"

"Increasingly, yes. I'm still not sure why I called you, for example."

"Perfect, let's look at that. Why do you think it might have been?"

"Well... For starters I quite fancy you," said Dalston with an optimistic smirk.

"That's nice, but if you were just looking to get laid I'm sure you know women far more likely to oblige you than I am. What else?"

"You're an easy person to talk to. You have a way of cutting to the chase that makes it easier for me to do the same."

"Good. Anything else?"

"You're completely different from me. You claim to not give a shit about money and pricey gear, although I'm still not convinced. Your life seems to be completely unstructured and you mainly do what you want. There's a growing part of me that is curious about what that would be like."

"Excellent. I'm impressed, Dave. You want to talk and learn, that's all I can ask. Look, we all get stuck in a rut. The first step towards doing something about it is to acknowledge the rut exists in the first place, which you seem to be in the process of doing."

"Am I? I don't know. I just know something's bothering me."

"I've only been doing this for a year or so, you know. A few years ago I was mucking about with some of the shit you're trying, except for me it was sexual politics. The intrinsic bias against women in society was all I could think of and it drove me mental. I would see people just getting on with their lives, without a care in the world, and their indifference to how screwed up society is made me want to slap them. I hated men for being men and women for not doing enough about it.

"I felt like I was the only person in the world who could see things as they really are, but that changed once I met a woman called Sally Pimienta. We agreed on pretty much everything, but before long she asked me what I was doing about it. I explained that I resist the patriarchy constantly but she kept asking me how. Eventually I realised I wasn't really doing anything useful, just shaking my first at the sky and seeking catharsis by being a bitch to everyone. Then she told me about Whistleblower Hotline."

"OK, that's ringing some bells so far, except for the hotline bit. What's the big deal about that?"

"It's an online community for people who are sick of just moaning and actually want to make a difference. It's partly a repository for leaked confidential documents, partly a forum and partly an internet university. I went there looking for material I could use against the patriarchy but got a lot more than I bargained for."

Davina paused and sipped from her tin as she recalled that pivotal moment in her life.

"Look, I still think society is biased against women, just not for the reasons I used to. Blokes like you will always manipulate and use women, but I realise you're programmed to do that to some extent. Women have to deal with a bunch of shit that men don't, like being pregnant, and society doesn't do nearly enough to compensate us for biologically taking one for the team. But, for example, when I looked for hard evidence of the gender pay gap I couldn't really find any. On top of that I learned about things like male depression and suicide, the disappearance of traditional industries and most recently this Id Card, which seems to be almost entirely designed to shit on male Canines. I realised I'd been so caught up in my own righteous indignation that it hadn't even occurred to me there might be another side to this victimhood narrative. We don't condemn male dogs for thinking with their dicks, so why do it to Canine blokes?"

"Ha! Thanks, I think," laughed Dalston. "So what are you saying, that there's no point in getting too worked up about stuff?"

"Not quite, more that getting worked up about stuff alone doesn't achieve anything, it just stresses you out. Also, just because something works you up doesn't mean it's wrong, at least not to anyone else. Who are you to say your way of thinking or acting is the best way? And even more importantly who are you to impose your will on someone else? That's what it really comes down to for me: I believe all people are equal, so while that means I fight inequality it also means I don't think I'm superior to anyone else. What gives me the right to force anyone to do anything? What's the moral case? There isn't one, so if I try to I'm basically being an egomaniacal bully, imposing my will on other people just because I feel like it, and I don't want to be that sort of person."

At that moment Dev Sharma happened to walk past.

"Alright, Lezbeth. Still trying to turn you into a bird is she Dave?" he shouted when he recognised them. "Don't fucking fall for it bruv! And also, what's that fucking noise?"

"Imperium, Machine Head," said Davina.

"I didn't ask about your politics, dick head."

"No Dev, that's the music I think," said Dalston. "Anyway we were just chatting about stuff. I've been trying to change, to get some of this Id Card heat off me, but it's stressing me out so I was asking Davina for advice."

"Yeah I bet you fucking were, you dirty cunt. Nothing will sort your head out like converting a tasty dyke, innit."

"Jesus Christ," said Davina. "Not that it's any of your business Ali, but I'm heterosexual. I'm just one of the overwhelming majority of women who find you as appealing as a bad case of thrush. In fact, now I come to think of it, all this talk of homosexuals makes me wonder what you're hiding, girlfriend."

"You cheeky bitch! I fuck loads of birds and they all love it. You better watch your mouth or I might be forced to teach you some manners."

"Oh, so it's alright for you to call me a lesbian, but when I suggest you might be gay you threaten me?"

Appalled at the way this was going, Dalston tried to steer the conversation in a more constructive direction.

"Dev, we were just talking about how hard I've been finding trying to fit in with the Felians and not get myself in the shit," he said. "Davina was saying I need to get to know myself better before I can change anything."

"Get to know yourself?" sneered Dev. "Of course you know yourself man. Who the fuck knows you better than you know yourself? Listen, I've been following your shit on social media and, don't take this the wrong way, but you're a fucking embarrassment, my friend. I've got no problem with what you're trying – if they're going to fuck you over for being honest then lie through your arse, innit – but you've got to be all-in, you hear what I'm saying. I can see you've had a look at Vertoo, but right now you're just being a pussy and getting no respect. You've got to be a fucking alpha, blad, go big or go home. Most other people on the internet know about Vertoo as well, so they're going to be wise to your entry-level bullshit, you get me."

"So that's your advice, lie better?" said Davina.

"It's a fuck-load better than yours, that's for sure," said Dev. "Look, you're totally over-complicating it with all this spiritual crap, man. There's nothing wrong with him, he just needs to get better at putting on a front, know what I mean. Even I have to bite my tongue every now and then in the shop, and that's why I've got the stall, innit."

"There we have rare common ground Dev, we both have stalls in the market because we want to do our own thing and we both think Dave should be true to himself. The difference is I think he can only do so by being honest with himself and you think he's better off lying."

"I think it's fairly fucking obvious you should give your enemies nothing to work with and right now the whole world is Dave's enemy, unless I'm missing something. Also, why can't he do both, man? So long as he builds up a good, strong front first, then he can get on with whatever self-improvement bullshit you lay on him. I'm telling you, bruv, strength is the only language these people understand and you've got to get a lot better at showing some. I know it's a bit confusing these days, with the biggest pussies getting all the sympathy on Twitter, but you've just got to learn the rules and fucking exploit them, innit. Look at who's winning, it's the people playing the victim game the best, blad. They're pretty fucking far from victims themselves though, they're just the biggest pros, know what I mean."

"I hear you Dev, I have been trying but I guess I need to double-down," said Dalston. "It's totally doing my head in though."

"Luckily I have a solution for that too," said Dev. "This skunk I got in my pocket is guaranteed to make you not give a fuck about anything else for hours. By happy coincidence it's on special offer for worthy causes and you can have a nice big bag for a ton."

The process of exchanging five twenty-pound notes for a bag of skunk was conducted with a theatrical degree of furtiveness almost designed to attract suspicion, but somehow they pulled it off. Davina was unimpressed.

"I genuinely thought we were getting somewhere Dave, and then this chancer turns up, dangles a short-term fix in front of you and you're biting his arm off," she said. "I've got to say I'm disappointed."

"Please don't be Davina," said Dalston. "I heard every word you said and I'm really grateful for you chatting to me, but I've just got to do this my way. It's clear the long-term solution is for me to sort my head out, but I also need the heat off me right now, and that means doing this Felian shit properly."

Chapter 14 – Inappropriateness

Dalston's chat with Davina and Dev posed as many questions as it answered, which he wasn't in the mood to confront. Fortunately his friends had already announced they were drinking around the corner at the Hawley Arms and when he arrived they were indulging in the time-honoured pastime of pontificating about football.

"We're two or three big signings short of being able to compete with the top teams," lamented Al Blake as he reflected on a recent defeat suffered by his team, Arsenal. "We're sorted out wide but our spine's too weak, we need a midfield enforcer and a solid centre-back or we'll keep losing these kinds of games."

"It feels like we've been saying this forever," said Dalston, a fellow Gooner, once he'd got a round in. "The fucking owners need to put their hands in their pockets for once. When you've got your Man Cities and your Liverpools spending fifty million on a defender you've got to match them or you've got no chance."

"Definitely, but no amount of money can help us when we get decisions like that."

"For fuck's sake did you see it? There's no way in a million years that's a penalty."

"I've seen them given," said Morrison, a Spurs fan.

"Fuck off!" said Dalston. "He's gone into the box looking for any contact and goes down like he's been shot in the head when there's nobody anywhere near him. It's a fucking disgrace Jack, and you know it. This is what's ruining the game and if it had happened against Spurs you'd be crying like a bitch."

"Well it happened against Arsenal and now you're crying like a bitch," said Morrison. "If you ask me your defender was an idiot going in like that and the lad was entitled to go down. In today's game you can't make any contact in the area and everyone knows it. Besides, Arsenal has had plenty of decisions in its favour and it all evens out over the course of the season."

"I've got a simple question for you, have a look at this and tell me if there's any contact whatsoever." Dalston found the incident on YouTube and held his Cosmic Phone in front of Morrison.

"There, he clearly makes contact. I'm sorry mate but you can't do that in this day and age," said Morrison.

"Are you trying to fucking wind me up? He's nowhere near him and anyway the cunt's already on his way down by the time he gets there. Help me out here Al."

"You're talking shit Jack and you know it," said Blake. "If you think that's a penalty then you should've gone to Specsavers, mate."

"Nick?" said Morrison.

"Well, you can't deny the defender came in hard and then the lad went down," said Georgiou. "Even if there was no contact what do you want the ref to do? He's got to protect the striker, innit."

"Typical fucking Hammer, always siding with the Yids," said Dalston. "If that's a penalty then let's just come out and say it: football is a non-contact sport and we might as well be playing netball."

"Calm down Dave, you know I'm not that bothered about football. I wasn't even joining in the conversation but then you asked me what I thought and got all arsey when I didn't give you the answer you wanted. Anyway, what does it matter what I think? The penalty was given and converted and Arsenal lost. End of."

"Meanwhile a stonewall penalty shout is turned down at the other end just before. We should have been a goal and a man up before that diving cunt cheated the ref. As far as I'm concerned we won."

"What the fuck's the matter with you Dave? 'As far as I'm concerned we won'? Have you lost your god damn mind? I know you're gutted about the result but you need to get a grip, my friend."

"Alright we're clearly not going to agree on this, no matter how fucking obvious it is, so let's change the subject," said Blake. "I don't know about you lot but I've been getting all kinds of grief from this Id Card shit. Not only is it blatantly racist, but now I've got everyone telling me to join the Felians just because the fuckers have stuck 'Simian' in my name. But I've never given a shit about politics and it seems to be worse than ever now. It's giving me the arsehole and I wish everyone would just shut the fuck up about it."

"Hold on Al, last time we got a drink you were giving me the whole 'it's for the greater good of society' routine and bollocked me for not getting into the spirit of it," said Georgiou. "Now you suddenly don't give a fuck, which is it?"

"Look, I'm still up for anything that tries to have a go at fixing our broken society and I still think the Id Card is worth sticking with for a while. What's winding me up is all this factional stuff; now suddenly everyone's got to pick a team and if you don't fancy doing that, you get even more grief. One minute I'm defined by being a soldier, or black, or whatever, the next minute the only thing that matters is some test has decided I'm a monkey-boy. Why can't I just be Al Blake?"

"Mate, you're preaching to the fucking converted here. If you remember rightly I've been warning about this from the start and nothing that's happened remotely surprises me. I'm Delphine so I'm getting grief flying at me from all directions, with the Felians and Canines both hassling me to join them and saying I'm a collaborator, or some shit like that, when I won't."

"I don't get it though, what's wrong with people? We've got the government actually trying to do something about greedy bankers, inequality and all that stuff, and these nutters have turned it into some psychotic power grab for themselves."

"It's what always happens when you create teams, Al, especially when you define them by characteristics people have no control over and can't change. Before all this everyone was talking about race but I hope you'll agree that while we've still got a way to go, society has definitely been improving on that issue."

"Yeah, we're getting there. In the 70s you had bananas and shit being chucked on to football pitches. Now people are shocked if anyone even says something racist in the stadium. I can tell plenty of people would still chuck bananas if they thought they would get away with it, though."

"Actually that raises a really good point. If we accept that most people are cunts to some degree, what stops them acting like cunts all of the time? Culture, that's what. On top of basic laws, we all instinctively know what's acceptable behaviour. But culture evolves over time, like attitudes to racism since the 70s. The problem with this Id Card stuff is it was suddenly imposed on everyone and there's been no opportunity to smooth out the rough edges. So it's black and white, if you see what I mean, with most people just picking a team and going all-in."

"But I still don't see why that means we need to have so much aggro."

"Basic psychology, mate. We look after ourselves first, then our family, then our mates, then our tribe. Because of the Id Card people are cutting out the family and friends bit and making the tribe everything. So families are arguing, mates are falling out, new alliances are being made up on the fly, it's fucking chaos, all because the government decided to arbitrarily slice and dice society on the back of some bright idea a couple of them had over a pint."

"You would say that though Nick," said Dalston. "You've never been into politics, or any kind of team effort for that matter. It's easy to just sit on the sidelines and take the piss, it's a lot harder to actually get off your arse and do something."

"You sound just like Al did when we were arguing the toss about this last time Dave," said Georgiou. "But now he can see it's not as simple as just 'doing something' and that the law of unintended consequences means it's sometimes better to do fuck all."

"Well that just sounds like an excuse to me. The financial crisis was brought about by Canines, fact. The insurrection was started by Canines, fact. Canines just want to fuck things up, fact. Thanks to the Id Card more than half of society has got together to put a stop to it and we should be celebrating that, not picking holes in it."

"But you're a Canine, Dave," said Morrison. "Doesn't it strike you as a bit retarded to be going against your own team? Would you stop supporting Arsenal just because some fucking survey said Gooners are, on average, bigger cunts than the rest of us?"

"Most people worked that out for themselves ages ago Jack," said Georgiou.

"Fuck off, both of you," said Dalston. "You still don't get it do you Jack? This is bigger than me picking a team, this is me doing what's best for society even if it's difficult for me personally. It's called altruism mate, look it up."

"Do me a favour. It's blatantly obvious what you're up to," said Morrison. "You shat yourself after you got suspended and now you're trying to make up for lost time by sucking up to the Felians to show what a fucking reformed character you are."

"You think you've got it all sussed out don't you? Maybe if you'd been a proper mate when all this started then I wouldn't have got suspended in the first place."

"What am I, your Dad? To be honest I couldn't believe what a fucking idiot you were. We were told a million times to wind our necks in and you just carried on like nothing had changed. You're a big boy Dave, it's not my job to hold your hand and stop you fucking your career up. And while we're on the subject you haven't exactly got off to a flyer since you came back. Everyone knows you spend half the day getting into bitch-fights on Twitter and it's not doing your numbers any favours. You need to snap out of it, mate, and sharpish."

Dalston didn't take Morrison's diatribe well and stood up abruptly, knocking the table and spilling their pints as he did. He appeared ready to hit Morrison but was gently restrained by Blake and Georgiou.

"Do you know what, you've turned into a right prick, Jack," he said. "The bloke I used to know would not only have shown some balls in the first place, but wouldn't have been such a selfish cunt when his mate needed some help. Some things are more important than money Jack, but it looks like you'll never realise that. Sorry about the pints lads, but I can't sit at the same table as this wanker."

Pausing only to chuck a couple of tenners onto the dripping table, he stormed out of the pub. As he stomped towards Camden Town tube station he muttered to himself about what a superficial, selfish prick Jack Morrison was. As far as he was concerned that argument put into perspective how much he had grown and developed since the Id Card was launched, while Morrison had clearly stood still.

By the time he left the tube he had calmed down enough to remember to check his phone and saw a bunch of Twitter notifications, so he turned on his laptop to investigate as soon as he got home. As it booted-up he reflected on the familiar combination of excitement and anxiety he felt in anticipation of what had ignited his Twitter account. It turned out to be mainly responses to some routine trolling he had done prior to his recent online encounter with Amy, in which he had denounced a prominent Canine for complaining about his treatment at the hands of the Felians.

@DalstonDave

@k9andproud the Nazis literally thought they were victims too

Looking at the timestamps on the responses to his comment, Dalston noticed they were snowballing. Nobody had even liked his comment for an hour or two after he made it and even then it was just a trickle. The interactions only really gathered momentum once *@woke_a_f* quote-tweeted it with the comment "*This.*" The vast majority of them were either simple agreements, GIFs of crying babies or links to stories about recent Canine transgressions, but some attempted to escalate his response and hold Canines collectively responsible for a wide range of current social ills and historical atrocities. The biggest source of activity on the thread, however, was *@k9andproud*, who attracted a frenzy of vitriol every time they commented.

@k9andproud

@DalstonDave The Nazis literally breathed, ate and went to the bog too, so what?

@woke_a_f

@k9andproud *If you can't see how being a Canine apologist is an act of violence against society then you're no better than the Nazis, that's what.*

@k9andproud

@woke_a_f *So you're saying any Canines who defend themselves are automatically Nazis, but any that admit to being Nazis are also Nazis? Why can't you see how retarded that is?*

@woke_a_f

@k9andproud *OMG as if you hadn't done enough damage you're now inflicting your hate onto mentally underprivileged people. Even the Nazis didn't do that.*

Dalston was pretty sure they did, but he wasn't about to undermine a key Twitter ally. The spat eventually ran out of steam and he remembered what Davina had told him about Whistleblower Hotline, so he opened a new browser tab to check it out. The loose layout of the site reminded him a bit of Reddit and, after peering into a few esoteric rabbit holes, he identified an especially active 'hotline' about the Felian movement. Initially it consisted mainly of generic political debate, but after a while he started to encounter actual leaked documents, such as the FLAP mission statement and minutes from Imperium meetings. He couldn't be bothered to read the whole FLAP document but it appeared to be fairly uncontroversial, as did the few Imperium minutes he was inclined to scan, but some threads contained links to further reading, which was where things started to get interesting.

An email sent by one member of the Triumvirate to the other two not long after the commencement of the Id Card scheme read as follows:

Fellow Triumvirs,

I'm sure it goes without saying that the societal reorganisation made inevitable by the Id Card experiment represents a once in a generation opportunity for our cause. To date all our efforts, though tireless and heroic, have yielded limited societal change. As we all know, this was largely due to the underprivileged being kept ignorant of their plight by the oppressive elite. We simply lacked the resources to wake people up in sufficient numbers to give our movement the momentum it needed and were reduced to praying for a miracle.

The Imperium Manifesto calls for the fracturing of society into at least three factions to facilitate the manufacture of a super-faction representing the clear majority of the population and thus claim a permanent popular mandate.

Our electoral system is the single biggest impediment to real progress, with the system favouring the incumbent elites. The only solution to this is through electoral control of the majority of the population and the Id Card represents the best opportunity we're ever going to have to achieve that.

Accordingly I propose the following strategy:

- *Identify one faction to associate intimately with the financial crisis*

- *Initiate a dark PR campaign with the aim of linking that faction with as many other social crimes as possible*

- *Identify a 'good' faction to position as the antagonist and opposition to the 'bad' faction*

- *Through a system of incentives and threats, ensure one of the remaining factions operates in alliance with the good faction*

- *Once this super-faction has been created we will be able to claim a popular mandate by default and the majority of the fourth faction is likely to join the winning team*

- *Momentum must be maintained at this point in the form of a campaign designed to pressure the incumbent political elites into acknowledging our mandate and allowing us representation in Parliament*

- *The end game will be to force a general election and get an Imperium member installed as Prime Minister*

I therefore put this plan of action before the quorum for approval, upon receipt of which I propose we convene to elaborate, determine initial actions and draft a presentation for P.

Further digging revealed 'P' was widely suspected to be Susan Percilious, the civil servant charged with implementing the Id Card scheme. Dalston didn't need to be the most rabid conspiracy theorist to be struck by the clear conflict of interest this presented. Civil servants supposed to be politically neutral and if the person running the Id Card also had a parallel agenda hinging on exploiting political opportunities created by it, corruption was inevitable. This revelation also called into question the provenance of the Felian movement. The Canines had clearly been designated the 'bad' faction and the Felines the 'good' one, with the Simians successfully corralled as allies.

While he began publicly supporting the Felian movement in a desperate bid to socially redeem himself, Dalston had started to believe it might bring about real, positive change. Even he could see the need to reform the system that brought about the financial crisis and the Payshus insurrection, and he found himself persuaded by Blake's argument in favour of getting behind whatever efforts were being made in that respect. But if the whole thing was manufactured solely to serve a narrow political agenda, then not only had everyone been lied to but Dalston strongly suspected the resulting political environment wouldn't be very different to the previous one.

His Twitter alerts had abated so he decided to see what else Whistleblower Hotline had to offer. Another hotline focused on the financial sector and well-known examples of historical misbehaviour. He discovered a section focusing on recent developments and was drawn to a thread discussing the latest financial derivatives. A lot of the information on offer was stuff he already knew regarding the provenance of the ARSE, the toxic debt hidden within SHITs and so on, but one section did catch his eye. It was concerned with the leak of a confidential government report into the social consequences of the surge in high interest payday loans made possible by the booming ARSE trade. There were several case-studies concerning individuals and families who had accumulated so much of this debt that the interest payments alone exceeded their collective incomes.

New financial services were rapidly evolving whose sole purpose was to provide additional sticking plasters to these people by offering further credit on ever more unfavourable terms. Contracts requiring borrowers to put forward novel forms of collateral were becoming commonplace. Some demanded a proportion of their future earnings or benefits, and even those of their relatives or children. Others called for a legal commitment to prioritise the lender in the event of any future capital gains, including inheritance, and there was even a contract making the lender the primary beneficiary of the borrower's will. Many people were being forced to literally sign their lives away just to keep themselves afloat.

For the first time in his career he started to think about the broader context of his profession. Until now he had been almost totally blinkered and focused only on the incentives placed in front of him. Regular financial windfalls not only ensured his commitment to this course of action, but also kept him so distracted he was almost totally insulated from the outside world. Even the financial crisis was only of interest as a problem to be endured and overcome as efficiently as possible, so the gravy train could embark once more. But the Payshus Insurrection and consequent social upheaval had not just caused him a fair bit of anxiety and inconvenience, it had forced him to look at the bigger picture. This new perspective made him regard the material he was now reading in a new way.

The ARSE industry was clearly parasitic, bordering on vampiric. While he didn't question the critical role credit plays in all functional economies, he knew there was also a point of diminishing returns after which it becomes counterproductive, and the people caught in this SHIT-induced debt spiral were clearly way beyond that. Not only would they never be able to repay this debt, but they would also clearly ruin their lives and those of their families trying, so why was this situation allowed to continue?

Dalston had previously thought of his work as just exploiting rich people by moving their money around in vaguely plausible ways, but now it increasingly looked like his two hundred quid jeans were paid for by people who could barely afford to buy clothes at all. He found that thought unsettling and couldn't help reflecting on how both the current political and financial situations amounted to a few people at the top manipulating and exploiting everyone else.

He was spared further introspection by another surge of Twitter alerts. Initially he was confused, as hundreds of people were adding *@DalstonDave* to their replies on threads that seemed to have nothing to do with him. Further investigation revealed the source of all this activity was the following tweet:

@suedenim83

So, this just happened. A close friend of mine confided in me that @FelianMovement activist @DalstonDave was TOTALLY INAPPROPRIATE when they dated a few years ago. And yet this person is still allowed to be on Twitter spreading his misogynist hate and making my friend relive her trauma.

Dalston had no idea who Sue Denim was, and suspected that wasn't her real name anyway. But he had no trouble believing he had behaved as insinuated many times in the past.

@woke_a_f

@suedenim83 @FelianMovement If this is true then @DalstonDave has gone against everything we stand for. We have a zero-tolerance policy towards inappropriateness and will take appropriate action when we deem it appropriate.

@Baizuo

@suedenim83 @FelianMovement @DalstonDave Inappropriateness is literally the greatest threat faced by women today and anyone who commits it is a misogynistic cunt.

@vajustice

Ban @DalstonDave

@FelianMovement

@suedenim83 we will investigate your shocking claim and have suspended @DalstonDave from the party while this process is underway.

Dalston checked his emails but found no communication from the Felian party. He tried to direct message some Felian contacts through Twitter but most had already blocked him and those that hadn't, did so immediately after receiving his DM. A similar process of rapid ostracization was playing out on Facebook, which generated its own social media pile-on. A few former allies even found the courage to share their own previously undisclosed experiences of his inappropriateness in the name of solidarity and stamping out that sort of thing. Back on Twitter the hashtag *#myturn* began trending, involving a mixture of people offended on behalf of those wronged, those traumatised by the mere reminder that inappropriateness still exists in the 21st century, those outraged at Dalston's reluctance to publicly defend himself, and those denouncing him for 'just not getting it' when he did.

When he tried to point out that he neither knew his accuser, nor the nature of the inappropriateness he was accused of, he found the momentum against him was irreversible. Requests for evidence, he was told, served only to amplify and perpetuate the initial crime and any attempt to question the validity of the claim was, apparently, victim-blaming. When one last attempt to defend himself resulted in a long thread consisting entirely of replies that simply read 'Nazi,' he gently closed his laptop and devoted his attention entirely to a bottle of Middleton Very Rare he had been saving for a special occasion.

Chapter 15 – Inspiration

Half the bottle and a few hours of agonised self-recrimination later, Dalston decided he needed a distraction so he slumped in front of the TV with a large bag of lime Doritos. As usual there was absolutely nothing on any of the regular channels he found even tolerable, let alone entertaining, but he remembered hearing that Netflix had picked up the rights to the experiment Raymond Payshus was currently running at Hill Street School. It was shot in a low-budget, fly-on-the-wall documentary style and was only onto its third episode, the first two having covered what he had mostly read about on the Payshus blog.

Driven by the creation of a currency unique to the school – the Hill – which rewarded them for approved behaviour, pupils organised themselves into three cabals run by the most politically ambitious. The leaders used some of the Hills they accumulated to employ tough kids to protect their interests. Those tough kids were in turn able to spend some of their Hills on paying academic kids to do their school work for them so, while the system significantly distorted the natural way of things at school, Payshus considered the resulting peace and prosperity to be a distinct step forward. It needed some fine tuning, but early experiments in unilaterally changing the criteria by which Hills were paid usually resulted in violent resistance from the kids.

Payshus realised he needed to be more sophisticated in his methods and once more dipped into his finance experience to introduce a system of taxes and subsidies. Once more he had some initial success in achieving his immediate goals, but also created new problems that forced further tweaks to his system. This process of fiscal whack-a-mole continued until eventually Payshus decided to interfere as little as possible and see how things played out. He had always been instinctively *laissez faire* and realised he had been given the perfect opportunity to indulge his instincts in a controlled environment. He convened a meeting of the school parliament and told the three leaders, Isabella, Bertie and Katty, that he wanted them to become a lot more autonomous. The system of incentives and sanctions based on the Hill currency would continue, but how they went about earning them would be left largely to the kids.

The first decision they made was to increase the reward level ten-fold across the board, thus allowing kids to buy much more from the school shops, whose shelves were quickly emptied in the resulting retail frenzy. Payshus took the opportunity to delay their replenishment and increase prices twelve-fold, thus teaching the kids important lessons about supply-and-demand and inflation. This shared macroeconomic challenge gave the three cabals a common purpose. To circumvent the hyperinflation occurring in their immediate environment, Hill

Street started trading with neighbouring schools it had inspired to join the currency experiment. This, in turn, created the new problem of how to spend 'foreign' money. There was talk of creating a new common currency for them all to use but rampant manipulation soon led to its collapse. Eventually the kids came to the conclusion the only reserve currency they could trust was real money – the pound.

Once more the Hill Street leaders took the initiative and presented their case to Payshus, effectively asking him to be their central bank. Payshus immediately detected the opportunity to regain some control and agreed, on the condition he retained control over the exchange rate between Hills and real money. So excited was he by this development that he committed some of his own funds to the Hill Street reserve and reset the value of the Hill to a level that ensured the collective wealth of each cabal remained at a reasonable level. Not all the local schools were being run by former bankers, however, and one started paying generous interest on deposits of its own currency. This caused great demand for it at other schools, with some kids even using pounds to buy ever greater quantities of that school's currency in the expectation of making an easy profit when they exchanged it back after its value inflated further.

The speculative bubble burst when the other school realised what was happening and suddenly stopped paying interest on its currency, which in turn resulted in a collapse in its relative value. The kids at the school from which it was issued were largely shielded from the effects of this devaluation as it had retained its internal fiscal discipline, but external speculators were significantly out of pocket. Since those were largely Hill Street pupils Payshus was forced to bail out some of them with his own money in order to prevent their bankruptcy. The latest episode of the documentary concluded with the interviewer reflecting on the irony of Payshus presiding over yet another financial misadventure and resulting bailout.

Dalston was drawn to a news alert from the BBC News app on his phone. The Hill Street experiment had apparently influenced even the UK government, which had developed its own new currency to augment the Id Card. As he saw at Gold & Mackenzie, a common reaction to the Id Card was pure pragmatism – focusing entirely on the bare minimum response required to placate the Ministry of Optimisation. Not long before her resignation Permanent Undersecretary for Personality Monitoring, Susan Percilious, worried about her new system being gamed. So she introduced Idcoin – a new currency that would run parallel to the pound and be awarded specifically for correct behaviour.

Britain's extensive network of security cameras, coupled with the presence of personality police answerable to the government in all organisations, meant it was possible to extensively monitor the behaviour of the population. New legislation made internet companies legally liable for all activity on their platforms, which in turn made them very receptive to cooperating with the UK government. As a consequence not only was the Ministry of Optimisation given full access to all internet platform APIs and back-ends, but the companies who ran them contributed to the algorithm required to calculate Idcoin credits.

Having seen the dangers of giving bespoke currency real monetary value at Hill Street School, Percilious decided Idcoins should not be exchangeable for material goods at all, but instead a range of 'experiences' ranging from cinema tickets to holidays. The digital tracking technology used to calculate Idcoin credits was used to make them non-transferable, by linking them to an individual's Id Card, thus preventing their use in any barter system.

Soon after the launch of Idcoin, however, it became apparent the main beneficiaries were people who were already behaving in the approved way, with the rest of the population apparently indifferent to the matter. So it was decided there needed to be a punitive element through which Idcoins could be fined for attitudes deemed problematic. This was of little use against miscreants who had accumulated no Idcoin credit, so the scope of the scheme was extended beyond mere experiences to cover privileges too. Idcoin thus became a measure of social credit, with high levels conferring privileges while going into the red resulted in restrictions on movement, access to services, etc. An individual's Idcoin balance was constantly updated and accessed through the Id Card app, which it was illegal not to display when requested.

Once the debit element was introduced the Idcoin scheme became a lot more effective, largely due to the prominent role it immediately played in social media interactions. Online disputes were increasingly concluded via a mutual show of Idcoin credit, with the higher tally considered proof also of moral superiority. Since problematic behaviour was punished by loss of Idcoin credit, this in turn fostered a culture of informing on other users for what soon became known as Idcrime, which was essentially the same behaviour previously designated hatethink, but with evolved nomenclature in recognition of the raised stakes. This community policing had the unintended consequence of massively increasing reported rates of Idcrime on social media due to a surge in frivolous accusations, often fuelled by coordinated activism.

Imperium was the most vigorous of the activist groups in this regard. Once more, if it could have designed a socio-political development to support its strategic aims it couldn't have done better than the introduction of Idcoin. The rudimentary, hashtag-based direct democracy Imperium and FLAP had been instrumental in instigating was massively augmented by the role of Idcoin as the primary measure of online status. As a result FLAP was soon able to completely dictate the parliamentary agenda, despite still having no MPs, and kept requesting votes of no confidence in the Prime Minister until one was won.

Once that happened FLAP was able to ensure no leadership candidate from the incumbent party gained sufficient support, thus necessitating a general election. FLAP chose one of the Imperium Triumvirate – Mary Onette – as its leader, and was able to pressure Parliament into replacing the traditional voting system with its Twitter-based direct democracy model. As a consequence much of the UK electorate was effectively disenfranchised and every single candidate FLAP put forward was elected, giving it a narrow majority in Parliament and thus control of the government.

Soon after, Onette made her first appearance on Iain Tegritie's radio programme and Dalston listened in.

"So, Ms Onette, yours is quite the meteoric rise isn't it?" opened Tegritie.

"I think the real story, Iain, is about how FLAP's message resonated with the ordinary voter after the catastrophic failures of the traditional political parties," said Onette. "This isn't about me any more than it is about any other member of FLAP or Imperium or the countless other activists without whom this could never have happened. I am merely the first among equals."

"And yet it's you in front of me, representing all those other people, having been a complete political unknown just a few months ago. You must be doing something right."

"To be honest I feel like my whole life has been leading up to this moment. Not necessarily talking to you Iain, with all due respect, but having the opportunity to correct the centuries of oppression suffered by my people."

"Your people?"

"Yes, the Felians," said Onette. "Throughout history we've had to endure a Canarchy in which Canines have had all the privilege and power. Felophobia is a recurring theme of the Canarchy, which defines itself by the exploitation and violent oppression of Felians. This has been criminally ignored by society until now and FLAP are proud to be leading the movement to right those wrongs. We're on the right side of history."

"But how could society have done anything about it when Felians didn't even exist until a few months ago?"

"That's deeply felophobic, Iain. Felians have always existed, it just took until now for them to be officially recognised. Are you saying characteristics like fear, conscientiousness and pessimism didn't exist previously? Of course they did and I think you should apologise for implying otherwise."

"I will do no such thing and I stand by my statement. But I couldn't help noticing the traits you mentioned are all associated with Felines. You seem to have forgotten about the Simian half of your supposedly oppressed group. Are Simians not oppressed or is their oppression just less important than that of the Felines?"

"Attempting to sow division between Felines and Simians is a classic anti-Felianic trope and further evidence of your appalling bigotry. That you're a Simian yourself in no way changes that and, in fact, reveals a toxic level of internalised felophobia. Of course traits like assertiveness have always been present too and without them the Felians couldn't have been so effective in overturning the Canarchy. Although judging by your problematic attitude Iain we still have a long way to go in our struggle for emancipation."

"It's interesting you feel so strongly about sowing division Ms Onette, since that's exactly the technique FLAP and Imperium have used to take power. Your strategy has been to demonise Canines and Delphines and exploit that fear for popularity. Furthermore you've bullied politicians, businesses and individuals on social media into submitting to your will in much the same way you're attempting to do to me now. I put it to you, Ms Onette, that far from adopting a principled stance you are cynically playing people off against each other in order to increase your own power."

"As I keep explaining, that division wasn't created by us. The history of all hitherto existing society is the history of factional struggles. Canine and Feline, Delphine and Simian, in a word, oppressor and oppressed, have stood in constant opposition to one another and carried on an uninterrupted, once hidden, now open fight. But what the Canines produce, above all, are their own grave-diggers. Their fall and the victory of the Felians are equally inevitable."

"Repurposing the communist manifesto to make your point doesn't make it any more correct Ms Onette. Let's see if you can use your own words this time: what evidence do you have that Canines and Delphines are historical oppressors and Felians their victims?"

"Even asking that question is felophobic but I'm happy to educate you, Iain. It's universally accepted that Canines are violent, amoral predators who exist solely to prey on more peaceful factions. But we don't hate them for this – it's not their fault – we only ask that they acknowledge this fundamental flaw in their psychological makeup and seek to correct it. History is littered with problematic Canine behaviour and FLAP seeks only to solve that problem."

"You like that word don't you?"

"What?"

"Problematic. You constantly use it to describe Canines and earlier you even said my attitude was problematic. But it's not clear to me what the word even means so perhaps you could define it for us."

"I think everyone knows what I mean by 'problematic' Iain."

"I don't."

"Well then we'll just have to agree to disagree won't we?"

"No. I don't know what you mean by 'problematic' so, by definition, your statement about everyone knowing what it means is incorrect."

"Obviously I didn't mean absolutely everyone."

"Why did you say it then?"

"OK I should have said 'nearly everyone.'"

"Good, so for the sake of those few who don't know what you mean, please define 'problematic' for us."

"I think it's fairly obvious, it describes things that cause problems."

"Problems for who?"

"For everyone."

"Really?"

"Alright, for the vast majority of people then."

"How do you know when something causes problems for the vast majority of people?"

"Again it's fairly obvious. Felophobia, for example, not only causes problems for Felians but is a form of idcrime."

"So felophobia is problematic. OK. Could you then define felophobia for us?"

"I don't need to, it's defined in law as 'any activity which is perceived by the victim or any other person, to be motivated by oppression based on a person's faction or perceived faction.'"

"That's the legal definition of Idcrime, which could surely apply to all factions."

"No Iain, as you know full well it's impossible for an Idcrime to be committed against Canines as they are the historical oppressors. Conversely, as historical victims, it's impossible for Felians to commit Idcrime."

"So what you seem to be saying, Ms Onette, is that 'problematic' is defined as pretty much all Canine behaviour, and yet you justify your persecution of Canines by pointing to their problematic behaviour. I put it to you, therefore, that your use of the term 'problematic' is entirely redundant and you simply believe Canines should be punished for being Canines."

"We don't punish, we rehabilitate."

"OK, how about this then? A few months ago you were quoted as saying the following: 'Simians are stupid, primitive people fit only to serve the Felines.' Do you stand by that statement?"

"That's a shameless slander. I could never have said anything like that and certainly have no recollection of doing so."

"Perhaps this recording will jog your memory," said Tegritie and played a clip of an audio recording in which Onette appeared to be saying those exact words.

"That could be anyone, or at least any woman," said Onette, after an awkward pause.

"The recording is clearly identified at the start as a meeting of the Imperium Triumvirate, of which you are the only female member."

"That was a confidential meeting and whoever gave you that recording committed an Idcrime, as have you by receiving it and again by playing it."

"Maybe, but I'm happy to let our lawyers deal with that. Do you still deny saying those words?"

"What I may or may not have said in a private meeting is not your concern."

"Oh really? You've just been elected Prime Minister of this country so I think you'll find your attitudes, however we come to know about them, are a matter of public concern. By definition that makes them the concern of this and every other journalist. What did you mean by those words?"

"We do not comment on what is discussed at policy meetings."

"You seemed to be saying you think Simians are inferior to Felines."

By this stage Onette was visibly losing her composure and her team were desperately urging her to end the interview via increasingly frantic throat-slitting gestures.

"There's no way I would have agreed to appear on your show if I'd known I would have been subjected to this felophobic ambush," said Onette.

"It wouldn't have been much of an ambush if you had known, would it?" said Tegritie. "I ask you again, is it your opinion that Simians are inferior to Felines?"

"That clip has been played entirely out of context and doesn't represent my current view."

"I see, so what made you stop believing Simians are inferior to Felines?"

"Now you're putting words into my mouth and I refuse to be subjected to this misogynistic felophobia for a moment longer."

With that Onette removed her headphones and stormed out of the radio studio.

Chapter 16 – Inquisition

The Onette interview served to accelerate Dalston's growing antipathy towards the Felian movement. His continued efforts to address the still anonymous accusation of inappropriateness against him were backfiring horribly, resulting in him being accused of 'doubling down' and told to 'stop digging.' In an instant he found himself transformed from celebrated Id Justice Warrior to irredeemable pariah. The same people who leapt to his defence online now denounced identical behaviour as felophobic, problematic and the sort of thing Adolf Hitler would get up to if he was alive today and inclined to kill time on social media in between atrocities.

He concluded there was no path to redemption. For a while he adopted a strategy of keeping his head down and not actively participating in social media in the hope the whole thing would eventually blow over, but the Felian activists he had been closest to prior to Inappropriategate were the most persistent and vicious in their denunciation. His sudden silence was considered 'deafening' and further evidence of his moral corruption. When he tried to defend himself by pointing out the severe consequences of having spoken out previously, he was met with ripostes such as "Oh so it's our fault is it?"

It became clear the exceptional hostility from his former allies was fuelled by their fear of contagion. Past public dialogue between them and Dalston was being dug up by offence archaeologists and weaponised by their own adversaries for ad hominem attacks on them. It wasn't enough, therefore, for them to merely match the normal levels of vitriol against him, they had to exceed them conspicuously to earn extra social credit as Torquemadas of the Dalston Inquisition.

The last straw came when Dalston was told that if he really wanted to show his support for the Felian movement he needed to 'take a step back' and prove, through self-sacrifice, that he 'gets it' and will 'do better.' Polite enquiries about what form this might take, while initially thrown back in his face as further evidence of wanton bigotry, eventually resulted in a steady stream of suggestions ranging from apologies to donating his job and house to a Felian. Dalston attempted some acts of self-abasement but when even the people who suggested them accused him of insincerity, ridiculed him and even laughed at his willingness to be humiliated, he realised the whole exercise was designed to extend his torture and the gratification of his tormentors.

One evening, when he was especially drunk, Dalston snapped. In an extended Twitter thread he started by reflecting on the total absence of due process. He then questioned the motives of those denouncing him, before concluding with review of how his attempts to redeem himself had been constantly undermined by the very people calling for them. When the Twittersphere gave him exactly the uniformly hysterical and vindictive response he anticipated, his final psychological restraint broke and he decided to fight fire with fire.

Since even the slightest attempt at reason or compromise resulted in vicious abuse, Dalston concluded he had nothing to lose by giving his antagonists a taste of their own medicine. He drew on every cussing competition he'd ever had with his mates to deliver the foulest insults he could think of. Nothing was off-limits; politics, race, gender, physical appearance, relatives, sexual preference, whatever came to mind was corrupted and derided with the sole aim of inflicting maximum damage on the target.

The response was spectacular, as social media users strove to out-do each other in expressing their outrage. Comparisons with Hitler became hopelessly obsolete almost immediately, so the world's literature and religions were scoured for even more extreme personifications of evil. He was even trending across multiple media at one stage, after a prominent YouTuber published a video charting his 'meltdown,' while even politicians were tripping over each other to join the mass denunciation.

To his surprise he found the whole experience exhilarating. Having already been so thoroughly abused, the new personal attacks felt unexceptional. Furthermore they followed the pattern he had become very familiar with, just with different language, and he had become so desensitised it almost felt like he was watching the whole thing from afar. He knew the mob was attacking a figment of their imagination who happened to share his name, so his psyche began to view the object of their scorn as a different person entirely, even allowing him to feel schadenfreude at this poor sod's plight. Soon he reached a state of indifference; he truly didn't care what was being said about him. It was as if the barbs they were throwing at him were bouncing off an invisible force field. He felt invulnerable.

Then a strange thing happened. After a few days of whipping the internet into a frenzy his taunts started to lose their ability to trigger. Even his core enemies had moved their tone from outrage to pity, retweeting him infrequently and then only to confirm his mental and moral decline. Even when he directly goaded them, claiming this was evidence of their capitulation and therefore his victory, they seldom rose to the bait. This enraged him in a way even his original defenestration failed to. He was enjoying his transition from supplicant lackey to notorious troll and was not at all psychologically prepared for this sudden irrelevance.

It turned out social media outrage was a fleeting thing and people needed fresh sources of it on a regular basis. There was little social credit to be earned from re-denouncing historical crimes. Dalston's fall was old news and in the eyes of the mob he had sunk so low that nothing he now said or did, however depraved, was noteworthy. He had been dealt with and there were always fresh heretics to be put to the torch. If you had told him, even a week previously, that he would soon be able say what he wanted online without consequence he would have wept with gratitude and yet here he was craving malevolent attention.

The solution presented itself by chance. In one of his attempts to rile his enemies Dalston accused them of behaving like savages. This was far from his worst taunt, yet it triggered them to the extent reminiscent of the good old days. When he asked why that bothered them so much he was told he obviously knew or he wouldn't have said it. Since his public profile was now so toxic that no third party, however neutral, would risk contamination by being seen to assist him with his enquiry, he took to Google. The imperialist and racist connotations of the word were obvious to him but he had said far worse things of that kind so he ruled it out as a reason for the disproportionate response.

It was only when he Googled 'Felian savage' that he found a story on an obscure blog about a nascent social movement called the Savages. His subsequent research revealed it was composed largely of young Canines following a YouTuber called Dick Savage, who made a name for himself railing against the injustices and hypocrisies of the Felians. This initially made him a hate figure for the Felian movement but, much as happened with Dalston himself, Savage's crimes were so persistently grave the mob had largely given up denouncing them. In one video, however, Savage documented his own physical assault at the hands of the Anticanes, a militia that appeared at the time of the Payshus Insurrection with the stated aim of combating the Canine threat.

The Anticanes initially operated as an extra-legal vigilante force, brought together by a desire to conduct 'safety patrols' of the streets to protect citizens from marauding Canines. When the insurrection died down the Anticanes became affiliated with the Felian movement and, counter-intuitively, intensified their activities. The Anticanes were given uniforms and had their remit extended to the identification of Canine 'precrime'. There was little point in confronting Canines once they committed a crime, reasoned the Felian leadership, as the harm had already been done. Acting in anticipation of it not only prevented the harm from taking place, it was also more efficient as precriminals were much easier to catch, since they were not aware they had done anything wrong. Further moral justification was derived from the view that this prophylactic approach to policing also served to protect Canines from their own intrinsically corrupt and feral nature by intervening before they were able to act upon it. Since it was intrinsically impossible to present solid evidence of precrime the Anticanes were largely exempt from legal due process and required only 'reasonable suspicion' to justify using their extensive powers.

Savage initially made a name for himself documenting the Payshus Insurrection from the ground by recording incidents on his phone and uploading them to YouTube. While the enforcement actions of the Anticanes had the tacit approval of FLAP, the arbitrary nature of some of their arrests and spot punishments had led to disquiet, even among card-carrying Felians. They were therefore very sensitive to being filmed and Savage, who at first took a neutral editorial line and was sometimes even critical of the excesses of his own Canine faction, started to find his activities opposed by the Anticanes.

On one occasion Savage filmed an Anticane patrol conducting a purge of a young Canine couple that degenerated into a humiliating sexual assault. As soon as it was completed the patrol turned on Savage and administered a further purge that resulted in the destruction of his phone. Unfortunately for them, not only was Savage live-streaming, but one of the assaulted couple regained their composure quickly enough to film the attack on Savage with their phone. The combined footage made Savage an instant celebrity in the corner of YouTube dedicated to opposing Felian authoritarianism and that, together with the experience itself, radicalised him. Savage's YouTube videos evolved from documenting and denouncing injustices perpetrated by Anticanes to calling for organised resistance and thus his group of followers known as the Savages was formed. Soon they were conducting regular counter-patrols designed to protect Canines and Delphines as well as directly confronting Anticanes whenever they could find them.

In the Savage movement Dalston felt he had not only discovered a group that shared his current aims, he saw a solution to the factional oppression he had been suffering since the advent of the Id Card. There was no way the Felians would ever relinquish the extraordinary power the Id Card scheme had given them, especially since they were now in charge of the country, so the choice was to capitulate or resist. He had tried the former and it hadn't ended end well so he decided it was time for the latter. He threw himself into the Savage movement with even greater commitment than he had previously shown to the Felians. His devotion to the Felian cause had always been forced but the Savage movement unlocked something much more visceral and instinctive in him. Where previously he only wanted to seem morally correct, he now knew he was, which gave him a whole new level of conviction.

It was still a big step to take, however, and once more he wanted a second opinion. He hadn't left either his mates or Davina Jones on good terms the last time he saw them, so he got in touch with Dev Sharma and arranged to meet him at the Camden Assembly.

"Savage is a fucking legend, blad," said Dev after Dalston brought him up to speed. "That geezer just doesn't give a fuck."

"Yeah that's it, isn't it?" Dalston replied. "After the Id Card kicked off I just totally shat myself. They were basically saying it was against the law to be Dave Dalston and I figured if I didn't convince them I was a different person then I'd lose everything. I tried, but they weren't having it, and it was only when I found out about Dick Savage that I realised they only have the power you give them, and if you don't give a fuck they've got nothing."

"That's what I was trying to tell you, bruv."

"Actually so was Davina, but I guess I had to work it out for myself."

"I feel you. So what's the deal with these Savages then? What are you saying?"

"I'm not sure. Their main thing seems to be to fuck with Felians, especially Anticanes, as much as they can. I don't think I'm up for fighting them in the streets but I'll certainly do my bit online, as I sort of have been anyway."

"Why don't you want to fight them, man? I thought you hated them."

"I do, but physical violence is a step too far."

"Not for them, innit. They're battering Canines all over the fucking shop. You think a bit of lip on Twitter matters to them? There's only one language they understand, know what I mean."

"Hmm, you do have a point. I at least want to be able to defend myself if they start on me."

"Listen, let me introduce you to a bloke I know – Frank Stein. One of the things he does is train and promote boxers and he's pretty fucking handy himself, you get me. He'll get you bang in shape and put you in touch with some other tasty types, if you want to go there."

"That's much appreciated Dev, but is it alright if I give it a bit of thought first? This feels like a big step and I don't want to dick this bloke about."

"I hear you, bruv, but fucking watch yourself out there. Now you've started banging on about the Savages on Twitter you've got a fucking target on your back, you get me."

Chapter 17 – Infiltration

Lost in thought as he left the pub, Dalston was struck by how much the prospect of physically hurting his Felian antagonists suddenly appealed to him. Graphic fantasies about the injuries he would inflict on them and Bond-style put-downs he would deliver to their prostrate forms filled his mind. When these escalated to physically acting out some of the lethal moves he would use, he decided he needed a second opinion and once more sought out Davina at her nearby stall.

"I've got to say it still sounds like you've just traded one group of nutters for another to me," said Davina after he reassured her that he'd taken her previous advice on board and updated her on his personal journey.

"It's a lot more complicated than that Davina," he replied. "You were right, trying to suck up to the Felians was a complete waste of time, and I learnt that the hard way, but it's different with the Savages. Firstly I don't have to pretend I'm something I'm not – they're Canines just like me – and secondly I genuinely believe in their cause. Are you telling me you approve of all this Anticane shit?"

"Definitely not. What they're doing goes against everything I stand for when it comes to basic civil liberties. But I also don't see what going out and scrapping with them in the street is going to achieve. Do you think it will persuade them to back off? What do you get out of it apart from fleeting catharsis? But the bigger issue I have is with you jumping from one dogma to another. You're still deriving all your views, motivation and self-worth externally and you'll never really progress until you stop."

"What do you mean?"

"Look, you're Dave Dalston, for better or worse. Yes, you're a bloke, a Canine, an Arsenal supporter, a trader, but those are all just components of you as an individual and they don't define you. What about the football team you support offers any insight into your politics, or sexual preferences, or favourite food? Nothing. The same goes for your immutable characteristics. In many ways you're a typical bloke who thinks with his dick half the time, but that doesn't determine all of your behaviour. The same goes of all this Id Card stuff. The government tried to reduce everyone down to one of four personality types but there are enormous variations within each one and they only cover a fraction of what makes us individuals."

"I do get that Davina, which is why being rejected by the Felians was such a release. Not only did I find out I didn't need them, I realised that trying to fit in with them had been holding me back. That's why the Savages are so perfect for me. I don't even need to try, these are my people and we have the same agenda. I didn't pick them, I'm just naturally one of them."

"It's still a distraction, Dave. You're still putting your energy into supporting them instead of yourself. It might seem like there's no difference but I promise you there is. Anyway, just like with the Felians you need to find all this out for yourself. Why don't you at least check Savage out on Whistleblower Hotline and see if he's all he claims to be?"

He followed Davina's advice, logged onto the site and had a browse, but apart from a general track record of saying offensive stuff in public and various accusations of shitty behaviour from ex-girlfriends he couldn't find any evidence that Savage was anything other then what he appeared. In fact that was his strength: he didn't claim to be virtuous or adopt any strong moral or even political stance. He defined himself in opposition to the Felians and that was good enough for him.

While he was there he decided to carry on reading around the damage being done by the ARSE financial derivative. One thread explored the circumstances behind its creation, questioning how such a thing could be possible while the country was still recovering from the damage done by very similar financial instruments. It all came down to convincing regulators things were different this time, that the banking sector had learned its lesson and that this was a fundamentally new type of derivative. The critical component was the CRAP, the corporate responsibility credential created specifically to distract regulators from the debased nature of the SHITs. To Dalston this was an obvious stitch-up. The payday loans that comprised the increasing majority of SHITs were the most toxic of debt and it was just a matter of time before the whole house of cards collapsed, just as it had with subprime mortgages. Yet the whole financial sector, its regulators and the broader investment community were committed to not just disguising this economic time bomb, but compounding its eventual damage by passing it between each other in what amounted to a white-collar game of Russian Roulette.

Further digging revealed the CRAP was itself a heavily traded derivative, principally by banks looking to stockpile them in order to cover their own ARSEs. SHITs were plentiful and regulators had so little ability or inclination to analyse them that, so long as each one was accompanied by a CRAP, that they were happy to provide the final component of an ARSE – the TURD. As a result CRAPs had become the most craved commodity in the investment world but, since they were also a derivative, Dalston was puzzled by their relative scarcity. He assumed any company with a decent corporate responsibility track record would be issuing these things as quickly as its compliance departments could print them, yet their spiralling value indicated they were thin on the ground.

On the discussion thread around the Whistleblower Hotline ARSE-dump he read some speculation about the reason for this. More than one commenter asserted the UK financial regulator didn't issue TURDs for just any old CRAP and that one supplier had a monopoly on the production of them. His heart was in his mouth when he saw the name Gold & Mackenzie come up in the subsequent speculation, and it got him thinking. He hadn't asked any questions when he was instructed to focus on trading ARSEs once he went back to work, mainly because he was just grateful to be there at all, but also because there was nothing unusual about being ordered to chase a quick buck. But, in hindsight, there had been an even stronger conspiratorial air about the place than usual.

The next time he was in the office Dalston engaged as many colleagues as possible in what he hoped seemed like casual chit-chat about ARSEs. Gold & Mackenzie was making obscene amounts of money from trading these new derivatives and had lapsed back into cocky exuberance. As a consequence people were happy to detail how they discovered the ARSE, with every trader keen to infer they were among the first to spot the opportunity.

"So how did you know this would be such a massive earner?" he asked one colleague.

"It's all down to the CRAP, mate, the corporate responsibility paper," said the colleague.

"What do you mean?"

"We were trying to sell SHITs by themselves but nobody was buying. They were like 'hold on a fucking minute, I don't like the look of this one little bit.' Even the biggest suckers reckoned it was a dud, so we had to disguise it. We'd been noticing the share price boost companies with spotless corporate responsibility were getting for a while and figured that could also be applied to derivatives."

"OK I'm with you, but the tricky bit must have been turning those good vibes into something liquid and transferable, right?"

"Egg-fuckin-zackly, my friend; you hit the nail on the head. There was no shortage of companies pretending to give a fuck about poofs, or whatever, just to get their CR score up, and it was easy enough to produce the CRAP to commoditise that score, but so long as it was just some bit of paper with a G&M letterhead nobody else would take it seriously."

"Yes, I can picture it. The thing you thought up to make SHITs look legit still needed something else to make *it* look legit. Nightmare."

At this point Dalston's colleague lowered his voice, peered around the office, and beckoned him closer.

"Let me ask you something. How did we get away with all that bollocks last time?"

"You mean subprime mortgages and all that?"

"Yeah."

"Well no-one really knew what the fuck was going on did they? It got so complicated that even the cunts doing the trading didn't know what they were selling. But the price kept going up so no-one gave a fuck."

"Right, and whose job was it to give a fuck more than anyone else?"

"The regulators, I suppose."

"Spot on again. But we realised that this time it wouldn't be enough just to confuse the regulators, we had to get them on board. It so happened they just as obsessed with CR so they bit our fucking hands off when we told them about the CRAP. Then it was just a matter of drafting up the TURD for them to sign and Robert's your father's brother."

"Brilliant!"

"No mate, the brilliant bit was persuading the regulator that only our CRAP was legit. There was nothing to stop all the other banks producing their own and if they had, the value of ARSEs would've gone down the toilet. If we were going to make any decent wedge out of this we needed to control the supply and that meant controlling the regulator."

"How did you do that?"

"I've got to be honest, that stuff is above my pay grade. But whoever did the deal is a fucking legend."

Once he knew what he was looking for, Dalston was amazed at how easy it was to trawl the corporate archives for documents and email trails concerning the negotiations between the CEO of Gold & Mackenzie and her counterpart at the regulator. The critical exchange pointed unequivocally towards an agreement between the two of them that promised considerable rewards for the regulator boss if he ensured no other banks were issued TURDs. Despite being a grizzled trader himself, Dalston was still shocked at the gall of this move. His company had successfully conspired with the regulator to rig the entire financial market.

He downloaded as much documentation as he could onto his laptop and was pleasantly surprised to be able to walk out of his office without so much as a sidelong glance from any colleagues or security staff. Once home, he logged in to his Whistleblower Hotline account and prepared to upload everything he knew about Gold & Mackenzie's role in the creation and proliferation of the ARSE. Just as he was about to pull the trigger he paused to reflect on the consequences. While he had a degree of anonymity thanks to his username of 'diamond_geezer85,' he knew the upload could be traced to him eventually. If this happened he would lose his job at the very least and it occurred to him maybe that was one of the main reasons he was doing it. Maybe his subconscious was desperate to leave Gold & Mackenzie but his conscious mind was too chicken-shit to just resign.

All the bullshit he had been dealing with, such as the Id Card scheme, had been brought about by the financial crisis and here was his own company revealed as the prime mover in a process that would surely result in another. Furthermore this one was almost certain to be worse than the last, since all the tools governments and central bankers had at their disposal for mitigating economic downturns remained spent after the last crisis. As a result of his many humbling experiences since all this started, something resembling a conscience had been slowly growing in an unused corner of his mind. It was one thing ripping off other big companies or funds, but with SHITs they were basically exploiting the poorest in society while pretending to help them. A large part of him was still happy living in a dog-eat-dog world, but sometimes the people at the bottom of the pile were so hapless and wretched that ripping them off left a bad taste in his mouth.

Lastly, he reflected on the triumphant smugness of his colleagues, especially the senior managers at Gold & Mackenzie, who thought they were so clever for ripping off the British underclass and corrupting its financial regulators. It was clear to him there was nothing so low, underhand or exploitative they wouldn't passionately embrace it if it might result in a quick buck and he hated them for it, in no small part because he recognised that tendency in himself. He physically shuddered when he realised he was about to embark on a moral act and wondered if other people felt like this all the time. Driven by disgust at his company's utter lack of ethics, decency and compassion and his own complicity in that culture, he clicked the upload button.

Chapter 18 – Impact

Davina, a Whistleblower Hotline administrator, saw what Dalston had done almost immediately and phoned to praise him for his courage. She told him Sally Pimienta, the founder of the organisation behind the site, wanted to talk to him in person so they arranged to meet. Dev also called to comment on the size and lustre of his testicles and to stress it was more important than ever for him to learn how to take care of himself. It was starting to dawn on Dalston that he had massively underestimated the significance of his action, so he accepted Dev's offer to introduce him to Frank Stein. Not long afterwards Amy surprised him with a video call.

"Hello Daddy," she said.

"Amy! It's great to speak to you again and even better to see you," he beamed. "You look great, darling, how are you?"

"I'm really good actually and I wanted to call to say how proud I am of you doing the right thing with all those secrets you put on the internet about the bank stuff. Mummy says what those people are doing is very greedy and naughty and will make a lot of people poor, so what you did is really important."

Dalston started choking up.

"Are you OK Daddy, did I say something wrong?"

"No, no! I'm just really happy to see you, that's all," he whispered.

"Mummy said something about you turning a corner but I don't know how she knows that when we haven't seen you for ages."

"Maybe she doesn't mean it literally and is trying to say she thinks I'm getting my life in order."

He noticed there was rock music playing in the background of wherever Amy was calling from. He felt he recognised it but couldn't place it. He even managed to make out a few lyrics.

...wreckage of all my twisted dreams...can't stifle all my screams...waiting at the crossroads...

"What's that music, baby?" he asked.

"Yes maybe that's what she meant," said Amy, "I hope so, because it might mean she will let you come and visit us again. I really miss you Daddy."

It was as if Amy hadn't heard his question at all, so Dalston presumed she was just wrapped up in digesting his previous statement.

"So do I sweetheart, do you really think I'm doing the right stuff to get back in Mummy's good books?"

"Yes, you should have seen her face when she saw the news, she laughed."

"The news? What do you mean?"

"You know, all those stories on the telly about the thing called hot whistle or whatever. Mummy said, 'I bet that was Daddy' and when that man from your company was interviewed and said your name we couldn't believe it."

"Shit!"

"Daddy! What did you say?"

"Sorry, baby, I just can't believe how big this has got so quickly."

"Isn't that what you thought would happen when you put those things on the internet?"

"To be honest Amy, I didn't really think about it much at all."

"Well I know you did the right thing, Daddy. I think you realised being greedy is bad so you decided to do something about it."

"Yeah, maybe."

"Please keep doing this sort of thing Daddy. I really want to see you again and it looks like you're starting to remind Mummy how nice you are."

"I will baby, I promise. Now I'd better go and find out what's going on."

Dalston switched on the TV and saw 'ARSEgate' was the lead evening news item on all channels. He had a few new missed calls from unidentified numbers and figured they must be the media. He felt dizzy. Then he got a message from Jack Morrison.

What the fuck have you done?

What do you mean?

Don't take the piss. You've fucked us. Why?

Mate, I looked into that shit we're selling and it's all bollocks.

No fucking shit Sherlock, you just realised?

Yeah but this is a whole new level of bollocks man. The whole gig is corrupt to the top. I couldn't believe it.

Jesus Christ you're naive. If you want to play by the rules go and work in the fucking Post Office you soppy cunt. This is how we've always coined it, you just got an attack of conscience because you got in trouble and now you've decided to fuck it up for the rest of us. Thanks a lot 'mate'.

It's a lot more complicated than that Jack, but I wouldn't expect a corporate suck-arse like you to even be capable of understanding, so I won't bother trying to explain. What's going on in the office?

That's fine, there's nothing to explain. You're a traitor, end of. And the rest of the office agrees, since you ask, but that's the only inside info you'll get from me, Judas.

Yeah, I figured you wouldn't want to risk getting into trouble with teacher. Well enjoy the ride mate and let me know when you get your head out of your arse.

Fuck you.

That seemed like a fairly conclusive statement so Dalston decided to leave it there. He figured he might as well see if he'd been sacked yet but when he attempted to log on to his work email he found himself blocked. However, his personal email revealed a short message from the head of HR at Gold & Mackenzie with the subject field 'Immediate termination.' It simply said, "In the light of recent acts concerning the release of confidential documents into the public domain, your employment at Gold & Mackenzie is hereby terminated with immediate effect due to gross misconduct. You will be hearing from our lawyers shortly."

Even though he knew this was the inevitable consequence of his actions he still felt stunned. Gold & Mackenzie had been his life for years and a large part of his identity was defined by being a trader. What was he going to do now? In the absence of many alternatives, he judged this was as good a time as any to meet the owner of Whistleblower Hotline.

***

He met Davina outside Chalk Farm tube station and she led him to Chamomile Cafe in England's Lane where Pimienta was already tucking into a cream tea. Affectionately known as Aunt Sally, she was a rotund late-middle-aged woman who dressed like an accident in a knitwear factory. She smiled when she saw them arrive and invited him to join her. For a moment she just watched him with a mischievous glint in her eye.

"Mr Dalston I presume," she said.

"The very same, Ms Pimienta."

"Sally is fine, may I call you Dave?"

"Please do."

"So, Dave, you've got yourself in a right old pickle haven't you?"

"You could say that, yeah."

"Why did you do it?"

"To be honest Sally I'm still struggling to find a good answer to that question. On one level I was genuinely pissed off when I saw what a stitch up the ARSE was. Not only were we repeating the behaviour that led to the financial crisis, but we were targeting the skintest people in the country to do it. The specific thing that triggered me, though, was being back in the office after my suspension and seeing how fucking pleased with themselves everyone was, like they were doing something really clever instead of just being selfish, dirty bastards. They were so smug, they were even talking openly about the stitch-up with the regulators and I just thought – 'I'm not having this'– and decided to shut it down."

"But you worked there during the last financial crisis, didn't you? Why didn't it trouble your conscience then, or if it did, why didn't you act on it?"

"Yeah that's something I've been wrestling with and I reckon it comes down to me being suspended. I wasn't really doing anything wrong, certainly nothing I hadn't been doing for years without anyone batting an eyelid, but as soon as the Id Card and the Simpson-Oxford Act came along they just threw me under the bus. I know I didn't help myself much but the more I thought about it, especially the way people like my mate Jack just went along with the Id Card like it was no big deal, the more I realised it was all bollocks."

"Elegantly stated," Pimienta smiled.

"I think what really crystalised it was my experience with the Felians," he continued. "When they turned on me over fuck-all it felt like the same situation. Well, not exactly the same; the Felians were much more vicious, but somehow it hurt less, maybe because I didn't know them very well and never really felt part of their group. Gold & Mackenzie are my people, man. I worked there for years and

I'm a City boy at heart, so to find out absolutely nobody had my back and they were only concerned with protecting themselves was a real blow."

"So it wasn't about doing the right thing, then, you just wanted to get your own back?"

"No, there's definitely more to it than that. It's like the betrayal opened my eyes and made me look at them in a different way. Just like with the Felians, once they booted me out, and I stopped trying to please them, I saw them for the stupid, nasty little bullies they are. Being treated that way at G&M made me look at its activities like an outsider. In the build up to the last crisis I was just laser-focused on making money and, to be honest, I didn't even consider any other implications of what we were doing. Once I did, I could see how out of order it was and I didn't like what it said about me that I was part of it."

"Fair enough. Well whatever your reasons you're in deep doo-doo now, young man. It won't just be your former employer that comes after you, it will be the whole establishment."

"Why? I would've thought they'd be happy I exposed what G&M was up to."

"Oh dear, my poor naive child, you really have no idea what you've got yourself into do you? Do you think the creation of the ARSE is some kind of outlier?"

"Isn't it?"

"Right, I think we need another round of tea and scones."

Pimienta gestured to Davina who dealt with the order.

"Pay attention, sweetie," she said. "The establishment isn't some shady elite cabal of people like the Illuminati who meet in secret to decide how the world should be run – it's a mindset. It's basically everyone who is afraid of change and uncertainty, everyone who just wants to fit in and is offended by people who are different. These are the people who rarely think for themselves, instead they read the approved papers, watch the approved news and think what they're told to think. They willingly surrender independence and freedom in return for the comfort and security of mainstream society."

"Hadn't thought of it that way," Dalston mused.

"The people who run the establishment are just the ones who have climbed the greasy pole the highest, but they know how precarious their position is, which is why they never rock the boat when they get to the top. On the contrary, they're the ones with the greatest interest in maintaining the status quo and will use all their considerable power to crush anything that threatens it. You haven't just declared war on the senior management of G&M, Dave, you've declared war on the entire establishment."

"I don't get it," he interjected. "The last financial crisis, which basically fucked the country, was caused by bankers cheating, right? And I just exposed another lot of almost identical cheating, but before it had a chance to do serious damage, right? So it seems to me I just saved the country from another macroeconomic disaster, which would have rocked the fuck out of the boat, so surely I've done the establishment a favour."

"Yes and no. You need to understand how interconnected everything in the establishment is. All the money being generated by ARSE trading doesn't just end up in the pockets of traders like you, it percolates across the whole system. Wealth isn't the accumulation of money, it's the flow of it, and the establishment likes anything that makes money flow. Everyone else knows that while the money's flowing some of it's likely to trickle their way and politicians know they're much more likely to win elections if everyone's getting paid.

"The financial crisis happened because the establishment was reluctant to take away the punch bowl while the party was in full swing. You could have been stopped at any time. In that respect speculative bubbles are like a game of musical chairs; everyone knows the music's going to stop sooner or later, but as long as they have a chair when it does they're not bothered. What you've done by leaking this stuff is make the music stop much sooner than everyone was ready for, so they'll be scared. You've also given them someone to blame for the resulting catastrophe."

"Me? How is it my fault when I'm the one calling it out?"

"Because now everyone can claim it wouldn't even have happened if it wasn't for you. The banks can claim they were on the verge of detoxifying the ARSE and were thwarted by your actions. The politicians can claim they were always on top of the situation and you just threw a spanner in the works, while the journalists will question your motives and do anything else they can to discredit you for delivering a scoop far bigger than anything they will ever manage. This will all lead to the establishment, which is most people, preferring to view you as some kind of threat to society, than the hero we know you to be."

"Fuck. I wish I'd chatted to you before I did this now."

"Why? Do you think you would have acted differently if you had?"

"I might have, yeah!"

"Well if it's any consolation I probably would have worked that out for myself and fed you some bullshit about how you would be anonymous or whatever it took to make you go ahead."

"You would've lied just to get me to publish the documents?"

"Of course. Look sweetie, you seem like a nice enough chap in a rough-and-ready kind of way, but this is much bigger than any individual. How many personal sacrifices do you think everyone at Whistleblower has made to make sure the world knows about all the stuff we publish? Everyone's happy to hear about it when some big leak hits the news, but hardly anyone is prepared to put their bum on the line to make it happen. If a few white lies had been required to make you do the right thing then I wouldn't have hesitated."

"So I'm fucked then am I? Great!"

"Yes and no. Your old life is gone, but judging by what Davina has told me that's no great loss. You've just got to make some adjustments. Have you ever heard of 'Rules for Radicals'?"

"No."

"It's a book, written in the golden era of civil disobedience. It offers some good advice about fighting the establishment and general top tips on dealing with the challenges you're going to have to deal with. It's like Machiavelli for normal people."

"OK, I'll check it out, thanks."

"Good. Now, since you've got no idea what you've just got yourself into I'm guessing you don't know what all this is really about."

"I'm starting to think not."

"You know the government created the Id Card scheme in an attempt to prevent anything like the financial crisis happening again, right? And that created all sorts of unintended consequences, including the faction system you found yourself in the middle of. So far so obvious, but what you may not have fully understood was that in so doing they also opened up humanity's biggest Pandora's box: top-down versus bottom-up."

"Really? What's that? I don't get it."

"That's fine, have a scone and just try to take in what I'm telling you, sweetie. There are basically two ways of looking at the world. The top-down way says there are one or more eternal, absolute ideals and everything else is subservient to them. Historically this has usually meant religion; if you followed the word of God you were good and if you didn't you were bad. This kind of stripped down, simplistic philosophy was very attractive to uneducated people, which was nearly all of them until the 20th century, because it not only gave them a rule book, it also compensated them for their horrid lives with the promise of heaven, or whatever, so long as they obeyed the rules. But it was even more appealing to the ruling class. Their superior education meant they were the only ones capable of fully interpreting the word of God, which allowed them to control everyone else by promising them paradise in afterlife and whatever else they needed to hear to make them put up with their appalling lot in life."

"When regular folk began to get more educated they started asking why, if God was so benevolent, they were constantly drawing the short straw. So religion became less popular, but with nothing to replace it a crisis of meaning resulted. That brings us to more contemporary dogma such as environmentalism, identity politics, Felianism, and so on, which perform more or less the same function as religion, but with secular, contemporary gods. So long as there's a set of rules, a self-appointed elite to enforce them and the promise of some kind of reward if you're a good boy, then you have a dogma that ticks all the top-down boxes. The Id Card scheme skewed UK society in a top-down direction by creating a new dogmatic framework everyone submitted to."

"So if top-down is all about rules and dogma and control, what's bottom-up?"

"Bottom-up is about evidence, experience and seeing things as they really are, rather than how you think they should be. It's about provable truth as opposed to comforting lies, it's empiricism versus idealism, individualism versus collectivism, principles versus ideals. The whole of human history is defined by this dichotomy. The people at the top always promote a top-down view of things for obvious reasons, but the people at the bottom usually go along with it because they don't know any better, or they want to believe the comforting lies, or they're just scared not to. Viewing the world in a bottom-up way is scary; there are no reassurances, no light at the end of the tunnel, no grand plan, just life and sensations and problems and pain. There's no obvious point to it all and most people find that concept just too difficult to accept."

"I can see how that might be a hard sell."

"But it's more natural to approach the world in a bottom-up way because we're all just animals at the end of the day," Pimienta continued. "Do you think dogs ponder the philosophical implications of sniffing each others' bums? Of course not, they just do it because they feel like it. That's bottom-up – quite literally! It's how we interact with the world when we're babies – touching, tasting, seeing. But then, for some reason, we spend the rest of our lives trying to make ourselves top-down by learning conventions, laws and belief systems, even though none of that can change the fact we're still individuals, essentially alone in the world. The crowning irony of the Id Card is that it's essentially a bottom-up tool in so much as it documents your core nature, but the way it has been used has resulted in a very much top-down outcome."

"I've never heard things put quite like that but it makes sense. I'm always torn between doing what the fuck I want and what I should be doing. But surely we have to have rules and laws or it would be chaos."

"Yes, but it's a bit more complicated than that. A lot of the rules we have in society might seem top-down, but they were actually arrived at by centuries of precedent, negotiation and consensus. This sort of thing is often called a social contract and it's basically a set of rules we all follow voluntarily because we know it just makes life easier. Similarly you impose certain rules on yourself, such as hygiene and basic discipline, for the same reason. These are all very different to top-down rules, which tend to be arbitrary and imposed by some third party. Their justification nearly always comes down to safety – imposing rules for your own protection – and for that to fly they need a source of danger. Historically that was the Devil, who you would fall prey to unless you did what you were told. Now it can be nearly anything: Nazis, global warming, bankers, Canines, it doesn't matter so long as there's sufficient consensus the thing is dangerous and we need protecting from it."

"Alright, but why should I care about this top-down/bottom-up stuff?"

"Because, whether you acknowledge it or not, the Id Card is making you choose between them. Top-down thinking relies on a grand, overarching narrative accepted as an article of faith. The mortal enemy of the narrative is any demand for evidence, as hardly any of them stand up to close scrutiny. Bottom-up thinking is all about building on foundations made by provable facts and principles, which makes it toxic to the very essence of top-down. That's why you can't have both. Before the Id Card you were living your life in a bottom-up way, basically doing what you wanted and only adapting your behaviour when specific incentives presented themselves. Then, because you were in unfamiliar territory, you decided to give top-down a go by signing up for the Felians and all their authoritarian nonsense. Now you've seen what a bad idea that was, you're at a crossroads, Dave; you can try top-down again or you can be true to yourself, for better or worse."

"Obviously I want to be true to myself, but there's still the problem that the Dalston brand isn't in great demand right now."

"Are you sure?"

"Egotistical, superficial, materialistic, selfish, are you having a laugh? I'm in the fucking Id Card instruction manual under the heading 'what not to do'."

"Is that really how you view yourself?"

"Not really but I know it's how I come over."

"Why do you think that?"

"Because that's how I behave, I guess."

"So it seems to me the answer to your problems is for you to find a way to behave differently. Not because you've been told to or because you're trying to fit into some stupid group, but because you want to."

"I do want to!"

"Then what are you waiting for?"

"When you put it like that…"

"Do you mind if I give you some extra advice, sweetie?"

"Go for it."

"Try to get to know yourself."

"That sounds familiar," said Dalston, rolling his eyes towards Davina.

"You've already given him the speech have you?" Pimienta asked Davina.

"Just a taste, I thought I'd leave the full version to you," said Davina.

"Thanks. Look, you've just revealed you don't know yourself that well; you don't know whether you're an arrogant prick or a decent bloke and you don't even seem to know how you go about picking one over the other," said Pimienta. "I suspect you're the latter or we wouldn't be sitting here now, but you could still go either way. My feeling is you're still too influenced by external events and you need to block as much of that rubbish out as possible. That's what I mean by getting to know yourself: try to find out the real reasons you think and do things. Once you really start being honest with yourself you'll start to realise a depressing amount of your behaviour is reacting to external events rather than doing what you really want."

"Like what?"

"Well, I know you've fallen out with the people you care most about. Why do you think that is?"

"Do you really want me to go into all the rows we've had?"

"No, I want you to try to view yourself from the outside and assess your role in these conflicts objectively. If it was one of your friends rather than you, what advice would you give them? Don't answer, just think about it. I'll give you a clue though: all people experience constant internal conflict between their instinctive self and their cerebral self. Nearly all disagreements come when the people involved have surrendered to the former and are behaving in an emotional, feral way. If you can get really good at tapping into your higher self you'll rise above the tempers and anxieties that make you fall out with people and instead strive to meet them in the middle."

"But what if they're wrong? Why should I give in?"

"How can you be so sure they are?"

"Sometimes they just are – it's fucking clear as day."

"It might seem that way but maybe it's just your instinctive self telling you so. Often it's impossible to prove someone else is wrong, it's just your gut-feel. But what if they feel just as strongly that you're the one who's wrong? Not only is it impossible to definitively resolve that dispute but your opposing positions almost guarantee conflict unless at least one of you is prepared to compromise. Imagine having the kind of mind that doesn't take it personally when someone proves you wrong or even insults you. Consider how much pain and conflict that would save you."

"That would be great, but I'm not like that."

"OK, let me just leave you with one last word then: humility. If you're not on a pedestal then you can't get knocked off it. If you've no pride then it can't be dented. If you have little that needs protecting then there's not much to be defensive about. Humility allows you to not sweat the small stuff and rise above petty conflicts. Humility means you value learning over winning and makes you actively embrace being proved wrong as a necessary step on that road. A humble person is willing to forgo small victories in pursuit of much bigger prizes like happiness, enlightenment and meaning."

Chapter 19 – Infamy

As he walked back towards Camden Town, Dalston was so immersed in reflecting on his conversation with Sally Pimienta that he didn't notice the group of Anticanes until it was too late. They had just come out of Chalk Farm tube station and started shouting taunts and jibes as soon as they recognised him. They were on the other side of the road so he tried to ignore them, but they followed him and eventually crossed over to confront him. Their insults were nothing new – the standard stuff about being a traitor, a Nazi and a Felophobe – but this was the first time his social media experiences had caught up with him in real life.

He tried to brush it off by congratulating them on their wit and commenting on the great courage of six people harassing one individual without provocation, but the abuse continued. Eventually he suggested they fuck off and get a life, but they rejected his advice. Instead they took turns in obstructing him by standing in his path with their hands by their sides, inviting him to walk into them. He could tell this was a crude way of trying to induce him into initiating physical contact and was determined not to fall for it, but they persisted. Passers-by not only declined to intervene, some even followed the scene, laughing nervously and filming it with their phones.

At one point a pair of community support officers approached and asked what was going on. Dalston attempted to explain he was being harassed but was drowned out by the Anticanes, who insisted they were just minding their own business and had no idea what Dalston's problem was. Eventually one of the officers asked the Anticanes to walk away but they refused, insisting they were doing nothing wrong. The officer asked once more and the leader of the group inquired what they would do if they refused. The officer had to concede there was nothing they could do, at which point the Anticanes demanded they fuck off, which they did.

The harassment recommenced with added intensity now that Dalston had added snitching to his already heinous rap sheet. The Anticanes were now performing spasmodic over-reactions and football-style dives whenever he so much as brushed past them. They also started getting their faces as close as possible to his without making contact and shouting "Nazi snitch!" as loudly as they could. Eventually he snapped and pushed one of them, who threw himself to the ground and writhed around in theatrical agony. Not only was this further evidence of his Nazism, but also the pretext the rest needed to retaliate physically. One of them was carrying a milkshake, which he threw in his face, and others retrieved concealed weapons such as bike locks, and rained blows on his head and body. Blinded by the milkshake and unable to identify a single assailant for long enough to attempt a counter-punch, he staggered on until he spotted a pub doorway and burst through it.

Battered and bleeding he shouted, "These cunts are trying to kill me, someone stop them for fuck's sake!" Nobody came to his aid, however, with most patrons staring intently at their phones, pints or companions to avoid acknowledging his existence. The barman eventually told Dalston he didn't want any trouble and demanded he leave, but since the Anticanes hadn't followed him into the pub he wouldn't have obeyed him even at gunpoint. He spotted a sign to the toilets, followed it and locked himself in a cubicle. As he slumped on the seatless toilet in agony, he swore he would never allow himself to be in a situation like this again.

More immediately, however, there was the matter of the Anticanes, who no doubt would wait outside the pub indefinitely. He needed help and that clearly wasn't going to come from anyone inside. He immediately thought of Dev Sharma, who would likely be tending his nearby stall and didn't seem the type to shy away from confrontation. He was relieved almost to the point of tears when Dev answered his phone and after he explained the situation Dev told him to stay right where he was and within 30 minutes came in to the pub bog and reassured him it was now safe to leave.

As he walked back through the pub he thanked the barman and patrons for nothing and met a couple of Dev's friends outside the pub, at least one of whom appeared to have been injured. "You should see the other cunt," said the friend as he wiped blood from his cheek. Outnumbered two to one, Dev and his friends hadn't even bothered speaking to the Anticanes when they arrived and just started swinging immediately. A couple of the Anticanes went down straight away but one managed to land a couple of blows before all six of them ran away. Dev berated Dalston for not having met Frank Stein yet and he meekly accepted the rebuke. They took him to the Royal Free Hospital for some stitches and then home to get cleaned up, then it was straight to Stein's gym in Holloway.

"Those slags wouldn't know a proper fight if it fucked them up the arse," growled Stein after they were introduced. "But listen, son, what were you thinking, walking around by yourself after everything you've done to wind them up?"

"I guess I wasn't thinking, Mr Stein," Dalston replied. "But I just never thought internet bullshit would turn into real life violence."

"You can call me Frank. Dev told me you had chatted about the Savages going up against the Anticanes. What did you think they were going to do, challenge them to a fucking dance-off?"

"I said they wasn't fucking about, innit." said Dev.

"Yeah you did Dev, and you were right," said Dalston. "I guess it just didn't sink in, but it certainly has now, don't you worry about that."

"So how do you feel now?" said Stein. "I know you've got some bumps and bruises, but I want to know what you feel about what they did to you."

"I'm fucking fuming to be honest. They seriously crossed a line Frank, and right now I just want to find them and kill them."

"Woah! Strong words, son, and ones you shouldn't use lightly, especially in here. Look, most of the blokes in here know they're not going to be world champions but all of them know how to take care of themselves. I'm going to let you in, on the back of Dev's recommendation, but don't waste my time. I'll train you to be a hundred times harder than you are right now, but I need to know you're up for it."

"Take my word for it, I am."

"I'll be the judge of that. What do you think boxing and martial arts are all about?"

"Well, they're ultimately like any other sport I guess – getting good at something and then competing against other people."

"No. Fighting's not like any other sport. For a start no other sports have hurting the other cunt as the main point and therefore aren't as risky, but even that's not what it's really all about. Your professional fighter is the ultimate individual. He can walk down the street knowing that if anyone fucks with him they're in a world of shit. That knowledge affects everything else you do and how you act. Most fighters never have to fight because of how they carry themselves and most people just don't fancy the aggro. Look around the gym Dave, look at all those blokes training. I'd back any of them against ten Anticanes if they had their back against the wall. I'm not saying I'll make a boxer out of you, but you stick with me and I'll make it so the next Anticane cunt who gets in your face will regret it for the rest of his life."

"That's all I can ask for Frank, I'm really grateful and I promise I won't dick you around."

"No, you fucking won't."

"One last thing, I was wondering if you have a middle name?"

Stein looked up sharply and stared into his eyes for a few seconds before responding.

"What the fuck's that got to do with anything?"

Dalston had wanted to leave their meeting on a lighter note, but realised he had totally misjudged the situation.

"Oh, erm, nothing Frank, I was just talking shit. Ignore me."

"It's Neville, since you ask. Is that a fucking problem?"

Behind Stein, Dalston made eye contact with Dev, who was frantically shaking his head and making a throat-cutting gesture with his hand.

"Look Frank, I'm sorry, I just talk shit when I'm nervous," he said, shaken by the speed with which the atmosphere in the room had chilled. "Please forget I mentioned it and thanks again for your time."

Stein stared him down once more, apparently looking for any trace of insincerity or disrespect.

"Alright then," he said. "Now sling your hook and if you're not here tomorrow at seven don't fucking bother coming back."

Dalston left the gym with Dev, who was furious with him.

"What the fuck's the matter with you, blad?" he said. "You just had your head kicked in so you thought it would be a laugh to wind up one of the most dangerous cunts in London. Level with me, bruv, are you suicidal or something? Because if you are I'll just leave you to it, know what I mean."

"No I'm not Dev," said Dalston. "I don't know why I said that. I just couldn't get it out of my head how funny it would be if his middle initial was 'N' and the comment just came out."

"Well thank fuck you didn't laugh when he told you or we wouldn't be standing here right now, you get me. He probably would've battered me just for being your mate, for fuck's sake."

"I hear you. Look you've got nothing to worry about. I'm going to turn up early every day and keep my gob shut and my head down."

"You fucking better had."

Chapter 20 – Interviews

By the time Dalston got home, footage of his assault at the hands of the Anticanes had already made its way onto social media, with many websites soon following and even some TV news already running with it under headlines such as 'ARSE whistleblower in street brawl.' He was stunned that not a single report portrayed him as the victim, despite conceding the attack was unprovoked, that he was outnumbered six-to-one and his assailants were armed while he wasn't. Nearly all reports opened with characterisations of him as a 'Felophobe leaker,' or 'Controversial Canine firebrand' and inferred he was to blame for the attack. "Self-styled Canine troll Dave Dalston, not content with spouting toxic hate on Twitter, sought to provoke the Felians further by brazenly strolling through their home turf of Camden Town and got more than he bargained for," opened one report.

A concrete narrative quickly formed, with various media apparently just copying each other's reports and rearranging the words a bit. There was mainstream consensus that, while violence should never be condoned, this wouldn't have happened if Dalston hadn't provoked his assailants so gratuitously. While the attack was regrettable, went the narrative, it was morally equivalent to Dalston's own verbal assaults, so at worst the two things cancelled each other out. The assumption seemed to be that Anticanes only used violence against their most egregious antagonists and it could be avoided if people were simply more deferential.

Dalston was incensed. He had never been a fan of the term 'victim blaming,' seeing it as a cynical concept designed to negate due process by insisting every accusation be taken at face value, but now it took on a whole new meaning. Why were the media all being so hostile towards him and dropping all pretence at objectivity? The answer, of course, was that he was not only a Canine but a symbol of all that was worst about them and thus a pariah to the Felians. The vast majority of the UK mainstream media was pro Felian and, now that its post-election honeymoon period was over, were increasingly protective of FLAP. Their behaviour reminded him of his own period of sucking up to the Felians and some of the more moderate publications were already being criticized for lacking zeal.

Independent bloggers and YouTubers seemed to operate in a totally different environment, however. While there were plenty of Felian supporters on the internet, there was also a substantial community of commentators willing to attack them with a disinhibition impossible to imagine from the traditional press. These ranged from people devoted to opposing everything Felian to generalist commentators calling out excesses on all sides. The most influential of the latter category was a YouTuber and podcaster known as Jive Robin, who specialised in broadcasting extended conversations often lasting several hours. While browsing YouTube Dalston found a clip of Jive Robin discussing the Anticane phenomenon with his guest and his heart raced when he heard his own case discussed at length. He was upset to hear himself positioned once more as a troll and a provocateur, but relieved when they concluded no amount of verbal provocation in any way justifies physical violence.

Being publicly discussed in this way was a new experience for him, simultaneously exhilarating and frustrating. There was an undoubted thrill and sense of validation from being considered important enough to be mentioned, but at the same time the casual voyeurism of the commentary left him feeling used. It was therefore with considerable surprise and relief that soon afterwards he received emails from the producers of both Iain Tegritie's radio show and the Jive Robin podcast, inviting him on to be interviewed about the Anticane attack. While intimidated at the prospect, especially of being cross-examined by the formidable Tegritie, his desire for vindication moved him to accept both.

Tegritie's studio was housed inside the headquarters of one of the UK's main terrestrial broadcasters in Central London. As she led him to the green room a production assistant told Dalston how lucky he was to have landed the prime interview slot, thus ensuring himself a full four-and-a-half minutes of airtime. Tegritie visited him briefly to go over what they were going to discuss and seemed a lot more sympathetic towards his situation than he expected. Reassured that Tegritie intended to act with a level of journalistic rigour and impartiality seldom seen from his contemporaries, Dalston relaxed and awaited the interview with excitement.

"Now I'm delighted to announce, in his first broadcast interview, Dave Dalston, the man at the centre of the recent Anticane altercation in North West London," said Tegritie. "Mr Dalston, it has been widely reported that you initiated this contretemps yourself, why would you do such a thing?"

"The truth is I didn't initiate anything and six people assaulted me in broad daylight with no provocation whatsoever. The thing you have to understand about Anticanes is…"

"Yes, yes, we'll come to that. Are you suggesting those reports are lies?"

"Well they're certainly mistaken. Whether that's the result of conscious lying or just incompetence I couldn't possibly say, but…"

"That's a very arrogant position."

"Look, I know what happened and those reporters don't. All of them, as far as I can tell, interviewed the leader of the Anticane group and none of them have even approached me. That's not balanced reporting, which is why I'm grateful you've given me the opportunity to tell my side of the story…"

"'Anticanes are a bunch of pussies who wouldn't know a fight if it bit them on the arse.' You recently posted those words on Twitter. They seem like pretty clear provocation to me."

"You've taken that tweet out of context…"

"OK, how about this one? 'Felians make Nazis look like Boy Scouts.' That's very offensive to at least half of the population."

Dalston was becoming flustered and exasperated. The interview was going completely contrary to his expectations. He still held out hope it could be steered in a more constructive direction, however, so he attempted to meet Tegritie halfway.

"I suppose it could be but, again, the context is important as I'd previously been accused of being a Nazi myself and was retaliating in kind."

"Regardless of the context, on many occasions you chose to make comments on social media that were clearly designed to provoke the Anticanes and offend not just all Felians but people of other factions who support FLAP," said Tegritie. "It's frankly absurd for you to then come here and play the victim after falling foul of the entirely predictable consequences of your actions."

It was now clear Tegritie had no intention of giving him a fair hearing so he decided to make a stand.

"Even if what I said was offensive to some people I don't see how that justifies what happened to me."

"So you're saying it's OK for anyone to say whatever they want to whoever they want with no consequences," said Tegritie.

"No I'm not, I'm saying offensive words aren't morally equivalent to physical violence."

"So you're saying words can't physically harm people."

"Yes."

"So you're saying it's OK for me to say, live on air, that people should hurt you. Or that I should be allowed to shout 'fire!' in a crowded theatre when there isn't one, even though the resulting panicked stampede would almost certainly result in physical harm being done."

"No, words that directly incite physical harm are a different matter."

"Your words directly resulted in physical harm to yourself though, didn't they?

"Eventually yes, but…"

"So by your own logic you brought that attack upon yourself with your offensive words."

"Hold on, are you saying that physically attacking people is OK if the attacker feels offended by something they said."

"I was very clear, Mr Dalston, and I'm offended by your attempt to put words in my mouth."

"I guess that means you're entitled to hit me then."

"That would doubtlessly suit your attention-seeking agenda but I won't stoop to your level, even though your presence here today makes me question the severity of your injuries."

"My level? My injuries? I find that pretty offensive to be honest. Does that mean I get to hit you?"

"Nice try, but the offense you claim is clearly false and manufactured to make a childish point."

"So you're saying your offense and that of anyone responding to my words is legitimate but mine isn't. Who decides what is legitimate?

"These are society's rules, not mine. Nobody questions that Canines were responsible for nearly all historical crimes and injustices and are thus denied victim status under any circumstances. You are therefore not permitted to take offense at anything a Feline such as myself might say or do. In fact even claiming offense is, in itself, an offensive act."

"I see. Perhaps you could provide me with a list of other words and phrases I should avoid."

"There's no need. It will be made clear to you when you've crossed the line and failure to act on these warnings will result in further consequences, as you've already discovered."

"But anyone can claim to be offended by anything, surely that's a terrible way of deciding what should be allowed to be said and by who."

"It's the only way of ensuring the world is protected from Canine hatecrime."

"So you're calling for unlimited censorship of at least a quarter of UK society. I think that's a remarkable position for a journalist to adopt."

"On the contrary, journalists play a vital role in protecting the public from harmful speech and information. Our gatekeeping is essential to the safe functioning of society and, in that capacity, I must now terminate this interview to spare me and my audience from further offence."

And that was that.

***

Jive Robin's studio was only a tube ride away but Dalston was so shaken by the Tegritie interview that all his instincts were telling him to cancel the podcast. He walked past Oxford Circus tube to get a beer and a chaser at The Clachan, partly to organise his thoughts but mainly because he just seriously needed a drink. What had just happened? Tegritie had seemed so reasonable and supportive of his position before the interview, but became hostile as soon as they went live. What had he done to antagonise him? As he went back over the entire conversation he came to the conclusion Tegritie had predetermined the tone of the interview and would have adopted an adversarial stance regardless of anything Dalston said.

He understood Tegritie couldn't be seen to give him an easy ride, but there had been no attempt at balance, nor any apparent desire to uncover the truth about the attack and the circumstances surrounding it. Tegritie had already made his mind up and seemed to be interested only in playing to the Felian gallery. Having come to this conclusion Dalston was more determined than ever to publicise his side of the story and, ideally, get back at Tegritie. The best platform to do this was just a tube ride away so he knocked back his drinks and set off with renewed purpose.

Jive Robin had converted the garage of his house into a studio and green room into which he was led by one of Robin's staff, who gestured towards a fridge full of drinks, both soft and alcoholic. Dalston thought he might as well have a beer, but was only a few sips into it when Robin himself arrived, smoking what smelt a lot like a joint.

"Dave, great to meet you, thanks a lot for coming," he said.

"You too Jive. I nearly didn't."

"Why's that, dude?"

"Did you hear my interview with Iain Tegritie?"

"No, how was it?"

"A fucking car crash. The bloke had it in for me from the start."

"Sorry to hear it – he can be a pretty tough guy. Here, this should help you get back in the mood."

Robin handed Dalston his joint.

"I don't know if it's a good idea for me to get stoned before we record, Jive," said Dalston. "I want to stay coherent, know what I mean?"

"And yet you're having a beer," laughed Robin. "But it's cool, man, whatever works for you. Shall we get cracking?"

Dalston was wrong-footed by the lack of preamble, but within a few minutes they were sat opposite each other in the recording studio. The only other person in the room was the producer, and once Robin got the green light from him he jumped straight into it.

"I'm joined today by Dave Dalston, a guy who made the news recently after being attacked by a bunch of dudes in the street," he said. "What the fuck happened, man?"

Dalston spent the next few minutes describing the attack, uninterrupted.

"Now come on, groups of guys don't just go around beating people up for no reason," said Robin, once the account was complete. "You must have done something to make them so mad at you."

"Yes, I was guilty of being an unapologetic Canine. The scum who attacked me were part of a group called the Anticanes, whose stated mission is to protect the world from Canines."

"Yeah I've heard about them – kind of vigilantes, right? But isn't that sort of thing the police's job?"

"Yes, and it's also their job to stop vigilante gangs but none of them have been arrested."

"Shit, man, that's heavy. Any idea why?"

"I think the police are scared. The Anticanes have the backing of FLAP and they're worried about being called Felophobes if they so much as reprimand them."

"So a bunch of dudes are going around beating motherfuckers up, without any legal reason, and the police are just letting them do it? That sounds like fucking bullshit, man."

"Totally. And the thing that's really freaking me out is nobody else seems to give a fuck either. You should listen to the interview I just did, Tegritie is supposed to be a journalist but he didn't show any interest in getting to the truth or informing his audience. He only cared about making the whole thing my fault and attacking Canines. I know he's a Feline, but journalists should be above that kind of tribal shit."

"I agree, mate. I'm Delphine so I haven't had it as bad as you Canines, but I know some Felians look down their nose at me. That just seems so crazy. Before this Id Card stuff they wouldn't have done that, or at least if they did it would have been for different reasons. But now they've found themselves in this gang that's running the country because of some bullshit test, they suddenly think they're better than me. What the fuck?"

"I'm telling you Jive, it runs deeper than that. They've decided Canines are responsible for all the bad shit that has happened throughout history, so existing Canines have to make up for it through some kind of reparations. And on top of that we're having our right to do things like defend ourselves, equality under the law and even our status as fellow human beings being taken away. It's like these factions now define everything, not just now but retrospectively. How the fuck is that possible?

"So is that it then, is that how it's going to be from now on? Felians calling all the shots and the rest of us just doing what we're told or else? Sounds a fuck of a lot like Nazi Germany or Communist Russia to me."

"I reckon there are two main reasons to hope it's not," Dalston said. "Firstly not all Felines and Simians are Felians in a political sense. A lot of people of all types think this Id Card scheme is bullshit and they're not interested in factional bollocks. They don't care what it says on your Id Card so long as you're cool to hang out with. Felian activists actually account for a small proportion of all Felines and Simians and they're being increasingly vindictive even to their own factions if they don't toe the FLAP line. What happened to me on social media is increasingly happening to full-blown Felines and Simians and a lot of those new exiles are feeling pretty fucking aggrieved. They've realised FLAP and Imperium don't actually give a toss about them and are just abusing their position to advance their own agendas."

"Yeah I hear you. I've got quite a few mates who are Felians or Simians who don't like all this stuff, but they're too afraid to speak up because they know they'll get in the shit. It looks like the Felians have got everything totally under control if you ask me."

"Not totally, which brings me onto my second point. The Canines are fighting back, both politically and physically."

"You mean the Savages, right?"

"Yes. If it wasn't for the Anticanes nobody would have heard of Dick Savage, but they were so out of order in those videos they turned loads of people against them. The thing is, most people aren't radicals or activists, but that doesn't mean they don't have a strong sense of right and wrong. They're not going to waste their time kicking off over every little issue but when they're presented with a clear injustice they're sometimes moved to act."

"A bit like you with that Whistleblower Hotline stuff eh?"

"Very much so. I just couldn't let them get away with that shit."

"But you did for a while, didn't you?"

"Yes, that's a fair point."

"So what changed?"

"Let's just say relations with my former employer had deteriorated somewhat, which made me look at what they were doing in a different way."

"I see. That's very interesting. You're saying the same thing can look very different depending on your point of view."

"I guess I am. While everything was going well at work I was definitely inclined to give G&M the benefit of the doubt, not least because I was making loads of money. But once that changed it was like the Emperor's New Clothes."

"Do you know what, Dave? Your story kind of sums this whole factional thing up. Everything is being viewed from a very subjective and entrenched point of view and everyone thinks they're right, but they can't all be. And the really crazy thing is people are switching from one team to the other quite often, and when they do they're just as biased in favour of their new team as they were the old one."

"When you put it like that it is totally nuts, but when you're in the middle of it, it all makes sense. Probably because we're talking about emotions and instincts rather than higher thought."

"I think you've nailed it, mate. Picking a team is an instinctive thing and actually saves you having to engage your higher brain at all. Whether it's a political faction, a religion or a football team, all you need to know is that you love your team and hate the other team. Focusing on that is a lot simpler than actually trying to work stuff out."

"I was aware of that when I was thinking about leaking those documents but in the end I felt totally justified. They were wrong and I was right."

"How did you know?"

"That's a fucking good question. I guess it's just back to the instinctive, emotional stuff. My feelings on the matter were totally clear and uncomplicated. I just knew."

"I don't doubt it mate, and I totally understand. I feel so strongly about some things that I really don't understand anyone who thinks differently. But doing this podcast has taught me that people can fundamentally disagree and still get on with each other. One thing I am sure of is if more people understood that the world would be a better place."

"That's hard to argue with but, getting back to my assault, all those groovy sentiments don't do you much good when a bunch of people are trying to kick the shit out of you."

"I hear you brother. Are you worried it might happen again?"

"Of course"

"That must be scary."

"It is, but I refuse to run scared from those pricks. I've started doing some training and I really like some of the stuff the Savages are doing. I hear what you're saying about the downsides of picking a team, but there's no reasoning with these motherfuckers and there's only one language they understand."

"OK, man. I don't think violence solves anything but obviously you have to defend yourself. Stay safe, brother."

Chapter 21 – Infatuation

Once the dust settled on the Anticane drama Dalston had to address the matter of his employment or, more specifically, lack of it. Having recently read a profile of Poppy Syndrome's philanthropic approach to banking at Clark's, he checked out its website. Clark's Inclusive Banking for a Better Society strategy was still paying dividends – figuratively for customers and Clark's employees and literally for its government owners – and Dalston hoped his recent exposure of the corrupt nature of the ARSE derivative would stand him in good stead with this most ethical of banks. The website revealed plenty of vacancies but none for traders, so he emailed Syndrome directly to appeal for a role. She responded by saying she had been following his situation closely and invited him to meet her at the Clark's offices.

Introductions done, Syndrome was keen to get a sense of his experiences and specifically what had driven him to do what he did. She seemed to view his transformation from superficial materialist to ethical activist as emblematic of the kind of change she was trying to bring to the whole financial sector and was keen to find a role for him. His Canine egotype ruled out any kind of outward-facing position, so she offered him a role in the support team of the Nice and Ethical Fund, managed by a former social worker. While the fund was still a fixture on the portfolios of many institutional investors looking to tick the corporate responsibility box, it was commercially underperforming to such an extent that some were openly contemplating removing it. Syndrome wanted Dalston to use his experience to improve the fund's performance and was prepared to make an exception and introduce a financial element to his bonus structure, understanding that you have to be prepared to pay for the best talent.

Compared to the cut-throat City environment Dalston was used to, his job at Clark's felt almost comically pedestrian. His main function was to give commercial advice to a fund manager who was concerned almost entirely with moral considerations. As a result of the way the Nice and Ethical Fund had been run it was almost impossible not to improve its commercial performance and his influence was felt almost immediately, especially since Syndrome instructed the manager to follow his recommendations. In spite of his Damascene conversion he soon realised his own ethical standards were still significantly less rigorous than his manager's, so he made a point of understanding her priorities, which he learned were both superficial and rudimentary. So long as he could demonstrate some vague concession to one of his manager's pet causes and that no fluffy animals were harmed in the making of the investment, there were few questions asked. Once this mutual understanding was achieved he was almost entirely unsupervised and his job was very easy indeed.

Syndrome herself spent nearly all her time managing her own SPIV fund, which she was able to grow more rapidly than ever thanks to Dalston's advice and her decision to live in the Channel Islands for tax purposes. Until recently she would have considered such a move to be profoundly immoral, but since she was doing so much good for society through her philanthropic work she now considered taxation of those activities to be regressive.

Since Dalston was soon earning more money than ever for a fraction of the work he was used to putting in, he was able to devote considerable time to training and contributing to the Savage resistance. He was going to Stein's gym on a daily basis, getting in decent shape and developing his nascent boxing skills. Stein ignored him initially, but after observing one sparring session in which he handled himself well, invited him to his office.

"Like fighting do you?" he asked.

"More than I thought I would, to be honest," Dalston replied. "I'd never really thought about learning it properly as I'm not a big fan of violence, but getting fucked over by the Anticanes changed everything and I never want to feel that helpless again."

"Good, good. You've hit the nail on the head, my son. Violence is the purest type of force – the ultimate extension of your personality. If you can protect yourself from physical force then you never need to do anything you don't want. Also, if you can use physical force yourself then you can get other people to do what you want. A proper hard man doesn't need to be big or mouthy, it's just the way you carry yourself. You can't fake it and once you have it you're in a special club your average fella doesn't even know about."

"Do you mean the Savages?"

"No, son. A few of them might think they're a bit tasty but they're just weekend warriors like those Anticane muppets what slapped you about. I'm talking about proper geezers, men you do not want to cross."

"Right, I see what you mean. I've spotted a few of them in the gym."

"You're learning. Why do you think I run this place?"

"Because you love boxing?"

"Well yes, I'm a fan of the sport, but what I really love about it is what it does to people. Boxing teaches you so much: discipline, endurance, ruthlessness, independence. I get soft cunts like you in here and make men of them."

"Sounds like you're a bit of a philanthropist then."

"You taking the fucking piss?" asked Stein, with a sudden edge to his voice and steel in his eyes.

"No Frank, I didn't mean any disrespect," said Dalston, acutely aware of how far short of being one of Stein's hard men he still was. "I just meant you seem to be keen on helping people out."

"That's alright then," said Stein. "You could say that, yes, but I expect plenty in return. The main reason I have this gym is to keep a constant supply of muscle. Like you I'm a businessman, but I don't do office work if you know what I mean. In my line of work strength is everything and the moment you show any weakness you're fucked. I need people around me who understand that and are capable of acting if the situation calls for it. Most of those hard men you saw in the gym work for me and get well paid for it. All I expect in return is unquestioning obedience and loyalty, that's not so much to ask is it, Dave?"

"Well, I guess that depends really," ventured Dalston, with trepidation. "Didn't you say one of the things learning to take care of yourself gives you is independence? But at the same time you're saying your fighters have to be unquestioningly obedient and loyal to you. That doesn't sound much like independence to me."

There was an uncomfortably long silence as Stein regarded him through narrowed eyes, but eventually they softened and he laughed. "You're a smart cunt aren't you?" he said. "Fair point, son, and you've dug up another important thing about strength: it's not just physical. Another part of it is will, how far are you willing to go? Those lads respect me because I've done my time – literally – and shown I don't take a backwards step. That's your reputation and it can take you a long way but it also puts a target on your back, as you just found out. So just because you've got yourself in a bit of shape and learnt a couple of moves, don't go thinking you're Mike fucking Tyson all of a sudden. It's different out on the street, but what you've been taught might at least help you get out of trouble if you bump into those pricks again."

Dalston found it exhilarating to associate with such an old-school alpha male. He thought of the big, swinging dicks at Gold & Mackenzie and laughed at the thought of any of them trying to impose their will on Stein. They'd shit themselves the first time he laid eyes on them. He also realised Stein was right about hardness: it seemed to be a full-time job and Dalston was pretty sure he didn't have the balls for it. But while he'd never be Stein muscle, which was fine with him, he felt he was definitely an order of magnitude harder than when the Anticanes attacked him, and still longed to avenge his humiliation. So once he was back at his flat he found a group called the London Savages on Facebook, introduced himself, and was invited to a face-to-face meeting.

It took place in the back of the Assembly House in Kentish Town. Around thirty people attended, mostly young, Canine men, although there were some women, a few Delphines and even a couple of Simians. Dalston was one of three first-timers and one of the others was a stunning young woman called Prosecca. He longed to get to know her, but was determined to stay focused on the meeting. It seemed like a cross between Alcoholics Anonymous and a war room. Most of the meeting was spent hearing each attendee's experiences of the Felians: their own persecution, that of someone they knew or simply venting about them in general. Once everyone unburdened themselves there was a 'call for activists' and around half the room left, but Dalston wasn't sure what to do. One of the veteran members noticed his confusion, approached him, and explained that Savage activists were those willing to go on to the streets and counter the Anticane scourge. Dalston didn't hesitate to get involved and he was delighted to see Prosecca also step up to the plate.

The purpose of the call for activists was to form and coordinate patrol groups in the NW1, NW3 and NW5 postcodes. Best practice limited the size of each group to six people, as any more than that tended to attract the attention of the police. So, of the 17 people left Dalston was assigned to the NW3 group, along with five veterans, Prosecca got a similar gig in NW5 and a group of five veterans was assigned to NW1. While it was stressed that no Savage patrol group should initiate violence, it was also considered vital that, if such an event did occur, they prevail. The purpose of the patrols wasn't just to protect Canines and Delphines from Felian persecution, it was to draw a line in the sand and let the Anticanes know they had met their match.

Dalston's first patrol was almost entirely uneventful, but such was his heightened level of anxiety and adrenaline throughout that he was exhausted by the end. In a subsequent patrol not long after, however, there was an encounter as they were walking along Mansfield Road towards Gospel Oak. A group of people came out of a mini market right in front of his group and one of them did a visible double-take when he recognised Dalston and quickly alerted the rest, who approached and confronted him directly. The leader of Dalston's group said if anyone was going to be beaten up this time, it was them.

There followed a standoff so protracted and surreal it bordered on comical. The leader of each group attempted to goad the other into initiating the fight, getting as far into their space as possible without actually touching them. Dalston realised this was, at least in part, because at least one person from each group was filming the encounter with their phone. Eventually one of the Anticane group cracked and threw something at Dalston, which missed but was considered sufficient provocation for the Savage leader to swing a punch at his Anticane counterpart. A brief skirmish ensued in which Dalston blocked and dodged a few attempted blows, before landing a solid one of his own, after which the Anticanes ran away.

Hyper-adrenalized, Dalston demanded they be chased down and, when that was rejected, expressed a strong desire to find more people in need of being taught some manners. The Savage leader explained that was not how they did things so he spent the rest of the uneventful patrol boasting about how much worse things would have gone for those Anticanes had they not legged it like the pussies they were. At the end of the evening the Savage activists compared notes in the pub. The NW5 group had also stumbled upon some Anticanes, but the encounter did not progress past the goading phase, which was not unusual. As people began to disperse Dalston seized the opportunity to offer Prosecca a drink, which she accepted, and they got to know each other better by comparing their respective journeys to this point.

Prosecca was a Delphine, but when the Id Card scheme first came into effect she largely ignored it, figuring it was just one of those stupid political fads that would blow over before long. It was only when the faction system became entrenched and FLAP came into power that she started feeling profound concerns about the broader implications of it all. As a Delphine and, to a lesser extent, as a woman, she felt partly protected from Felian fervour, but she also felt like a second-class citizen and didn't want to live in a country that only treated half of its population with dignity and respect.

Conversation turned to the evening's events and he realised Prosecca was no less excited than he about their encounters with the Anticanes. They agreed there was no reasoning with them and violence was the only language they understood. While there was satisfaction from taking the fight to the Felians, both of them eventually confessed that the best part of it was the thrill and danger of confrontation itself. Prosecca had been disappointed at the lack of physical contact from her group's encounter and said she had to be restrained from initiating it herself. Dalston described his encounter vividly but she still pressed him for more detail, especially concerning the punch he managed to land. She wanted to know how it felt to physically hurt someone and exert raw power over another person. He was only too happy to oblige when he saw how his tale excited her.

As closing time loomed Prosecca said she didn't think she'd be able to sleep after such drama and Dalston said he felt the same. He revealed he had recently restocked his drinks cabinet and invited her to help him deplete it, which she accepted. They managed a couple of beers and Tequila shots before their first kiss and were ripping each other's clothes off soon after. They had sex on the sofa, then a couple more shots before moving to the bedroom where they carried on until dawn, assisted by a couple of grams of coke she had stashed in her bra.

When they woke up around midday he cooked them both bacon and eggs and was relieved to see sobriety hadn't doused their fire. Just as he was getting his hopes up Prosecca insisted she had to go, so he took her mobile number, promised to be in touch very soon and saw her to the door. He then collapsed on his sofa and reflected on the best sex he'd had in ages. He couldn't get her out of his head and dreamily wondered if it could be love at first sight. She had everything: beautiful, passionate, strong and most importantly of all, she fancied him.

Before long they were inseparable. Dalston invited Prosecca to quit her hated government-imposed job as he was earning enough money for both of them and was able to adapt the needs of his own job to their almost entirely nocturnal lifestyle. They were typically only on patrol with the Savages once or twice a week, but they had become such adrenaline junkies that most other days were spent partying into the small hours followed by coke-fuelled sex-athons. In fact cocaine became so synonymous with their affair that before long they were chopping-up as soon as they met. Dalston needed to buy coke in greater quantities than Nick Georgiou was able to provide reliably and, furthermore, he felt self-conscious about revealing his rapidly escalating consumption to his friend. So he got in touch with Dev Sharma, who he figured would at least know some decent dealers, and went to meet him at his stall in Camden.

"So how's it going, bruv?" said Dev. "I heard you gave some back to those cunts the other day."

"Yeah, I joined the Savages and we've been out looking for Anticanes. The training I've been doing at Frank's came in pretty handy, so thanks again for the intro, mate."

"Think nothing of it my friend, but what's with the sudden need for so much Charlie? Sounds like you've got enough excitement already, innit."

"You don't know the half of it, man. I met this bird in the Savages and she's knackering me out, know what I mean?"

"Yeah, yeah, yeah!" laughed Dev, extending his hand for a slap. "Nice one, fam, I told you that Cosmic Phone would get you some action innit. Is she a dirty bitch?"

"While it's none of your fucking business, let's just say I'm going to struggle if you don't sort me out."

"Alright, alright, I didn't realise you was already in love, bruv. The C is not a problem, just let me know how much you need a week and I know a bloke who knows a bloke, you get me."

"I owe you big time Dev, you're a fucking life saver."

"Well it's funny you mention that man, because I've got some free advice for you. I'm the last bloke to tell anyone to slow down, but to me it looks like you're jumping in at the deep-end big time. You're only human, blad, and you need to pace yourself or it could all end up going Pete Tong, hear what I'm saying."

"Know what Dev, you're probably right but right now I genuinely don't give a fuck. I was having a nightmare and now everything's going cushty so I'm going to make the most of it. After all, you never know when it's all going to go tits up again."

"I'm with you all the way, geezer, you fucking go for it. I'm just saying don't go 100 percent, keep a bit back just in case. Think of it as insurance, know what I mean."

Later that day Dalston was back at his flat, chopping-up a couple of lines in anticipation of Prosecca's arrival, when his phone rang and he saw it was from Amy.

"Hello darling, great to hear from you," he said. "How are you?"

"I'm sad, Daddy," she said.

"Why, baby?"

"I heard you got beaten up."

While there was no music in the background this time, Dalston thought he could hear angry shouting in the distance.

"Sorry, I should have called you to say I was OK. Look it was just some nasty people looking to cause trouble. They wanted to beat me up but I managed to get away from them, so there's nothing to be sad about. Is that shouting I can hear? Are you OK?"

"But what if they try to do it again?" said Amy, apparently oblivious to his question.

"I thought of that too, so I've joined up with a group of people and we all walk around together, so if any of the nasty people try to attack one of us then the others help them. Also we go around and help other people if they're going through the same kind of thing I did. That's good isn't it?"

"I suppose so, but doesn't that mean you get in a lot more fights?"

"Not necessarily, but it also means I'm much more likely to win them."

The background shouting seemed to be getting louder and more aggressive, and he was concerned.

"Baby, is someone there with you?" he asked.

"But isn't fighting bad?" said Amy, disregarding his concern once more.

"Yes, starting fights is bad, but if you never defend yourself from nasty people then they've got no reason to stop being horrible to you."

"You're doing more than defending yourself though, aren't you? You're going and looking for nasty people."

"Sometimes it's better to find them before they find you. Listen, did you hear me a minute ago? Is there someone there I should be worried about?"

"Mummy says you never return her emails anymore."

Aside from making sure he did the bare minimum to keep his job, since meeting Prosecca Dalston had been neglecting everything else. He hadn't even checked his personal emails or told Mel about his new job.

"I'm really sorry," he said. "Please tell her I'll get back to her straight away?"

"OK Daddy," said Amy. "I really hope you do because Mummy is quite cross and now I don't think she wants me to see you anymore. Anyway I've got to go now."

The background shouting hadn't abated, but he assumed it must be something on the TV and didn't pursue the matter any further.

"Don't worry baby, I'll make everything better," he said. "Bye bye, I love you."

"I love you too," said Amy.

As soon as he hung up Dalston fired up his laptop to review his emails and was shocked to find hundreds unread, including several from Mel. Embarrassed by how he had let things slip he clicked on her latest and started writing a reply, but soon after Prosecca arrived and he was distracted by her immediate demands for cocaine and sex. Unable to think of a good enough reason to deny her either, he closed his laptop with his response to Mel still in draft form, resolved to finish the email as soon as he got the chance.

Chapter 22 – Incitement

Although everything else now took second place to the pleasures of the flesh, Dalston kept up to date with major political developments through his membership of the Savages, which drew him to an article that analysed the movement's strategy. Dick Savage himself had rapidly become a prominent political figure thanks to the support of every Canine and Delphine who had fallen foul of the Felians, which was most of them but constituted only about a quarter of the electorate. Savage calculated there was another large constituency sympathetic to at least part of his cause, but afraid of Felian punishment and hesitant to show public support. He decided their timidity could be overcome by a similar kind of direct democracy system to the one FLAP rode to power, but anonymised and taken further.

During his early political campaigning Savage developed a smartphone app designed to help petition Parliament. It experienced some early success but was soon superseded by FLAP's social media-based system. Once FLAP took power Savage adapted the app to be used as a hub for protest and dissent. He regularly polled its users on the latest socio-political developments and then published the results. The tricky bit was giving the polls popular legitimacy, while at the same time ensuring the anonymity of the participants.

Fortunately the ability to do so had already been created by the lobbying efforts of FLAP itself during its rise to power, in the form of a law granting all political parties electronic access to much of the data that comprised each Id Card, via its API. While the information was anonymised at the point of delivery, it did provide demographic metadata such as age, sex, parliamentary constituency and, most importantly, egotype, which allowed Savage to add a lot more substance to his poll results. While they still had no legal or electoral weight, the polls often caused awkwardness for FLAP when it could be demonstrated a significant number of Felines and Simians opposed one of its policies.

Savage had known there was no way FLAP would allow his app to form part of its direct democracy programme, so he introduced it instead at the local government level, which was still dominated by the traditional political parties. The adapted Savage app was renamed YouChoose and, through it, people were regularly polled on local government decisions such as frequency of bin collection and investment in local infrastructure. Unsurprisingly, given the traditional apathy towards local politics, participation was initially so low as to render outcomes invalid, so Savage realised people needed further incentives to participate. Once more the Id Card API presented the answer as participation in local politics was considered an act of civic virtue worthy of Idcoin rewards. It followed, therefore, that failure to participate in YouChoose was punishable by Idcoin fines. As soon as that mechanism was introduced, app engagement soared.

The final masterstroke was to hand over ownership of the app to reality TV king Sven Garlic, who not only brought his user-experience and game theory expertise to the project but also installed YouChoose as the only way of voting on Britain's Got Issues. Even more importantly it removed Savage's direct association with YouChoose, thus creating the impression of political neutrality. This gave YouChoose significant popular legitimacy via the back door and by the time FLAP understood the severity of the threat it posed, it was too late. Imperium did have some initial success in hacking its API to obtain the identities of some users, then doxxing them via social media, but a leak to Whistleblower Hotline exposed those activities and the resulting public outcry was so severe that FLAP was forced to publicly support YouChoose in order to distance itself from Imperium and mitigate the PR damage.

Before long YouChoose had such influence it was able to resume national political lobbying, and FLAP realised the genie was truly out of the bottle when some of its own decisions came under such severe public scrutiny through the app that it was forced to amend them. This served to fuel Savage's ambition, which nothing short of running the country could now satisfy. He calculated his best chance was not only to force another general election, but to have it conducted via YouChoose. There being no way FLAP would ever allow such a thing to happen under normal circumstances, he had to create abnormal ones. He immersed himself in the tactical teachings of history, from Sun Tzu to Saul Alinsky, Musashi to Machiavelli, and concluded he had to use the Felians' strengths against them to provoke them into a critical mistake. Once he worked out the best way to do so he couldn't believe it hadn't occurred to him sooner.

Felian political strategy was based on ensuring a state of constant outrage at everything Canine. Inspired by the Id Card concept, Imperium also concluded that if you ensure people are largely beholden to their base selves they're almost entirely predictable and thus easy to control. Not only were feral emotions such as fear, anger and disgust easy to maintain among Felines and Simians through constant demonisation of Canines, it also ensured Canines, and to a large extent Delphines too, were too busy defending themselves to pose any significant challenge. But that very predictability was also the key to countering the Felians, as their response to Canine provocation was entirely predictable.

Once he understood this Savage realised that if you can predict how your opponent will behave in certain circumstances, you can also engineer outcomes. So he used Twitter to bait the Felians, sometimes saying the most outrageous things he could, other times creating the impression of trying to be conciliatory.

While was always denounced, he started to notice patterns within the denunciation. His milder posts seemed to draw the ire of the FLAP inner party and its most devout followers, but relative indifference from Canines and Delphines and little mainstream media coverage. His most deliberately provocative posts, however, not only elicited a far greater volume of apoplectic responses but could sometimes even dominate the immediate news cycle. Furthermore he was pleasantly surprised by the number of likes, retweets and even supportive comments those posts received. It seemed his audacity emboldened others, perhaps because Felian fury was briefly so focused on him that it barely registered all other heretics.

Since the entire basis of his political movement was to oppose the draconian excesses of the FLAP regime, he concluded the best use of his observations would be to provoke the inner party into such outrageous public displays that even their most committed supporters would struggle to defend them. While direct attacks elicited predictable outrage from FLAP, comments about Felines or Simians in general yielded much more useful results. The resulting outcry often extended far beyond the narrow boundaries of party politics, into hysterical comparisons with Hitler, Judas, Satan, and so on. To Savage's surprise, however, the richest source of provocation was any kind of comment about Delphines. Anything derogatory was pounced upon as proof that his malevolent depravity knew no bounds, while anything positive was condemned as a cynical attempt to cast his sinister spell over the hapless Delphines in order to use them as pawns in his nefarious machinations.

Dalston was already following him on Twitter, but after reading that article he set up alerts to follow Savage's tweets closely, and so was one of the first to see a sequence that proved pivotal.

@dicksavage

Is it just me or is FLAP losing the plot?

@Felianmovement

@dicksavage The very act of sending this tweet is proof you are the one losing the plot. Delete your account.

@vajustice

@Felianmovement Dick head Savage inflicts severe psychological damage on the world every time he tweets. @TwitterSupport is criminally negligent for allowing him to spread his poison but I'm actually pleased, because it will be great evidence when I sue.

@suedenim83

@vajustice *Your courage is an inspiration to us all. You have my total support in your fight against hate. They know we're winning and they're scared!*

@k9andproud

@suedenim83 *The only thing FLAP is winning is unpopularity. Thank God somebody has the balls to call out this repressive, authoritarian regime. #flapfail*

@supersavages

@k9andproud *Well said. Fuck them! #flapfail*

@woke_a_j

@k9andproud @supersavages *Typical cabbages, they moan about being oppressed but don't hesitate to oppress others when it suits them #hypocrites #flapftw #safetynothate #bollockstocabbages*

Dalston was tempted to get involved in the thread but judged he had nothing to say that hadn't been said already. It made him reflect that his previous social media behaviour had been largely exhibitionist and attention-seeking. Most comments on Twitter, especially those responding to very prominent tweets such as those sent by Dick Savage, were almost entirely redundant. Watching the constant venom and hysteria play out, he realised very little of it really mattered and any contribution he might make would be a drop in the ocean. Those thoughts were vindicated when Savage sent another tweet, which immediately rendered the previous one and every thread resulting from it obsolete.

@dicksavage

It is my considered opinion, and I don't say this lightly, that the majority of Felines and Simians are losers. But hey, maybe I'm wrong, change my mind!

@suedenim83

@dicksavage *if your definition of a loser is someone who wants to change the world and isn't a greedy, violent, fat bastard then I guess we are.*

@supersavages

@suedenim83 *Typical Felians, rather than debate they resort immediately to crude personal attacks. That's why they're losing and* @dicksavage *is right.*

@woke_a_j

@supersavages *It's not a personal attack when it's clearly correct, you moron. And what's wrong with wanting to change the world anyway?*

@k9andproud

How can an opinion be "correct" @woke_a_f you fucking retard? And there's a lot wrong with wanting to change the world when the aim is to make it worse, Nazi.

@Felianmovement

Spoiler alert, @k9andproud, it is an empirical fact beyond question that @dicksavage is greedy, violent, fat, a bastard and those are the least of his failings as a human. He is the real Nazi and is a threat to society that we need to find a solution to.

@dicksavage

@Felianmovement Would a temporary solution do?

@Felianmovement

@dicksavage No, your level of evil requires a final solution.

Dalston was astounded at the ease with which Savage was able to manipulate the FLAP inner party into making public statements of the most potentially catastrophic kind. He was also fascinated to see Savage follow the exact playbook detailed in the article and couldn't wait to see how the denouement phase, in which he attacked the Delphines, played out. Would FLAP walk into his trap?

@dicksavage

Literally nobody:

Delphines: FLAP just wants the best for us!

@suedenim83

@dicksavage They say that because they're grateful for the protection we give them from you and your hate.

@woke_a_f

You're so right @suedenim83. But even your brave resistance on Twitter isn't stopping him. I think more needs to be done.

@vajustice

Don't worry @woke_a_f, we know where he lives. It's time to mobilise the Anticanes. This is the moment of truth @Felianmovement, if you're not part of the solution you're part of the problem. How much longer are you going to allow @dicksavage to harm Delphines with his Twitter violence?

@Felianmovement

FLAP condemns @dicksavage on behalf of all Delphines, who are clearly too afraid to speak out against him themselves. We won't stand for his bigotry, hatred and digital violence a moment longer and call on the Anticanes to intervene directly for the good of society.

The Felian tweet, which broke the ratio record recently set when a Canine celebrity asked people to be kinder to him on Twitter, was understood as a call for Dick Savage to be physically attacked. Bizarrely, given the level of vitriol routinely directed at him, this seemed to cross some kind of arbitrary line. The first prominent non-Canine tweeter to condemn the FLAP tweet performed the function of the proverbial child who observed the Emperor wasn't wearing any clothes.

Before long there were widespread calls for a retraction and apology, which would probably have marked the end of the matter had they been accepted. But FLAP instead chose to double down, insisting that physical violence was justified when used to combat an even greater evil and it would never apologise for doing the right thing. This prompted a surprisingly elevated online debate on the definitions of good and evil, which concluded FLAP was insufficiently qualified to make such lofty claims. By the time FLAP finally understood that the only way out of the hole it was in was to stop digging, it had done itself significant reputational damage and, more importantly, had signalled to the world that it could be faced down.

Savage used that incident as the platform to formally launch his own political campaign. The call for violence against him was portrayed as typifying how FLAP had always operated behind the scenes. Savage drew heavily on precedent, from the Spanish Inquisition to present day North Korea, to illustrate FLAP's defining philosophy. This was especially effective whenever FLAP tried to defend itself by claiming to act in the public interest, as Savage was able to accuse it of using the doublespeak favoured by despots throughout history. Savage's goading accelerated the increasing public hostility towards FLAP to such an extent that it felt compelled to accept his calls for a general election, in the hope of drawing a line under the debacle.

FLAP had the advantage of a supportive mainstream media, most of which were so afraid of being branded Felophobic that they never refused a request by one of its politicians to be interviewed and asked only the most anodyne questions. Savage seized on this to demonize the mainstream media as biased and dishonest, and refused to speak to any of them himself. He also noticed he had a far more sympathetic audience online, with many YouTubers daring to compare him favourably to FLAP. One such figure was the podcaster Jive Robin, to whom

Savage granted one of the few public interviews he gave during his election campaign.

Dalston tuned in eagerly, but a lot of the discussion was nothing new for him, with Savage recapping the origin story of his assault by the Anticanes, positioning himself as the only significant obstacle to outright Felian despotism and restating his political positions. The only time Savage seemed uncomfortable was when Jive Robin challenged him over his adversarial attitude.

"Listen dude, I've got a lot of sympathy with your position, especially when I see good friends of mine scared to speak their minds," said Robin. "But I think people are getting sick of everyone shouting the whole time and calling each other Nazis and shit. I'd have a lot more time for your political position if it was more focused on bringing people together rather than just slagging off the Felians the whole time."

"I hear you, Jive, but they give me no choice," said Savage. "They're the ones persecuting the rest of the country, they're the ones attacking me every day, and they're the ones I'm looking to kick out of power. I have to attack them."

"That's bullshit, man. You don't have to do anything – you choose to act this way and you could choose to reach out to them."

"OK, let's say you're right and it's my choice, what do you think would happen if I chose not to attack them and tried to meet them in the middle?"

"I have no idea, but isn't it worth trying?"

"No, because I do know what would happen. Plenty of people have tried and they end up being attacked, victimized and sometimes even arrested. Let me put a question back to you: how many times do you need to be attacked before you retaliate?"

"OK, I think I know where you're going with this – you can't just be a pussy all the time and sometimes you need to stand up for yourself. I totally agree with that, but there's a difference between self-defence and taking the fight to them."

"Agreed, but Canines have been defending themselves ever since the Felians were created and there's no sign of the attacks ever stopping. Furthermore, the law is being corrupted is making it harder for us to defend ourselves through legal means, which is why you get groups like the Savages."

"So you concede that the Savages act illegally?"

"They're not being protected by the law so they're forced to take matters into their own hands. But I'd prefer to resolve this stuff the democratic way, which is why I'm running in this election."

"Which gets us back to the way you're going about it, man. Yes, you're entitled to feel provoked, but from my point of view you're no better than them when all you can do is slag them off. Why not show there's another way?"

"Because I don't think it would work. Look, our whole system is designed to be adversarial – we sit opposite each other in the House of Commons, nearly all political careers end in scandal and the media only care about the bad stuff. If I just sat there trying to be John Lennon and saying, 'all you need is love,' not only would I get shat on by the Felians but I also wouldn't get any coverage."

"Maybe it's only like that because nobody will try anything different. And anyway, you're getting plenty of coverage by talking to me now."

"Yes and I'm very grateful. I like you and respect where you're coming from. I tell you what, I'll give it a go and maybe I can come back on to talk about how it worked out. Fair enough?"

"You've got yourself a deal, my friend."

Savage was true to his word and did send a few conciliatory tweets towards the Felians, but seemed always to do so just after they had been publicly fulminating about some Canine outrage or other. Perhaps as a consequence of this unfortunate timing, his tweets tended to be poorly received and assumed by Felians to be at least some kind of fresh intrigue. To the neutral observer, however, their spiteful reactions seemed to be a totally unjustified response to tweets that were, at worst, playful. While Savage didn't receive much personal benefit from his experiment with reaching across the aisle, it did give him yet another strategic victory by triggering the Felians into entrenching their reputation for arbitrary cruelty.

As general election day approached even the mainstream media began to turn against FLAP, with a series of articles chronicling other examples of Felian poor form, many of them based on anonymous accounts first published on Whistleblower Hotline. One of them even accused Mary Onette, the Prime Minister, of behaving inappropriately at some time in the past with a person who refused to come out of anonymity, which gave Dalston a delicious sense of schadenfreude. Even so, polling on the eve of the election still gave FLAP a slender lead over the Savage Party and even exit polls indicated a FLAP win. When the votes were counted, however, Dick Savage just managed to secure the largest share of the vote, which, under the new voting system, made him Prime Minister.

Chapter 23 – Incoherence

The elation Dalston felt after Savage's victory was second only to his exultant schadenfreude at the suffering of the Felians. All his pent up frustration and resentment came to the surface in a surge that bordered on the orgasmic and his affair with Prosecca scaled new orgiastic heights. Eventually they had to return to their regular lives, which threatened an epic come-down. So he sought to perpetuate his triumph by gloating, goading and trolling on social media, an undertaking greatly facilitated by being off his tits nearly all of the time.

This provided good sport for a while, as he was able to whip Felians into ever greater froths of outrage but, just as happened when he last devoted himself to trolling, his predictable taunts were soon discounted by opponents grown tired of his shtick. One evening, out of coke and thus merely drunk, he slipped into a melancholy mood in which it occurred to him his behaviour was dangerously similar to his opponents', and that maybe the only difference between oppressor and oppressed was opportunity.

The next morning, after soothing his hangover with a stiff vodka and orange, he was still troubled by the previous night's insight and felt a need to discuss it. Normally that would have involved his mates, but he still wasn't speaking to Jack Morrison and didn't want to put Al Blake and Nick Georgiou in an awkward position by trying to meet without him. He hadn't seen Dev or Davina since the election so he got in touch with them. They were both at their stalls in Camden Market so he ventured forth, blinking in the unfamiliar daylight. When he arrived Dev was talking to Frank Stein, so he invited them to a drink at Dingwalls. It was a nice day, so they sat on the terrace.

"I bet you're fucking buzzing now, innit." said Dev.

"Damn right I am," said Dalston. "Kind of restores your faith in humanity."

"So you been celebrating ever since, is it? Because you're looking a bit rough, if you don't mind me saying."

"Yeah you could say that. The thing is I met this bird and I've never known anything like it, mate. She makes me feel old, man, and it's getting so I'm grateful when she's not around just so I can get some kip."

"I'm amazed you can kip at all with all that Charlie you're getting through, know what I mean."

Dalston glanced nervously at Stein, but still had to ask the question. "Now that you mention it Dev, I'm running a bit low. Can you have another word with your mates?"

"You want to knock that fucking shit on the head, son," said Stein, "it's making you weak."

"I'm sure you're right Frank, but it's not forever," Dalston replied. "I was on such a high with the Savages stuff, winning the election and all, that I never wanted to come down. So I'm just easing myself off it."

"You dopey cunt, do you have any idea how many times I've heard fighters come out with that bollocks? Look, son, I don't give a fuck what you do in your spare time, and I've certainly got off my head plenty over the years, but this is becoming the main event for you and that's a mug's game."

"OK, but I bet you've seen a lot of fighters celebrate wins for a while and eventually get back into training, right?"

"They do but you've been at it for weeks. Anyway that's beside the point, you've won and now you've got to work out what you're going to do next. You might feel like you're having a religious experience when you stick your cock in that bird and coke up your nose, but you're just putting off thinking about more important stuff. And I promise you this: the longer you do it, the harder it will be to stop."

"Alright, alright, I hear you, but if we can just leave my lifestyle out of it for a moment, why shouldn't I enjoy my victory over those Felian fuckers?"

"I never said you shouldn't, but do me a favour and consider a couple of things. Do you ever see a fighter stand over his opponent and rub it in? No. Once the bout's over the two fighters congratulate each other on a good scrap and it's all done and dusted. Apart from respecting a fellow warrior the fighter does this because he knows it could easily have gone the other way and on another night it probably will. Triumph is fleeting, son, and so is defeat. Tomorrow's a new day and you need to start preparing for the next fight. If you're lucky your next opponent will be some fat, knackered cunt who spent too long dining out on his last victory and isn't ready for you. Do you understand what I'm saying?"

"Yes."

"The other reason to knock this shit on the head is that, while you may have beaten your opponent, you didn't kill them."

"Is that bad?"

"Well that depends, but the fact remains you didn't and that means they'll be back at you one day. The more you rub their noses in it now, the more they're going to want to fuck you over when they're back in the game. They might want to do that anyway, just because you beat them, but then again they might not. By being a prick you guarantee it, and you also give them the motivation to get up at four in the morning to get into the best shape of their life just to kick the maximum amount of shit out of you when they get the chance. Take it from me, son, if you create enough of those people you'll never be able to leave the house again."

Dalston finished his pint and, as Dev went to get another round, asked him for a double Jameson's to go with it. Stein's look of renewed disapproval at this request antagonised Dalston and Dev's absence somehow made him feel more uninhibited.

"Look Frank, that all seems like good advice, but you seem to be forgetting what monumental cunts those people have been, not just to me but the whole fucking country. So with all due respect, it's their turn to feel the burn, if you take my meaning."

"Of course I do, son, do you think I've never felt that way? I've got my revenge plenty of times but I promise you this, it's never as satisfying as you think it will be. Now don't get me wrong, sometimes you've got to send a message. If someone fucks with you, you've got to sort them out or the next cunt will think he can take liberties, but that's business, not personal. You don't do it because it makes you feel like a big man, you do it because by stomping on that geezer you save yourself having to do the same to ten others. It's a funny thing, once you get enough of a reputation for violence you end up never having to use it at all."

"You'll never fucking guess who I bumped into at the bar, your rug-muncher mate and her Mum, innit," said Dev, when he returned with the drinks.

"For fuck's sake," said Dalston, irritated by Dev's casual disrespect. "I guess you mean Davina, but I've got no idea who she's brought with her."

As Davina walked out onto the terrace Dalston saw her companion was Sally Pimienta and felt anxious at the prospect of introducing her to Stein. But it could not be avoided and he completed the formalities promptly.

"When you said you wanted a chat, Dave, I didn't think you meant group therapy," said Davina as they sat down.

"Well I only called you and Dev but it turns out everyone's out Camden today so the more the merrier," he said.

"That remains to be seen," said Davina, giving Dev an unaccommodating sidelong glance. "It's been a while, what have you been up to?"

Dalston recounted the Anticane attack that followed their last meeting, joining the gym and the Savages, meeting Prosecca and his joy at unseating the Felians from power.

"You have been a busy boy, haven't you?" said Davina. "So, now what?"

"Well I've been fucking appalled at the way the Felians have responded to losing the election so I'm feeling pretty motivated to keep reminding them who won and generally making sure they've learnt their lesson."

"And I told him that unless he's prepared to kill them he'd better wind his fucking neck in," interrupted Stein.

"Did you now?" said Pimienta. "Is that generally how you resolve disagreements, Mr Stein, by killing people?"

"Not these days, it's not really necessary anymore. But as I was just saying to the lad, a real man doesn't stand over his vanquished opponent and gloat unless he intends to finish the job off."

"That's one way of looking at it I suppose, but I can think of many better reasons to be magnanimous in victory. Firstly, it's not yours, Dave, and it says something about where your head is right now that you think it is. This political change was the result of a massive collective effort, of which you were a tiny, almost inconsequential part. The sooner you make this whole thing a bit less personal the better, in my humble opinion."

"In your humble opinion eh – that's a good one," said Stein.

"Excuse me?" said Pimienta.

"You turn up here, not even knowing what happened to the lad right after he last met you, and start telling him how he should just brush it off like nothing happened. I just think you've got a bit of a fucking nerve, that's all."

"Really? And I suppose you advised him to get his revenge and beat them up did you? Violence solves nothing Mr Stein and I have nothing but contempt for anyone who thinks it does."

"Well I have nothing but contempt for people who allow themselves to be pushed around. Weakness invites aggression, I think you'll find."

"There are non-violent ways of resisting, but I wouldn't expect a man like you to understand that."

"You know nothing about me."

"I know enough."

"You, madam, are a very presumptuous and rude person."

"And you, sir, are a cunt, sir."

The conversation had reached an impasse. All the people from whom Dalston hoped to seek counsel were now staring grimly at their drinks, avoiding eye contact, so he tried to get the conversation back on track.

"This is what I mean," he said. "You two are giving me all this advice about being a good winner and being the bigger man, but as soon as you disagree about something you start calling each other names. So fuck the Felians and the Anticanes, they've brought this shit on themselves, they cheated and lied and threatened but lost anyway. So, you know what, this chat has helped, just not in the way I thought it would. I think I was hoping you'd convince me to find a better way of dealing with this stuff, but now I realise there isn't. The only way to survive in the world is to pick a team and defend it at all costs. To the winners go the spoils."

"Hold on a moment," said Pimienta. "Think about what you're saying. By all means pick a team, but if you defend it at all costs then you're saying the team is the most important thing. What about you? Aren't you important? A team is still a collection of individuals, each with their own unique needs and opinions. It's impossible for any team to be all things to all people so you always need to leave some time for yourself."

"I have to say the old girl's right on this one," said Stein. "What if the group you're part of asks you to do something you don't want to do? What if you want something and the group says you can't have it, what do you do then?"

"That's the trade-off isn't it?" said Dalston. "Yeah, your tribe isn't always going to meet your expectations but what about those times you get benefits you would never have got by yourself? And what about the protection you get from being part of a tribe? I've finally found a group of people who share my values and hate my enemies and I've never felt stronger as a result."

"Didn't you feel that when you decided the Felians were your team though?" said Davina. "You felt strong then, right up until the moment they turned on you. Then you suddenly felt weaker and more vulnerable than ever. I have to agree with Frank that if you invest too much in your team, you neglect yourself. Then, if it doesn't work out with the team, you're screwed."

"Seriously bruv, you've got to look after numero uno, innit," said Dev. "Don't get me wrong, it's wicked when your team wins but that doesn't pay the fucking bills, you get me. You won the cup final, well fucking done. Nobody's saying you can't have an open-top bus parade and get mashed, but the world keeps spinning and in a few months you'll be back, starting all over again, hear what I'm saying."

"Amazing!" Dalston laughed. "One minute you're all calling each other cunts and the next you all agree I'm full of shit. I'm so pleased my flaws have been the thing to bring you all together."

"Stop blubbing like a fucking poof," said Stein. "Be a man and take good advice when it's offered to you. What I'm saying is that depending too much on other people makes you weak, not strong. Yeah, you can join a load of groups, but only to get what you need from them and nothing more. As soon as you start thinking other people will solve all your problems you're inviting them to start taking the piss. Strength isn't about submitting to a cult, son, real strength is about defending your own without making too many enemies in the process. You need to be able to live with other people but have the strength to push back when one of them starts taking liberties."

"I do agree that you need to prioritise yourself, because if you don't then nobody else will," said Pimienta. "But you also need to have the humility to acknowledge you're just one individual among millions of others, each with their own needs. Just as you need to stick up for yourself, you also should try not to impose your will on others. You might feel justified in punishing your opponents after what they've done to you, but if you do are you any better than them? I suggest you try to refine your own personal moral compass instead of delegating that task to your tribe. Stop trying to win. Focus on making yourself happy, not on making other people unhappy."

"Unbelievable! I never thought I'd see the day when all four of you agreed with each other but here you are, united in your conviction that I'm living my life the wrong way. Well you know what, I'm going to take your advice and prioritise myself. I think you can be an individual and commit to a group at the same time. You said it yourselves: take what you need from it. Well I'm a hundred percent sure I'm stronger as part of the Savages than I could ever be by myself and what's more it's through them that I met Prosecca, who makes me feel better than anyone else ever has. So, with all due respect, you can all shove your advice. See you later."

With that Dalston necked his Jamesons, defiantly downed the remaining third of his pint and flounced off. He didn't have too long to reflect on the unsettling cooling of relations with his new friends, however, as he had agreed to be a spokesman for the Savages and a request had come in for someone to appear on Iain Tegritie's radio programme. He was delighted to accept the opportunity, mainly because he wanted to reinforce his commitment to the Savages, but also because he felt he had unfinished business from his previous appearance. He was scheduled to appear the next morning so he limited himself to just a few beers and a couple of whiskeys that evening to ensure he would be on top form.

***

"The recent electoral shock didn't surprise everyone, of course," said Tegritie in his introduction. "One of the most prominent members of the Savage campaign was Dave Dalston, a one-time Felian supporter whose spectacular fall from grace culminated in a physical altercation with members of the so-called Anticanes. Mr Dalston, you must be very happy with the result."

"Hello Iain," said Dalston. "I certainly am, and consider it a vindication not just of what Dick Savage stands for but of everyone who suffered under the Felian tyranny."

"I see. And you think things will be better now, do you?"

"Of course. They couldn't be much worse, could they?"

"That remains to be seen, but it's hardly a resounding endorsement of your own side is it? Perhaps you could highlight the Savage policies you think will do the most to improve the lot of the average UK citizen."

"Well, for a start, they're going to repeal every law the Felians introduced that discriminated against Canines and Delphines."

"That might please you and your Canine buddies, but surely it will upset a lot of Felines and Simians. I don't see how it will benefit the whole country."

"Surely you can see how laws that discriminate against half the country are bad though, Iain."

"I guess it depends. But what I really want to know is what new policies the Savages have, as opposed to simply repealing Felian ones, that we should be getting excited about."

"I can't think of any specific ones right now, but I have total confidence Dick Savage will be a massive improvement on Mary Onette as the leader of this country."

"How can you be, though, when you don't know any of his policies?"

"I'll tell you how, because he's not a fucking Fascist," said Dalston, beginning to get flustered.

"I see," said Tegritie, smiling. "And you presumably think Onette is. Perhaps, then, you could tell us what defines a Fascist."

"Surely everyone knows that."

"Maybe, but since your main argument in favour of Dick Savage is that he's not a Fascist, it would be instructive to know what you think a Fascist is."

"OK, I'm thinking of the kind of stuff the Nazis got up to in the Second World War."

"So the Felians want to conquer Europe and create a master race by murdering millions of people?"

"Well not yet, but I wouldn't put it past them! Which is why it was so important they were taken out of power."

"What other Nazi stuff did they do?"

"Look, you got me Iain, I'm not an expert on the Nazis either. But I do know they were tyrants who violently discriminated against anyone they didn't like – just like the Felians."

"One of Savage's policies is for reparations to be paid by Felines and Simians to Canines and Delphines for the abuse they suffered under the Felians."

"That's totally fair enough, why shouldn't there be some justice for us?"

"How much do you think you should be paid?"

"No amount of money can undo what they did."

"So why bother with reparations at all?"

"Because they can't be allowed to get away with it."

"OK, another policy is an extension of the Id Card scheme that will see wholesale replacement of Felines and Simians by Canines in influential jobs."

"Again, fair enough. They've had a go at this stuff and they fucked it up. Now it's our turn."

"I see. A moment ago you told me any policy which discriminates against half the country must be bad, now you're saying exactly the opposite. I put it to you, Mr Dalston, that you have no interest in fairness or the common good. You are, in fact, no better than the people you claim to oppose and are in many ways the same. With the Savages winning the election you now feel it's your turn to behave in exactly the way you found so heinous on the part of the Felians."

"No, it's not like that, you're twisting my words."

"I'm doing no such thing. I'm merely repeating back to you what you've said to me. Isn't it funny how much worse that made it sound? You may feel justified in exacting revenge on the Felians, but surely that's how they felt about you when they came to power. Your attempts to sugar-coat your petty self-interest with a veneer of morality are transparent, vulgar and offensive. I would have more respect for you if you just admitted you want your turn wielding the whip, but that would require a degree of self-reflection you're clearly incapable of. Thank you for your time Mr Dalston."

With that Tegritie terminated the interview and turned to his notes without even making eye contact with Dalston, who was so stunned by the fait accompli he missed the opportunity to tell Tegritie what he thought of him before being ushered from the studio. He hadn't expected an easy ride but couldn't help feeling appalled and upset at how quickly the interview had turned against him. As he replayed it in his mind on the way home he was forced to reflect on Tegritie's observations about his attitudes towards the vanquished Felians. Was it wrong to want payback when you've suffered such injustice? Was he really no better than them? Did it matter if he was not?

The public dressing-down had really hit his confidence and left a bad taste in his mouth at a time when he should have been on top of the world, and for that he resented Tegritie bitterly. To his relief the opportunity to get rid of the bad taste took little time to present itself, when a representative of Jive Robin got in touch through Twitter to invite him back on his podcast. The abrupt, adversarial nature of his encounter with Tegritie left him yearning for a proper, long form, conversation, so he gratefully accepted.

Chapter 24 – Ignominy

The Green Room at Robin's recording studio now offered a cornucopia of recreational drugs. While tempted, Dalston was determined to represent himself as well as possible during this precious opportunity for public redemption. Coke might make him gibber, joints and edibles could slow his thinking and probably render him paranoid and, as he had never been a fan of hallucinogens, this was certainly not the time to experiment. On the other hand a drink to calm the nerves wouldn't kill him and, delighted to find a bottle of Eagle Rare, he helped himself to a generous slug. He was allowed to take his drink into the studio and, seeing his preference, Robin called for the bottle to be brought in so they could drink together.

The start of the conversation consisted of Robin enquiring about Dalston's vice inclinations, which rapidly evolved from illicit substances to sexual tastes. Seeing this was making Dalston uncomfortable he moved onto the matter at hand – his most recent Tegritie interview. Dalston gave a comprehensive account of the encounter and thought he did a good job of criticising Tegritie's interview style, and anti-Savage agenda, without being excessively adversarial. Robin shared his dislike of the way the interview concluded and explained that one of the main reasons he got into podcasting was because he wanted to offer an alternative to the compressed, forced, adversarial style of mainstream media interviews. Having said that, Robin also thought Tegritie made some good points about the dangers of tribalism and moral relativism, so challenged Dalston to explain his position.

"For me it all comes down to justice," said Dalston. "The Felians used their power to persecute Canines and Delphines and I don't see why they should be allowed to get away with it."

"OK, but looking at it from their perspective, they thought they were acting to correct hundreds of years of historical injustice perpetrated by Canines," said Robin. "So, as Tegritie asked in your most recent interview, how is your current vengeful attitude any more justified than theirs was? The only motivation I can see is blind tribalism, which I thought we agreed in our previous conversation was not cool. So what changed, dude?"

"The big difference is that the Felians are all about collective punishment. They have attributed a whole range of past misdeeds to Canines and decided today's Canines need to pay the price for them in order to even the score. The stuff I'm referring to is much more recent, specific and tangible. Individual Felians committed acts of injustice, for which there is incontrovertible proof. I'm not looking for collective punishment, only the justice that comes with the individuals responsible being held to account."

"I completely agree with you on the matter of collective punishment. Not only is it unfair to hold people accountable for things they didn't do, it also does nothing to undo the original act. Many terrible things have happened throughout history but what's done is done and can't be changed. And while we're talking about the past, how the fuck can we talk about historical Canines when they only got invented recently? Are we saying anyone who was a dick in the past must have been Canine? Because that's clearly bullshit and also far too handy for anyone looking to score points against them. I apply the same logic to present-day collective punishment; just because one Canine is an asshole doesn't mean the rest of them are. The only reason I can think of for collective punishment is vindictiveness or an underlying political agenda."

"I think it's both, Jive. From the moment the Felians were formed they made it clear they wanted to impose their will on the rest of the country and were prepared to use any amount of force to do so. Their politics were merely the formal expression of that desire."

"Sure, but at the end of the day we're splitting hairs, mate. You're still behaving in the tribal way we previously agreed was counterproductive. So I'm still left wondering what changed."

"Last time I was here I felt like an innocent victim, I felt vulnerable, but the political environment has totally changed since then and now I feel a lot stronger and ready to fight back."

"That's what I'm fucking saying though! You're not using any moral principles. You're saying the only thing that determines whether something is good or bad is power. When you're vulnerable you're all about mercy, understanding and forgiveness, but when you're on top you just want to punish anyone who's ever fucked with you. Can't you see what a double standard that is?"

"When you put it like that, yes, but maybe that whole experience has taught me there's no point in trying to get through to some people. There will always be cunts and the only language they understand is strength. The only way to stop them shitting on you is to do it to them first."

"But what if they're thinking exactly the same about you and the only reason they shit on you is to get their retaliation in first? This vendetta bullshit has to stop somewhere, dude, or everyone ends up dead. Someone has to start the confrontation, but what if the people you attack never intended to do anything to you in the first place? They sure as hell will want to fuck you over after though, won't they? It's a self-fulfilling prophecy."

"In an abstract sense I agree, but in the real world I definitely didn't do anything to those Anticanes that battered me, did I?"

"Well I don't think that's entirely true. It might not have justified physical violence, but you had been winding up the Felians for quite a while, hadn't you?

"Jive, I hope you're not saying we shouldn't speak openly in case we get attacked. Surely that's encouraging aggression and ensuring only the most powerful people get to speak."

"No, I'm not saying that. I agree with you that violent censors need to be resisted, but at the same time we can't pretend words don't have any consequences at all. I'm just saying that if you hadn't chosen to get in the face of these people, all the other stuff wouldn't have happened."

"It still sounds to me like you're asking me to be a pussy."

"I'm not, I promise. Of course you need to stick up for yourself. I'm just saying that strength without humility usually leads to conflict, that's all."

"And I'm saying that humility without strength invites aggression."

"I hear you brother, but we got kind of blown off course there. What I really want to know is: why do you need to pick a team at all?"

"I never set out to. But circumstances seemed to always force me into one group or other. It wasn't always this way though, and I blame the Id Card thing. A mate of mine said at the start it would force people into political factions and he was fucking spot on. At first I went along with it, tried to downplay my status as a Canine, and to suck up to the Felians. But when that blew up in my face I went looking for whatever group was most opposed to them."

"So your enemy's enemy was your friend?"

"I guess so."

"OK, I can see how that's justified tactically, but not strategically. Let me explain. Circumstances compel you to pick a team because it helps you achieve an aim, in this case combating an adversary. But that team doesn't exist solely to help you and has plenty of other priorities that have nothing to do with yours. So you effectively enter into a contract with them in which they promise to help you achieve your aims in return for you adopting theirs. You may well end up achieving your immediate aim, but now you've got to deal with a bunch of other shit that you didn't give a fuck about before. So in a sense you've just swapped one problem for a bunch of others."

"That's one way of looking at it."

"Don't get me wrong, not all interactions are so transactional. Friendship and love make people do stuff for each other just because they want to. The reward is the other person's happiness or safety or whatever. But those kinds of relationships are rare and we often take them for granted. Think about all the things people closest to you do without asking for anything in return other than for you to not be too much of a dick."

Dalston's thoughts at once turned to Amy and Mel and the reason he hadn't seen them for so long – no doubt about it, it was because he had been a dick. He also thought of Prosecca and wondered how transactional their relationship was. He was sure they really cared for each other, but their time together was almost entirely defined by partying and sex, which neither of them would have nearly so much of without the other. Were they just using each other? The answer was probably yes and that was fine, but it did make it the kind of transactional relationship Robin was talking about?

He also thought about the other people closest to him and realised he was estranged from nearly all of them. As well as Mel, he wasn't talking to Jack, and as a consequence hardly ever saw Al and Nick either. And then there were his parents. They brought him into the world and gave him so much else, but he hardly ever went to see them and always considered it a massive drag when he did. Was he being too much of a dick to them too?

"Looks like I got you thinking, brother," said Robin.

"You certainly have, mate, and that's why you're so good at what you do. I'm a bit confused now though, are you saying I should stick to myself and try to avoid other people or what?"

"No I'm not saying that, I'm suggesting you examine the relationships and groups you get into and ask yourself why you do so. If you're in a group because it serves some immediate purpose, do you still want to be in it after that purpose is served? And the same goes for relationships with other individuals: is it simply transactional or something more profound?"

"How can I tell?"

"By having a conversation with yourself. Often we don't know our own motives and need to dig deep to find them. There's an old saying that goes 'virtue is its own reward.' If you do something just because it feels right, then I reckon that makes it a pure act. If you expect payment in kind, whether money, stuff, sex or status, then it's a transaction, isn't it?"

"I'd never really thought of it like that, Jive. Have a conversation with yourself eh? Sounds a bit nuts but I'll give it a go."

"Do it, dude, and then come back and tell us how it went."

***

Dalston met up with Prosecca after the Jive Robin podcast and was keen to get her take on all the thoughts and ideas his recent experiences had brought to the front of his mind. She admitted she hadn't listened to either interview, but said she had no doubt he was amazing in both. She asked if he had any coke, which he did, so she challenged him to multitask enough to chop up a couple of lines while he spoke. As soon as they snorted, she interrupted him to declare that everything he said was cause for celebration, poured them both a massive drink and demanded they go out.

He was determined to make the most of the euphoric mood and remembered seeing a poster for live comedy when he was at Dingwalls. Prosecca thought that was a great idea so they necked their drinks, did another line each and burst into the North London evening. They arrived at Dingwalls early, so were able to stock up on drinks, do one more cheeky line in the toilets and grab prime spots near the front. The warmup act was fairly mediocre, which resulted in Dalston and Prosecca spending much of the time groping each other and giggling incongruously, to the irritation of all those around them. By the time the main act came on he was pissed, buzzing and convinced he could have done a better job than the warmup. After about five minutes he decided this comedian was no better and lost patience.

"You're fucking shit!" he shouted at the comedian.

"Ah, I remember my first beer," retorted the comedian, getting his first big laugh of the set.

Dalston was indignant at the gall of the comedian and the impertinence of the crowd for siding with him. "It's whiskey actually, but no amount would make you funny, you cunt," he said, exasperated at having to double down on his reprimand.

"OK, that's how you want to play it do you?" said the comedian. "I can see I'm going to have to work up a number six on you." Dalston never got a chance to deliver a third heckle.

"I'm not surprised you're such a prick because your face looks like a blind kid tried to draw his nightmares," said the comedian, to a fresh round of laughter. "You're so ugly you make onions cry. You're so ugly, when you were born the midwife slapped your Mum. If I had a face like yours I'd sue my parents. I heard your birth certificate is an apology letter from the condom factory. I don't know what makes you so ugly, but it's doing a great job. I never forget a face, but in your case I'll make an exception."

By this stage the entire room was roaring with laughter and the comedian was showing no signs of slowing down. Dalston looked beside him to Prosecca for moral support but she was too busy dabbing tears of mirth from her eyes. He could make out a man in the audience who had stood up and was actually pointing at him as he convulsed with laughter and fought for breath. His mood transformed from euphoric to despondent in a matter of seconds, he just stared darkly at the comedian in a futile attempt to intimidate him into ending his assault.

"Keep rolling your eyes mate, you might find your brain," continued the comedian. "Do you know what, I'm actually jealous of people who have never met you. Did your parents ever beg you to run away from home? Your family tree must be a cactus because everybody on it is a prick. Did you get that top off Amazon? I bet if I looked it up it would say 'people who bought this also bought extra small condoms, inflatable sheep and a life.' They don't make men like you anymore, but just to be safe you'd better get your tubes tied. Acting like a prick doesn't make yours grow bigger you know. Mind you, the smartest thing that ever came out of your mouth was a cock so fair enough. Don't worry mate, you haven't got a tiny cock, just massive balls, keep telling yourself that."

By now Dalston was almost crying with humiliation and, with no end to the torture in sight, he got up to leave. "Aww don't leave, mate, we were just getting to know each other," taunted the comedian. "Listen you've got it all wrong, I'm not trying to insult you, I'm just describing you. But look on the bright side, at least you bring happiness whenever you go."

As Dalston worked his way slowly through the baying crowd and reached the exit the comedian delivered one last parting shot. "Not so fucking funny when you're on the receiving end is it, mate?" he said. Dalston ordered the largest whiskey the bar would give him and downed it in one. Before long Prosecca came out and, to his utter incredulity, asked him why he had walked out.

"What, you mean apart from being publicly humiliated for the past ten minutes?" he seethed.

"It's just banter isn't it?" said Prosecca. "I figured that's what you were looking for when you started heckling him."

"No, I was telling him he was shit because he was."

"And what the fuck did you expect him to do with that feedback, Dave, invite you backstage to give him some comedy lessons? Do you know what, I think he was right, you can dish it out just fine but as soon as you get a bit back you fucking shit yourself."

He felt a strong urge to hit her and if they hadn't been in a public place he might have. Instead, he launched into a tirade about how he didn't think a bit of support was too much to ask for from his bird, especially when he's recently paid for her to stick half of Colombia up her nose. She retorted that she didn't owe him anything and hadn't heard him complaining until now. When he persisted she stood up, saying she was bored of his whining bullshit and was going to find someone more fun to stay out with. He grabbed her arm and felt the red mist descend once more, tinged with possessive jealousy. She screamed at him to let go of her, which he did, and walked off without looking back. As he slumped back into his chair, only the threat of further public humiliation prevented him sobbing with self pity and he resolved instead to drink his problems away.

When he woke up in a police cell the next day with a banging headache, he had no recollection of what he had got up to after his row with Prosecca, but was gloomily unsurprised to see it had landed him in trouble. He was alone in the cell and could see nobody else in his bit of the police station. His increasingly loud demands to have his current predicament explained to him were ignored for a considerable period of time but eventually someone arrived bearing a plastic cup of water with a couple of Alka Seltzer tablets fizzing in the bottom. "Drink it and I'll be back in an hour," said the policewoman with bored indifference, before handing the cup through the bars and then walking off, unmoved by his continuing pleas.

A few minutes after gratefully downing the drink he started to feel a little bit more normal and attempted to remember what happened. He discovered fresh bruises and saw an Electric Ballroom ink stamp on the back of his hand, but other than that had no idea what he had been up to. It must have been pretty exceptional, though, to be so much worse than everyone else in night-time Camden that the police had taken special interest in him.

As his headache started to subside the self-recriminatory phase of his hangover kicked in. In what was supposed to be his moment of triumph following the Savage victory he was instead locked in a cage, feeling like shit, having alienated his girlfriend, most of his friends and probably a large portion of North West London. This wasn't how it was supposed to be. After all, his team had won, he had won! So why wasn't everything else sorted?

Then he remembered his humiliation at the hands of the comedian and the lack of support from Prosecca that had made him so angry. He started muttering about what an ungrateful bitch she was under his breath, but immediately struggled to identify precisely what he expected her to be grateful for. Yes, he'd bought her a few meals and probably paid for the majority of the drugs they shared, but he had enjoyed every minute of it and certainly expected nothing in return other than a continuation of their hedonistic coexistence.

Could he really blame Prosecca for walking off after his sense of humour failure at the comedy club? And why had that gone so badly? The comedian had certainly given him both barrels, but he had asked for it. The more he thought about it the more he was inclined to conclude he had arrived at the comedy club on such a literal and metaphorical high he felt invulnerable. It hadn't even occurred to him the comedian would hit back at his artless heckling and it had come as a massive blow to his ego to be handled with such effortless contempt.

The most uncomfortable feature of his jail cell introspection was arriving at the conclusion he didn't like the person he was having a conversation with very much. That person was a superficial egomaniac who used people to fulfil his immediate needs and then disposed of them as soon as they had the temerity to challenge him. The Savages weren't his friends, they were just a collection of people he had allied himself to because that suited his aim of striking back at the Felians and Anticanes. He concluded that individuality and group membership were opposites and the more committed to a team you are, the more of your individuality you have to surrender. He realised the neutrals were actually much freer than he was; free to make informed choices depending on the unique characteristics of a given issue, free to join several teams, even if some of them were at times in direct opposition to each other – in sum, free to be themselves.

Eventually the policewoman came back and told him he had a visitor. Dalston assumed Prosecca had come to remonstrate with him for being such a prick and he was ready to apologise unconditionally. But the people he found waiting for him when he got to the visiting booth were the very last he expected to see.

Chapter 25 – Introspection

For several seconds Dalston could only stand and stare at the smiling face of Amy, so delighted to see her he almost sobbed. As he fought to compose himself he considered the environment to which he had exposed his daughter and felt deeply ashamed. That this was the first time he had been in the same room as her for months compounded his disgrace, especially since they were still separated by plexiglass, but it also gave him the motivation to try to extract any positive from this ignominy.

Bizarrely, the same music he had heard the last time he spoke to Amy appeared to be playing somewhere in the police station. It seemed to be coming from everywhere but he couldn't see any speakers. It was almost as if the music was following her.

...Home is where the heart is... you don't need a doctor, no one else can heal your soul...

"Hello Daddy," said Amy.

"Hello baby, what are you doing here?"

"There was a video of you getting in trouble on YouTube and I heard about it, so I begged Mummy to bring me down here."

Dalston looked around and saw Mel sitting in the background of the visiting area. He waved apologetically at her and she reciprocated with a half wave, half shrug as though to say, 'what the hell are you doing with your life?' He wasn't surprised to hear somebody had filmed his drunken display and published it.

"Oh my God I'm so sorry you had to see that Amy, I'm so ashamed. Don't worry I'm not in big trouble, I was just feeling upset about something yesterday and then drank too much. I know you must be so disappointed in me but I promise it will never happen again."

"I believe you Daddy."

Amy's unconditional support nearly set him off again but he mustered all his self-discipline to keep it together as he didn't want to upset her.

"I bet your Mum will never let me see you properly now," he said.

"Actually she was saying on the way here that she thinks this might do you some good and I do too," said Amy. "I bet you've been doing a lot of thinking this morning, haven't you, Daddy? Why don't you tell me about it?"

Amy spoke in such a knowing way that Dalston almost suspected she had been spying on him. He was also surprised by how grateful he was at this opportunity to share some of his recent ruminations.

"Well, I've been wondering whether I got it all wrong by joining these groups and being so competitive," he said. "Every time I think I've won, things just seem to have got worse for me, so I'm starting to think I would have been better off not bothering with all of it."

"What else?"

"I reckon I need to rethink what's really important. Maybe I've been spending all this time with complete strangers because for some reason I found it easier than sorting things out with the people closest to me. I just seemed to always screw things up, like I did with your Mum, so I think I was running away."

"Do you still want to run away?"

"That's such a good question and the answer is no, I don't. I really want another chance to do things right and that starts with you, baby."

"I'm so happy to hear that, Daddy, and I can see in your eyes that you really mean it."

"In that case I've got a really big job for you. You need to talk to Mummy and tell her what you've seen in my eyes. I am never, ever going to let myself get in a situation like this again. I'm going to clean up my act, stop hanging around with people I don't care about, and do everything I can to be a good Dad. Can you do that for me?"

"I will, you leave it with me. And the big job I ask of you is to run back to the people you feel closest to."

"Thank you, I will. I love you very much, you know that don't you?"

"Yes and I love you too."

With that Amy blew him a kiss, went back to Mel and the two of them walked towards the exit of the visiting room, with the music fading as they got further away. When the door opened he thought he could make out angry shouting, which he found unsettling and intimidating. He was close to calling for help until he saw the two of them smiling and hugging as they walked through the door, but his response to the imagined danger deepened his determination to organise his life so he could be there to protect Amy when needed.

The revelation that his desire to be a good parent was such a decisive motivating force steered Dalston's thoughts towards the concept of parenting in general once he was alone again. Why hadn't that instinct been stronger in him previously? Perhaps it was but he had allowed it to be drowned out by his own immediate needs and desires. That got him thinking about his relationship with his own parents, which had broken down somewhat in recent years mainly due to his difficult relationship with his mother. Of course he still loved her and always assumed any severing of diplomatic relations would be temporary, but he was still compelled to reflect to on the paradoxical relationship between parent and child that made them simultaneously resentful of but dependent on each other.

Perhaps that was what love is, he mused – enduring mutual dependence. There had been times he felt dependent on Prosecca but he could already see it was a fleeting thing, strongly implying he had confused infatuation for love. He was deeply shocked when she walked out on him, but he could already detect a growing sense indifference towards her. He still craved her, but what was it he actually wanted? The sex and the partying, certainly, but there were countless other women who could perform the same function in his life.

The more he thought about it, the more he was sure that what he missed most about Prosecca was her beauty. Just being around such a gorgeous woman lifted his spirits, but it was addictive. It wasn't enough to just appreciate her beauty and personality, he had to own it, to consume it. It had to be his. The very qualities that made her attractive became massive liabilities once he had her. If he valued them, it stood to reason other men would too and would want to take her from him, which he couldn't allow.

But why? When the answer presented itself, his heart sank at the pathetic inevitability of it. Being Prosecca's lover made him feel better about himself, and that was what he most needed. Every time he walked into a pub with his arm around this exquisite creature and every time she looked into his eyes as she orgasmed was a validation of him as a man. She made him feel special, but only so long as she was his. Like any addiction the high required constant topping up and the longer it lasted, the bigger the come-down. Furthermore whenever she so much as looked at another person, even a woman, the fragile spell was in danger of breaking. If she laughed at another man's joke that might mean she fancied him a bit, which would mean she fancied Dalston a bit less.

As he contemplated that revelation, Dalston was confronted by the fact that his thoughts had moved seamlessly from his mother to his lover. He writhed in oedipal agony for a short time, before eventually convincing himself the reason for such a disturbing segue was that he was mulling the nature of love and contrasting familial with romantic love was justified in that context, or so he hoped. But did he really love either his mother or his lover? Just because he was biologically stuck with his Mum, did that automatically translate into love? Conversely was a strong desire to be with a person the same as loving them?

Dalston started imagining pairs of people in burning buildings and being confronted with the dilemma of which to save first, or at all, in each case. Before long the concept of duty started to play an increasingly prominent role in his hypothesising. It was joined by other sentiments, which coalesced into an ad hoc decision-making framework in which immediate family always took priority over lovers and friends. Tie-breakers between close family were resolved by reflecting on how much affection and protectiveness he felt for each person, such that he would save his Dad before his Mum, but Amy before either of them. Among friends, he found shared history to be the decider. He would save any of his three closest friends before Prosecca, whose chances of surviving the conflagration were diminishing by the second.

The wild-card in Dalston's macabre mental game was Mel. She wasn't currently a lover or even really a friend, but had been both in the past. As the mother of his daughter she was technically family, but they had no blood relationship and recent months had shown their mutual dependence to be far from enduring. In the end a combination of their shared history, his continued affection for her and, most importantly, her status as Amy's mother and guardian, placed Mel in her own category below his parents, but above his closest friends.

Eventually let out of the police station with a caution, Dalston checked his phone for messages from Prosecca, but there were none. There was also no sign of her when he got home, which he realised he was quite relieved about since he really didn't feel like being shouted at, or doing whatever Prosecca would demand they do after she deemed him sufficiently contrite. He had that classic hungover feeling of genuinely never wanting to drink or do drugs again, utterly humbled by the last 24 hours. He ate some cold pizza straight from the box, took another couple of pain-killers and slunk off to bed.

When he woke up Dalston felt a lot less sorry for himself and a lot more purposeful. His ultimate aim of being reunited with his family seemed so daunting at that moment that he decided to target some lower-hanging fruit first. Once more Prosecca sprang to mind, as she was wont to do, so Dalston decided that situation needed attending before he could move on to more involved matters.

To his delight she responded to his text message with 'hello stranger' and they arranged to meet a couple of days later at The Flask in Hampstead. He got there first, in time to lean on the bar and observe Prosecca walking into the pub, at which point his hard-won indifference towards her evaporated immediately. For the few moments before they made eye contact he drank in her beauty. It was effortless to the point of mockery, as if she only visited the pub to rub everyone else's noses in how plain and flawed they were. Even the way she surveyed the room, her lips parted to somehow combine innocent anticipation with erotic promise, was mesmerizing.

She soon spotted Dalston and came over to him. Neither of them was sure of the correct greeting. Usually it would have been a lingering kiss on the lips, but things hadn't concluded well the last time they were together and it was clear neither of them was of a mind to just carry on as if nothing had happened. His recent conclusions about the superficial nature of their relationship were vindicated by the fact he felt like he was meeting a stranger on a blind date – all nerves and awkward formality – and the feeling appeared to be mutual.

It was as if their intimacy required constant maintenance and it started diminishing the moment they were parted. Dalston realised there was nothing intrinsically enduring about their relationship and it was only as good as the last meeting. It was the diametric opposite of his relationship with close family and friends, which existed whether he liked it or not and was largely unaffected by time apart.

"I got you your usual," he said.

"Cheers," said Prosecca.

They clinked glasses and found a table. For a short time they both surveyed the pub as if they were planning to buy it, before her eyes turned to Dalston. He probably would have lost himself in them if they weren't so clearly communicating a desire for him to get to the point.

"OK," he said. "Thanks a lot for coming out, Prosecca, it's really good to see you."

"You too," she said in a clipped manner implying 'is this what you dragged me out of the house for, you time-wasting twat?'

"Firstly I want to say sorry for being such a dick that night in Camden, I don't know what came over me. Did you know I got arrested after you left?"

"Yup," she replied, her lack of sympathy perfectly conveyed in a solitary syllable.

Even though he expected it, Dalston was still hurt by her apparent indifference to his suffering, but he forced himself to stay on track.

"I did a lot of thinking in my cell," he said, unable to keep the final two words entirely free of reproach. "I thought about what I'm doing with my life and what I really want from it. I realised one of the reasons I acted like I did was because my head was wrecked and it turns out a spell of forced isolation was just what I needed. Anyway, none of that was your problem and you didn't deserve to be spoken to the way I did, so I'm very sorry. Will you accept my apology?

She extended one of her hands across the table and he took it, cringing inwardly to feel grateful for the physical contact.

"To be honest, Dave, I'd pretty much forgotten about the whole thing until you brought it up just now. So there's really no need for an apology, but if it will make you happy then of course I accept it."

At last he fully understood how little they had in common. This probably wasn't such an exceptional scenario for Prosecca. If she aroused such passions in him, she had presumably done so to loads of other blokes. Most people would do anything to have people fall head-over-heels for them, but for her it was probably more remarkable if they didn't. Dramatic displays by besotted lovers were just a regular day at the office for her and not especially noteworthy.

"Thank you," he said, squeezing her hand briefly, before removing his own. "I think we should call it a day."

"You're not chucking me are you?" she asked with a cheeky smirk, as if the very concept was ridiculous.

"Look, I'm still crazy about you. I just think things have run their course. We've had loads of fun, but I think I need more than that right now."

"More than fun? Like what?"

"I'm not entirely sure. More structure, more substance, more trust, more commitment, more meaning."

"Don't want much, do you?"

"Yes, turns out I'm the high maintenance one. But don't you want any of those things?"

"I thought I did, but then I realised for most blokes commitment is a one-way thing and they're not so keen on applying it to themselves. Also commitment only really matters if you're going to get married and have kids. If that's not on the cards then what's the point in laying all those rules and restrictions on each other just because you're having sex. You don't expect your mates to not have a laugh with other people, do you? You don't get all stroppy when they don't call you for a couple of days, so why lay that stuff on someone you're shagging?"

"You must fall for people a bit though. Didn't you fall for me?"

"Of course I did, darling, but if I fall for someone it's my problem, not theirs. Just because I can't get some bloke out of my head doesn't mean he owes me anything. I want people to do things for me because they feel like it, not because I've hassled them into it or because they're afraid I'll throw my toys out of the pram if they don't. That was why I walked off that night and didn't get back in touch, not because you were being a stroppy little git, but because you started acting like I owed you something. I don't, Dave, and I hope you realise that now."

"I do. I also realise there is someone I do owe my commitment to and it's not you."

"Mel?"

"Yes and no. I was really thinking of Amy, but Mel is part of the package. The reason Mel doesn't want me around Amy is she thinks I'll do more harm than good. For a while I thought she was just being a spiteful bitch, looking to punish me for sleeping around, and maybe there was a bit of that to it, but I realise now she always had Amy's interests as her first priority. I'm ashamed to admit I didn't."

"What, just because you saw other women?"

"It was more the way I did it. I could have been discreet and I could have treated Mel with more respect. Also I shouldn't have used new relationships as a reason not to act like a proper Dad. It's just too easy to be all-in when you start seeing someone, just like I did with you in fact, but it's actually an incredibly selfish approach. You go around introducing this new bird to everyone you know, banging on about how amazing she is and getting the arsehole if they're not enthusiastic enough. I used to try to get women I'd only been seeing for a few days to start acting like a Mum to Amy, what kind of bollocks was that?"

"Blokes tend to go all-in, in my experience. It's all or nothing with you lot. You get a taste of sweet loving and you go all gooey and teenagery, like you've never had sex before. Before long you get possessive and controlling and start acting like it's your time of the month half the time. Then, one day, you meet some new girl who you decide has all the qualities suddenly lacking in your current girlfriend so you upgrade. Rinse and repeat, my friend. That's why I decided not to take things too seriously – men are most fun in the first few weeks and more often than not I'm happy for them to clear off after that anyway."

"Fucking hell Prosecca, that's some pretty cold shit right there."

"Is it though? Or is it just sensible? What would you have me do, beg not to be chucked? That's undignified if you ask me and, anyway, what's the point? If the man has already started looking around it's just a matter of time, so you might as well just let him get on with it."

"When you put it like that it's hard to argue with and you could be fucking spot on. Where my situation is different is it's not really about Mel, at least not just her. I really want to be a big part of Amy's life again and Mel's not going to fall for me just telling her whatever bullshit I think she wants to hear. The only way I'm going to convince her is to change my whole attitude to being Amy's Dad and that includes how I conduct my private life. In short, I don't think it would kill me to be celibate for a bit."

"Jesus Christ, Dave, that's a bit drastic isn't it? You'll be telling me you're going to stop wanking next."

"It's not about how and where I shoot my load, Prosecca, it's about where my mind is. Maybe it's different for you, but I've realised I can only focus on one relationship at a time and this is the one I've picked."

"Well fair enough and I wish you all the best in getting your ex back – I hope she's worth it. Feel like a last quickie for old time's sake?"

Under normal circumstances Dalston would have started ripping his kit off in the pub, but now he paused. What possible harm could it do? He still had a bit of coke left too, so they could go out with a bang, so to speak. The activity itself had nothing but upside, but it just didn't feel right. The reason why, he quickly realised, was because it would be a massive psychological step backwards. Partying with Prosecca, even if it was definitely the last time, would represent a regression to the mindset he had just been congratulating himself for leaving behind. Old Dave would have jumped at the chance, but new Dave was made of sterner stuff.

"Thanks a lot for the offer Prosecca, but I'll pass. A hug would be nice though."

They stood up, shared a warm, lingering embrace and left the pub in different directions.

Chapter 26 - Ingenuousness

As Dalston walked towards Hampstead tube station the clock tower at the entrance to Holly Hill made him think of the Holly Bush pub, the site of so many great evenings with his friends. Emboldened by the positive outcome of his chat with Prosecca he decided to strike while the iron was hot and called Nick Georgiou. His suggestion that the four of them have a drink was fielded cautiously by Georgiou, who wanted to know if he was OK but also to gauge what frame of mind he was in, as he had no desire to gather if he and Morrison were just going to have another domestic. Dalston reassured him he was fine and only wanted to patch things up, so Georgiou offered to contact Morrison while Dalston invited Blake.

He arrived at the Holly Bush early, grabbed their usual table and bought a round. Morrison was the last to arrive and all they could manage by way of greeting was to say "alright?" to each other accompanied by the most fleeting of eye contact. Dalston had already decided what he was going to say when they sat down.

"Lads, this evening is on me to say sorry for being such a prick last time we met up," he said. "I've been through a lot since then and it really got me thinking – I miss you guys."

"Cheers!" said Georgiou and raised his glass. The other three all clinked each other's glasses but eye contact from Morrison was still elusive. Georgiou noted this and figured things would relax a bit once everyone had a few drinks. So, against all prevailing small-talk wisdom, he decided to start a conversation about politics.

"So Savage went and did it eh?" said Georgiou. "I've got to admit, I think he's a nutter but I still voted for him."

"You're the nutter mate, how could you bring yourself to put an X in the Savage box, man?" said Blake.

"Because anything was better than those FLAP psychos. They were tearing the country apart and he was the only bloke standing up to them. I didn't so much vote for Savage, but against FLAP, innit."

"Look, I'm the first to admit FLAP lost their way. I think the power went to their heads, if I'm honest. But at the end of the day they still want to make the country fairer for everyone. All that Savage prick wants to do is sow division and spread hate."

"Fairer for everyone?" said Dalston. "Are you fucking mad? They only care about half the country, if that, the clue's in the name mate."

"Equality is good for everyone Dave," said Blake. "They're just trying to restore equality after years of everything being biased in favour of the Canines."

"I sincerely hope you don't actually believe that, Al."

"Al, even if that was true at the start, power always corrupts and it was never going to be enough for the Felians to just level the playing field," Georgiou chipped in. "You must have seen all that shit they came out with, about it being impossible for a Felian to be wrong and for a Canine to be right. That's not equality by any definition of the word."

"Look lads, you can't make an omelette without breaking eggs," said Blake. "I've already agreed there was an over-correction, but that was bound to happen and it's not forever. Shit was just starting to settle down when that cunt Savage came in and stirred it all up again."

"I think it really depends on your perspective Al," said Morrison. "As a Canine I was prepared to keep my head down and put up with it for a while, but I disagree with you about it settling down. If anything, it was getting worse and hardly a day goes by at work right now without a Felian accusing me of some thought crime or other. They don't want equality, they want subjugation and they want it permanently. You can only push a bloke so much and Savage is a product of Felian excess, nothing more."

"So are you saying that because I'm a Simian I'm biased in favour of the Felians?"

"You might not be actively biased, but I don't see many Simians speaking out about it. It could just be a matter of not realising what it's like to be on the receiving end of this kind of shit."

"Are you having a laugh, Jack? Have you ever noticed the colour of my skin? I've been putting up with this sort of shit all my life, bruv."

"Well then you know what I'm talking about don't you? Even after all the discrimination you faced, you never went around saying white people should be punished for being white. So how come it's alright to shit all over Canines just for being Canines?"

"This always happens whenever power imbalances are created, the sociopaths appropriate the original good cause to impose their will on everyone else," said Georgiou. "Let's not forget the Felians are mostly Felines. They started it and only invited the Simians into the club so they could out-number the Canines.

The top Felians certainly don't give a fuck about Simians, and I bet the same even applies to most Felines. All of you are just tools to legitimise their personal agenda when they claim to act on your behalf. Just look at what happened to Dave, who thought he was saying all the right things, as soon as he became an inconvenience."

"Yeah, but he was being a bit of a tool though," said Blake.

"You know what Al, you're fucking spot on, that's exactly what I was being," said Dalston. "But that doesn't undermine Nick's point. I did everything they could possibly have asked of me and I still ended up getting spat out. I realise now I was always walking a tightrope with them and was only one move away from being fucked over."

"That happened just after we met up in Camden didn't it?" said Morrison. "I must admit I pissed myself when I first found out."

This was the first time anyone directly addressed the fractious ending to their last get-together and Morrison's words were far from conciliatory. Blake and Georgiou held their breath and Dalston felt a flash of anger, but he checked himself and realised this could just have been Morrison's way of breaking the ice while saving face and making it clear he was still pissed off. He also remembered he deserved it.

"Fair enough Jack, if I'd been in your position I probably would have felt the same," he replied. "But you've got to understand I genuinely thought I was in the right at the time. I realise now you were much more sensible and pragmatic in your response to the Id Card and I should have followed your lead. The thing is, it all escalated so quickly; one minute we were staying up all night, doing coke in strip club bogs and whatever the fuck else we felt like, the next I was spending half my time in HR. And I know it was the same for you, but you seemed to adapt so easily. How did you manage it?"

"Psychology mate, I just got inside the heads of those Id Card cunts and worked out what they needed to see. The biggest difference between me and you was that I totally got into the role and while I was in the office I never left character because I knew the fuckers were watching me 24/7. You didn't join the dots from thought police to Big Brother, so your mask kept slipping and they nailed you every time."

"That's interesting and, in hindsight, I think it's what I found most difficult; it felt like you turned against me but you were just trying to get by. I made it about me and also judged you for not being more defiant. But since then I've realised we're just different people and judging you for not being more like me is a fucking bullshit position. In fact, I reckon I've learnt a lot about my attitude to other people since then."

"What do you mean?"

"I was expecting too much from you, and I don't mean that in a shitty way. The fault was mine, I had no right to expect you to support me unconditionally, no matter how many times I fucked up. That got me thinking about my expectations of other people too – why should anyone do anything for me? My time with the Felians and then the Savages was entirely transactional; we only supported each other for as long as there was clear mutual benefit. But the fucked-up thing is that even when those kinds of relationships end there's usually the kind of melodrama you normally associate with splitting up with a bird."

"I've noticed that too," said Georgiou. "It's really easy to join groups but a lot harder to leave them. In theory it shouldn't be a big deal; we didn't have a relationship before and now we don't again, but someone nearly always throws their toys out of the pram. I reckon it's to do with ego and rejection. Someone always takes shit personally and gets bent out of shape. It sounds like that's what's happened with you, Dave."

"Yes, and the closer you are to someone the more you feel like they owe you something, but that's bollocks," said Dalston. "I've learnt that I've got no right to expect anything and I should be more grateful for what I do get. I used to take so much shit for granted and that includes you guys. You could argue we have a transactional relationship based around drinking and talking shit, but it's a lot more than that."

"You're making me well up here with your poof talk, Dave," said Blake. "But joking aside, of course it is, you soppy twat. The army teaches you the importance of relationships, comradeship, having each others' backs, but it's not unconditional. Anyone who decides they can't be arsed one day finds that out soon enough, I can tell you. But there's no substitute for shared history. You and I have known each other since school and the four of us have been hanging out for what, ten or fifteen years? We know each other fucking well and share a lot of unique memories. You can't fake that, man."

"Before you two get a room, it's worth pointing out this works both ways," said Georgiou. "Other people don't have any right to expect stuff from you either. That was always my problem with this Id Card, it created the platform for one lot of people to start demanding shit from everyone else and to use force if they didn't get it. Relationships only work when the people involved want to do things for each other, not when they feel compelled to. A really good relationship is one in which you know the other people have got your back, but you trust them so much that you don't need them to prove it the whole time. You just know you're better off with them in your life."

"That's a fucking good point Nick," said Dalston. "In fact you've articulated what I've been thinking better than I could. Too many people have lost sight of what proper relationships are all about and just go around using each other. Maybe the biggest thing I learned from joining those tribes is that I've never felt more alone. The only reason I joined them was to address some immediate concern, but I never thought about what I would do even if I got what I wanted. I think that really hit home when Savage won. I expected to be ecstatic but in the end it was a massive anti-climax. One group of people I didn't know just managed to beat another bunch of cunts I didn't know, in a contest I had almost no control over but which was supposed to change my life. It might as well have been a game of fucking football."

The conversation then turned to football banter, which served as the final ice-breaker for the group. Dalston realised the Anticanes and the Savages were no better than football hooligans, using arbitrary tribalism as a pretext for pointless conflict. He had always been an Arsenal fan, but that said absolutely nothing about him other than the team he rooted for on a Saturday afternoon. Equally, the fact that Morrison was a Spurs fan said nothing about him and had never been a serious point of serious conflict between them before.

Dalston reflected on the bickering about football that preceded their falling out and concluded it was merely a symptom of the way his view of the world had been corrupted by the Id Card. He now felt such renewed regard and love for his friends he knew he would never fall into that trap again. At the end of the evening Blake goaded Morrison and Dalston into hugging it out and they eventually obliged, which then degenerated into a highly unstable group hug. On his way home Dalston felt more content than he had for a long time.

Chapter 27 – Imperiousness

Dalston was still feeling on top of the world the next day. He marvelled at how easy it is to get on with people once you have your head straight and therefore saw no reason not to move onto trickier relationships, so he grabbed his phone and messaged Mel. She didn't seem to be holding the recent events against him and replied with "I thought you would never ask!" He asked if she would let him treat her to dinner and once more resistance failed to materialise, so they set a date for Odette's in Primrose Hill a few days later.

Dalston started the evening by apologising for the police incident and explained it was the culmination of a long journey of self discovery.

"If that was the culmination I'd hate to see what the rest of the trip was like," said Mel.

"Yeah, good point," he replied. "But I think I needed to be knocked off my pedestal for the journey to be complete."

"How do you mean?"

"Well it all started with the fucking Id Card. I realised I was just the kind of cocky prick it was designed to root out, so I decided to try and reinvent myself as an Id Justice Warrior, hassling people on social media and generally playing the sanctimonious prick."

"I remember the phase only too well Dave, don't forget I never stopped following you on social media, I just stopped posting myself."

"Really? Fuck! I just assumed you'd cut me off totally."

"Hey, you might be a cocky prick, but you're still Amy's Dad. I had to keep an eye on you if only for her."

"OK, so you saw the kind of shit I was into and can I assume you tracked my fall from grace too?"

"Yes, and I thought it was bullshit. But at the same time I was pleased because I didn't like what you were turning into when you were trying to suck up to those Felians."

"Well, that's how I came to view it too. I obviously wasn't being myself, but it took something brutal to snap me out of it. So having been chucked out of the Felians I started hanging out with fellow Canines who were resisting the Felian tyranny."

"And how did that go?"

"Fucking great, to be honest. I met some cool people, was able to do my bit, and then we ended up winning the election. Job done."

"Yet here you are saying you needed to be knocked down a peg or two, and being locked up was the best thing for you."

"Yes. It started to dawn on me when I was in that cell and seeing you and Amy confirmed it. My mistake had been thinking I needed to join any kind of group at all. All I did was switch from the red team to the blue team, but I was still trying to win the same game."

"Which is?"

"The power game. The struggle to impose your will on other people. Joining a team comes with the condition that you help them beat the other team, but there will always be new opponents. When I was locked up I realised it's impossible to decisively 'win' at life and trying to do so is at best a waste of time. I mean, when can you say you've won, when you have a billion quid? When you've shagged the fittest bird in the world? When? Suddenly it seemed so obvious: the very desire to win is a massive cause of unhappiness and life is a lot simpler when you just stop."

"Well you've already shagged the fittest bird in the world anyway, haven't you?"

Dalston smirked and narrowed his eyes. He still thought Mel was gorgeous and their shared history meant his feelings towards her remained far more profound than anything he had with Prosecca. If he was to have any chance of reconciling with Mel he would have to choose his next words very carefully.

"I wouldn't mind doing it again, if I'm honest," he leered.

"Wow, you really know how to make a girl feel special Dave," she replied. "What the fuck makes you think you're in with a hope in hell?"

"I saw the way you just looked at me. I know you're still up for it."

"Dear, oh dear, oh dear. What a shit effort. I guess I knew tonight would come to this eventually but I thought you might be a bit more subtle after all this time."

"Subtlety is overrated."

"Not by you, clearly. So, tell me a bit more about the people you met when you joined the Savages."

"Well, like I said, they were opposed to the Felians and the Anticanes, so that was the main thing we had in common. But they were just good, honest people trying to cope with all the bullshit Canines had to put up with."

"Any women?"

"Sure, of course."

"And did you sleep with any of them?"

"What the fuck has that got to do with you?"

"Because, Dave, you seem to think we can just pick up where we left off while you're still going around shagging anything in a skirt. That's what the fuck it has to do with me."

"But that's what I wanted to say to you. I'm not interested in all that anymore. I know I fucked up with you before but I'm different now. Just give me the chance to prove how I've changed."

"OK, I will."

"Cool. Feel like coming back to mine then?"

Mel threw her head back and let out an exasperated laugh. "Not so fast, keen boy," she said. "That's, like, stage ten of me letting you back into my life and you haven't even started stage one yet. Try keeping your cock in your pants for a bit and then maybe I'll start believing you're serious."

"Alright Mel. Any other shit you want to ban while you're at it?"

"It wouldn't kill you to have a sober night every now and then either."

"Yeah, sure. I tell you what, I'll go and become a Buddhist monk and flagellate myself ten times a day, how does that sound?"

"Dave, look at me. I'm not fucking around here. The only reason I met you is because Amy begged me to and told me you had changed. We're doing just fine without you, and certainly don't need some pissed liability staggering back into our lives just because he's feeling a bit sorry for himself, but I think everyone deserves a second chance. You've got a simple choice: carry on behaving like a goddamn student with a trust fund or grow the fuck up. The ball's in your court, mate, and you can start by getting the bill and calling me a cab."

Reviewing his dinner with Mel at home over a nightcap, Dalston mulled this unexpected obstacle on his road to redemption. Mel hadn't really told him anything he didn't already know, although apparently he needed to hear it again. What did appal him, however, was the apparent inability of his higher brain to rein in his base self. He knew his clumsy flirtations would be rejected and yet he went ahead with them regardless. If anything he was even more oafish than usual, for reasons he couldn't fathom.

The best theory he could come up with during his second nightcap was self-sabotage. Maybe the stakes were so high his subconscious bottled it and decided to get the failure over and done with nice and quickly, rather than risk the torture of rejection after trying his best. Dalston was dejected by this possibility. He felt he had made so much progress in getting to know himself as an individual rather than a member of a group and wrongly assumed it meant from now on his higher brain would always prevail.

The next morning Dalston was awoken by an incoming message alert on his phone. It was Amy.

Good morning daddy how was your dinner with mummy?

It was really good to see her, baby, and thanks a lot for persuading her to come out.

Do you think things are getting better between you?

I'm not sure. Why, did Mummy say anything?

Not really but she looked a bit funny you know like when someone tells you everything is alright when they know it isn't

Yes, I can imagine. Look Amy, the truth is I didn't handle our meeting very well. I rushed into trying to get us back together when I should have just relaxed and listened to Mummy.

Why do you think you did that?

I'm not really sure and even I was kind of surprised when I did it. I guess maybe I haven't progressed as much as you thought I had.

I don't think that's true it's just you weren't quite ready. You're not going to be able to persuade mummy unless you really mean it she will know if you don't

You're right as usual. I think I need to spend a bit more time thinking about what I'm really trying to achieve.

OK I understand but don't take too long daddy I really miss you

I really, really miss you too, baby.

As ever Dalston felt simultaneously humbled and emboldened by his contact with Amy. It made him want to do better and to have something to feel proud of the next time he spoke to her. The best way to ensure it would be to win back the trust of her mother, but Dalston still didn't feel he'd worked out how. That led him to consider the case of his own mother again. She was pretty far from perfect as a parent, but there had never been a time when he was growing up when he had wanted someone to take him away from her. Yes, he had wished her harm and even death from time to time as a child, but he never really meant it and she was still his Mum at the end of the day.

Doris Dalston was not an easy person to like. Her demeanour conveyed a sense of mild disgust at pretty much everything and she seemed to spend most of her time looking for people to belittle, at which her acute mind and sharp tongue made her very effective. For most of his childhood he had been in awe of her, as she appeared to have total command over her environment. Through sheer force of will she always got what she wanted and God help anyone who defied to her. Men tended to retreat quickly at the sight of her bared teeth, but Dalston remembered protracted disputes with other women that made the Hatfield-McCoy feud seem like a minor misunderstanding.

During his teenage years he experimented with standing up to her. Each time he did she would increase the intensity of her verbal barbs until he was too upset to continue, which she seemed to consider a victory. But this process also served to toughen his emotional skin until he reached the point where he saw his mother's verbal viciousness as a massive bluff. She wasn't strong; she was scared and compensated for it by getting her retaliation in first. After that he found her verbal barbs more pathetic than hurtful, so Doris resorted to pathos and attempted to portray herself as a victim, cruelly scorned by an ungrateful son she just wanted to nurture and protect. Completely wrong-footed, for a while guilt made him compliant once more. But Doris soon began to overplay her hand so egregiously that he called bullshit, leading to their most spectacular falling out yet.

His father, Derek, was largely a bystander in this domestic civil war. A contrastingly passive and gentle man, he seemed baffled by their inability to get on with each other. Any attempt to play the peacemaker usually resulted in him being verbally slapped down by Doris, which provoked Dave to defend him, thus fanning the flames of conflict even more, so he tended to retreat to the other end of the house when things kicked off. Dalston had a lot of affection for his Dad but was appalled by his weakness in the face of his Mum's tyranny. When they were alone he often implored him to stand up to her, without success.

During one such melodrama something snapped and Dalston became aware of the utter futility of all this conflict. He and Doris had been locked in a battle of wills for his entire adolescence and he was damned if it was going to extend into his adulthood. From that moment on he became laser focused on creating the circumstances to leave home on his own terms. The desire to escape his toxic domestic environment, more than raw ambition, drove him to pursue a career in the City, and as soon as he was earning enough to rent a shitty flat he left.

That was many years ago and, while he kept in touch with his parents, he had never fully repaired his relationship with Doris. Such conversations as they had were usually curt and superficial, as if they both feared anything more substantial would burst the fragile bubble of civility. At some stage in a typical visit Doris usually remembered some pressing errand and left the two men alone, after which Derek relaxed and came out of his shell. While Dalston treasured the time alone with his Dad, he battled with feelings of contempt towards the docile old man, who was increasingly compromised by arthritis and early dementia. How could he stand to live such a limited, cowed life? He seemed to exist only to placate his wife, a Sisyphean task with no apparent hope of success. The resulting confusion, exasperation and shame led his visits to become increasingly infrequent.

Everything that had happened since the launch of the Id Card had given him fresh resolve to risk seeing his parents once more. Nonetheless, when he phoned home he was relieved it was his Dad who picked up. After the customary exchange of pleasantries, during which Dalston assured him he was fine and his Dad described at length the discomforts and indignities age was inflicting on him, the negotiation over dates and times for a visit was annoyingly complicated by Derek's need to consult Doris at every juncture. At one stage Dalston nearly hung up when his Dad shouted the same question at his distant wife several times. But they got there in the end and, after hanging up and collapsing in an emotionally spent heap, he concluded the call was probably a good dress rehearsal.

Doris answered the door and greeted Dalston with an exuberance that belonged on the amateur dramatic stage. They exchanged familial kisses in which both puckered their lips to one side as far from the opposing cheek as possible. The doorstep greeting was protracted while he was thoroughly interrogated. Only once he provided a sufficient account of how busy he had been, how healthy he nonetheless remained and how sorry he was for his many failings as a son since they last met, was the visit allowed to progress to the interior of his parents' house.

Derek was sitting in the living room in his easy chair. Dalston interrupted his clearly painful attempt to get up by bending over to hug him. When Dalston asked after him, Derek insisted he couldn't complain but Doris didn't concur.

"To be quite honest, David, he's a full-time job," she said. "He can't do anything for himself these days so I have to do everything. I wouldn't mind but I told him for years to go to the doctor over his arthritis and now it's too late. And as if I didn't have enough on my plate, now he's going soft in the head."

Doris didn't actually speak the last four words, instead mouthing them at Dalston while tapping her temple with her index finger to remove any chance of misinterpretation.

Dalston immediately felt the blood rushing to his own head as decades of emotional scars combined with protectiveness towards his Dad and revulsion at such a display of casual cruelty.

"He seems fine to me Mum," he replied, drawing on all his self discipline.

"Well you would say that wouldn't you?" said Doris. "You're hardly ever here and don't know what it's like. Would it kill you to visit a bit more often, or are you too busy getting drunk and thrown in prison?"

There was no way Dalston could just brush off that provocation, but he was still determined to retain some decorum.

"Wow, that didn't take long Mum, even for you," he said.

"And what's that supposed to mean?"

He knew he was getting sucked into a Doris Dalston psychodrama, but somehow he couldn't resist. He even whispered "here we go again" to himself before answering her.

"It means that's why I don't visit more often, because you always cause a fucking scene whenever I do."

"How dare you use language like that in this house? It might be acceptable among your drinking buddies, but not under my roof."

"Oh for God's sake, what does it matter? It's been ages since we've seen each other and you're not the only one to have had it tough in the intervening time, you know. If you must know I deeply regret getting arrested but one positive to come from it was a reminder of how important family is, which is why I got in touch. But you make it so fucking difficult, Mum, and I still don't know why. It's like you're allergic to getting on with people."

"I see. So you were sitting, hungover, in your cell and started crying for Mummy did you? Well it doesn't work that way David, you don't get to just flit in and out of people's lives and act like nothing's changed. You might think I'm a bad mother, but have you ever thought about how good a son you are? Look, you've already upset your father."

Before he could wipe it away a tear trickled down Derek's cheek. His claim to have something in his eye just served to emphasise the pathos of the situation and brought Dalston close to tears himself. The sight of his Dad's quiet sorrow put his latest spat with his Mum into instant perspective and instantly sucked the fight out of him.

"I'm really sorry Dad, I wanted more than anything to just have a friendly, happy time with you both today but it looks like it just wasn't meant to be," he said. "So I think I'd better just go now."

He bent down once more to hug the old man, who seemed barely to have the strength to reciprocate. When he stood up, he tried to face his Mum but was so appalled at the utter dysfunction of their relationship he couldn't bring himself to. Instead he just flicked his gaze to the door, opened it and walked out. As the door was closing he heard Doris say, "Goodbye David," in a voice prickling with defiance, but in which he thought he detected a slight quiver.

As he sat at home contemplating the failed visit over a large glass of 2005 La Rioja Alta Gran Reserva 890, Dalston felt utterly conflicted. His internal dialogue oscillated between self-reproach and bitter resentment towards Doris. Before long he found himself reverse-engineering their relationship in a futile attempt to identify some kind of sliding-doors moment when, if things had gone differently, the entire subsequent trajectory would have been fundamentally better. Had he ever felt loved by Doris as a child? The answer had to be yes; barbed tongue and emotional distance aside, his Mum had always looked after him, made sure he was clothed, sheltered, protected and educated. In fact it was Doris, not Derek, who provided the structure and discipline kids need, with his Dad's indulgent benevolence a stark contrast.

The more he thought about it, the more he realised she had been fairly consistent throughout his life and it was he who changed. As he grew into adulthood and became more independent, she clung to her historical role with ever greater desperation, as if she objected to the whole process. The result was a fractious impasse, the characteristics of which remained more or less the same since he left home. He knew his Mum felt the need to control her environment, and to some extent he empathised, but after all these years he still had no idea how to reconcile it with his equally strong desire not to be controlled.

Perhaps his encounters with Doris and Mel had both failed for the same reason, he posed. If his higher brain had been calling the shots during his parental visit would he have responded the same way? While there he felt he had been the model of self-restraint and only buckled under overwhelming provocation – but was that really what had happened? Was it not more accurate to say he arrived with a chip on his shoulder and was all too ready to be triggered when his Mum behaved in exactly the way he expected?

A second glass yielded an epiphany. Yes, he was evolving in a positive direction, but he expected the rest of the world to evolve with him. In hindsight what upset him most about the encounter with his Mum was that she was exactly the same as ever, while he felt he was a different person. She was also too concerned with her own needs, and with the predicament she felt she was in, to notice and change in him. In her unpleasant, acerbic way she was signalling this, but Dalston himself couldn't see past his own agenda and emotional baggage. Neither of them was therefore inclined to give each other the benefit of the doubt.

Chapter 28 – Individuality

The setbacks with Mel and his Mum hit Dalston hard. He had been so sure he had turned the corner but now it felt like he was back to square one. Perhaps that was it – his early wins made him cocky and complacent, assuming the same formula would work for all his relationships. Put like that, his approach represented a ridiculous oversimplification of two distinct and complicated matters. He decided introspection alone had taken him as far as it could for the time being and also reminded himself that he had forgotten to make amends for storming off the last time he met Davina, Dev, Pimienta and Stein. After considerable pleading, cajoling and reassuring he managed to persuade all four of them to meet him at the same place.

"Heard about you getting nicked, bruv," said Dev once they all sat down with their drinks. "I told you to watch yourself. I don't know why I fucking bother sometimes, know what I mean."

"Well it was Frank who said it, if I remember rightly. But that doesn't really matter, you were both right and I didn't listen. I guess I needed to find out the hard way."

"The hard way, are you fucking having a laugh?" Stein snorted. "A couple of bruises and a caution, you jammy bastard."

"Fair enough Frank, but that's not what I mean," Dalston replied. "Sitting in that police cell, feeling as shit as I did at a time when I was supposed to be on top of the world, got me thinking properly for the first time in ages. Then having Amy and Mel come and see me there was the last straw. The penny dropped that I'd been doing it all wrong and the energy I'd been putting into trying to fit in was worse than wasted, it was doing real harm."

"In what way?" asked Pimienta.

"Trying to be what other people want you to be is basically like lying – it takes a massive psychological toll. Not only is there the effort of keeping up with the lies and making sure you don't slip up, but you start to lose track of what's real and what's bullshit. And it gets more complicated the longer you do it, so much so that eventually you have to remain in character the whole time, even when you're alone, which is enough to drive you mental. To be fair to you Sally, you did warn me about all that shit the first time we met, but for some reason I still had to work it all out for myself."

"Don't worry about it, sweetie, experience is the only way to truly learn, but it's high risk. That's why I came here today and I'm so delighted to hear what you're saying about your experiences. It shows the gamble has paid off, for now. But you're not out of the woods yet."

"What do you mean?"

"I hate to be the one to break it to you, but realising the futility of trying to define yourself by other people's standards is just the start. You've just backed yourself into a philosophical corner in which you're now forced to confront yourself as an individual. Don't get me wrong, you've done well to get even that far – many people never do – but now the hard work really starts."

"Fuck! I thought I was doing so well."

"You are, honestly. You've been trying to resolve your relationship with the outside world and maybe you've hit a bit of a wall, so I think it's time to take things back to first principles – in other words, some bottom-up thinking. Hopefully you've realised a top-down approach to exploring your social self just made things worse, which is really important. But I don't think you've spent much time on the bottom-up approach, am I right?"

"How would I know if I had?"

"Well, have you spent much time thinking about freedom of speech, due process and objective truth?"

"I guess not."

"OK, then listen carefully, because this is important stuff. Individuals still need to live in harmony with their environment and it just so happens that, over time, people have developed ground rules for doing just that. Just as top-down thinking relies on universal ideals, such as God, or equality of outcome, or saving the planet, bottom-up relies on underlying principles that everyone buys into. The most obvious example is the US Declaration of Independence, which says 'We hold these truths to be self-evident, that all men are created equal.' That is probably the single most important bottom-up principle, although I'd rather they'd said 'people' but such were the times. It was used as the foundational statement of possibly the best-known struggle against top-down control in history."

"I think I see where you're going with this – a principle is a hard starting point, while an ideal is an absolute end point – and you're saying principles are better than ideals."

"Definitely, because principles don't predetermine outcomes, they're just a set of tools designed to improve the chances of you working out the best outcome for your own circumstances. They guide the means but not the end. Ideals are all about the goal and implicitly justify any means in pursuit of it, which raises a couple of major issues. Firstly, if all people are created equal, who gets to decide which ideals are best? How can one person claim to be more right than everyone else? And secondly, if the ends justify the means, then any act can be excused in pursuit of the ideal? The starkest illustration of that was the behaviour of the Nazis. One of their ideals was genetic purity, so they justified almost any amount of atrocity in pursuit of it. So if we agree we should focus on principles then, in a social context, freedom of speech, due process and objective truth are the three most important ones."

"I can see why they're important, but it's not immediately obvious to me why they're so much more important than all other principles."

"It's because they're the three that do the most to protect the individual. If you don't have freedom of speech you're effectively excluded from public discussion, meaning you've no say in public matters. Also, any decision to censor must ultimately be taken by an individual who thinks they know better than everyone else which speech is undesirable. But how can we possibly be sure their view is the best one if all people are created equal? Even more important, however, is that censorship must always be accompanied by coercion, force and ultimately violence. This leads back to the core top-down problem of the ends justifying the means, and it's also a great illustration of how a top-down social approach always results in tyranny. The first thing anyone who has the power of censorship does is persecute people who say things they don't like."

"But we need some censorship, right? Didn't I read something about shouting fire in a crowded theatre and the resulting panic leading to physical harm? I mean I can't just walk around in the street telling people to attack you, can I? You need some protection, surely."

"Yes and those kinds of things are covered by the law. Any censorship beyond that required by law is arbitrary and therefore oppressive, because it will always favour those calling for the censorship. That's not to say your point about harmful speech isn't a good one, and it's usually the one adopted by the would-be censors. So let me say one more thing about the choice between freedom and safety, which underpins most social decisions. Since it's clear no individual is qualified to be the arbiter of good speech, we have to accept that we can't guarantee only good speech will exist, so the question is then what to do about bad speech. Again that's a subjective concept and attempting to define and police it will always end in tyranny, so the best we can hope for is mitigation. This is best done by individuals calling out the bad speech and explaining why they think it's bad. The result is public conversation, which is usually messy and often inconclusive, but it's the only non-tyrannical way of challenging speech you don't like."

"Yup, that all makes sense. But what if the law starts poking its nose into speech that doesn't incite violence or whatever? Or what if it starts messing with the definition of things like violence or harm, to ensure all the speech it doesn't like is defined that way?"

"I'm so pleased you asked that Dave, because it leads naturally to the other two principles. Due process describes the principle of everyone being entitled to the same legal protections regardless of who they are, but it extends to all civil processes and most closely represents the 'all people are created equal' principle."

"Kind of depends on how good a lawyer you can afford though, doesn't it?"

"Yes, which is probably the single biggest weakness of our system. But again, what can you do about it that wouldn't have oppressive outcomes? You can't ban lawyers entirely, you can't prevent some from being better than the others, and you can't prevent people from paying a premium for the best ones if they choose. All you can do is make public funds available for people who can't afford legal representation at all, but the big money is always going to be in the private sector, so that's where the best lawyers will go."

"But isn't that an argument against due process?"

"Not a good one when you consider the alternatives. If we didn't have due process then all legal judgments would just be made unilaterally by whoever has put themselves in charge. As well as the problems we already discussed about one individual's views having supremacy over everyone else's, all historical precedent says power will be used by whoever possesses it to bolster their position and persecute anyone they view as a threat. So it's a lot like the speech situation, nobody likes bad speech but since the process of identifying it and trying to get rid of it is so much more damaging than the speech itself, it's better not to try. Similarly, it's better to have unequal legal representation than none at all and it's better to have the legal system based on principles rather than ideals."

"It sounds like you're saying it's the least shit system."

"Pretty much. And that's generally the view of the other vital form of due process – democracy – which Churchill famously said is the worst form of government except for all other forms that have been tried from time to time. As we're currently seeing, the chances are democracy will put someone deeply flawed in charge of the country, but the good news is we only have to put up with them for a few years, during which they're subject to intense public scrutiny, another strong argument in favour of free speech, at the end of which we get to pass judgment on them in another general election. As Churchill implied, every time we've tried any other way of determining who runs the country it has ended in despotism. No leader ever wants to stand down and if they know the only threat to their power comes from rivals, or journalists, or whoever, they invariably imprison or kill however many they think necessary to remove the threat."

"But that's just a system of government isn't it? What's it got to do with due process?"

"Due process is what makes democracy the least shit type of government. It's founded on the principle that all people are created equal, so everyone gets a vote and each vote carries equal weight. To fully grasp what a powerful concept this is you just need to look at how long it took even relatively sophisticated countries like England to implement it. It's clearly the only fair way to run a free country, but it's also very inconvenient for the elite. It's to the credit of every democratic country that, at some point in its history, its elite chose to acknowledge that all people are equal by massively diluting their own power and influence. Democratic elections rely on strict enforcement of due process to protect the one-person-one-vote system and prevent electoral fraud, as well as the assumption that the losers concede defeat. That's the most important due process of all. All other aspects of democracy rest on that one principle because if the losers don't concede then the whole electoral process is negated."

"Fair enough. There was one more principle, wasn't there?"

"Yes, objective truth, which is the most fundamental of all. Let me ask you, how can you tell something is true?"

"I guess I usually count on the judgment of an expert. Either that, or if everyone else thinks it's true I assume it must be."

"That's totally reasonable. You can't be an expert on everything so you have to rely on others. But what if, one day, something everyone accepts as true doesn't feel right to you. How would you go about finding out for sure, one way or the other."

"I'd probably get on the internet and look for evidence. And I'd also speak to people I trust, even if they're not especially clued up on the matter, just to get their gut-feel take."

"Good! Evidence is the foundation of objective truth. It can be mathematically proven that two plus two equals four and anyone who tried to argue they equal five would quite rightly be dismissed."

"Everyone agrees that two plus two equals four though, don't they?"

"Yes but very few of them realise what a powerful position that puts them in. Try to imagine what it would be like to live in a country where the people in charge said it equals five. What would you do?"

"I'd tell them they were talking shit."

"What if it was illegal to challenge the people in charge?"

"Well I'd still know they were full of shit, I'd just be more careful about saying so."

"What if they had cameras, microphones and informants everywhere?"

"Then I wouldn't say it at all."

"What if one of the people in charge asked you what two plus two equals?"

"In that case I guess I'd have to say five, but I'd know I didn't mean it."

"What if you knew they were going to inject you with a truth drug and if you said four they would torture you?"

"Fuck, I see where you're going with this. That's hardcore, man. I would have to unlearn that two plus two equals four and totally convince myself it equals five, or else get tortured."

"So the people in charge would have such total control over you that they could not just make you lie, but make you totally believe the lie to the extent you no longer thought it was a lie. Once they control your mind they control you entirely and you have no individuality left whatsoever. That's why Orwell wrote 'Freedom is the freedom to say two plus two make four. If that is granted, all else follows.' He was referring more to freedom of speech, but if you change 'say' to 'know' it applies equally to objective truth.

"Any time someone tries to deny something you know to be objectively true, what they're actually trying to do is take away your most basic freedoms and strip you of all individual identity. Your ability to think independently and work things out for yourself relies entirely on the quest for objective truth and in its absence you're just a worker drone. You can only thrive as an individual in a society that respects the principles of freedom of speech, due process and objective truth. Where any of these are absent you have tyranny in which the people at the top control everyone else through force."

"And that, if I can get a word in edgeways, is why you need to take care of yourself," said Stein.

"What, so you can be the one who controls everyone else?" said Dalston.

"You know what, son, that's exactly how I used to think. I saw life as a zero-sum game in which people were either predators or prey. I basically got shat on for my whole childhood, so when I became an adult I swore nobody would do that to me ever again. I've been pretty successful but I've had to be a bit of a cunt in the process. Let me tell you a story: one day I told the lads to break the legs of some poor fucker who'd let me down and I could tell by the looks on their faces they thought I was out of order. I was on the verge of getting a new crew in just to kneecap my regular lot for their cheek, when I took a step back and asked myself what the fuck I was up to. What kind of a person needs to go around constantly kicking the shit out of everyone even slightly disagrees with them? I suddenly saw all the people I'd hurt as individuals, rather than threats, and realised what a psycho I'd become."

"Well I didn't want to say anything…"

"It's alright, I actually like being disagreed with now. You see I realised that needing to impose your will on everyone else is actually a sign of weakness, not strength. Real strength comes from being able to control yourself, not other people, and it's only people who are scared of confronting themselves that go around trying to change everyone else. If you're always comparing yourself to everyone else then there are two ways to do better. The most obvious way is to improve yourself, which is difficult and you might fail. The alternative is to try to bring everyone else down by inventing a set of rules that miraculously puts you at the top of the pile."

"That sounds a lot like the Felians."

"It certainly does, but if you think about it, it applies to almost every tribe. You think your Savages are any different? They define themselves in opposition to the Felians, which means all they need to do to feel good about themselves is shit on Felians. I realised that acting like I was the only geezer on earth was actually making me weaker. My crew was trying to tell me something in the only way they dared and, for once, I listened to them. When I told them to call off the beating and let the guy know it was his lucky day, the lads looked at me in a way they never had before, and it was because they respected me and not just my power. It was then I realised respect was what I'd been looking for all the time and I was confusing it with fear and obedience."

"That sounds quite ironic to me Frank. You'd spent all your life trying to be totally self reliant, but when push came to shove what you wanted most relied on other people."

"You're right to a certain extent. The thing about dealing with other people is it's dangerous. When you only have to look after numero uno everything's under control, but as soon as you introduce other punters into the equation it often goes Pete Tong. Life's all about balancing safety with freedom. The freer you want to be, the more you expose yourself to risk, so it's down to each individual to decide where the right balance is for them."

"Surely you can be free and safe though."

"I'm afraid not, son. Imagine you lived in a country where there were no laws, no taxes, no government – anarchy – that's about as free as it gets, right? But then you'd be spending half your time fending off predators and the rest of it just trying to get basic stuff done. So we willingly give up a bunch of freedom in the name of safety and a bunch of our cash in the name of efficiency. Politics is ultimately about how much of their own cash people are willing to put into the public pot and what they want in return, but nobody talks about how much freedom we're expected to give up. Be very wary of anyone who claims to care about your safety son, because I guarantee you what they really want to do is take away your freedom."

"Alright, that makes sense. Is that what you meant about me only being right to a certain extent; that you still need to be wary of other people?"

"Not quite, and that brings me to the last point I want to make before I'll shut up too," said Stein, shooting Pimienta a cheeky wink. "I've got to say the old girl has grown on me and she spoke a lot of sense just now, but I want to add one more thing: self-respect. I'll happily admit I hadn't realised how important being respected was to me, but I could still live without it so long as I respected myself. Ultimately, the only person on this earth you absolutely have to get on with is yourself, and if you don't then everything else falls to shit. I realised on the day I called the lads off that I didn't like the person I'd become and wanted to do something about it. Once you realise you can have a dialogue with yourself without being a nut-case, and you have a lot more control over yourself than you ever imagined, a whole load of new stuff becomes possible."

"Frank is spot on, I'm pleasantly surprised to say," said Davina. "I would just like to add another layer of Sally wisdom on top if that's OK.

"Go for it, love," said Stein.

"Sally spoke about top-down versus bottom-up ways of looking at society and I think it can equally be applied to how you view yourself within society. The top-down way is to derive your self-worth from the approval of others. Some people are very good at this and some even make a career out of it, such as politicians. But you can't please all the people all the time and, even if you could, when do you do stuff only for yourself? Most people who take that approach end up joining tribes where the rules are clearly defined. That's a classic example of giving up freedom for safety – they exchange the freedom to make their own choices for a simplified existence."

"OK I get that top-down thinking puts people in tribes and echo chambers where the choices are simplified, but what's the bottom-up view of yourself in society?" said Dalston.

"An individual, nothing more. You know those alphabet people who talk about the LGBTQIWXYZ+ community? The reason they keep having to add new letters, but still have a plus on the end, is that people keep identifying themselves in slightly different ways and they're chasing their tails trying to represent them all. I'm not a lesbian, no matter what Dev thinks, but if I was it wouldn't define me. Not even white, tall, straight, Aspergic, able-bodied, activist would define me because that would still ignore everything else. The basic unit of society is the individual and the bottom-up view of yourself within society is as an individual. You're Dave Dalston and don't let anyone tell you otherwise."

"But nobody's ever come up to me and said, 'you're not Dave Dalston'."

"Not in so many words, but you'll have encountered client-seekers regularly."

"That rings a bell. I think they mention it on Vertoo."

"I'm not at all surprised. It's a classic technique for stripping people of their individuality and accumulating power through unwitting proxies. It's very straightforward; you just identify a group of people that can be labelled vulnerable or disadvantaged or whatever and then unilaterally claim to represent them. In one easy move you rob that entire group of their agency and individuality, and at the same time elevate yourself both in terms of popular mandate and moral standing. In other words you instantly acquire power without having to earn it. It's entirely parasitic, bordering on vampiric."

"But client-seekers don't have real power do they?"

"What do you think power is, Dave? In a social context power is simply the ability to bend people to your will. Money is probably the simplest way to do that and being good-looking certainly helps, but what do you do if you're ugly and skint but still want people to do what you say? The answer for a lot of people is to adopt clients among the population. It confers power in two main ways: direct influence over the clients and the use of their cause as proxy moral authority. The ugly, skint person is now transformed into a leader and a champion of the oppressed. That's basically why politicians want to be elected isn't it? I guarantee you've been subject to the will of a client-seeker at some stage."

"Too fucking right, you can start with the goddamn Felians."

"Exactly, so my final point is similar to Frank's. You live in a society but you are an individual and should define yourself accordingly. Once you have a strong sense of yourself you can investigate which groups might be a good fit for you. But it doesn't work the other way around and you can never derive your own identity from other people."

"I think that's spot-on Davina and it certainly chimes with my recent experiences. What about you Dev? You've been pretty quiet, mate."

"To be honest I've been enjoying hearing all these pearls of wisdom, innit," said Dev. "The birds use some pretty fucking big words but they know what they're talking about. Listen man, it ain't rocket science, just take care of your shit and try not to be too much of a dick to everyone else, know what I mean. But life isn't as simple as that is it? There's just too many pricks out there trying to fuck you over so you need to give some of them a slap every now and then. People have got to know you're no push-over, but for that to happen you've got to know it yourself. Apart from that, so long as I've got the cash to tell anyone who's winding me up to go and fuck themselves, then I'm a free man and that's all that matters, you feel me."

"Well I'm really grateful to all of you. I had no right to expect you to turn up after the way I acted the other day and on top of that you've taken the time to give me some really great advice, so thanks a lot. But I think the most gratifying thing of all is seeing you all get on so well. It's almost like having the common challenge of helping me is all you needed to overcome your differences. If all four of you are pointing me in the same direction then that must be the right way to go."

Chapter 29 – Innovation

Politics, partying and penitence had left little time for the day job but, luckily, nobody at Clark's seemed to have seen his arrest video, so the obligatory claims of illness passed uncontested. His first day back in the office was dominated by what amounted to an ad hoc therapy session, in which all the managers and brokers associated with the Nice and Ethical Fund lamented how difficult their jobs had become.

Their main issue was that the nature of the election had caused the very concept of ethics to be called into question. The process had been so vitriolic and conducted in such bad faith that the wider public were disgusted with everyone involved. The media had taken to calling it the Vertoo Election as the two main protagonists both seemed to derive all their tactics from the internet warfare website. Consequently both of the election campaigns had been devoted almost entirely to denouncing every word and act committed by the other team in the most hysterical and hyperbolic manner possible.

Most election post-mortems were coming to the conclusion that Savage won only because he was able to produce more solid evidence of his opponent's depravity by virtue of them having been in power. As a result it seemed many votes were not so much for Savage but against FLAP, and as a result the public mood had darkened and distrust towards nearly all other prominent institutions was endemic. The opprobrium directed towards the financial sector had metastasised, with social media-driven boycotts of companies for even the slightest perceived moral transgression becoming commonplace. The usual technique of pandering to the grievance until the drama blew over was no longer effective, thanks to an atmosphere so febrile that corporate virtue-signalling had become an unpredictable minefield.

Even before the briefing concluded Dalston could see a clear business opportunity. The online mob had become the primary security threat to large companies and they lacked adequate defences. While trading in the ARSE derivative ceased soon after it was exposed on Whistleblower Hotline, he felt the underlying concept of laundering while-collar ordure by packaging it alongside commoditised corporate responsibility credentials remained sound. During his time as an Id Justice Warrior he had been acutely aware of the influence of certain campaigning organisations, which seemed to perform a similar role to credit-rating agencies but assessed moral rather than financial risk. An endorsement from one of those organisations provided a massive injection of moral capital, while their condemnation usually guaranteed the cancellation of the recipient from public life.

Inevitably there was a hierarchy among these groups, measured by their relative influence, and one called Safety Not Freedom had emerged as the most influential moral-rating agency. He concluded that if he could find a way of commoditising Safety Not Freedom endorsements, he could package them into a financial derivative that would perform the function of modern-day indulgences for corporate misdeeds. The derivative could be deployed in defence by any company finding itself in the crosshairs of the online mob.

Dalston pitched the idea to his manager, being sure to position it primarily as a way to encourage higher standards of ethical conduct in the corporate world, and it was well received. Asked for advice on persuading Safety Not Freedom to get on-board with the scheme, he noted such organisations always seem to struggle for funding and paying a commission for the sale of each financial product to which it gave the moral stamp of approval would provide it with valuable resources to expand its crusade against hatethink.

So not only would Clark's be improving corporate ethics through this new derivative, it would be directly contributing to a general reduction in harmful thought – a win-win. The final piece of the puzzle was to find a way of making the new product impossible for competitors to copy. As well as adding an exclusivity clause to the contract with Safety Not Freedom, Dalston got his company's legal team to draft a Byzantine set of rules, parameters and criteria effectively giving Clark's the sole power to determine which causes qualified for inclusion in the derivative. Thus the Corporate Offsetting Note was born.

Reputation management was a challenge the world's major companies had been throwing money at for decades, but the undermining of establishment media gatekeepers by the internet had resulted in diminishing returns from the usual technique of bribing them to write puff-pieces. The arrival of a commoditised form of corporate absolution was therefore greeted with unconstrained relief and exuberance by every company large enough to consider its ethical profile worth investing in. Within days demand for CONs had gone exponential.

Dalston advised the Nice and Ethical Fund team to restrict the supply and peg the price to the secondary market, which caused it to go through the roof. All other banks and financial institutions tried to sell their own corporate indulgences but a combination of first-mover advantage, Clark's new public reputation for high ethical standards and the continuing monogamy of Safety Not Freedom ensured the CON remained the blue-ribbon ethical product. Clark's competitors were left to compete in the cheaper tiers of the market, occupied by companies prepared to settle for a lower grade of absolution for their sins.

Clark's didn't emerge entirely unscathed from this competition, however, as the existence of different tiers of indulgence belatedly brought public attention to the entirely transactional nature of the whole product category. Eventually the business press started to question whether it was even possible for virtue to be bought and sold. Dalston knew the CON, like almost all novel financial derivatives, would generate its own boom and bust cycle, so he was determined to stash as much cash as he could while the going was good.

***

Since his own income was now directly linked to political currents, Dalston allowed himself to check back in with that world. He was disappointed to see the Id Card experiment was showing no signs of ending, as he had expected its abolition to be one of the first things Savage would do once in power. The reason for this became apparent in Savage's first interview since winning the election, on Iain Tegritie's radio show, which had taken place a week previously, so Dalston listened to it via a catch-up service.

"Welcome Prime Minister and congratulations on your election victory," said Tegritie. "It seems like only weeks ago that you were an obscure YouTuber. It has been quite the meteoric rise."

"Yes, although the same could be said of FLAP and Mary Onette," said Savage. "Literally nobody had heard of her before she became PM."

"That's a bit of an exaggeration but I take your point. A significant unintended consequence of the Id Card scheme has been the disruption of the established political order, propelling hitherto unknowns to positions of extreme prominence at bewildering speed."

"I would say it was long overdue. I mean, what has the establishment ever done for us? And while we're on the subject, on closer inspection you might find FLAP isn't quite the unheralded force you might imagine."

"What do you mean?"

"Well firstly it's headed up by Susan Percilious, who is about as establishment as it's possible to be. Secondly most of big business, the media and pretty much every public figure you can think of are behind them. But most importantly its political strategy is the same tried-and-tested formula of recruiting political clients the traditional political parties have always employed."

"You mean Felines and Simians?"

"Yes. Once you can create the impression that it's in the interests of at least half the country for you to be in power, winning elections is a piece of piss. It's almost like Percilious devised the whole Id Card scheme solely to create this political opportunity for herself. You should look into that Iain."

"I'll decide what I cover, thank you Mr Savage, and your suggestion is clearly preposterous. After all, FLAP just lost the election. How does your conspiracy theory account for that?"

"For the same reason all parties that try to manufacture a loyal electorate always fail in the end; their clientele is fickle and ungrateful. If your whole proposition is 'vote for me and I'll give you stuff,' then you create a situation where you have to constantly raise your level of bribery to maintain electoral loyalty. FLAP's great achievement was to squander such a strong position so quickly but, as is so often the case, they'll think their mistake was to be too moderate. That's why they're doubling down on the Felian rhetoric even now; they don't have a plan B."

"But haven't you done just the same as them by claiming to represent the Canines and Delphines?"

"No, I've done the opposite. I opposed the FLAP strategy and stood for everyone, regardless of faction. That's why I also got a significant number of Feline and Simian votes too. Only I know what's best for the whole country and the electorate clearly understands that."

"And yet I can't help noticing your entire cabinet and pretty much every person of significance in your administration is a Canine."

"Look, almost since the Id Card started I've been getting shit from Felines and Simians. I never even had any plans to get into politics but the factional apartheid created by FLAP forced my hand. Against all odds I managed to win an incredible victory so forgive me if I'm not tripping over myself to offer them top jobs straight away."

"Them?"

"Yeah, Felines and Simians. I don't remember seeing many Canines milling around FLAP HQ so let's see how they like it now the shoe's on the other foot."

"Didn't you just say you stand for everyone?"

"I do, but there has to be some reckoning for the injustices perpetrated by the Felians. You can't expect us to just forget all that and turn the other cheek. They were as oppressive as they could be while they had the power. Now it's our turn."

"Your turn to be oppressive?"

"Stop putting words in my mouth Iain. You wouldn't be any different if you were in my position. To the victor goes the spoils and I've got big plans for this country. But if I'm going to undo all the harm done by the Felians I can hardly have Felines and Simians involved in the process can I? Don't worry though, they'll be taken care of, but the Canines are calling the shots now."

"And the Delphines, surely."

"Yes, and the Delphines, of course."

It was clear to Dalston that Savage was already becoming corrupted by his new power, making him more convinced than ever he was better off out of politics entirely. But politics has a habit of sticking its nose into your life whether you like it or not and his job compelled him to further research how Savage was putting his power to use.

After the interview Savage faced heavy criticism for his antagonistic attitude towards Felines and Simians, especially since it ran contrary to his earlier unifying rhetoric. In an apparent bid to repair the damage he made a point of peppering his administration with members of non-Canine factions, while still being careful not to compromise the factional purity of his inner circle.

Having put out that fire, he turned his attention to the project intended to define his premiership: wresting power from ideologically possessed public institutions. Wholesale transfactionalisation of those institutions wasn't a viable option in the short term so Savage decided instead to investigate ways of bypassing them, eventually concluding this could be done via the YouChoose app. It had already been shown that a system of incentives and sanctions deployed through the app was very effective at getting people to vote, so why couldn't its role be expanded to encourage other types of behaviour?

The first set of initiatives he put into place involved a system of micro-incentives using artificial intelligence to mine the YouChoose database in order to anticipate people's needs. This enabled the app to present offers, vouchers, etc, tailored to the individual and at their time of greatest need, thus making the process of political bribery far more efficient.

The scheme was well received but equivalent attempts to introduce negative incentives in the form of micro-fines were complete failures as they just resulted in people uninstalling the app. This was a major blow as negative incentives were a big part of Savage's plan to sideline the loathed police. Having established the effectiveness of micro-bribes, it then occurred to him people could be incentivised to do the policing themselves. YouChoose started introducing rewards for 'public order intelligence,' which varied according to how useful the information was. A viral campaign targeted at children and teenagers labelled #snitchinisbitchin was especially successful and before long the government had an army of youthful informants at its disposal.

Only after this intermediate step had been taken was Savage able to introduce a punitive element to YouChoose. He phased out the micro-bribes in favour of a new Social Standing system, in which people were granted merits and demerits depending on their behaviour. Much of this could be calculated automatically by tracking things like voting records, philanthropic activities and minor crimes. For the self-policing system to be most effective the rewards for citizen informants ('Good Neighbours' as they were referred to on YouChoose) needed to be as generous as possible. Conversely the demerits imposed for being denounced by a Good Neighbour had to be an order of magnitude greater than those for regular misdemeanours. The net total of a person's merits and demerits determined their Social Standing – a simple index that dynamically updated and was made public via the YouChoose site.

Incentivising people to denounce each other struck Dalston as dangerous and wrong. It reminded him of the perverse incentive structure used to encourage the police to victimise Canines while FLAP was in power. The difference this time was that the few institutional checks and balances still restraining the police did not extend to the general populace, so there was no protection from vexatious or malicious accusations. Furthermore, since any accusation was automatically fed into the YouChoose algorithm, those accused were effectively guilty until proven innocent through the byzantine appeals process.

Even the most generous appraisal of what Savage had done couldn't fail to conclude that in his desperation to sideline the police, he had replaced them with mob rule. Dalston was pleased to see Iain Tegritie had more recently challenged Savage on this very matter, so he streamed that interview too.

"So, Prime Minister, you think you can run the country by smartphone app do you?" opened Tegritie.

"No." said Savage.

"Well you certainly seem to be concentrating a lot of power in YouChoose."

"YouChoose is just a tool designed to empower individuals. Previously the people's democratic voice was only heard once every four or five years and then only for a crude binary choice between continuity and change. I was one of many people in the country who found that state of affairs unacceptable, which is why I was delighted when FLAP first introduced direct democracy. Unfortunately they immediately abused it by trying to rig the election in their favour and it was only by switching from social media to the YouChoose app that we were able to ensure the people's will was properly represented."

"Whether it does or not remains to be seen, but the change clearly benefited you."

"Only because I was offering what the people wanted. They were sick of the feeble pretence at choice presented by the old way of doing things. They knew no politician ever intended to deliver on any of their election promises, but in the absence of an alternative most of them trudged to the polling station anyway to select the person and party they found least repellent. As much as people may have voted for me, they also voted to scrap the old system."

"You keep talking about 'the people,' but they're fundamentally ill-qualified to make such decisions. The big problem with your direct democracy system, Prime Minister, is that it shamefully relinquishes responsibility. Even if we accept electoral reform was overdue, it doesn't justify extending the same mechanism to running the country. You are in charge, you are the government, it should be you making the important decisions, not some white van man sitting in a pub."

"Did you know the very first democracy, in Ancient Greece, was a direct democracy, Iain? The definition of democracy is 'rule by the people,' so surely I'm just being true to that."

"As you well know, ours is a representative democracy, in which people vote for their representatives, then leave them to it. There's a reason for that."

"I'm sure there are loads of reasons, but how good are any of them? As for leaving us to it, I'd say that's the opposite of what your profession does."

"But surely you agree that, in a democracy, power needs to be held to account."

"Yes, but why should it only be journalists who do it? The only people who hold power to account in between general elections are the very same people who are dependent on access to politicians to do their jobs. Seems like a massive conflict of interest to me."

"I'll overlook the slight on my profession and simply ask you this: how can you trust the unqualified, uneducated, unenlightened man on the street to make the correct decision?

"Why should I trust them any less than corrupt politicians and biased journalists? But you pose an important question, which brings us back to YouChoose and the incentive schemes built into it. Essentially we're using nudge theory to help people arrive at the correct decisions."

"Which implies you don't trust them to make the right decision without being nudged."

"It's a matter of education, Iain. Not everyone is as privileged as you and, as a consequence, many people lack the knowledge required to make informed choices. It's clearly not practical to try to re-educate the entire population, so instead we simply give them access to the most pertinent information as and when they need it."

"I get your point about democracy but not many people are qualified, or even capable, of making important decisions. Countries are like families; parents pretend to let the kids have their say and then do what they think is best regardless. If you let kids run the house then everything would collapse! Which brings me back to your new policy, specifically #snitchinisbitchin. How's that going?

"We're delighted. Who better to keep an eye on everyone than our pure, innocent children?"

"So it's working then? Crime is down as a result?"

"Well, reported crime spiked initially because the kids were flagging up many unnoticed crimes through their YouChoose Junior accounts. But the great news is they soon fell as people adapted their behaviour, which is to say they stopped committing crimes."

"Last I heard crime rates were once more on the rise, though."

"It seems some children have taken it upon themselves to be somewhat creative in their interpretation of criminal behaviour in order to fraudulently claim rewards. So we created another scheme to incentivise kids to report on other kids they suspect of abusing the system."

"Presumably you then need a further set of kids to keep an eye on those kids, and so on. Sounds fun. One other problem would seem to present itself, however, which is what to do with the first set of kids who informed on their parents."

"What do you mean?"

"Well, their parents are criminals now aren't they? Even if they're not imprisoned, surely that raises serious questions about their suitability as guardians of their children."

"Are you suggesting we take the kids away from their parents?"

"I'm just saying this seems like a great opportunity to optimise the way our children are raised. A great reset, if you like. I think it's time the state stepped in and took charge of raising those kids clearly being badly served by sub-standard parents."

"Hmm. As you know I don't really trust the state to do anything, but I also have to agree with your point about protecting children. I tell you what, I'll have my app people look into ways we could raise those kids remotely through the app. Judging by their response to #snitchinisbitchin, I reckon kids would be really receptive to an expansion of their relationship with YouChoose."

"On behalf of the country I thank you for that but your plans may be overtaken by events. Can I ask what the government's strategy is for dealing with the novel Diademvirus outbreak?"

"Of course we are monitoring the situation very closely, but our experts believe there's no need to panic."

"That won't offer much reassurance to people seeing reports of overwhelmed hospitals and thousands of deaths. Surely you should lock down the whole country just to be safe."

"Come on Iain, I'm not about to let the country grind to a halt just to prevent a few people getting a cold."

"I sincerely hope you don't come to regret that position."

Chapter 30 – Indoctrination

Dalston made a mental note to look into the Diademvirus as he wasn't at all reassured by Savage's complacent downplaying of this potential plague. But first, all the talk of raising kids by smartphone reminded him to catch up with what Ray Payshus had doing at Hill Street School. He fired up Netflix and was pleased to see the fly-on-the-wall documentary series was still running. The latest episode continued from Payshus's experiment with micro-currency in a bid to find novel ways to incentivise and control the children. He had partially abandoned it after extensive speculation in a currency developed by a neighbouring school resulted in some of his own pupils losing such large amounts of real-world money that he was forced to bail them out from his own pocket.

While proven totally correct in assuming the kids would be motivated by the prospect of accumulating wealth, Payshus soon realised only around half of them sought to do so by performing the tasks he wanted to incentivise. The rest of the kids participated entirely in a secondary economy created by trading the Hill currency. These were split evenly into the alpha kids, who the political leaders employed for security, and an underclass that accepted payments from one of the pupil cabals in return for their loyalty when it came to major political events such as school parliament elections.

When one cabal came up with the idea of a social safety net for disadvantaged pupils, the other two soon recognised this as a very effective way to buy loyalty, so they copied it. There then followed an arms race as each cabal tried to politically elevate themselves by raising the height of their social safety net. It was obvious this would lead to the financial ruin of all three as they promised far more in social payments then they could raise in revenue, so Payshus had to admit defeat and go back to the drawing board when it came to designing systems to optimise outcomes at the school. It occurred to him that, rather than trying to reinvent the wheel, he should instead have studied the domestic circumstances of his students. Parents' evenings provided a great opportunity for him to do just that.

The common factor among the parents of the most under-achieving kids was their apparent indifference to schooling on the whole. They were loosely divided into two groups. The first treated their child's poor performance as a deliberate provocation, rather than a problem to be addressed. Upon being given the latest poor report they tended to round on the sheepish child, saying helpful things like "I hope you're proud of yourself," and "I always said you were a useless little shit." The second group consisted of strangely passive and fatalistic parents who usually had a cowed, meek air about them and tended to start by apologising on behalf of their child as soon as they sat down. They would present feeble mitigation for their failure to push their child and often clung to the best grade like a piece of driftwood floating in a sea of failure.

In stark contrast what the highest achieving kids had in common was the commitment, engagement and love of their parents. Just as important was a healthy balance in their relationships, striking the right balance between discipline and support. The child needed to be sufficiently wary of their parents to check their behaviour, but still receive the encouragement needed to be confident and motivated. Payshus concluded the most effective way of raising standards at the school was through the parents. He became fascinated by different parenting styles and their effect on the kids. Some just had malevolent parents and, sad though that was, he felt it was beyond his power to do anything about those situations, so he turned his attention to the parents he had classified as negligent but benign.

Reviewing his notes from the parents' evening, he sorted them into four sub-categories: weak, in denial, entitled, and compromised. Weak parents were mainly those who allowed their kids to walk all over them. They were afraid of confrontation and generally overwhelmed by the job of parenting. They knew they weren't doing a great job but seemed to lack either the tools or inclination to improve. There was some overlap between the weak parents and those in denial as they shared a disinclination to see their children as others did. But the denial-type parents were possessed by tribal instincts and unconditionally defended their kids regardless of the circumstances. Payshus concluded that, to those parents, the kids were proxy manifestations of their own egos and thus any criticism of the kid was, by definition, a criticism of them. It was therefore impossible for the parent to view the behaviour of the child objectively and they had an overwhelming psychological incentive to disregard their children's failings and weaknesses.

Denial parents in turn had some overlap with the entitled ones, in so much as they were the types most likely to counter-attack when their child was criticised. The main difference between them was that the entitled ones took any deficiency on the part of their child as evidence of systemic failure. Entitled parents tended to be the most politically engaged, always in the collectivist direction, and viewed the educational system through a political lens. This allowed them to not only inject their political agendas onto the school, for example positioning its failings as the result of negligence on the part of their political opponents, but to exonerate both their child and themselves from responsibility for underperformance and bad behaviour by blaming it on 'the system.'

The last category had some overlap with all the others, but was made distinct by the circumstances the parents found themselves in. Compromised parents were largely single mothers or mothers with unsupportive partners. These were people who, on the whole, seemed to be trying to do their best, but were still falling way short of the mark. This was usually due to having such extensive wage-earning and domestic commitments that their children were left unattended much of the time. Payshus found himself most intrigued by this parent group because he suspected just a minor improvement in their personal circumstances would allow them to fulfil their clear potential as parents. But in the absence of outside intervention Payshus couldn't see any way improvement could happen.

While this ad hoc categorisation helped him organise his thoughts, something about it rankled. He realised what it was when he found himself trying to further sub-categorise the compromised parents along sex, marital status, occupation and even personality-type lines. It wasn't that he found it difficult to do, but it became increasingly obvious it was a total waste of time. No matter how precisely he was able to categorise an individual, he was no closer to coming up with concrete measures to help them.

Before long he came to recognise the whole thing as a quintessential exercise in procrastination, through which he could kid himself he was making progress. It did serve one important purpose, which was to highlight that the process of continual sub-categorisation can only ever conclude at one point: the individual. A given parent wasn't a nervous single mother who worked in sales, she was Victoria, or Raveena, or Beatriz. Payshus realised the only way he could really understand the unique needs of his pupil's parents was to talk to them. So he set up a new parents' evening discuss their needs rather than those of their children.

He felt he learnt more from those conversations than he had from weeks of tinkering, experimenting and social engineering. All the parents of the good kids turned up, of course, because they were so invested in them. Some were competitive, others constantly concerned about their child's future and many were simply loving, but one thing they all seemed to have in common was a stable domestic situation. They weren't necessarily wealthy, although they did tend to be better off than average, and not all of them were a nuclear family, but he got a sense they were relatively content with their lives. They were no less busy and still had to contend with the kinds of obstacles and setbacks everyone does, but they seemed to be more or less on top of things. In turn that meant they had spare time and emotional capacity to devote to their children, which Payshus realised was a significant factor in their behaviour and performance.

Conversely those who left the most negative impression at the previous parents' evening seemed permanently angry. They complained about having to come to the school in the first place and then moaned about what they saw as the futility of the exercise. When Payshus explained he was trying to learn how to best support them as parents he was advised the best way would be for him to dramatically improve his performance as head teacher, especially when it came to their own children. Even the gentlest enquiries about their personal circumstances were met with hostility and most of them treated any such questioning as an attempt to dodge his own professional responsibilities.

He realised most of the worst parents were scared of their own inadequacies and how their children reflected them, but chose to counter their fear with aggression. It was as if they were at war with themselves, a conflict that sapped their energy and goodwill, leaving little for their kids. Payshus concluded he was very unlikely to have any positive direct influence on those parents so he kept meetings with them as brief as possible, to allow more time for those with whom he felt he had a chance of making a difference.

The children of compromised parents were largely left to bring themselves up and thus free to make bad choices. Clearly Payshus couldn't simply bankroll those parents, but he decided the most efficient way of helping them would be to buy them some time through extra facilities at the school. As well as a Breakfast Club and After School Club, he also created a Common Room for each year group in which kids were free just to socialise if they wanted to. The only catch was that the same rules applied as during the regular school day, which meant no phones or electronic devices were allowed to be used at the clubs. This not only meant kids tended to pursue studies and hobbies rather than just stare at the wall, it also forced them to develop their core social skills. In addition to the clubs Payshus also introduced school buses, a crèche and a room full of workstations to allow parents to work remotely from the school if they needed to.

His most radical invention, however, was the creation of the Extracurricular Day. Payshus had come to the conclusion that the obsession with the National Curriculum and GCSE grades was detrimental to the kids. In the name of jostling for a place on school league tables, they were continually force-fed chunks of obscure information in the hope they could regurgitate them on demand. He decided they needed a break from the GCSE production line and devoted every Friday entirely to the pursuit of non-academic interests. Some alternative studies, such as philosophy, civics, journalism or auto mechanics, took place within the school, but the really clever bit involved letting the kids take part in off-site activities if they chose to.

To enable this, Payshus devised a voucher system to allow the kids to pay for approved activities, such as courses, museum visits, activity groups and sports clubs, via their school smartphone app. However, the kids had to maintain an acceptable level of behaviour for the preceding week on a 'three strikes and you're out' basis. Pupils who received three strikes were stripped of their Extracurricular Day for the week, which reverted instead to a regular school day. These experiments were still in their early stages but there were signs they were having a much more profoundly positive effect than anything Payshus had tried previously. By giving pupils more support, while at the same time granting them individual agency, he felt he had finally found a winning formula.

Chapter 31 – Interrelations

There was no more putting it off. Political turmoil and impending pestilence gave Dalston a renewed sense of urgency about patching things up with his family. He hadn't got around to asking for specific advice on the matter when he last met Davina and Dev as the conversation had taken a broader philosophical turn, so he got in touch with them again and arranged to meet at the Black Heart in Camden. Davina was the first to arrive so he brought her up to speed on his state of mind following the difficult meetings with his parents and his ex. He confided he was frustrated because he felt so close to being able to repair those relationships but had somehow stumbled at the final hurdle.

"OK, let's start with your parents," said Davina. "It sounds like your Mum is pretty hard work, why do you think she's like that?"

"Just her personality I guess," said Dalston.

"Maybe, but do you really think she's incapable of being any other way? There must have been times when you were growing up when she was softer."

"No doubt, but I'm fucked if I can remember many of them. I mean, I don't remember my childhood being unhappy, but as I got older the dynamic between my parents definitely started to bother me."

"In what way?"

"Mainly the way she would snap at my Dad and he would just take it, or even worse apologise and pander to her. It was just pathetic to watch and made me despise them both when it happened."

"Your Mum for being overbearing and your Dad for being weak?"

"Exactly."

"Do you think it would have been any easier to take if the roles had been reversed and your Dad was the overbearing one?"

"That's a good question. It would have been different; I would have felt more protective than contemptuous towards a victimised Mum and, on the flip side, once I got big enough I could have physically protected her by telling my Dad to pick on someone his own size."

"It sounds like those more traditional sex roles would have at least been easier to get your head around."

"Yes, I guess so."

"And it seems your Dad's apparent weakness bothers you more because he's a man."

"You may well be onto something there and maybe that's why I'm extra twitchy with my Mum. I could be compensating for my Dad, not just because I can't stand to see him pushed about, but because I'm effectively trying to lend him the self-respect he doesn't seem to be able to find within himself."

"Sounds very plausible but let me ask you one more thing: has it ever occurred to you that your Dad does have strength and self-respect, but is willingly submissive to your Mum?"

"No. Why the fuck would he do that?"

"Well, there could be a number of reasons. He might have decided to let her have some small victories while still asserting himself over big stuff you don't see. Or maybe he just loves her and wants her to be happy."

"She doesn't look very god damn happy to me."

"As you said earlier, coming to terms with the fact some people are just fundamentally different from you can be tricky."

"So bitching and moaning about everything and being a general pain in the arse makes her happy?"

"Maybe, but that's your characterisation of her behaviour. Perhaps she doesn't see it the same way and just thinks she's being strong and decisive."

"Are you saying I've just got a problem with strong women, then?"

"I like to think I'm quite strong and you certainly seemed to have a problem with me when we first met. In fact I reckon I've got a pretty good idea how you acted during your dinner with Mel on the basis of my experience of you. But you came around fairly quickly when you realised I wasn't going to stand for any of your bullshit, so maybe you're more like your Dad than you like to admit and you're actually provoking women into standing up to you."

"Jesus fucking Christ, Davina, that's below the belt."

"The truth hurts, Dave."

At that moment Dev Sharma turned up and joined them.

"A'ight. What's the emergency then?" he said.

Dalston brought him up to speed, including the conversation he and Davina just had.

"Birds are a fucking liability, bruv," said Dev, prompting a snort of derision from Davina. "No offense, love, I don't mean it in a bad way. I'm just saying everything gets a fuck of a lot more complicated when birds are involved, hear what I'm saying."

"Like what?" said Davina.

"Like the stuff Dave was just chatting about, innit. His Mum wrecks his head, then his ex wrecks his head too. Who needs that shit, man?"

"I assume that's a rhetorical question but it was actually a good one. Why do you think Dave is persisting with trying to develop those relationships when the women are such 'liabilities,' as you put it?"

"I don't know – I'm assuming he still fancies his ex and maybe he feels guilty about his Mum or something. Whatever, he needs to snap out of it sharpish."

"Why?"

"Because it's wrecking his head, like I keep saying, innit."

"So your answer to difficult situations is just to run away from them is it?"

"I don't fucking run away from nothing," Dev retorted.

"Well that's it, though, isn't it Dev?" said Dalston. "Yes they're doing my head in but I don't want to run away because they mean a lot to me."

"OK, fair enough. Look, I was partly just fucking about, because you both seemed so serious. But this is your Mother and the woman you love we're talking about, so of course they're going to do your head in and of course, if you're a real man, you've got to deal with it."

"God, you can be a prick sometimes," laughed Davina.

"You love it, you slag," Dev smiled.

"So, if you two have finished flirting, how about some answers?" said Dalston.

"I reckon Davina might have a point about strong women," said Dev. "Look, I like to wear the trousers, yeah, but if I'm honest I get bored if a bird can't stand up for herself. So I've got my cock telling me to be a caveman and my head telling me it's never going to last with someone I don't respect. I guess my heart's the bit in the middle deciding which one to listen to, you get me."

"And there you have Freudian theory, Dev Sharma style," said Davina. "His cock is the id, driving him to conquer and dominate. His brain is the superego, seeking peace and harmony, and his heart is the ego, mediating between the two."

"I like it," Dalston mused.

"But you don't really have the option of ignoring these two women just because your id can't be bothered with the hassle, as they're central parts of your life and I can see you love them both. So it looks like your choices are limited. The dilemma isn't whether or not you should keep trying to improve your relationships with them, but how best to do it."

"Yeah you're fucking stuck with them, blad," said Dev. "The thing is, respect is a two-way thing. You want to be around birds you respect, but you want them to respect you back. And then, on top of that, they want the same too, you get me."

"Damn, Dev, that's a lot of respect," said Dalston.

"You think I'm fucking around here, fam? This is no laughing matter. Look if I've got no time for some random bitch I'll treat her like I want and if she puts up with it that just proves my fucking point. But once you start giving a fuck everything changes. You're going to meet, like, five or six women, max, you properly care about in your life. They're fucking hard to find and if you don't make the most of it when you do that makes you an idiot in my book, you hear what I'm saying."

"But how do I know if Mel is one of those?"

"I'm not going to lie to you geezer, you're starting to wind me up now. What do you think we're chatting about right now? Why the fuck are we all here? Apart from your Mum this whole thing is about Mel, you dopey twat. What's the matter with you? Not only is she the mother of your daughter, but I reckon she's probably the only bird you've ever properly fallen for. You were going on about this Prosecca for a while, but I've seen that shit a million times. Now she's legged it, it's not her you're chasing around the gaff is it? I don't think you've mentioned her once."

"Hmm, you do have a point."

"Of course I fucking do. So can we cut to the chase and work out how you're going to convince Mel you're not a complete bellend?"

"I agree with you to a point, Dev," said Davina. "But you're still treating Mel like some kind of mark, to be coerced into falling for a con. This isn't about flowers and boxes of chocolates and cheap chat-up lines; we're not 16 years old for God's sake. If you ask me this is less about convincing Mel you're not a bellend and more about convincing yourself. Truly loving someone means wanting the best for them, even at cost to yourself. If you want the best for Mel, and also want to be in her life, then you better make damn sure you're the best man for the job."

"So are you saying that as long as I focus on trying to be the man Mel deserves, then everything else should sort itself out?" said Dalston.

"Yes!" said Davina and Dev, simultaneously.

***

Dalston opted to address the parent situation first. He decided not to call them in advance this time and surprise them at home. As he approached their house the curtains in their street-facing living room window were open. Derek was sitting, as ever, in his easy chair watching TV. Dalston was happy to just watch him from afar for a few minutes and contemplate the decades of shared history they had. This man had watched over him from the day he was born and offered nothing but unconditional love and support. He felt tears welling in his eyes when he considered how little his Dad had asked in return, and how he had not even given that in recent years.

With her usual impeccable timing, Doris chose that moment to enter the room and Dalston felt his lips purse with tension. If she dared to even raise her voice to his Dad, he would be in there like a shot. What happened next, however, completely blind-sided him. Doris crouched down beside the chair, her eye-level below Derek's, and appeared to ask him a question, to which he responded with a simple nod. She then left the room and came back with a steaming bowl on a tray. Doris set the tray down on an over-chair table she had positioned directly in front of Derek, tucked a napkin into his shirt collar and then took a spoonful of the soup. She blew gently on the spoon until she judged it to be cool enough to eat and put it to her husband's mouth.

It took around ten minutes for Derek to consume the entire bowl in this manner, including several instances in which Doris had to mop dribbled soup from Derek's mouth and chin. Not once did Dalston see any sign of impatience from his Mum, let alone a rebuke. Once the meal was complete Doris picked up the tray, the two of them had another brief conversation during which Derek stared gratefully into his wife's eyes throughout, and then she left the room. Dalston could see how much the simple gesture of being helped with his dinner contented his Dad and, by the time Derek had nodded off into a light sleep, he was wiping tears from his own cheeks.

Once he composed himself Dalston approached the house and knocked on the door. Doris opened it, raised her eyebrows, and simply remarked, "Oh, you again is it?" He knew his Mum too well to be surprised by the contrast between the tenderness he witnessed minutes ago and the frosty greeting he had just received. At any other time he would probably have still been triggered into returning fire with an unfriendly rhetorical question of his own, but now Doris's defensive demeanour just served to reinforce the conclusion that a lot of his Mum's antisocial behaviour stemmed from her insecure need to get her retaliation in first. She was never going to change and he now understood the only way to move past it was to let her win.

Suddenly he saw his Dad's lifelong capitulation in a whole new light; it wasn't weakness, quite the opposite. In granting his wife regular superficial victories, Derek ensured the two of them wasted as little time as possible on petty conflict and were able to get the best from each other. Doris had a flaw in her personality, which required her to feel she was on top in a given social interaction. Once she did, her deeper personality was free to emerge from hiding, secure in the knowledge it wasn't likely to be hurt.

"Is it OK if I come in?" said Dalston.

"Yes, I suppose so," said Doris. "Your father is, as ever, in the living room."

"Actually Mum, I'd really like to speak to you alone first, if that's alright."

"I see. Well after the way you behaved the last time you were here, David, I'm not sure it is."

"Please Mum, it's not what you think. I don't want to fight, just talk."

"OK, in you come then. Let's go to the kitchen. Would you like a cup of tea?"

"That would be great, thanks."

There was an awkward silence as the kettle boiled and tea bags were placed into cups

"Mum, I want to apologise," said Dalston once the ceremony was complete.

"Really? What on earth for?" said Doris, wrong-footed by the direction the conversation had taken.

"For everything. For fighting you all the time, for assuming the worst of you, for taking you for granted, for not keeping in touch, for being an ungrateful little shit. In summary, for being a bad son."

There was a pause as Doris struggled to process the unprecedented turn of events.

"I don't know what to say," she said, eventually.

"You don't have to say anything Mum. But I hope you'll accept my apology. I've been doing a lot of thinking and asked myself: since you are one of the people I love most in the world, why the hell don't I have a better relationship with you? It was only when I realised the fault was entirely mine that the solution presented itself, so I promise to do better from now on if you'll give me the chance."

"Of course Davey," said Doris, retrieving the term of endearment from decades in cold storage. "I just want us to get on, you know."

"Yes I do," he replied tenderly. "How about a hug then?"

Mother and son embraced for the first time either of them could remember. As soon as they parted both looked away, blinked repeatedly and sniffed. Doris broke the ice, saying "Your father will be wondering where I've got to."

"Can I bring his tea to him?"

"Yes, that would be lovely."

Derek's face lit up when he saw the surprise source of his evening cuppa, but he also couldn't hide his anxiety when his son and wife entered the room together. Instinctively Dalston put his arms around his Mum's shoulders and she responded by resting her head on his chest. The look of relief and pleasure on Derek's face was one both Dalston and his Mum knew they would never forget. The three of them spent the rest of the evening watching TV and exchanging small talk. It was great.

Chapter 32 – Inflection

After repairing his relationship with his Mum Dalston felt anything was possible. He was determined not become complacent this time, however, and still wasn't sure what form a reconciliation with Mel might take. He was sure he wanted more than to merely placate her enough to be granted access to Amy, but he was also struggling to visualise a classic, happy-families scenario. As much as anything he just felt the two of them had unfinished business. His toes curled at the prospect of once-a-fortnight weekend access to Amy, featuring trips to the zoo and silent restaurant meals. Significant improvement on the current situation though that would represent, it wasn't real parenting as far as he was concerned, which involved both of them working together for the good of the child.

Maybe that was what he wanted, a partnership. He had always thought it wanky and politically correct to refer to the person you were with as your 'partner,' but when he considered it as a concept, rather than just a label, it made a lot more sense. When he and Mel were still together, after Amy was born, he pretty much left all the boring parts of dealing with the baby to Mel. Shitty nappies didn't do it for him and he even viewed bath time as a chaotic pain in the arse. His idea of being a great Dad at the time was to stay in a couple of nights a week and watch telly with Amy on his lap.

Consequently he also wasn't much of a partner to Mel. He figured his job was to supply half of the genetic material and all of the day-to-day cash, and anything extra was a bonus. Even at the time he knew he could have done lots more, but he frankly couldn't be bothered. Now, having been starved of Amy's company for so long, he wanted to earn it back and knew that meant doing the hard yards. The nappy changing window was closed, but Amy still needed a Dad and he was now desperate to be one more than just in name. While that was impossible without a dramatic improvement in his relationship with Mel, it wasn't the only reason he was so keen on reconciliation.

While he had fallen for plenty of women before and after Mel, she was probably the only one he had thought of as a friend as well. He had never seen the point of platonic relationships, reasoning that if you liked a woman, you might as well sleep with her. Of course it was never as simple as that, with mutual expectations going through the roof, everyone concerned losing their sense of humour and, as he had just experienced with Prosecca, there was always a power imbalance. Some of the tension unique to relationships, as opposed to friendships, was because one person was usually more invested in the whole enterprise than the other. That didn't happen with mates, you never feel a mate is more or less into your friendship than you are, you just accept them for what they are and get on with having a laugh together.

Before Amy was born they seemed to have the balance just about right. Their respective levels of emotional investment seemed fairly equal and, on the whole, they did a great job of combining being great mates with an excellent sex life. That all changed when Amy came along as Mel seemed obsessed with her and she was all they ever spoke about. How can you spend literally a whole evening discussing baby shit, or lack of? And as for sex, forget it. Dalston understood that pushing out a sprog was no walk in the park, but Mel had put him on iron rations for months, which he considered an injustice. So he started to get restless, began flirting with other women, one thing led to another and before he knew it, he was out the door.

At the time he thought his behaviour, while out of order, was the result of severe provocation and thus at least understandable, so he was genuinely surprised at Mel's response when he shared this point of view with her. Only when it was too late, and she was refusing any contact with him, did he start trying to look at the situation from her perspective. When Amy was born Mel needed him to be her best friend more than ever. Friends help each other out and do so unconditionally, but not only was Dalston unhelpful when it came to the day-to-day grind of caring for an infant, he betrayed Mel when he felt insufficiently rewarded for what little he did. He didn't think of it as a betrayal at the time, of course, in fact he could remember justifying sleeping around to himself as a way of taking pressure off her.

It was clear to him now how terrible his attitude was after Amy was born. But while he was now desperate for a chance to redeem himself, he still drew the line at total capitulation. He might be prick, but Mel wasn't perfect, and he remembered feeling she was making no effort to meet him halfway. That didn't necessarily mean more sex, but she became obsessed with the baby to the extent that the rest of the world ceased to exist unless it had a part to play in fulfilling Amy's immediate needs. He recalled being given very few opportunities to demonstrate his parenting competence before he was relegated, first to lackey, then to nuisance, and ultimately to liability. All decisions concerning Amy, however trivial, were made unilaterally by Mel and the slightest dissent was suppressed with savage put-downs or spectacular histrionics.

Then, to add insult to injury, his lack of input into the process was often used as further evidence against him in future disputes. But that was all ancient history, surely, and what mattered was the present and the future. Determined to sell the concept to Mel, he got in touch with her and was relieved to hear she was receptive to meeting again. Amy, she said, was having a sleep-over at a friend's house, so Mel suggested he come to their flat, but also to make sure he didn't bring any funny ideas with him.

He was surprised to hear a barking when he rang the doorbell, followed by Mel's futile pleas for the source of the din to restrain itself. When she opened the door the barking became punctuated with judgmental growls from a mid-sized dog that looked capable of delivering a painful bite but little more. Only when Mel welcomed Dalston into the house with a peck on the cheek did the pugnacious pooch dial its protective histrionics down to DEFCON 2. They walked through to the kitchen, where Mel made them some tea, then moved to the living room where they sat opposite each other. After a minute or two more of tail-quivering hostility, the dog curled up at Mel's feet such that he was able to keep an uninterrupted eye on Dalston, about whom the hound clearly still harboured deep suspicions.

"So, how's it going?" opened Mel.

"Pretty well actually," he replied. "I patched things up with my Mum."

"Wow, that's amazing Dave, I'm so happy to hear it. Is she finally mellowing with age?"

"Not as far as I can tell, the change is mine. I started looking at our relationship from a fresh perspective, realised one of us had to give ground, and concluded it could only be me."

"Doesn't sound like you at all, no offence."

"Yeah, the really funny thing is it was my Dad who inspired me to do it. For so many years I hated the way he pandered to my Mum and tolerated her shitty behaviour, assuming it was because he was too weak to stand up to her. But then I saw something that made me understand Dad's indulgence was born of love, not fear. Mum needs to wear the trousers and can be a right bitch when her status is threatened, but once she doesn't feel she's in a pissing competition she chills the fuck out. So I just apologised to her for everything and next thing I knew we were having a hug and it was happy families all round."

"I see, very interesting," said Mel, leaning back in her chair and crossing her arms, causing the dog to sit up and give her a concerned stare.

"Yes, it was," said Dalston oblivious to Mel's defensive body language. "And I want to apologise to you too."

"To make me feel like I'm wearing the trousers?"

"Erm. no," he said, belatedly recognising how his parental anecdote could have been interpreted. "I'm being serious now Mel, I promise. Please just hear me out. I've been doing a lot of thinking about how things went with us, especially after Amy was born, and I realise now how little I did to help. Even though I loved Amy more than anything, for some reason I treated the whole thing as a massive pain in the arse most of the time. I think I was just too immature to understand what being a parent really meant and I was really slow to get my head around it all."

Mel stated at him in silence for a long time, as if she was trying to work out how sincere he was being.

"You were an unforgivable prick, Dave," she said at last. "Just when I needed you most you totally let me down. I was vulnerable, tired, hormonal and dependent on you and you threw it all back in my face. Your apology is far too little, too late, I'm afraid."

"I know, you're right," he replied. "I can't explain it and I don't defend the person I was then."

"I mean, it was like you were getting some kind of sadistic pleasure out of being as much of a dick as possible. I had to do everything myself, you only got involved with Amy when you felt like it and whenever I needed a bit of affection you were nowhere to be seen."

"Again, I can only apologise," he said, starting to feel exasperated. "But it does take two to tango, Mel."

"You what? Are you saying it was all my fault?"

"No, certainly not, but I am saying that when a relationship fails it can't only be down to one person."

"You are something else, you know that? You can't even apologize properly! You come in here, banging on about turning over a new leaf and even had me half convinced for a sec. Then, when I don't swoon gratefully into your arms straight away, the facade drops and you start acting like you were the victim all along. I think you'd better just fuck off."

The dog reacted to their raised voices by barking at Dalston, but Mel had hold of its collar and stroked its head. After a short hiatus it calmed down once more.

"There it is, it's all coming back to me now," Dalston said. "That's what you always do: take the worst possible interpretation of what I say, pad it out with some extra stuff you just made up, and then use it as proof that I'm a piece of shit. Well I'm going nowhere and if that little cunt's got a problem with it, then it had better be ready for a fucking good punting."

"Fido is not a little cunt and how the fuck else am I supposed to interpret it then?" said Mel in a calm but quivering tone.

"You say you had to do everything yourself, but do you remember what a fucking control freak you were? Any time I tried to help you used to cut me down. So, yes, I admit it, after a while I just thought 'fuck this'."

"Oh, poor little Davey, did I hurt your feelings? Was Melly Welly a bit too strict? Diddums."

"Thank you for proving my fucking point better than I ever could."

There was another extended pause as Mel looked out of the window for a bit, apparently lost in thought.

"OK, that was out of order," she said. "And I'm even willing to admit I may have a bit of an escalation problem, but you knew that before Amy was born. The bloke's job when a child is born is to be the faithful sidekick to the woman and help her in whatever way she needs. It's the one time in your fucking lives when you're not holding all the cards and it doesn't even last very long. Surely it's not too much to ask for you to be an emotional punch bag for a few weeks."

"No, it's not, and I wish more than anything I'd had the maturity to be that for you, but I didn't. All I can do is beg you to give me the chance to be the friend and father now I should have been all along."

"Why should I believe you when you've let me down so many times before?"

Now it was Dalston's turn to pause. It was a good question. Further pleading would prove nothing, so he racked his brains for anything to demonstrate his sincerity.

"Do you remember, when Amy was born, they gave her to me straight away to hold while they tended to you?"

"Yes, of course."

"When I looked down at that little pink grub and tried to warm up her tiny blue hands I had the most profound sense of purpose and belonging I'd ever experienced. That baby girl was totally vulnerable and dependent on me, and I knew immediately I would do anything to protect her. It was a calling of a kind no job ever came close to. My biggest mistake was forgetting that feeling when things got tricky."

Suddenly Dalston viewed Fido in a new light. They hadn't got off to a great start, but he was beginning to develop a grudging respect for the beast. Its life was simple; all it had to do was protect its family and in return it got food, shelter, love and a sense of meaning. That was it, no worrying about money, no trying to be cool, if a shagging opportunity presented itself when they were out for a walk, then great, but if not, no worries. The little fleabag didn't even need to think about clothes, for fuck's sake.

One thing was clear however; if anyone messed with Mel or Amy, that dog wouldn't hesitate to put his life on the line to protect them. He respected that and, more importantly, was grateful the two of them had this devoted ally. Then it struck him the real reason he wanted a second chance with Mel was to be the man of the house. Not in some, old-school, macho way, well not entirely, anyway. Yes, he wanted to be a protector and provider, but also a Dad, best friend and part of the team.

"I was selfish," he said, "and I'm not just talking about me being lazy or unfaithful. I didn't stop to consider what it takes to make a family and what my contribution needed to be. Being a proper parent is fucking difficult and I bottled it at the first sign of hassle. I'm ashamed of that Mel, and nothing I say can undo it, but you've got to believe me when I say the one thing in the world I want now is to be the father and partner I should have been back then."

Mel stared at him long and hard. "I think you actually mean it," she said, eventually, "and you might even believe it too. But these are still just words, Dave, and I need more. On the other hand there's no way you can prove yourself if I don't give you a shot, so I'm prepared to meet you in the middle. When Amy gets home I'll speak to her and, if she's keen, the three of us can get together. OK?"

"Thank you so much Mel, that's all I'm asking for," he said, his face split by a broad grin. "I fucking guarantee you won't regret this."

"Well that remains to be seen, young man, and don't start getting ideas about the sleeping arrangements either. That's a different conversation entirely, and one I can't be arsed to have right now, so don't chuck the box of tissues away just yet."

Dalston realised sleeping with Mel hadn't entered his mind once during the whole conversation. Furthermore, he realised he was totally relaxed about it. There were so many more important things he wanted and he would gladly live a life of monastic asceticism to achieve even half of them. If a bit of hanky-panky happened to be on offer occasionally then great, but it was way down his list of priorities.

"I think I'd better quit while I'm ahead," he said. "Believe it or not, Mel, I'm trying to learn when to shut the fuck up and I think this is a golden opportunity to do just that."

He stood up, prompting Fido to spring to his feet, followed by Mel.

"You've made a good start, mate," she said. "I've seldom regretted shutting the fuck up."

She walked him to the door and opened it. "I'll be in touch," she said, and gave him a warm hug. Fido got up on his hind legs and rested one forepaw on each of them while they were hugging, but there was no growling and it just seemed to want to join in the hug. Dalston even risked a tentative pat on the head, from which he was pleasantly surprised to emerge unscathed. He said goodbye to Mel and left with a spring in his step and a song in his heart.

The next day, when he calculated she was likely to be home, he messaged Amy, ostensibly to tell her about his visit but also to get indirect feedback.

Hello baby, did you speak to Mummy?

Im so happy you and mummy met up again daddy

So am I and I really enjoyed our chat

I think mummy did too she looked different than the last time and said you were going to visit me soon YAY!!!

The message was accompanied by a litany of emojis, the meaning of half of which Dalston couldn't even guess at, but which seemed to be very positive.

I know, amazing isn't it?

I'm sure Mummy wont mind if we have a video call seeing as we're meeting up soon is that ok

Great, I'll call you now.

Amy was in her room, lying on her front on her bed. There was music playing in the background which, to Dalston's surprise, sounded like classical piano.

"There you are," said Dalston when her smiling face appeared on the screen of his phone. "Is this the sort of thing you're listening to now?"

"Good to see you Daddy, especially after the last time," she said, once more ignoring his enquiry into her music tastes.

"Ah, yes. I'm really sorry about that. I was going through a difficult time but that's no excuse."

"Don't worry Daddy, we all make mistakes and it was good to see you, even though there was that window between us."

"Thank you for being so understanding. And the funny thing is, even though I should never have found myself in that police station, it did get me thinking about what I need to do to bring me back to you again, and it seemed to work, didn't it?"

"Yes it did. I guess sometimes good things happen when you least expect it, don't they?"

The music in the background had switched and sounded much more like rock now, albeit with a pure female voice singing over it. Dalston could briefly make out some lyrics: *...my spirit's sleeping somewhere cold, until you find it there and lead, it, back...* In addition he started to hear raised voices in the background. They sounded angry, which upset him to such an extent that words failed him.

"Are you OK Daddy?" asked Amy, reading his expression. "Did I say something wrong?"

"No, no, not at all," he replied, recovering his composure. "It's just that I can hear shouting."

"Oh, yes, that's Mummy and her boyfriend," said Amy, with a derisory emphasis on the final word and a roll of her eyes. "They do that a lot these days."

That revelation completely took the wind out of him. It had never occurred to him Mel might have another man in her life and she had certainly given no indication of it in either of their recent meetings. Having received this bombshell he was relieved to hear her other relationship was already under strain. Maybe that's why she had never mentioned him, because she was already thinking of dumping him. Perhaps seeing her old flame was what tipped her over the edge. Yes, that must be it. She thought she was happy with this new bloke until she saw Dalston again and remembered how good things could be. Of course she couldn't make it easy for him, and he didn't expect her to, but at the end of the day they had something special and she knew it.

No sooner had he settled on that optimistic narrative than it struck him Mel and Amy had a strange man in their house who sounded aggressive and unpleasant. He wanted to intervene and protect them, chucking the prick out of the house in the process and beating the shit out of him if he had a problem with it. But since they lived miles away and the danger was imminent, there was little he could do. Dalston had never felt so frustrated and impotent.

"I'm really worried Amy, I don't know what this person is capable of," he said. "Has he ever, you know, done more than shout at Mummy?

"What do you mean?"

"Has he ever hit either of you?"

"Oh no, definitely not. Don't worry Daddy, they just disagree a lot and when they do I come to my room, shut the door and play music."

At that moment he heard the now familiar sound of Fido's barking, followed by a male voice telling it to shut up and then a shouted reproach from Mel. Dalston's reappraisal of Fido was now complete, regarding him now as a paragon among dogs, a combination of Lassie, the Littlest Hobo and Hooch. As for the boyfriend, he was dead meat.

"What's his name Amy?"

"Iain," said Amy.

"Have I ever met him?

"Yes, I think you did a radio interview with him. He sounds Scottish."

This time the gut-shot hit him so hard he almost puked.

"Iain Tegritie?" he gasped. "Mummy's boyfriend is Iain Tegritie?"

"That's right," said Amy. "I don't really like him, to be honest. I wish you were here instead."

Chapter 33 – Isolation

Iain. Fucking. Tegritie. Dalston ended the video call soon after Amy's revelation as he was incapable of coherent thought, let alone speech. Hours later, he still didn't know what to feel about it. First he had to contend with the fact Mel had a boyfriend at all. Not too long ago it would have been a matter of near indifference to him, but now they were so close to reconciliation it felt like a betrayal, almost an infidelity. He knew he had no right to feel that way, especially when juxtaposed with his own eclectic love life, but he did nonetheless. That Mel had apparently gone out of her way to conceal this relationship during their recent meetings only fuelled his indignation. Did she think it was some trifling detail not worth bothering the father of her daughter with? Or was the aim to secure some kind of irreversible concession before dropping her bombshell?

Even worse was the possibility she pitied him and wanted to spare him the humiliation of being replaced by a big shot, which it most certainly was. Just as he had allowed himself to start falling for Mel all over again, even going so far as to dump a world-class girlfriend, he was brutally put back in his place, the insult compounded by the person in question. If Mel had just shacked up with, say, a game show host or a celebrity chef, Dalston could have discounted it as an experiment, to be abandoned once the irredeemable superficiality of the bloke became apparent. But Tegritie was a heavyweight, a man of influence and substance. He wasn't getting any younger but he was exceptionally smart, sharp and charismatic. How could he possibly compete?

He lunged despairingly at his drinks cabinet and swigged from the first thing to hand. This was bad. Why the hell would Mel even consider getting back with a loser like him when she had won the heart of Iain Fucking Tegritie? They had been arguing though, Dalston reminded himself, desperately clutching at any and all straws. If his radio persona was anything to go by then Tegritie must be a right stroppy twat to be around. Maybe, by some amazing fluke, what he happened to overhear was the ending of their relationship. Yes, that was it, Mel had asked Tegritie to visit her to tell him it was all over. Thanks for everything, it's not you it's me, I just have unfinished business, you'll always have a special place in my heart. Bad luck Iain, you can't win 'em all, mate. Some things just aren't meant to be, plenty more fish in the sea, and so on. Then it occurred to him it was time for Tegritie's radio show and he couldn't resist tuning in hoping to hear the defeat of rejection in his voice. Once more he was interviewing the Prime Minister, Dick Savage.

"As you know, Prime Minister, the Diademvirus has already spread to Europe and the first cases are being reported in the UK," said Tegritie in a tone indistinguishable from his previous hundred broadcasts, to Dalston's crushing disappointment. "What is the government doing to protect its citizens?"

"Thank you Iain," said Savage. "I am, of course, being kept fully up to date on the latest developments regarding the spread of the Diademvirus and nothing is more important to me than public safety. Every indication tells us this virus is only dangerous to the most vulnerable people, so we're doing everything in our power to protect them."

"And just leaving everyone else to die in the streets?"

"No. As I said, our expert advice is that the risk is very low to everyone bar the immunocompromised."

"Would one of those so-called experts be your own special advisor, Hugh Jenicks?"

"We have several committees containing experts in areas ranging from virology to epidemiology to national security."

"But Jenicks is the only one you really listen to, isn't he? Was it he who persuaded you to use the country as a giant medical experiment? To roll the dice on millions of lives?"

"I don't know why you've decided Hugh is the story here, Iain. This policy has been arrived at after exhaustive consultation with multiple governmental departments and is clearly the optimal response to the emerging situation."

"Maybe it's because tomorrow's papers are all leading with allegations about Mr Jenicks being seen leaving a house of ill-repute last night."

"I'm aware of that story, but I don't see what it has to do with the government's response to the Diademvirus."

"So you admit the stories are true?"

"No."

"Well you're not denying them."

"I have made no comment on them at all."

"Do you deny them?"

"No."

"So they're true!"

"I don't know."

"But you won't deny them, will you?"

"I can neither confirm nor deny the allegations."

"Well I think that scandalous."

"What, you think it scandalous I won't deny something I know nothing about?"

"No, the fact that you've come to this interview so ill-prepared is what's completely unacceptable."

"I came to this interview prepared to talk about the national emergency presented by the Diademvirus. Instead you insist on asking me about what one of my advisors may or may not have been up to over the weekend, and I'm the one who's out of order?"

"OK, since you insist on sidestepping the matter of Mr Jenicks' ability to do his job..."

"Hold on, I haven't done that. Please withdraw your statement."

"I will do no such thing!"

"OK, I'm off then."

There were various clicking and rustling sounds as Savage apparently attempted to disentangle himself from the recording equipment and leave the studio. Eventually Tegritie intervened.

"Really, Prime Minister, there's no need for this."

"Not if you withdraw your statement, there isn't."

"I stand by everything I've said."

"Then you can stand alone, you fucking prick."

The rustling continued.

"OK, I withdraw the statement," said Tegritie through gritted teeth, apparently at the urging of his producer.

"Which statement?" said Savage, amid yet more microphone buffeting, clearly antagonised and determined to maximise Tegritie's humiliation.

"That you sidestepped the matter of Mr Jenicks' ability to do his job. I didn't ask you a direct question on the matter, but now I will. In the light of the recent allegations, does he still have your confidence?"

"Yes."

"Why?"

"Coz."

"That's not much of an explanation."

"Well it's the only one you're fucking getting, so I suggest you either move on or call an end to this farce."

"I think your reluctance to more fully address the matter shows a serious misjudging of the public mood."

"How would you know?"

"It's my job to know."

"So you've been chatting to 'the public' about this have you?"

"No, but it's clear to anyone who's been paying attention..."

"I've been paying attention – I am the goddamn Prime Minister after all – and it's not clear to me."

"Well then you'll just have to take my word for it."

"No I don't."

"So have you been talking to 'the public' then?"

"No, but I don't claim to have been. What you're doing, Tegritie, is fabricating the illusion of consensus to add weight to your own personal position. For God's sake man, own your shit, don't take the coward's route of pretending you're just passing a memo on from the rest of the country."

"Fine. Back to the Diademvirus crisis then. We recently conducted an extensive survey, asking people what they think our national response should be, and the overwhelming majority said we should shut everything down to prevent its spread. Despite that, you insist on letting this plague run through the country unchecked. Why?"

"I appreciate their concern, but they don't have the information I do."

"Perhaps you could share it then."

"That would be completely impractical, as you well know. I have been elected to make decisions on the country's behalf and I've made my decision on the best approach to the Diademvirus."

"Prime Minister, people are dying! All over the country the citizens you claim to care so much about are losing mothers, fathers, grandparents, siblings, even children. Every second you delay the nationwide quarantine that anyone with half a brain can see you'll have to declare sooner or later means more blood on your hands. This isn't just some stupid policy decision, it's literally life or death. What the hell gives you the right to be so cavalier with the nation's health?"

"As I keep saying, it's my job…"

"It's not your job to murder pensioners and children," Tegritie interrupted. "It's your job to protect the country and you're refusing to do so, presumably on the insistence of the person really in charge, Hugh Jenicks."

"That's not true," said Savage, a plaintive, faltering tone creeping into his tone for the first time during the interview.

"Our survey says otherwise. Why are you so determined to go against the will of the nation at this critical time?"

"Your survey is just that, it can hardly be treated as a democratic mandate."

"Fair enough. If only we had a mechanism for consulting the country on critical matters."

Savage realised he had walked into a trap.

"I presume you're referring to YouChoose," said Savage.

"Of course," said Tegritie. "If you're so sure the country is behind you on this decision, then why not confirm it once and for all?"

"It would be pointless, the decision has been made."

"There you have it, people of Britain," said Tegritie, now addressing his audience directly. "Your Prime Minister is so insecure and drunk on power that even on this most critical of matters he no longer thinks your opinion is worthy of consideration."

"Hold on, I never said that," said Savage, now firmly on the back foot and desperate to regain control of the interview. "On reflection it does seem appropriate to take the nation's pulse on this matter. So I hereby pledge to convene an emergency cabinet meeting with a view to presenting our Diademvirus policy on YouChoose for public approval.

"Prime Minister Savage, the nation thanks you," said Tegritie before abruptly ending the interview.

While disappointed to have heard no reduction in Tegritie's arrogance, Dalston was even more concerned to learn the government was already contemplating restricting civil liberties to an extent not seen since World War

Two. Furthermore the decision to do so was apparently the result of the Prime Minister being browbeaten, live on air, into rethinking a painstakingly developed policy. Savage's instincts about the virus could be wrong, but surely it wasn't for some random journalist to make that call on behalf of the whole country.

On the other hand, the only firm concession Tegritie had extracted from Savage was a commitment to consider consulting the electorate on the matter. While that seemed fair enough, the UK's media was united in a state of total hysteria about the Diademvirus, seeking to out-do each other in their fear-mongering. Dalston had to assume public opinion would lean towards whichever course of action was most likely to protect them from this lethal blight.

The next day it was announced public policy on the Diademvirus threat would be decided by a national referendum conducted on YouChoose. The choice would be a binary one: continue with the course of action proposed by the government or place the entire country into quarantine. The latter choice meant ensuring no British individual came into direct contact with anyone other than the people they were living with. That meant the closure of all physical shops, offices and public transport, and a permanent ban on anyone leaving the house barring exceptional circumstances, which had yet to be defined.

In the days leading up to the referendum the media gave itself over entirely to campaigning for its desired outcome, which in nearly all cases was the full lockdown. At the forefront of this campaign was Tegritie himself, who had now taken to starting his radio show with a monologue portending the imminent apocalypse, followed by interviews with prominent campaigners for a more moderate response to the crisis, in which he hectored them with rhetorical questions, baseless accusations and the full spectrum of character assassinations.

In stark contrast most individual commentators on the internet were opposed to a full lockdown on the grounds it would wreck the economy, trample on civil liberties and generally do far more harm than even the very worst-case scenario associated with the virus. Most media now devoted significant time and resources to naming and shaming those commentators deemed most 'problematic,' which included lobbying the platform on which their heresy was published to sever all contact with them or be found guilty by association.

The Diademvirus crisis also marked the resurgence of FLAP, which not only identified an opportunity to damage its political nemesis but saw the binary referendum as a chance to back the winning horse and thus win back the trust of the UK public. Susan Percilious was universally lauded by the media as the only one who stood between the country and catastrophe, with some even going so far as to frame the public health crisis as some kind of divine retribution for voting her out of office. Her interviews with Tegritie were especially unctuous affairs, filled with mutual admiration and softball questions.

By the time of the referendum the combined efforts of the media, FLAP and countless pseudo-political organisations, of which Safety Not Freedom was the most prominent, had worked the nation into a froth of anxiety and dread. The result was a landslide result in favour of a full lockdown. Since Savage had publicly pledged to honour the outcome, he had no choice but to impose the will of the state on its citizens to an extent not seen for a century.

Dalston looked around his flat and contemplated being stuck there for weeks on end. His mind soon turned to more practical matters as he mulled the implications of takeaways being closed. He took an inventory of his fridge and cupboards and concluded that even if he was willing to subsist on sauces, condiments and preserves alone, he had less than a week's worth of food in the flat. Gingerly he crept towards his drinks cabinet and slowly opened one of its doors. The briefest of glimpses confirmed his worst fears and, pausing only to recite soothing mantras to himself, he sprinted out of the house towards the soon-to-be-closed shops.

The local supermarket had already been stripped bare of bog-roll and pasta and Dalston couldn't begin to guess what people might do with their resulting stockpiles. There was also a serious shortage of cooking lager, but the posher booze had been largely spared the ravages of the hoarding hordes, so he bought as much of it as he could transport home. The freezer cabinets were pillaged too, but some exotic crustaceans remained, which he claimed. Satisfied he wasn't going to starve to death and even if he did, he would at least be drunk when it happened, he retreated back to his flat, uncorked a 2010 Clos de Tart, and contemplated what had suddenly become of the world.

Halfway into the Burgundy he decided there was no point in worrying about what he couldn't control and concluded there were worse things than being stuck at home on full pay. He could catch up on some reading, and some sleep for that matter. His life had been absolutely hectic for months and he was long overdue a wind-down. Furthermore, recent experience had taught him leaving the house tended to end badly, so staying in seemed the most sensible thing to do.

Knowing he didn't have to venture outside also changed Dalston's perception of other broader societal matters. The factional conflict he had been immersed in for so long now seemed utterly trivial. Whether the Felines or the Canines had the upper hand at a given moment was of no consequence to his personal circumstances whatsoever. Neither of them was more likely than the other to supply him with food, drink or bog-roll and he had long ago relinquished his tribal investment in the Canines. After all, what had they ever done for him?

The front door was thus transformed from a gateway to the world to a barrier designed to keep it out. His flat evolved from a place to crash and bring back women, to a spiritual oasis in a desert of anxiety. It was still gutting that he wasn't going to be able to see Amy for a while yet, but maybe it was for the best. A few weeks of rest and recuperation were probably what he needed to smooth out his remaining rough edges and ensure he could present the best version of himself when he emerged. On the whole, he concluded, this lockdown was probably for the best. Better safe than sorry.

Chapter 34 – Inquiry

Having made his peace with the lockdown Dalston decided the rest of the world needed to be brought up to speed on his thinking. His followings on both Twitter and Facebook had diminished considerably since his Id Justice Warrior days so, after venturing a few unrequited posts of his own, he took to commenting on established threads. At first he limited himself to making brief affirmative comments on posts in support of the lockdown but, except for a few likes, they offered little gratification. Then he stumbled across a Facebook discussion praising Iain Tegritie for cajoling Savage into putting the matter of the lockdown to the people. He reflexively pushed back and called Tegritie's motives and character into question.

Soon he was being denounced from all sides. One person even called him racist, even though nothing to do with race, ethnicity or even complexion had come near the conversation. Dalston's protestations that he was happier than anyone about the lockdown were deemed far too little, too late, given the atrocity of his previous statements, and he was brutally reminded why he hadn't visited the site for weeks. A similar pattern played out on Twitter, where engagement was minimal until he pushed back on a banal piece of consensus, at which point he was set upon by one of the roving lynch mobs that policed the platform. This brief return to the social media quagmire just served to cement his sense that isolation was the best policy, so he uninstalled both apps and vowed never to return.

So, apart from occasional instant message enquiries into Amy's welfare, Dalston's only contact with the outside world was limited to TV, radio, and the non-social internet. It had been a while since he listened to a Jive Robin podcast and this seemed like a great opportunity to do some catching up. One of Robin's most popular guests was the public intellectual Phil O'Soficle and they spent much of their recent podcast discussing the difficulty of discerning truth.

"What do you think truth is?" asked O'Soficle.

"Well, it's when something is totally right, isn't it?" said Robin.

"Sure, but how do you know when something is totally right?"

"A combination of things I guess. Sometimes it's just because you've been taught it, or you just assume it's right because everyone else does too. Other times you weigh up the evidence yourself and make a call, and some things you just know, like a kind of gut feel or instinct."

"There's nothing wrong with any of those, but can you see how a degree of subjectivity comes into all of them, whether it's your environment or your perspective or just your personality?"

"I guess…"

"Let's go through them. Nobody knows everything, so your perception of truth will be influenced by what you've chosen to learn and how you learnt it. You'll then be influenced by other people who invest their own experiences, perspectives and biases in their teachings. The only way those can be avoided is by learning from primary experience, but that's very time consuming. Even then you can only view a thing from one perspective at a time and then there's the intrinsic uncertainty principle. So a lot of learning is a matter of exploring consensus, much of which we simply absorb from our environment. Most civics, such as the rule of law, democracy, common courtesy and so on fall into that category.

"Makes sense."

"But every now and then consensus is challenged and somebody calls bullshit, what do you do then? Is it, then, no longer consensus and if so is the matter in question no longer a fact? A consensus is essentially just the view of the majority, but does that mean the minority, no matter how large, is automatically wrong? Then we have your gut feel, how much validity does that have? You might feel something really strongly, but what do you do when faced by someone who feels the opposite with equal strength – fight it out? That's not very civilised is it? And what about when you get a new gut feel, do you just go with it, or do you stop to make sure it's correct? If it's the latter then you're back to square one – having to educate yourself or ask other people's views."

"Jesus Christ, dude, how the fuck does anyone know anything then?"

"Good question. The answer is there are very few absolute, objective truths and nearly all of them involve maths. It's not just consensus that two plus two equals four, it can be empirically proven, but most things can't be put into an equation. There's applied maths, but as you move up through the sciences things get harder to prove. We know for sure that water freezes when cold and evaporates when hot, but even the metrics we use to measure hot and cold are arbitrary. Once you get into the study of people, the so-called social sciences, pretty much everything is subjective and there are almost no absolutes. Look at how often expert sociologists or economists get things wrong and don't even get me started on politicians.

"Languages have certain absolutes, but they're man-made and constantly evolve. In some ways the purest truth comes from the arts, precisely because it's impossible to define them. A genuine piece of art claims to be nothing more than the true expression of an individual's creativity at a given moment. The short answer to your question is we know very few things for sure, so we have to pick what to study more deeply, what to just take on faith, what to ignore, and what to challenge."

"You seem to be saying nearly everything is subjective."

"Pretty much, which is why dogma is so futile and destructive. When you insist you're absolutely right, you're saying anyone who even slightly deviates from your position – i.e. everyone else – is wrong, and what happens when dogmas collide? Conflict. If everyone could just come to terms with the fact that they don't know much and what little they do know is mainly just an opinion, then the world would be a much more peaceful place."

"That's a really good point, man. Why do you think they don't?"

"Ego. It's as simple as that. We all have a desperate need to feel special. In its purest form it's just survival instinct. We don't judge animals for being egocentric, because we expect no better and it's literally survival of the fittest for them. But among civilised humans, where nearly everyone has enough to survive, this instinct still exists and therefore expresses itself in bizarre ways. Even that would be much less of a problem if our psychology wasn't so varied."

"So we've got a bunch of people who all need to feel special, but part of that involves shitting on everyone else. No wonder we're all so fucked up."

"Yes, but we do also share some balancing instincts with animals, such as nurturing and cooperation. Look at a wolf pack, for example, they all look out for each other because even they understand enlightened self-interest. The reason civilisation exists is we've learned life is better if we all try to get along, even if we think everyone else is barking mad. You can't go around fighting anyone you slightly disagree with, if only because you'd never get anything else done, so we tolerate each other most of the time."

"You say that, but it doesn't look like there has been much tolerance going on recently."

"You noticed that, did you? The social contract I just outlined is a very fragile one, you see, and our country decided to try to reinvent the wheel. This happens far more often than it should because people refuse to learn from history. A functional society is a bit like a chemical reaction in equilibrium, which has bounced from extreme to extreme, but eventually settled on a relatively stable middle ground. By implementing the Id Card scheme, the UK government shook up that social chemistry to see if a better equilibrium would result."

"That seems to summarise it quite well, but let's not forget why they did it – things were pretty fucked up."

"Yes, I call it the tower of sticking plasters. The Id Card scheme was created as a sticking plaster over the problems created by the Payshus insurrection, which was ultimately caused by excessive pandering to bankers after the sub-prime crisis, which in turn was made possible by low interest rates used to cushion the economic blow from the dotcom bubble bursting, and so on. To stretch the metaphor, each sticking plaster on the tower is less effective than the last, so it needs to be bigger. None of them properly deal with the underlying injury and serve only to numb the pain for a little while longer, while the wound continues to fester.

"The Id Card was presented as a carefully considered scientific proposition but it was actually a last desperate throw of the dice, born of panic about the insurrection. It served the purpose of making the government look like it was doing something, placated the protesters and generally did a great job of distracting everyone. But I think we can all agree by now it not only failed to resolve the matter of 'destructive greed' but it made a bunch of other stuff worse."

"I do agree, but I'm not sure why."

"My view is it created a new set of social tensions and gave them no time to reach equilibrium. We already had a bunch of them to do with class, race, sex, et cetera, but we had been dealing with those for thousands of years. So while lots of people were still unhappy about them, those varied grievances were at least in some kind of sustainable balance. Throw in a fresh lot and everyone is on edge because they don't know the new rules and they're afraid of coming out the wrong side of the shake-up."

"That's so true. It's one thing facing a specific threat and trying to work out what to do about it, but it's a whole lot scarier when you've got no idea which direction the danger is coming from."

"Yes, and the really insidious thing about it was that the government chose to divide us according to personality, rather than visible characteristics like race and sex. When you can't tell what team a person is on it makes you instinctively distrust them. They might as well have split us into red, blue, yellow and green teams randomly. Except each team they created had, by definition, a primary personality trait. It was inevitable, given the cause of the experiment, that the group largely defined by greed would become the scapegoats and, to a lesser extent, that the anxious people would ally with the aggressive ones to protect themselves."

"When you put it like that it seems obvious, why didn't they see it coming?"

"Hindsight is always 20-20, as they say, but mainly they failed to take account of the law of unintended consequences. They were so focused on the upside of what they wanted to do – taking the greedy people out of banking – they didn't think about the downsides. There also seems to have been a healthy dose of 'not invented here' syndrome, which was probably what led them to make up their own psychometrics instead of using tried and tested ones."

"Do you have any examples of those?"

"They could have gone with the Big Five personality traits or even Myers-Briggs. They would probably have identified certain personality types prevalent in banking and possibly even singled out more specific types most inclined to take excessive risk. I must stress, however, that if they had executed the scheme the way they did, even using different psychometrics, the outcome would probably have been roughly the same. Their biggest mistake wasn't so much in trying to identify buccaneering personality types, although that in itself is futile because surely all successful financiers are above average risk takers anyway. No, I would say all of the most catastrophic unintended consequences directly resulted from the decision to make the results of the test public and force people to be defined by them. The resulting factionalism was so inevitable I genuinely wonder whether it was unintentional at all."

"That's hard to argue with. If you force people into teams you can't be surprised when they end up competing with each other. It was probably also inevitable that two of them would gang up to try to form a majority and thus call the shots. If they'd done it with the big five we probably would have seen the neuroticism, conscientious and extraversion groups gang up on the agreeable and open ones. In fact there's probably a lot of direct correlation between Id Card categories and Big Five ones, don't you think?"

"I can't believe I hadn't thought about it but yes, you're probably right. Canine/extraversion, Feline/neuroticism, Simian/conscientiousness and Delphine/agreeableness. That just leaves openness, which is probably strongest among Delphines too. But that exercise also reminds me of another set of psychological categories they missed out: moral tastes. There are six of those: caring, fairness, authority, loyalty, purity and liberty and they don't necessarily overlap with the Big Five at all."

"Why is that, if they're also psychometrics?

"I must confess I haven't given that nearly as much thought as I should have either. The best I can manage for now is that the Big Five is a good descriptor of how people think, but moral tastes say more about their instincts and the strength of their visceral reactions to things. For example many political activists probably score highly on authority, loyalty and purity, but not so much on caring, fairness and liberty, because they're prepared to do whatever it takes to help their side win and are most inclined to believe the ends justify the means."

"So maybe we should have tested everyone's moral tastes and made sure those people hardwired towards fanaticism weren't put in charge of important shit."

"Sure, but the law of unintended consequences would have applied there too, because the fanatics are probably also the most productive when given the right incentives, so just locking them in a cupboard would have been wasteful and would probably have resulted in them becoming even more radicalised. But above all you have the problem that comes with all attempts at social engineering, which is they ultimately come down to one person's value judgments. If the person calling the shots was a Canine, or high in extraversion, or inclined towards authority, then they probably would have ended up favouring other people hardwired in a similar way because that's how the ego works – we are more warmly disposed towards people who are like us."

"OK, so let's recap. Hardly anything is absolutely true, everything outside of maths is subjective, everyone is fucked up, but in endlessly different ways, and any attempt to sort them out just makes things worse. Give me something to cling to, dude!"

"There are no easy answers, my friend. The best starting point is to only worry about what you can control, which is very little. You can, however, control yourself, probably more than you think, so start there. That's not to say you should be selfish, just that you're no good to anyone else until you get your own house in order. It's a bit like airplane emergency guidance telling parents to put their own oxygen masks on before trying to help their kids, because if they pass out then the whole family is screwed anyway.

"That's a great platform for seeking truth, right there. If you trust your own intuition, motives and intellect then you should gather as many sources as possible and make your own mind up. The result won't be absolute truth, but it will be as close to it as you can reasonably expect to get and at least it won't be somebody else's. But which truths should you seek? Those are unique to every individual and a big part of the challenge lies in working out what's most important to you. If I had to pick one thing that's really helped me in my search for truth it would be striving to remove desire from my mind."

"What, you mean stop fancying people?"

"Not really, I'm talking more about primal craving. It's one thing to fancy someone, but if you obsess about them it nearly always leads to pain, right?"

"Oh, yes. I've been there more often than I'd like to admit, man."

"And then there are material things. Desiring possessions leads to pain if you can't get them and only fleeting pleasure when you can. And even that pleasure is born mostly of the temporary relief from craving rather than any intrinsic qualities of the thing itself. It's like any addiction, most of which are psychological rather than physiological, the pain created by craving a thing is removed once the thing is acquired, but it soon returns and with greater strength each time. The only solution to this is cold turkey, hence working to eliminate desire."

"But you can't totally get rid of it can you. Everyone desires life, comfort, happiness and so on, don't they?"

"Yes, but you can strive to make your comfort and happiness as free from other desires as possible. Imagine if all you needed to make you feel happy was for the sun to rise in the morning. Then you'd be happy every day."

"Damn, that would be some fucking powerful shit, right there! So why isn't everyone doing this?

"Enlightenment can't just be bought; it has to be uniquely discovered by each individual. Hopefully some people will begin their search as a result of listening to this conversation, but many won't be ready, or will reject the idea entirely."

"OK, so do you have any last words you would like people to hear that might help them to help themselves?"

"As with so much else, the search for truth requires a balance of strength and humility. You should strive to find the strength to trust your own instincts, but also the humility to know your instincts don't necessarily apply to anyone else. No single person can be the bearer of absolute truth and no individual is intrinsically superior to any other. All you can do is seek truth and make your findings available to those who request them. In short, have the strength to find and defend what's important to you, but the humility not to impose it on others. Live a good life and hope to inspire a few people by your example. If everyone limited their ambitions to that, the world would be a much better place."

"Amen to that, brother."

Chapter 35 – Insurgence

Popular consensus over the lockdown began to crumble. Initially the country had revelled in the blitz spirit that came with the sense of collective struggle against a common enemy. In the absence of genuine social contact, people shouted conversations at each other from doorsteps and windows and sought solace in stuttering video conferences. There were even reports of impromptu, communal jamming sessions with pots, pans and assorted other household implements competing with legitimate musical instruments for prominence in the resulting din.

Once the initial wave of apocalyptic reporting about the Diademvirus subsided, however, people started to wonder whether the whole thing had been a bit of a storm in a teacup. Where questions about the necessity of the lockdown were once denounced as treason they now started to be, if not welcomed, then at least entertained. So long as people prefaced their statements with something like 'of course it's better to be safe than sorry,' the Overton Window eventually moved to accommodate outright dissent. As soon as the government, which had openly opposed a full lockdown during the referendum campaign, caught wind of this shift in public sentiment, it cautiously sought to nurture it. Prime Minister Savage began to question the very scientific experts he had previously deferred to on matters of epidemiological judgment and made much of his initial reluctance to lock down the country. The brief political calm that accompanied the start of the pandemic turned out to merely be the eye of the storm and, given a new issue to pick a team over, partisan business as usual returned with a vengeance.

FLAP, which had been licking the wounds from its Savage beating, sensed an opportunity to regain the political initiative and emphatically backed team lockdown. Apparently taking its lead from the Tegritie interview, FLAP's communications team dedicated itself to characterising Savage's desire to loosen the lockdown as homicidal folly. This, in turn, provoked Savage into doubling-down on his position, one manifestation of which involved him recording in-person interviews with small children about how much they missed their little friends and publishing the most emotive answers as video clips on twitter. FLAP denounced this appropriation of children for political purposes, augmenting its own position by asking even younger ones whether they were afraid of dying and publishing the videos of their hysterical responses. The virus itself was soon forgotten as politicians, activists and a rapidly growing army of bored, unemployed regular people lapsed back into the familiar territory of factional warfare over the issue of the day.

Savage was eventually provoked into proposing another referendum on the matter. FLAP initially opposed it on the grounds that it was something Savage was doing, but when even its own base bridled at the spectacle of the opposition opposing the opportunity to oppose government policy, it was forced to accede. The campaigning by both sides, as ever, focused entirely on smearing, slandering and sabotaging the other side, rather than putting their own case forward. Once more the public ignored the lot of them and made its own mind up. The result was a 52% majority in favour of lifting the lockdown.

Savage was jubilant, treating the outcome as a personal endorsement despite his reluctance to permit the vote in the first place, while FLAP retreated back to sullen silence. There was, however, an immediate backlash from many on the losing side of the referendum, who were concerned the ballot had been held prematurely and with insufficient consideration of the risks involved. Having campaigned successfully in favour of the original lockdown, activist group Safety Not Freedom once more took the lead in opposing its lifting. Their message was simple: it's still not safe and. since a small majority of the electorate had just demonstrated their failure to understand that undeniable fact, it fell to Safety Not Freedom to show them the error of their ways.

FLAP, in turn, saw an opportunity to snatch victory from the jaws of defeat and committed itself fully to the campaign to overturn the referendum. The addition of FLAP's political nous led to a strategy of contesting the legitimacy of the election itself. FLAP couldn't attack YouChoose and the concept of direct democracy as it had been instrumental in their creation, so instead it focused on the electorate. The 52% of the population who voted to lift the lockdown were characterised as either reckless hedonists, placing their desire to party above the nation's health, or hapless dupes, conned into voting the wrong way by Savage's devious machinations. While the former group were dismissed as Canines, and thus beyond the pale, it was assumed most of the latter group must have been confused at the time they voted. Hence the only way democracy could be properly represented would be for the stated will of the majority of the electorate to be overturned.

Opinion polls immediately began indicating sympathy for what became known as the People's Lockdown, which emboldened FLAP to pressure Savage to hold yet another referendum, on the grounds that the people had changed their mind. He countered that people change their minds all the time, but even direct democracy relies on the outcome of elections being honoured. It was impractical and unjust for decisions to be constantly litigated, he argued, especially since someone was always going to be unhappy with the outcome. The increasingly shrill calls were flatly denied by Savage, who had already declared people were free to leave the house so long as any who weren't feeling well wore a bell around their neck and declared themselves unclean.

Dalston was still enjoying the lockdown, but presumed the cause lost until he watched an Iain Tegritie interview with someone who claimed to have been deliberately infected. It was conducted remotely over video conference, with the Feline interviewee coughing, shivering and groaning throughout. Tegritie was able to establish that the biological assault was committed by a man in a bright red 'Proud To Be Savage' t-shirt. He apparently shouted 'justice for Canines' before grabbing the victim and coughing in her face repeatedly. As the interview went on her condition deteriorated rapidly, causing Tegritie to suggest, on several occasions, that they stop in order to seek medical help. Each time the interviewee refused, but she eventually embarked on a protracted coughing fit culminating in a gasping, throat-clutching, eye-bulging death rattle, all perfectly framed in the video-conference window, after which the broadcast cut out.

A bulletin by Tegritie just minutes later confirmed the woman had died, live on camera. He launched immediately into a touching obituary, which revealed the victim was a young altruist who had devoted her brief life to helping the under-fortunate. Her only crime was caring too much, the audience was told, and for that she had paid the ultimate price. "The question is what, if anything, can the rest of us do about it?" concluded Tegritie.

He was immediately answered by mass street demonstrations across the country calling for the People's Lockdown. In many cases they descended into riots in which Canine-owned shops were looted, Canine communities ransacked and anyone with a Savage t-shirt assaulted. FLAP's official communications channel said all the right things about not breaking the law, but at the same time various party spokespeople hinted that this is the sort of thing you can expect if you ignore the will of 48 percent of the population. While FLAP didn't condone the growing insurgence, it was forced to ask what alternative was left to frustrated lockdowners treated so badly by the democratic process.

Safety Not Freedom focused its activism on portraying the lifting of the lockdown as an act of violence, on the grounds that it increased the chance of Diademvirus infection. Bands of activists, comprised largely of Anticanes, began roaming the streets to take photos of anyone they found in order to shame them on social media. This vigilantism inevitably escalated to physical assaults, which Safety Not Freedom characterised as self-defence due to the intrinsic violence contained in the act of leaving the house. Savage initially responded by condemning the whole thing on social media, but when it became clear he was merely fanning the flames he retreated entirely from the public sphere. To all intents and purposes the country was being run by street gangs, loosely directed by the People's Lockdown campaign.

A direct consequence of this social turmoil was corporate panic. The rules of public engagement at this time were very fluid, but nonetheless fanatically policed, such that even the most switched-on corporate reputation management departments struggled to stay ahead of the baying mob. Staying silent wasn't an option either, as that too was considered a form of violence, but even the slightest mistake in brand positioning could be catastrophic. Worst of all Dalston's Corporate Offsetting Note and other such modern-day indulgences were no longer effective, having finally been recognised for the cynical window-dressing they were.

In an emergency video conference Dalston's boss at Clark's bank, Poppy Syndrome, lamented the collapse in revenues resulting from the failure of the CON and challenged him to come up with a replacement. An examination of the corporate reputation ecosystem revealed that, in their panic, companies had been exacerbating their collective problem by competing with each other for conspicuous virtue. An arms race had commenced, with brands seeking to out-do each other over the size of their donations to Safety Not Freedom, the extent of their pandering to the People's Lockdown, and the abjectness of their public self-flagellation.

Dalston could see this was unsustainable, so he set about designing a reputation management product to suit the current circumstances. He observed the most effective tactic seemed to be the corporate 'struggle session,' which typically involved the CEO recording an earnest, often tearful piece to camera, in which they apologised for everything they could think of and vowed to devote themselves to a life of philanthropy and monastic asceticism. The effectiveness of this performative grovelling was being rapidly diminished by the white-collar one-upmanship, so he concluded that standardizing the whole process would not only put a cap on the pathos arms race, but also create a new product. Soon afterwards he presented the Commoditized Exculpatory Struggle Session Platform for Institutional Transformation to Syndrome and she actually squealed with delight.

The CESSPIT consisted of a secure video publishing platform combined with an indulgence certification system. Customers were guided through the process, which included an approved script, a database of societal ills to apologise for and a b-roll library with a wide selection of generic acts of philanthropy set to stirring, aspirational music. As with the CON, Dalston knew the certification process would require validation by an acknowledged moral authority. If anything, Safety Not Freedom was more trusted than ever, so once more he got one of his team to approach them and they were no less keen to get involved this time, noting that anything which facilitates displays of repentance should be encouraged and supported. They did express concern at the administrative burden of blessing each CESSPIT performance, however, and suggested the problem could be resolved by a simple royalties system, in which the cut Safety Not Freedom received of every deal also signified its endorsement. Dalston advised his colleagues to make a show of negotiating, but to secure Safety Not Freedom's buy-in, whatever the cost.

As soon as the CESSPIT hit the market it was overwhelmed by such demand it made the CON look like a flash in the pan and Dalston himself richer than ever. But while those corporations that could afford a CESSPIT were shielded from the worst of the insurgence, small businesses and regular people weren't. In protest at the lifting of the lockdown, thousands of FLAP activists took to the streets. Any venues where people might congregate, such as pubs, restaurants and cinemas, were vandalised, even though they had yet to reopen. In many cases the protesters were literally climbing over each other to get to their latest target and those few people who dared to even suggest a possible hypocrisy in their actions immediately found themselves at the top of the hit-list.

Chapter 36 – Independence

Dalston began to suspect the People's Lockdown movement wasn't really about the lockdown or even the dead interviewee, but it was only when protesters started wearing green baseball caps with Safety Not Freedom on them that he smelled a rat. The suspicious whiff led him to research the organisation online, where he discovered its founding ideal was to safeguard the future of the human race by dismantling society in order to rebuild it with Safety Not Freedom in charge. Its website prominently featured the mantra Surrender is Freedom. Since individual agency led to bad outcomes, wasted productivity and emotional pain, explained the website, only through complete surrender could a person truly be free.

This philosophy overlapped considerably with FLAP's and soon the two decided to fully merge, forming what they simply called the Revolutionary Party. Its aim was very simple: to oppose everything. Since everything was corrupted by the chaos of individuality and millennia of Canine influence, it all had to be torn down. The resulting vacuum would be filled by the Revolutionary Party as a matter of historical inevitability.

To his horror Revolutionary Party dogma was taking hold among the general populace. Some were apparently genuine converts, but most seemed to think that by demonstrating fealty to the Party they might be spared the ravages of its activists. When CESSPIT videos began to beg forgiveness from the Revolutionary Party explicitly, Dalston realised he had been instrumental in creating this situation and therefore had to take responsibility for fixing it. The solution presented itself when it occurred to him that he had unwittingly built a self-destruct button into the whole CESSPIT system by involving Safety Not Freedom. A couple of phone calls were all it took to have possession of the full paper-trail detailing Safety Not Freedom's involvement, thus revealing the fundamental conflict of interests presented by them having a financial incentive to exonerate the very companies they claimed to be opposing.

He was on the verge of dumping the lot onto Whistleblower Hotline when it occurred to him he should at least check in with Sally Pimienta and Davina Jones to get their advice on the best way to go about it. He was able to get through to Davina, who insisted they continue the conversation in person due to its delicate nature. He found himself strangely excited at the prospect of physically socialising after his extended period of house arrest. Under normal circumstances, the prospect of meeting a woman, especially one as attractive as Davina, would always have been accompanied by the hope, however remote, that it may culminate in sex. After weeks of sleeping alone, however, Dalston realised he would cherish even the briefest hug. Since the pub situation was still dire he pocketed a half bottle of cooking bourbon he'd been keeping aside for emergencies and set off. They met at an empty and lifeless Camden Lock and decided to walk along the Regency Canal towpath.

"So, what have you got for me then?" said Davina.

"OK, this Revolutionary Party stuff is really doing my head in and, as I'm partially responsible, I want to do something about it," he replied.

"How's that then?"

"The fucking CESSPIT, man, that was my idea. I thought it would just be a cool way to fleece corporate virtue-signallers while they indulge in their pathetic, performative pandering. I didn't think anyone would take any of their videos seriously, but it turns out I was wrong. To crown it, each one that pledges support for the Revolutionary Party legitimises and promotes its agenda far more effectively than any regular campaigning could. It's a fucking nightmare and it's got to be stopped."

"I see. Before we go any further, why do you think its agenda needs to be stopped?"

"Are you having a laugh? They want to destroy everything, for God's sake!"

"But you have to admit things are pretty fucked up, though. Politicians are always promising to make things better and they never do. Maybe the only way to really change anything is through creative destruction."

"Jesus Christ, where do I start? Firstly things are getting better and have been for years. Everyone has the same rights and opportunities and even seventies bigotry is totally beyond the pale now. Of course there's still room for improvement, but I totally reject the suggestion that things are more fucked up than they've ever been. Yes, politicians are lying cunts, but they're still better than mob rule. That's what bothers me the most about this revolutionary shit: it's completely undemocratic and would only serve to put FLAP types in charge. They just got kicked out in a general election and they're trying to grab back power by getting into bed with these Safety Not Freedom Nazis. We've got more democratic power than ever thanks to YouChoose and I'm fucked if I'm going to surrender it to a band of chancers, fanatics and god damn commies."

"Good. I agree. I just wanted to make sure you really understood what's going on and weren't just acting out some bullshit Canine thing."

"No, I'm past all that, I promise. Factions can fuck off and this is about much more. Why do FLAP and its allies get to change everything just because they've got the arsehole? There's plenty of shit I don't like but can I get it changed just by stamping my feet and threatening to smash stuff up? No, so why should they?

"When Sally explained due process to me it really struck a chord. If we didn't have things like free and fair elections and equality under the law, then the only way to make collective decisions and resolve disputes would be force. We would effectively be in a perpetual civil war, with the strongest calling all the shots and everyone else having no rights at all, unless they successfully fight back. And even then, the new lot would probably be even worse, because they would want to have their turn with the whip hand. So if I'm fighting for anything it's for principles, which these Revolutionary cunts want to get rid of and replace with their own arbitrary ideals they just made up."

"Sally couldn't have said it better herself. So what have you got in mind?"

"What do you think has made the CESSPIT such a success?"

"Being in the right place at the right time, I assumed."

"Yes, but the secret sauce lies in making it unique, and difficult to copy. If all I'd done is come up with the bright idea of making a bespoke video platform for spineless corporations, it would have been copied within days. The reason these chicken shits will pay through the arse for the CESSPIT is because it's partnered with Safety Not Freedom. They are the current archbishops of secular religion and are thus in a position to hand out modern-day indulgences. Without them, the CESSPIT is nothing."

"OK, but I think I already knew that – it's no big secret, is it?"

"No, but their terms of engagement are."

"What do you mean, I thought they were there to 'facilitate the learning curve' or whatever your silly marketing guff says."

"Ha! Of course that's what we say, because if the truth came out the whole scheme would be fucked. Are you ready for this? Safety Not Hate gets ten percent of the fee paid for every CESSPIT video."

"Fuck off!"

"I shit you not, Davina, and what's more I've got a solid paper trail to prove it on this flash drive. That's how we're going to fuck the Revolutionary Party."

"Nice one. OK hand it over, but I'm going to give you a day to think about it. One we publish this shit it's game over for you in finance, my friend, possibly even the entire job market. This is the point of no return and I want you to be sure you fully understand that before I pull the trigger."

"I'm sure now, man. I've got fucking tons of money and I've been sick of this industry for a while. I only took the job at Clark's because I was skint and that's not going to be a problem for a very long time now."

"It's not just the loss of income, Dave, it's letting go of everything you've become used to, everything you know, everything that's safe."

"Freedom not safety, that's what I say Davina. But sure, let's give it a day, but even if you haven't heard back from me, stick it up tomorrow."

Dalston gave Davina the flash drive, said goodbye and pondered who he could speak to for a second opinion. He couldn't think of anyone more opposite to Davina Jones than Dev Sharma and sent him a message. Luckily Dev had been trying to make ends meet during the lockdown through a bit of light dealing around the stables, so they met at the eerily quiet and deserted Gin Alley.

"Nice to meet a normal human being for a change, know what I mean." said Dev.

"Nice to meet anyone at all, you mean." said Dalston.

"No bruv, I'm not letting some fuckin cold make me hide like a bitch, you get me. I've been out and about the whole time but there's been fuck-all action. The only punters I bump into are proper nutters, but at least some of them are looking for gear, innit."

"It's funny you say that, because I got quite used to the idea of being locked down. It just simplified everything and got rid of so much stress. So long as I had some grub, some booze and the door was shut I had no worries. As you say, once you leave the house there are nutters and Anticanes and all kinds of dangerous shit around. Much safer just to stay in."

"What the fuck's the matter with you, blad? That's some of the worst pussy talk I've ever heard and I'm fucking tempted to slap some sense into you right here. What happened to the Dave Dalston I used to know, who would train all day so he could take care of himself? One little sniffle and you stick your tail between your legs, is it?"

"I hear what you're saying, but it's not that I'm scared, I just realised that having fewer choices makes life a lot easier. It's just less fucking complicated."

"But you didn't have fewer choices, you just made different decisions. Listen to what I'm saying, man, the government said 'stay in' but you still had to choose to. You could have gone out any time, bruv, and what's more you don't have to wait for some prick in Westminster to give you the nod if you want to stay in the whole time either. Thousands of lazy cunts do that every day just because they can't be arsed, know what I mean."

"It sounds like you're talking about free will, which is something I've been thinking about a fair bit recently. I listened to this Jive Robin pod where he was talking to this really clever fella about personality types. We've got this Id Card thing now, but it turns out we've been trying to map people's personalities for ages and it just depends which bit you focus on."

"For real, bruv."

The thing that's been doing my head in is: if my personality is set in stone, then aren't my actions and even my thoughts just a product of what I am anyway? In other words, am I making any actual decisions at all, or am I just acting out what my personality type tells me to do."

"OK, looks like you haven't totally wasted the time you've been locked up after all. Listen, Frank told me this thing once, he might have got it from someone else, but it stuck with me as a great way to look at the whole nature, nurture, free-will thing. You know holdem poker yeah? Well the hole cards are like your genes – they're what you get at the start of life, you get me. There's nothing you can do about them, they're your nature. Some people are going to be tall, smart and beautiful and others are going to be short, thick and ugly. It's a shit deal for the second lot, but it is what it is.

"Then the board cards are the environment you were born into and your upbringing, in other words the nurture bit. You could say growing up in the inner city in a dump with a fucked-up family is a bad set of board cards, and for a lot of people it is, but it doesn't have to be. For example, what if you get rubbish hole cards and a shit board, but the two sets complement each other to give you a low pair or whatever, that's still something, yeah? But the whole point of poker is betting, and anyone can bet whatever they want. That's the free-will bit and nobody can take it away from you.

"Now don't get me wrong, your personality type definitely affects how you're likely to bet. Some people are cautious and others are mental, but you don't have to stick to your personality type. A clever cautious person will sometimes be aggressive, just to keep everyone on their toes, and even the most reckless gambler has to throw in a hand every now and then, innit. If poker was only about the cards then the law of averages says it would all even out over time, but some people are much better than everyone else at it, so why is that, bruv? The answer is they calculate odds better, they read the other players better and they just fucking play better.

"A great poker player can win a hand with seven-two, unsuited, and fuck-all to help them on the board, just by making everyone else shit themselves before the showdown. In the same way, someone who has been dealt a rubbish hand in life can still win at it by working hard, making good decisions and just wanting it more than the other cunt. That's free-will and it's the only part you can control, so you might as well go all-in on it, you get me."

"I like it – my compliments to Frank. So you're your will is something distinct from your genes and your upbringing, right?"

"Well, it can be. Your clever cunt from the podcast was probably right about a lot of people, because they don't think they have a choice. They've thrown in the towel and decided that because they're this, that and the other there's fuck all they can do about it and they might as well act the same way as everyone else who looks like them, or grew up near them, or whatever. But that's just a mental prison they made for themselves, innit.

"You got to realise the bars of the prison are illusions and then just walk through them. Like with this fucking virus, people would rather be a bit safer in prison than face all the risks that come with true freedom, but they don't know what they're giving up until it's too late. What's the point in living a few more years if you spend them shitting yourself?"

"I hear you, man, I do, which brings me onto the thing I wanted to chat to you about. You know this fucking Revolutionary Party everyone's suddenly sucking up to because of that bird who died? Well I've got some information that will properly fuck them over, but if I publish it everyone will know it came from me, which will probably screw my life up. So I guess what I wanted to know is, what would you do in my position?"

"What I would do is irrelevant, blad, and I think you're over-complicating the matter. The question seems to be: should you be a man or a fucking bitch? And if you don't know the right answer to that, my friend, then you got much bigger problems to worry about."

Chapter 37 – Investments

On his way home Dalston messaged Davina to tell her go ahead and pull the trigger on the CESSPIT leak. He immediately felt a lightness of spirit, bordering on euphoria, at having stepped off the edge of the precipice. Yes, he was terrified of the implications for his career, his reputation and his personal safety, but knowing there was now no turning back also greatly simplified things. He knew which direction all the bad stuff would be coming from, so he could prepare for it. Furthermore, he had so much recent experience of being a pariah and had built up such extensive emotional scar tissue as a result, he thought it very unlikely his new enemies could hurt him.

Within minutes of the leak being published on Whistleblower Hotline he received a message from Poppy Syndrome, his boss at Clark's bank, simply asking: "Was it you?" Once he confirmed she was referring to the leak, he said they needed to talk in person. It was a nice day and the lockdown conditions had loosened to allow outside drinking, so he suggested the Freemasons Arms in Hampstead where they could sit in the beer garden and maybe even go for a walk on the Heath afterwards if they fancied it.

"You know you have to leave Clark's now, don't you?" said Syndrome, after they sat down with their drinks.

"Yes," he replied. "And I just want you to know this was nothing personal. I just couldn't let those psychos at the Revolutionary Party complete their coup, especially with what I know about Safety Not Freedom. I agonised about whether to act and, in the end, realised I would never forgive myself if I didn't."

"Well I can't say I wasn't livid when I saw the leak and, by destroying the CESSPIT, you've given Clark's a hell of a cash flow problem. But at the same time I have to respect the brave and principled nature of what you did, and I can hardly claim to be totally surprised, given your track record of leaking your employer's confidential information."

"No, I guess not. So you see where I'm coming from?"

"To some extent. I suspect I have a bit more sympathy with FLAP and the Revolutionary Party than you do, but I do share your concerns about one group of people, however well-intentioned, imposing their will on the rest of the country through force. That said, I understand their outrage at the death of that Feline woman, the malevolence of the Savage government and general difficulty of bringing about positive change in society."

"I totally get your point about change. We definitely need it, but revolution isn't the way because it always ends up concentrating even more power in the hands of a new lot of nutters."

"I agree, which is why I've got a proposition for you. But first let me ask you something: do you know how much commission you've earned from CESSPIT sales?

"I know it's a lot, judging by their popularity, but no, I couldn't put a precise number on it."

"Nor can I, but I can be sure it's in eight figures, maybe even nine."

Dalston was so shocked he almost threw up. The sums were of a far greater order of magnitude than he had anticipated. A certain degree of long-term financial security had been one of his assumptions when deliberating over the CESSPIT leak, but he never imagined he was about to join the ranks of the mega-rich.

"Jesus fucking Christ!" he said, after an awestruck pause.

"Well, quite," said Syndrome. "Now, as you know, I've been increasingly focused on directing my own earnings from Clark's into philanthropic work. I haven't done too badly out of the CON and the CESSPIT either but, like you, I have found it increasingly hard to justify my active involvement in helping corporations deceive the public and get away with unethical behaviour. A proper Clark's CEO would file charges against you for what you've done but, if we're honest, I never was a proper CEO and I'll probably end up getting sacked myself over this anyway. I'm a head teacher – that's where all my skills and experience are and where my heart still lies.

"I think it's clear to everyone now the Id Card experiment has been a total failure and you can't just arbitrarily shuffle the deck like they did and think it will sort out all of society's problems. It's made things worse in so many ways that if it wasn't for all the cash I've made I would wish it had never happened."

"The money does change things a bit though, doesn't it?"

"It does, but my view has always been that any wealth I acquire, beyond what I need to live, comes with an obligation to use it to help society."

"Fair enough, so why don't you just hand it over to the government then?"

"I actually did do that, at first, when I started at Clark's, but running a commercial organization has completely changed my view of the public sector. It has exposed how corrupt, bloated and goddamn inefficient it all is. So little of the money that goes into the government finds its way to the people who need it most and even when it does, it's mainly used to grow the client-class directly dependent on state handouts. Seeing how much more of a difference I have been able to make through direct philanthropy, rather than just chucking a bit more cash into the governmental black hole, has made me determined to do more."

"OK, so what have you got in mind?"

"Catastrophe though the Id Card has been, it has at least caused a lot of people to look at the world in completely new ways. Just as being in charge of a bank introduced me to different ways of running things, watching some of the stuff Ray Payshus has been trying at my old school made me realise how unimaginative I was as a head teacher. I kept in close touch with Payshus this whole time, mainly to make sure he didn't wreck my school, and just as I have learnt ways in which the private sector does things better he has been taught its weaknesses while running Hill Street School.

"The only way he knew how to incentivise and control people was through money, but he soon reached the limit of that strategy in a school environment. On the other hand Payshus also learnt that he finds running a school a lot more rewarding than running a bank and, dare I say it, might even have developed a bit of a social conscience. Anyway, to cut a long story short, we've decided to set up and run a school together."

"Wow, that's amazing. I reckon you'll be fucking great at it too, especially with all the stuff you've both learnt."

"Thanks a lot, but here's the thing – we need a third investor. We're each putting in ten million, but we need thirty, and I can't think of a better partner than you."

"You want me to hand over ten million fucking quid so you can start a school?"

"Yes. I know you can comfortably afford it and I honestly think you'll find it rewarding. I can't guarantee any financial return, but you would be on the school board with us and playing a major part in creating the kind of place you would like Amy to attend."

There was a lengthy silence as Dalston contemplated everything he had just been told. Ten million pounds was a shit-load of money, but then again it sounded like he had it and then some. The most he had ever given to charity was whatever change he had in his pocket to get a beggar to clear off, but something about this proposition appealed to him. There was only so much you could spend on bling and getting off your tits, and getting involved in something not only profound but permanent seemed so much more meaningful. He knew it was superficial and vain, but the thought of creating something that would last after he died felt like a kind of immortality, which definitely added to the appeal.

After he expressed his initial interest to Syndrome they spoke at length about what this school would do to set it apart from others. They discussed the Payshus incentivisation experiments and the extra difficulty of helping kids whose parents were actively hindering them. Dalston realised he felt really strongly about vocational education and argued the ultimate point of the school should be more to prepare the kids for life itself, rather than just to be a steppingstone to a university that would probably just rip them off for a useless qualification. The best way to offset the intellectual snobbery associated with academia would be to pay the kids for vocational work.

The ideal combination of private and public sector, he concluded, would be for the school to act as an incubator for revenue-generating businesses and pay any kids who contributed to them. If others wanted to take a purely academic route it wouldn't be discouraged, but they wouldn't be paid for it. The key thing would be to encourage and reward the acquisition of practical and commercially useful skills as early as possible. Once that was agreed in principle Dalston said he was on board and he and Syndrome drank a toast to their new venture.

***

The credibility of Safety Not Freedom as an activist organisation was completely destroyed by the CESSPIT leak. Dalston was fascinated to see it wasn't the clear corruption or even the complicity in covering up corporate criminality that was deemed most unforgivable by its supporters, it was that Safety Not Freedom had cooperated with a bank in the first place. In the binary worldview of the Revolutionary Party there were goodies and baddies and no grey areas in between. The real damage done by the CESSPIT leak, therefore, was the cancer of denunciation it created within the heart of the Revolutionary Party itself, which metastasized so rapidly he could see the Party decompose before his eyes on social media.

But just as he was preparing to celebrate the demise of the group he so despised, another Whistleblower Hotline revelation threatened to undo all his good work. A stash of documents, emails and messages had been dumped onto the site implicating Prime Minister Savage in an orchestrated campaign to subvert democracy. It seemed he had decided too many decisions were being taken out of his hands during the lockdown referendum process. Since it was clear to him most people lacked the knowledge, intellect and judgment to make good decisions, Savage concluded the greater good would be best served if he relieved them of that responsibility.

The irony was that the very same direct democracy system he had ridden to power was now standing in the way of him fully exercising it. It was also clear he had no hope of winning a referendum on abandoning direct democracy, so he concluded the only solution available to him was to place his thumb on the scales to ensure the correct outcomes were delivered by the current system. Initially Savage went about this by manipulating the Social Standing system to reward those who voted in his favour and punish those who did otherwise. But he was appalled to find a significant proportion of the population valued their personal principles above their Social Standing and continued to vote against what he considered to be their own interests. That left him with no alternative but to bribe and bully the YouChoose developers into giving him direct access to the back-end of the platform, to enable him to control the outcome of votes himself. It seemed one of the developers had an attack of conscience, or pique, or both, because they were the likely source of the leak.

The Savage revelations not only distracted attention away from Dalston's Safety Not Freedom scandal, they provided the Revolutionary Party with the perfect platform to regain the moral high ground. It immediately moved to distance itself from Safety Not Freedom, even going so far as to attempt to rewrite history by claiming it was only ever a distant, very junior partner. Safety Not Freedom, in turn, redirected its campaigning efforts towards retaliating against the Revolutionary Party, accusing it of every conceivable form of bigotry, which was in turn paid back with interest. This undignified game of denunciation tennis was mildly entertaining for a short time, but ultimately sullied all involved as well as anyone who paid too close attention to it.

Savage, meanwhile, pulled out all the stops in his bid to discredit the Whistleblower Hotline leaks, but found himself backed into a corner when a couple of the few remaining traditional party MPs, one from each, actually questioned him in Parliament on matters of detail and evidence. Statistical studies were done of recent YouChoose voting patterns which indicated a sudden swing in favour of Savage's policies at odds with his declining performance in opinion polls, so a Parliamentary inquiry was launched. Sensing the opportunity and noting the damaging division within both the Savage and the Revolutionary parties, the leaders of the Conservative and Labour parties decided to form an unprecedented opposition coalition.

The move was predicated on their observation that the UK population was sick of the factionalism and polarisation brought about by the Id Card and now just craved a bit of peace and quiet. To reflect the spirit of compromise and reconciliation in which it had been formed the coalition was branded the Moderate Party but the traditional affiliation of its MPs and members was also acknowledged. Not only did that ease the formation of the party, it also emphasised the symbolism of two previously irreconcilable groups coming together in the name of national unity. It was even decided the Moderate Party would have joint leaders – one from each wing – and that they would have to agree on political decisions before they could be implemented.

In anticipation of the potential for stalemate presented by the joint leadership structure, the Moderate Party decided YouChoose, which would otherwise be involved in far fewer decisions, would provide the perfect tie-breaker at times when the two leaders just couldn't agree. When that happened they would put the matter to a simple binary referendum through YouChoose in which each wing would summarise their position in ten words or less and it would be left to the electorate to pick one of them. Furthermore, all campaigning over the issue would also take place exclusively on YouChoose in a standardised format. The Moderate Party would ban all political advertising and lobbying if it won power, with fund-raising once more carried out entirely on YouChoose. Its headline policy, however, was the abandonment of the Id Card scheme and everything that came with it, including forced job transfers and the faction system.

Chapter 38 – Immortality

Dalston was really encouraged by the formation of the Moderate Party as he was sick of all the adversarial bullshit. The decision to empower the electorate to be the arbiter of disputes within the coalition government seemed like a stroke of genius, with the added benefit of showing deference to a people sick of being represented by demagogues and egomaniacs. Excited though he was at the prospect of having grownups in charge for once, his mood was still depressed by the get-out-of-jail-free card given to the Revolutionary Party by the Savage leak. He considered it to be the greatest immediate threat and was determined to seek a new way of eliminating it from British public life. Before making any further plans he decided to check in with Davina Jones once more, to see if Whistleblower Hotline had any further surprises up its sleeve.

They met in the beer garden of the Pembroke Castle in Primrose Hill. Davina was taken aback at Dalston's reproachful tone and asked if he thought his personal agenda should have taken precedence over the public interest. He was forced to concede the point and congratulated her on the leak, but stressed his undiminished resolve to obstruct the Revolutionary Party in any way he could. Davina made it clear she shared his feelings, leading them to discuss the political promise of the Moderate Party, about which they were also in agreement. Conversation then turned to Dalston's meeting with Poppy Syndrome and the opportunity presented of helping set up a new school.

"It's very interesting to hear you're into philanthropy these days, Dave," said Davina.

"Is it now?" he replied, with an arched eyebrow. "You've got a project in sudden need of cash too, have you?"

"Yes and there's no need to be so arsey about it – it's called Whistleblower Hotline."

"I didn't know it needed much cash, but I'm certainly happy to chip in to keep it going."

"Great to hear, thanks a lot, but I think there's a lot more we could do. You must have noticed how pricks like Iain Tegritie are doing an increasingly shit job of actually telling the public what's going on."

"Totally. In fact they usually make things worse, working everyone up into a froth and making it seem like everything's even shitter than it actually is."

"That's because the media has forgotten what its job is and has been panicked by collapsing ad revenues into chasing increasingly niche audiences.

Social media has not only stolen most of their money, it has duped them into thinking they need to act like trolls to get an audience. There isn't a single topic they can't warp into some kind of factional conflict, which makes everyone think they're in a constant state of existential peril. That, in turn, means they reward politicians who make the boldest promises to protect them. But they've taken it too far because people are sick of the conflict now and are starting to see the media Emperor has no clothes on. The Moderate Party has identified this as an opportunity and so have we."

"Fair enough, but I still don't see how money alone can make a massive difference to Whistleblower Hotline. I mean, either you get given leaks or you don't, right?"

"Agreed, which is why we're branching out. We have thought of two other things we could do that would help the public conversation most: a fact-checking service and an alternative social media platform. The former to hold the media to account and the latter to do a better job of encouraging constructive public debate."

"OK, I like the sound of that but there are already fact-checking services aren't there? And the same goes for social media; loads of people have tried but they've all failed. What makes you lot so different?

"Excellent question, especially from a prospective investor. Let me take them one at a time. Nearly all fact-checking services are, themselves, biased and corrupt. Their business model is very similar to your CON and CESSPIT products – providing a veneer of third-party legitimacy for their clients' actions. They also face the same pressures and challenges as you did, especially regarding long-term sustainability. Biased media, which includes fact-checking services, always gets exposed in the end and trust in it evaporates. Once this happens most media learn the wrong lesson and double down on pandering to their shrinking audience. The same applies to fact-checkers as they will all be accused of bias eventually, regardless of any efforts not to be, and commercial pressures will inevitably drive them to try to accommodate their clients."

"Seems like a tough one to overcome."

"Yes, impossible in fact, unless you opt for total objectivity and transparency, which is what we propose to do. Our fact-checking will use independently acquired primary sources and direct reporting wherever possible. Every piece of reporting we do will be recorded on video, which will be live streamed and published in unedited form. Where named primary sources can't be obtained, we will perform a thorough audit of all public accounts of the matter in question and grade them solely according to evidence presented. To overcome the client issue we will be funded only by donations – no ads and no clients – and will publish the details of any donations in excess of a thousand pounds."

"Okay, that all seems to make sense. So what do you need the cash for?"

"People, simple as that. Proper fact checking is very expensive, which is why the media increasingly doesn't bother with it. We need resourceful, honest people on the ground and, for the service to be useful, we need them to work fast. If we can publish trustworthy fact-checking on hot topics quickly, we're confident there is a massive untapped market that will support us. We also need some breathing space to be able to develop our operation and reputation without having to worry about short-term revenue. Most investors are impatient and we need someone who understands results won't come overnight. Also we want to develop a journalistic outfit called CounterNarrative to write stories based on the fact-checking research, designed to offer an alternative view to the mainstream media consensus. Lastly an off-shoot, based on the same principle, will report on published podcasts. It will be called Podpast and will bring a journalistic perspective to the juiciest comments made on them."

"I've got to be honest, that sounds pretty cool. I've got a good idea of how much of my wedge I need to invest for short term revenue generation, so I'm happy to commit a good chunk of the rest into long-term projects."

"Good, because our social media idea has a higher probability of failure but if it doesn't it could be huge. Here's a question for you: if you could change anything about current social media, what would it be?"

"Get rid of all the cunts."

"Fair enough, but how do you define a cunt in this context and who would be in charge of that process?"

"Yes, it's the old censorship dilemma isn't it? A system designed to make sure it's free of people I don't like would only be good for me and would drive everyone else away. But you've got to admit trolls and bellends are ruining social media for everyone else."

"Exactly. Policing is the problem, but the current system of ad hoc censorship is the worst of both worlds. It pisses off more and more users but can never hope to keep the platform free of bad actors."

"But isn't the alternative just letting it be a free-for-all, which seems to always end up with those bad actors ruining it for everyone else anyway?"

"Indeed, so it comes down to the top-down versus bottom-up thing Sally talks about. The top-down approach to managing a community will always bring out the worst kind of censorship, with arbitrary decisions being made by a small group of people who will inevitably be biased. So the question is: what does bottom-up censorship look like and is it any better? We reckon we know the answers to both of those questions."

"I'm holding my breath!"

"It looks like community policing using a patronage model, in which people are only permitted access to the platform if they're invited by an existing member, who becomes their sponsor on the site. Complaints against a member are directed to their sponsor to investigate. How they deal with it is down to them, and they will have the power to suspend their client if they see fit, but further complaints will be referred to the next person up in the hierarchy, who will have the power to act against everyone below them in the tree, and so on. We think most incidents will be dealt with by the immediate sponsor, but this structure permits as much escalation as required."

"That's pretty fucking clever Davina. But it still seems to rely on people grassing each other up, which surely encourages the kind of malicious reporting you're trying to get rid of."

"Ah, but we're going to apply the system in the other direction too. A sponsor will be notified every time their client reports another member and will have the opportunity to ask them about it and intervene if it looks unjustified. We also hope to minimize the number of bad actors by limiting the number of invitations each new member is able to offer to two. With each month that passes in which their own clients record no unresolved incidents they get one more invitation. We think this network of direct accountability will resolve nearly all matters requiring policing on the platform, but we'll have an independent arbitration service for those who require it, which will act as the top of the hierarchical pyramid."

"It looks like you've got all the bases covered. OK, I'm sold."

"Great, nice one Dave, I knew I could count on you. Now, don't be cross, but I've got one more pitch for you."

"Damn Davina, you're rinsing me more than any bird I've ever known and I'm not even getting so much as a snog out of it."

"Not me, actually. This one's from Dev."

Dev Sharma arrived, invited by Davina and armed with three pints.

"Easy, DD, what are you saying?" he asked.

"I'm wondering what this little ambush is all about, if I'm honest Dev," said Dalston.

"Davina told me you were feeling flush so I've got a proposition for you, bruv."

"Fuck me, it's amazing how popular a bloke suddenly gets when people hear he's got a few spare quid. Go on then Dev, let's hear it."

"Don't do me no favours, blad, nobody's got a gun to your head, know what I mean. I'll tell you something else that comes with a bit of wedge: a dodgy fucking attitude. You too rich to give your mates a few minutes of your precious time now, is it?"

"Sorry Dev, it's just you're the third person to make me a proposition today. But you're right, that was out of order, please go ahead."

"Right, you know Frank's gym, yeah? Well he wants to make it about much more than just training hard-arses, you get me."

"So, what, turn it into a regular gym?

"No, man, much more than that. The thing is Frank's been on a bit of a personal journey, innit, and now he reckons there's no point in training your body unless you train your mind and your personality at the same time. Basically he reckons he only spent all those years fucking people up and ripping them off because he didn't know any better. If he'd known about psychology and philosophy and shit like that, he might have taken a different approach, he reckons."

"So he wants to make a gym for the mind as well as the body?"

"Spot on, man. That's why you get the big bucks, innit. I'm going to help him out and we're thinking of calling it Warrior Monks. It will still be a gym, but it will be all about the classes: martial arts, philosophy, logic, you name it – everything you need to sort your life and your head out."

"You know what, Dev, I think that sounds like a fucking awesome idea. If I'd had a bit more of that kind of training when I was younger I bet I wouldn't have made half the mistakes I did. I would love to get involved mate, but I do have one condition."

"Here we go; you want us to name it after you or some shit like that?

"No, I love Warrior Monks. Another project I've just committed myself to is a new type of secondary school that will focus on teaching the kids skills they need to make a living, but it occurs to me we should be looking to give them more of a head start on life in general. I think having a smaller version of Warrior Monks at the school, teaching all the same stuff, could make a massive difference to the pupils. And if you want to call it the Dalston Gym then I wouldn't have a problem with that."

"Sounds great to me, bruv. I'll have to run it past Frank, but as far as I'm concerned you've got yourself a deal."

"Nice one Dev, and sorry again for being a dick earlier."

"Already forgotten, my friend."

Chapter 39 – Identity

Reflecting on his new projects Dalston felt a great sense of satisfaction. In hindsight much of his historical boorish behaviour had just been mimicry. Blowing your cash in the most ostentatious, self-destructive way possible was just what you did if you worked in the city, wasn't it? But now he was grateful to have been given the opportunity to invest in useful, sustainable, substantial endeavours. The Dave Dalston of a few years ago would have viewed any activities that weren't overtly self-serving as a mug's game and a sign of weakness. Now he realised the real weakness lay in investing so much time and money in placating his ego and anaesthetising his soul. He was glad he now had increasingly little in common with the old Dave, and reflected on his progress with pleasure.

One person defined his journey more than any other – Amy. She had been a benign spirit, keeping an eye on him and showing him the correct path to take when he was most lost. She was the one thing that pulled him back from his most resolute folly and his desire to be reunited with her kept him going when he might otherwise have given up. Then, just when it looked like his destination was within reach the Diademvirus came along, isolating him not just from her once more, but from everyone else as well. He reflected in shame on how willing he had been to exchange his freedom, and all that came with it, for a secure padded cell.

Now he was more anxious than ever to see them both, but first he had to contend with the ubiquitous Iain Tegritie. Not content with humiliating him in interviews and generally making him feel intellectually inadequate, the bastard was trying to steal his family too. He had the consolation that Amy didn't seem to like Tegritie, which gave him hope Mel might be coming to the same conclusion, so he decided to call her. After a stilted exchange of pleasantries and small-talk, he cut to the chase and asked about Tegritie.

"Yeah, it's all great," said Mel airily. "Iain's such a smart guy and he's really great with Amy."

"Smart eh? That's nice," said Dalston.

"Yes, yes it is."

"And he's great with Amy is he?"

"Yes, really great."

"In what way?"

"Excuse me?"

"Tell me one of the ways in which Iain is great with Amy."

"I think I know where this is going. I know Amy doesn't think too much of him and, if I'm honest, that's probably a deal-breaker at the end of the day, okay? It's been so long since I had a decent bloke, and on one level he's such a catch that I've been trying to give it every chance to work. But not only is Amy far from convinced, I don't think Iain's that bothered about her either. He sort of goes through the motions when we're all together but I can tell his heart isn't in it and I'm not sure he even likes kids at all."

"And what about you? Do you still like him?"

"On one level yes – he's such a sharp, interesting person and has such an amazing lifestyle that I guess I got a bit starstruck. But I'm starting to see a darker side to his personality coming through. He's not violent or anything, but if you catch him at the wrong time he can be a complete prick until he catches himself and turns on the charm. Sometimes I hear him on the phone and he seems to think he's a movie star or something, acting like a complete prima donna half the time."

"Sounds a bit two-faced to me."

"Yes and there was this one conversation I heard... no I shouldn't mention it."

"What Mel? Look, I know your private life's none of my business, but surely I'm entitled to be notified if there's anything going on that might affect Amy."

"Alright. The other night I heard him talking to someone and it seemed to be about that interview he did when the woman died. Something about his tone really freaked me out, so I got as close as I could to the doorway and started recording with my phone. They only chatted for a couple of minutes but I've listened to the recording a few times and, I can't believe I'm saying this, I think the whole interview might have been a hoax."

"You what? Why?"

"Because, as far as I can tell, the person he was speaking to was the one who supposedly died on air. In fact the whole conversation seemed to be about that person panicking she might get found out and Iain trying to calm her down."

"Fuck me Mel, do you still have the recording?"

"Yes, it's on my phone."

"Do you think you could send it to me?"

"I knew you'd ask, that's why I hesitated. What are you planning to do with it?"

"If it shows what you think it does it has to go public, man. The UK is on the verge of civil war over this and if it turns out to be bollocks, people need to know."

"But there's only one place it could possibly have come from, Dave. If I send it to you and you publish it, then Iain will know I recorded it and will probably join the dots to you too."

"Well, yes."

"I'll need to think about this Dave. I will say one thing though, you may be a bit of a twat, but you love Amy and I think I'm only just starting to really appreciate how important that is to me."

"Don't doubt it Mel, I'd do anything for her and I think I've only recently fully understood that too."

"OK, leave it with me. I'll be in touch."

Several news alerts had pinged Dalston's phone while he was speaking to Mel. People were still rioting in protest over the woman presumed to have died during the Tegritie interview. The Revolutionary Party was doing everything it could to link the death to Dick Savage and the current UK government in general. It had started openly inciting the burgeoning mob to attack symbols of the Savage government, which included any people, buildings or statues suspected of having any connection to Canines. Even the police, passive to the point of tacit support in the face of the riots, were targeted as allies of the government.

It was also election day, which gave everything a heightened sense of urgency and drama. Savage had been forced to call a snap general election in response to the political pressure resulting from the Whistleblower Hotline electoral fraud leak. While forced to hand control of the YouChoose app to parliament as a result of the allegations against him, he still figured direct democracy represented his best chance of winning the election. In addition, to protect himself from what he perceived to be a hostile commentariat, he picked the earliest possible date to hold it, insisted it be conducted during working hours on a single day, and demanded the results be displayed in real time via the app. The party with the most total votes by 5pm that day would be the winner, regardless of how close or how many people voted.

Such was their hunger to get rid of Savage, the Revolutionary and Moderate parties agreed to his terms. Dalston fired up YouChoose on his phone for the first time in the late morning and saw the Revolutionary Party was comfortably ahead after a small proportion of the electorate had cast their vote. Its strategy of warning voters they could expect the riots to continue if they didn't vote for the only party that vowed to avenge the dead woman was paying off. The prospect of such a divisive, dishonest and destructive group of people taking over the country tortured Dalston's soul to the point he couldn't keep it to himself and contacted Davina and Dev. They arranged to meet at the Oxford Arms in Camden.

"This shit is fucking mental, blad," said Dev after Dalston got a round in.

"You know what I mean," said Dalston.

"Savage is a prick, yeah, but at least he's not crazy. Those Revolutionary cunts get in and it's game over, I'm telling you."

"I agree, but check this out: I was just chatting to my ex – Mel – and you know she's been seeing Iain Tegritie, right? Well she said she's got a recording of him talking to the bird who supposedly died on his show, after it happened."

"You what?" said Davina.

"It looks like the whole fucking thing was a hoax! Mel reckons the bird was losing her nerve on the call and Iain had to talk her down."

"Jesus Christ Dave, this could be huge. If we could get hold of that recording sharpish and put it on Whistleblower Hotline then it could even swing the election."

"Yes, I was looking on YouChoose and the Revolutionary Party is ahead, but that's mostly due to Feline votes. Savage is doing alright thanks to Canine votes, but it looks like most Simians and Delphines haven't voted yet. I don't reckon Savage stands a chance thanks to your leak, so maybe a lot of neutrals will vote for the Moderate Party, which is definitely the one I want to win."

"Me too," said Davina.

"Fuck yeah, it's time to get back to normal, innit," said Dev.

"But Mel's still not sure if she wants to share it," said Dalston. "We're running out of time and I don't see how I can force her."

"You can't, Dave," said Davina. "You're no better than those Felian pricks if you start trying to impose your will on other people just to get what you want."

"Listen Davina, sometimes you've got to do what it takes, you get me," said Dev. "This is more important than some ethical dilemma, at the end of the day."

"You're wrong Dev. Without your principles you're nothing."

"What good are your principles if that's all you got, though?"

An alert went off on Dalston's phone. It was a message from Mel that simply read 'check your email'. When he did he saw an email from an account he didn't recognise, with 'as discussed' in the subject field. It contained an attachment that turned out to be an MP3 file, which he downloaded and then played with the volume at maximum so Davina and Dev could hear it. A male voice was hissing pleas and threats at an unheard recipient, the intermittent pauses and outbursts suggesting he was either speaking to someone on the phone or having a severe schizophrenic episode. It sounded like Tegritie but it was impossible to tell until he said "Listen, bitch, this is Iain fucking Tegritie you're dealing with and don't you forget it."

He seemed to regret that approach immediately and reverted to a soothing, apologetic tone, apparently designed to take the emotion out of the exchange. There was lots of affirming and empathising before the man asked what it would take to resolve their dispute. Upon hearing the reply he sighed, but accepted it. "That's a fuck of a lot of money and for that I expect you to disappear permanently," said Tegritie. "And I promise you one thing: if I ever hear from you, or even about you, again you'll wish you really had died on my show."

As soon as it finished playing Davina told him to send it to her immediately, which he did. Within ten minutes she had forwarded it to Sally Pimienta with instructions on how to frame the audio file on Whistleblower Hotline. By the time he got another round in it was published so he made a rare visit to social media to promote it. Most of his remaining followers, especially on Twitter, were either people who despised him or journalists who preferred to report on contentious tweets rather than actually finding stuff out for themselves. As a result his tweet was greeted with derision but, crucially, plenty of it. In their haste to discredit his claim that the Tegritie interview tragedy was a hoax, the hacks and trolls did a better job of attracting traffic to the leak than a million pounds of advertising spend could have done.

Before long it was clear the furore around the Tegritie recording was even having an effect on the election. The Revolutionary Party had relied heavily on the tragedy to portray itself as the party of safety, which would keep the country locked down to ensure nothing like it ever happened again. But the possible hoax was not only negating that strategy but making some people question the severity of the Diademvirus epidemic entirely. Having maintained its position through to midday, the Revolutionary Party started to lose ground as soon as the leak went viral, and its lead was halved a couple of hours later. The main recipient of the swing was the Moderate Party, confirming the YouChoose scandal was too great for Savage to overcome.

Dalston's Twitter session was interrupted by a call from an unknown number, which he rejected, but when it came again immediately he picked it up.

"Dave Dalston," he said.

"Daddy?" said Amy.

"Amy? Oh my God! My phone didn't know it was you for some reason."

"That's because I'm calling from Iain's phone. He picked me up from school for some reason and I'm in his car but he left it when he went to the shops without me. He's acting strange, Daddy."

"Has he hurt you baby?"

"No, he just seems really manic and distracted and keeps talking to himself. When I asked him where Mummy is he told me to shut up and seemed really cross and now he won't talk to me at all. I don't know what to do, Daddy."

Dalston could hear some music, presumably coming from the car stereo, which he recognised but couldn't quite put a name to. He could even make out some lyrics.

...what do I got to do to wake you up, to shake you up, to break the structure up...

"OK, just keep quiet and try not to make him cross, I'll come and get you," he said. "Do you have any idea where you are?"

"Sorry Daddy, no. We can't be too far from school because he only picked me up a few minutes ago, but I don't recognise where we are. Hold on, I can see a street sign... Oh no! He's coming back, I've got to go."

"Wait! Just tell me what the sign..." said Dalston, until he realised he wasn't talking to anyone.

"FUCK!" he shouted, to the indignation of everyone else in the pub.

"What's going on, bruv," said Dev.

"Iain Tegritie has kidnapped my daughter."

"Oh shit," said Davina. "Do you think it's because of the leak?"

"That or Mel has chucked him, or both. I'd better call her."

Mel answered in a state of panic and immediately asked if he had seen Amy. He explained that Tegritie had her, at which point Mel started berating herself for sending the audio clip and Dalston for encouraging her to do so. He was in the middle of explaining how they needed to stay calm and try to guess where Tegritie may have taken her when he got another call from the mystery number, which he now knew to be Tegritie's, so he cut Mel off to answer it.

"Amy?" he said.

"I'm afraid not," said Iain Tegritie.

"Give me back my daughter!"

"I'm sorry Dave, I'm afraid I can't do that."

"Why not?"

"I think you know what the problem is, just as well as I do."

"Iain, I've got no idea what the fuck you're talking about."

"Well I'd be happy to explain in person. I have arranged for us to have a public conversation on Jive Robin's podcast, so I suggest you meet me there as soon as possible."

"If you fucking touch a hair on her head, I swear…" said Dalston before he realised Tegritie had already hung up.

Chapter 40 – Ideology

"You're not going to believe this, the cunt wants to do a podcast with me," Dalston told Davina and Dev after he put down his phone.

"Given how pissed off he must be, I doubt he just wants to kiss and make up," said Davina.

"I reckon he wants to cuss you down in public, know what I mean." said Dev.

"If he does I don't see what I can do about it. The bloke's sharp as anything and can run rings around me."

"Don't play his game then, innit."

"I've got to meet him – he's got Amy."

"Totally, bruv, but that doesn't mean you've got to just stand there and take his shit. He's made a strong move and you've got to counter it. You've got nothing to be afraid of if you're true to yourself, you get me. The geezer's a bluffer and you're not, which ultimately makes you stronger than him."

"I agree with Dev about not playing his game, but you've got to tread carefully because it sounds like he's lost his mind," said Davina. "I reckon you've got to at least act intimidated until you can get an idea of what he wants."

"That won't be difficult. Will you two come with me?"

"Damn right we will," said Davina and Dev in unison.

When they arrived at the studio, Jive Robin was waiting for Dalston in the green room.

"What the hell is going on, dude?" said Robin. "This motherfucker just turns up and says I've got to host a pod with you and him. I was about to set the dogs on him when he said your daughter's life depends on it. What the fuck?"

"It's a long story Jive, but he's got Amy somewhere and won't give her back unless we do this," said Dalston.

"Jesus Christ, what did you do to piss him off so much?"

"Did you hear about the leak that exposed he faked the death of that woman?"

"Yeah, like an hour ago, crazy."

"Well it was Amy's Mum recorded it and I got it published, so it looks like he wants to punish us both."

"Fuck, that's heavy. Shouldn't we just call the cops?

"I don't want to risk it, Jive. At least while it's just me and him I have some direct control over the Amy situation."

"OK, whatever you say, dude. Shall we get on with it then? Your friends can come in too if they keep quiet."

Iain Tegritie was sitting at the podcasting table with headphones already on and microphone poised. He gestured imperiously for Dalston and Robin to take the two vacant chairs on the other side of the table and ordered the producer to begin recording. The producer ignored Tegritie and shot an inquiring glance at his employer, who nodded.

"Thank you for joining me," said Tegritie as soon as live streaming began.

"You didn't give me a lot of choice did you?" said Dalston.

"I assure you Amy's quite alright, but I needed a way of making sure you would come. Once we're finished you have my word you'll be reunited."

"A pretty fucking psychotic way of arranging a meeting if you ask me, but here we are. So what do you want?"

"Psychotic, maybe, but you concede it was also effective?"

"Clearly."

"Power, Mister Dalston."

"Eh?"

"What do you think power is?"

"Erm, strength, influence, money?"

"Those are all manifestations of power. A man's power is measured by his ability to impose his will on another man. By holding your daughter captive I exerted power over you, just as you did over me when you leaked that forged recording of me speaking on the phone onto the internet."

"OK, so we're even, right?"

"I'm afraid that's not how power works Dave, it won't be shared. You've made it clear through your actions that you want to take power from me and I can't allow you to succeed."

"Listen man, the leak wasn't even about you, it was about preventing the Revolutionary Party winning the election on the strength of a lie."

"And who the fuck do you think runs the Revolutionary Party? Who do you think created the Felians? Who do you think put the conditions in place for the Id Card to be created? I have put a lot of money, effort and thought into this election and I'm not about to let some barrow-boy with an attack of conscience ruin it."

"I see. The last time I checked the tide was starting to turn against your party Iain, how are things now?"

They all checked their YouChoose apps, which revealed the Revolutionary Party still had a lead of around two percentage points with half an hour of polling left.

"It looks like you're just going to scrape home Iain, so what's the problem?" said Dalston.

"Let's just make sure shall we?" said Tegritie. "I would like you to confess, on this podcast, to fabricating that recording, in order to prevent any voters making the wrong decision on the back of your deception."

"Or you'll do something to Amy?"

"Power, Dave."

"OK, but first just answer me this. Why do you crave power so much?"

"To improve things, of course. Even you must be able to see how imperfect everything is, how flawed people are. We lack leaders with clear vision and the will to implement it, but I am just such a person. This is much bigger than me Dave, it's about making the world a better place."

"So the Id Card, the faction system, all that shit, was all part of your grand plan?"

"Is it such a stretch to accept there should be more order in the world and that there's a natural pecking order? Yes, the factions created by the Id Card system were arbitrary, but that was the point. I needed to shake up society so much that the traditional centres of power were neutralised, allowing me to fill the vacuum and engineer my great reset. I still needed allies in big business and the government, of course, which was where Ray Payshus and Sue Percilious came in, but Payshus seems to have gone native at that school of his and Percilious lacked the will to do what was necessary. When push came to shove they were weak, so good riddance to them."

"Shit, man, that was a fucking long game you were playing. So you're saying you set up the Payshus interview in order to have the Destructive Greed report, which then led to the Id Card scheme and the factions and the breakdown of society. Damn, that's a lot of moving parts."

"Much as I'd like to say I orchestrated every last detail, that wasn't the case. It's very difficult to seize power in a stable environment. You need to throw a healthy dose of chaos and misery in there and then be the knight in shining armour promising to restore order. I calculated the Payshus interview would cause considerable social upheaval, which the government would be forced to address, and then I used my contacts to steer the government towards the Id Card scheme once it went down the social engineering path. Then it was just a matter of keeping an eye on how things developed and picking the faction most suited to my purposes. Once it became clear the Canines were to be the scapegoats for all of society's ills it was inevitable that the neurotic Felines would become radicalised by their desire to crush them. The Simians were always likely to join whoever was in the ascendancy and Delphines were just irrelevant, as they remain to this day."

"And it would have all worked if it wasn't for those meddling Savages."

"Yes. If there's one lesson I've learnt it's that client groups are seldom as loyal as they should be. Some Simians and Delphines voted against their own interests, bewitched by Savage's demagoguery. Thankfully the Diademvirus not only presented the opportunity to regain control of the narrative, but to disrupt society once more in order to build back better. My mistake was leaving anything to chance, one I don't intend to repeat, which brings us back to your confession. Time is short and this is your last chance to save Amy.

"OK, OK, stay calm," said Dalston as he turned to look directly into the camera. "The audio clip uploaded, by me, to Whistleblower Hotline today, was a fake. That wasn't Iain Tegritie's voice and I have no evidence to suggest his interview with the woman who died of Diademvirus was anything other than genuine."

"Now apologise."

"I apologise for my deception and for any harm it may have caused."

"And who, therefore, should people vote for?"

"The Revolutionary Party. Happy now?"

"Yes and I will return Amy to you just as soon as my, sorry *our*, victory is secured."

There were fifteen minutes left before the close of voting and the Revolutionary Party's lead had been reduced to a percentage point ahead of the Moderate Party, but the clock was on its side.

"We might as well keep talking then I suppose," said Dalston. "Iain, it strikes me you're all about top-down power, aren't you?"

"What do you mean?" said Tegritie.

"I've learnt there are two types of people when it comes to how they interact with the world. Top-down people pick an ideal and then engineer everything else to try to achieve it. Meanwhile, bottom-up people start with a foundation of basic principles and then allow things to organically build from there. The very concept of power as you see it is top-down, because it's concentrated in one place, from where everything else is controlled. In effect you see your will as the ideal because you're a goddamn megalomaniac. That's what makes democracy so important – it's bottom up. The simple principle of one person, one vote states that everyone is absolutely equal in the ballot box and is the perfect counterbalance to top-down nutters like you."

"It is somewhat inconvenient isn't it? People sometimes need some extra help to make them choose the correct path, which is where force comes in. Nobody regrets the need for it more than I, which is why I've come to know the real mistake is to allow people any power in the first place. When I win this election my first priority will be to ensure I have no opposition whatsoever, thus freeing the country from the agony of choice."

"Now there's a fucking shock."

"I don't think you understand. Force is only required when people have the opportunity to make incorrect decisions. Eliminate that and you remove the need for force. So, you see, removing all opposition is actually the peaceful thing to do, in the long run."

"Jesus Christ, you really are a lunatic."

"On the contrary I'm the sanest person in this country, which is why it's imperative that I run it. If there must be some collateral damage in the short term, it's an acceptable price to pay. After all, you can't make an omelette without breaking eggs."

"OK Thanos, let's say you are the fucking chosen one. What if someone else comes along just as convinced they're the messiah and is just as determined to do whatever it takes to call all the shots. What happens then?"

"I would attempt to reason with them, but if that failed then conflict would be unavoidable. Once more this highlights the need to concentrate power in one place, to prevent costly war. Without any prospect of victory, your challenger would soon see sense and redirect their ambitions towards supporting me.

"So how come you lost to Savage then?"

"That's what I've been trying to make you understand. I was too soft on the Canines and allowed them to organise. Dick Savage was a product of my weakness and his rise serves as confirmation that power cannot be shared. I thought it would be enough just to persecute the Canines, but I mistakenly left them a glimmer of hope. This time I will ensure all of them are completely crushed, with just a few left to personify their defeat at branches of the Chestnut Tree Café that I intend to build. Only then will safety be ensured."

"But what if someone, regardless of their faction, doesn't want to do what you tell them to?"

"Well that would depend on their reason."

"Would it?"

"Ultimately not, I suppose, but their reason may affect which methods would be required to persuade them to comply."

"You're just a glorified playground bully at the end of the day aren't you? Everything's about pushing people around and forcing them to do what you want."

"As I keep trying to make you understand, I take no pleasure from the use of force, but regrettably it's sometimes necessary."

"...to make people do what you want."

"To make people do the right thing."

He looked Tegritie in the eyes and saw pure, unblinking zealotry. The man seemed totally convinced he was infallible. That gave him enormous strength, but Dalston had come to understand that strength without humility was brittle.

"What if you're wrong?" he asked.

"What?" said Tegritie.

"It's a simple question Iain. What if your vision is wrong? What if someone else is right? What if you're not the chosen one?"

"Don't be ridiculous."

"Why is the prospect of you being wrong ridiculous? Surely it's far more ridiculous for the rest of the world to be wrong. The only moral justification you have for imposing your will on everyone else is that you're right, so if you're not then everything collapses. So how can you be so sure you're right?"

"I just am."

"That's a bit of a shit answer, isn't it? OK then, I'm sure you're a pointless little dick. How do you like them apples?"

"I see where you're going with this Dave. Yes, ultimately it comes down to power and that alone. The only way I can prove I'm right is if I have the power to mold society according to my vision. Morality is irrelevant, there's only power. Whoever holds power by definition holds the moral high ground because they dictate its location."

"What about free speech, due process and objective truth? Surely some things are absolute and eternal, above fleeting power games."

"Nothing is absolute apart from power. With enough power I can force you to accept that black is white and up is down. Speech always has limits and consequences determined by the powerful and the same is true of due process. Just look at the many countries around the world ruled with real power – top-down as you put it – look how peaceful and efficient they are. Their leaders don't have to waste time trying to persuade and compromise; they simply make decisions and those become reality. In those countries the objective truth is what the powerful deem it to be, because they control the narrative and there is no capacity for their will to be contested. You see, there's ultimately no such thing as objective truth, only narratives imposed by force. When people are given no alternatives to choose between, concepts like truth become meaningless. Soon that will be the case here too and, in time, the people will learn to be grateful for being released from the many dilemmas and torments their supposed freedom inflicted on them. Then they will finally be free to live truly safe lives."

"I wouldn't be so sure, dude," interjected Robin. "There are only a couple of minutes to go and the Moderate Party is in the lead."

The conversation paused for everyone to fire up YouChoose on their phones once more, which revealed the Moderate Party had a lead over the Revolutionary Party of three tenths of a percentage point. It seemed the live-streamed exchange between Tegritie and Dalston had made the decisive difference. They lapsed into entranced silence as they watched the live scores and Robin filled the remaining minutes with running commentary. By the close of voting the Moderate Party's lead had extended to half a percentage point – a clear if narrow victory. Dalston cheered and high-fived Robin, who had Champagne delivered to the table.

"I guess the people didn't get the memo, mate," said Robin to Tegritie as he poured the bubbly.

Tegritie didn't seem to hear him. He was still staring at his phone.

"So, erm, that went well," said Dalston. "Turns out you're not the Messiah after all, just a very naughty boy."

Robin laughed at the jibe and the two of them clinked glasses in a mutual toast, the sound of which seemed to snap Tegritie out of his catatonia. He looked up, saw the smiling, jubilant faces of Dalston and Robin, looked at his own glass of water and backhanded it across the studio, where it eventually exploded against a wall, covering Robin's producer in glass fragments. Robin immediately jumped up to confront Tegritie, but Dalston urged him to sit back down and let him deal with it.

"What a fucking prick," said Robin.

"Who the hell do you think you are to judge me? You're not even a proper journalist," countered Tegritie.

"Maybe not, loser, but at least I don't make shit up just to get my own way."

"I didn't make anything up, I controlled the narrative. That's what you do, that's how you get power. The narrative is the truth, it's everything."

"But you didn't, did you?" said Dalston. "It turned out people aren't as gullible as you think and they can make their own minds up. This is why your moronic grand plan will never work, Iain, people would rather have difficult lives on their own terms than be forced to live in a cage made by some fucking psycho. At the end of the day you're nothing more than a regular bloke, with no more right to tell people what to do than anyone else. Your ego might think you're something special, but it turns out most of the country disagrees."

"Do you think this is over, you ignorant fool? You clearly stole the election with your lies, so we'll just have another and keep having them until we get the correct outcome."

"Jesus Christ, this is just tragic now. It's over Iain, you gave it your best shot and you fell just short, it happens. Now give me back my daughter."

"Ah, yes, thank you for reminding me. So long as I have her this most certainly isn't over. I may not have power over the country, but I very much have it over you."

Now giggling maniacally to himself, Tegritie stood up, put his hand into his trouser pocket and pulled out a car key.

"This is power Dave," said Tegritie, dangling the key across the table towards Dalston. "This is why people like me always win and people like you always lose. This key symbolises my strength and your weakness and there's nothing you can do about it."

Dalston stood up and walked slowly around the table towards Tegritie.

"So you've got Amy locked in your car, have you?" he said. "I'm going to give you one chance to give me the key, or I will take it from you. How's that for power?"

"You don't have the balls," sneered Tegritie.

By this stage everyone in the studio was standing, alarmed by the rapid escalation of tensions.

"Dave, think carefully about what you're doing," said Davina. "He's trying to provoke you into acting irrationally. If you physically attack him then how can you say you're any better than him?"

"Dev?" said Dalston, without taking his eyes from Tegritie.

"Fucking twat the cunt," said Dev.

All Dalston now saw in Tegritie was a maniac who had completely lost his composure, revealing his last card in his desperation to extract some small victory from the devastation of his plans. Freedom from Tegritie was within his grasp, all he had to do was find the strength to take it.

"I don't need to be better than him," he said, stepping forward and punching Tegritie hard in the mouth. Tegritie fell to the floor and Dalston stood over the quivering wreck of the man who would be king. He grabbed the car key from his hand and walked out of the studio to find Tegritie's car parked right outside it.

Inside, on the back seat, he could see Amy, once more separated from him by a pane of glass. When she saw him approaching she placed both of her palms against the window and shouted "Daddy!" It felt like everything that had happened since the Id Card was created was a test to see if he was worthy of being reunited with his daughter. In overcoming Tegritie, intellectually and physically, Dalston knew he had passed the final test, so he unlocked the car and opened the door.

Chapter 41 – Epilogue

When Dalston woke up, the antiseptic smell and sound of beeping machinery led him to conclude he had somehow ended up in hospital. He had no recollection of getting there or of what happened to make it necessary. He didn't seem to be in pain, but his head was swimming, so he assumed he must be emerging from some kind of anaesthetic. Unsure of his physical status, he kept his eyes closed and his body still while he gathered his thoughts. He remembered his confrontation with Iain Tegritie on the Jive Robin podcast, at the end of which he hit him in order to get his car key and free his daughter. The last thing he remembered was opening the car door to get Amy out.

The most obvious explanation was that Tegritie had attacked him and knocked him out, but that would have resulted in some kind of head injury. Just as he was contemplating trying to move an arm to inspect his skull, he heard voices he vaguely recognised but couldn't quite identify. Despite dreading what he might see, he risked opening his eyes.

The undecorated walls and guard rails around the bed he was lying on confirmed his suspicions about where was, but he needed to see the rest of the room to make sure. As soon as he raised his head he heard several people gasping and shushing, followed by a flurry of activity. Then he heard Amy's voice.

"Daddy, you're awake!" shrieked Amy, who was only prevented from throwing herself onto him by the rails.

She was closely followed by Mel, who gently restrained her. Dalston attempted to lift himself up onto his elbows but felt very weak, which he once more put down to whatever drugs he had been given. He also noticed that he was attached to a drip and what looked like a life support unit, so Tegritie must have really lamped him. He started to enquire what had happened but his throat was incredibly dry and his voice so hoarse it was unintelligible. Observing this, Mel poured some water into a small plastic beaker and lifted it to his mouth. He drank gratefully and gasped with relief.

He heard another familiar voice say they were going to get a doctor. By the time he finished his water and collapsed back onto his pillows, which had been adjusted to prop up his head, he noticed his parents had approached his bed. Both of them were crying. Mel made the executive decision to lower the guard rail and Amy fell immediately into Dalston's embrace, at which time they both started crying uncontrollably.

"I thought you were never going to wake up," said Amy, between sobs.

That confirmed his suspicion he had somehow been seriously injured, but he could still see no bandages or feel any pain.

"What happened?" he croaked.

Mel and his parents exchanged furtive looks.

"Don't you remember?" asked Mel.

"I was doing the podcast with Tegritie and he had Amy locked in a car. So I got the key off him and the last thing I remember is going to get Amy out of the car."

Another round of looks was exchanged and he gave Amy one more squeeze before he released her from his hug. Finally making physical contact with his daughter had restored some of his strength, such that he was now able to raise himself up on his elbows. Once he did he could see his friends Jack Morrison and Al Blake across the room.

"Lads!" Dalston cried.

They approached the bed and each shook his hand.

"Great to hear your voice again, mate," said Morrison.

"Can someone tell me what the fuck is going on?"

At that moment Nick Georgiou entered the room along with the doctor he had summoned.

"Hey Nick," said Dalston.

"Hey Dave, looking good, my friend," said Georgiou, before giving ground to the doctor.

The rest of Dalston's family and friends also retreated to allow the doctor to pull a curtain around the bed and begin her examination.

"So are you going to tell me what happened to put me in here?" said Dalston.

"Do you have no memory of it at all?" said the doctor as she took his pulse.

"I just remember going to get Amy out of a car and the next thing I know I'm in hospital, with everyone acting like they know something I don't."

"How long ago was it that you were getting Amy out of the car?"

"It feels like it was just a minute ago."

"Hmm," said the doctor, while looking into his eyes for an uncomfortably long time, before continuing her checks.

"Mister Dalston I'm going to tell you something you may find difficult to accept but is nonetheless true," she said eventually. "You've been in a coma for several months."

"Fuck off!"

"It's common for people emerging from comas to feel disoriented and dislocated. Take as long as you need."

"Look, there must be some mistake, there's no way I've been unconscious for more than a few hours. Are you sure you've got the right bloke?"

"Yes."

"But it doesn't make any sense. I mean…"

"I wasn't here when you were brought in, but I'm very familiar with your records. When you were released you were already in a catatonic state, but otherwise physically unharmed. You've been a bit of a mystery, to be honest."

"You said released. From what?"

"Ah, so I did. Look, I don't really know the details but you were apparently held captive for some time before you arrived here. Our assumption has been that whatever you experienced during that period was sufficiently traumatic to effectively shut your brain down in self defence. I'm afraid I don't know anything about the circumstances of your captivity, but maybe your friends and family can shed some light on it."

The doctor finished her examination and pulled back the curtains.

"He seems to be in good physical health," the doctor told Dalston's well-wishers. "But he is very disoriented and seems to have no recollection of the circumstances that brought him here. I think the best thing for him is to be with people he knows and trusts, but please be patient and gentle; he has a lot of catching up to do."

"OK I'm freaking out here," he said after the doctor left. "Hands up who wants to tell me what the hell is going on."

Everyone appeared to be waiting for someone else to take charge and eventually Nick Georgiou stepped forward.

"What did the doc say, mate?" said Georgiou.

"That I've been in a coma for fucking months, man. She's talking shit, right?"

"I wish she was. We thought you were never going to pull through..."

When Georgiou's eyes welled up Dalston knew he meant it. He extended his hand and Georgiou held it tightly. Dalston beckoned for everyone else to return to his bedside and he hugged them all in turn, with Amy refusing to disengage from hers. There wasn't a dry eye in the house. Once tissues had been deployed and composure regained, he turned once more to Georgiou.

"OK mate, it looks like you've volunteered to tell me what I presume everyone else knows. Don't be shy, I can handle it."

"Alright, what's the last thing you remember?"

"The podcast I did with Iain Tegritie when I lamped him to get his car key and free Amy. It was Jive Robin's show and I had Davina Jones and Dev Sharma with me."

"Mate, apart from Amy I don't even know who those people are. Maybe you met them before you were captured or something."

"There we go again. The doctor mentioned me being released and now you're talking about me being captured. I've got no memory of any of that shit so how about we start there, yeah?"

"OK. The last time anyone saw you was in your office. At some time between you leaving and the next morning, when your colleagues started asking Jack if he knew where you were, you disappeared. Nobody had a fucking scooby, your phone was turned off and it looked like you never made it home."

"Jesus. How long ago was that?"

"Like, June, mate. It's November now."

"So I've been in a coma for five months?"

"At least three or four, because it was weeks before you turned up here."

"You say 'turned up...'"

"You were dumped at Accident and Emergency. They just found you in a heap, already out for the count."

"Jesus Christ. Do we know who brought me here?"

"Not for sure, but we've got a pretty good idea. There's this group of domestic terrorists that call themselves The Chosen Ones. They reckon some random higher power has given them the responsibility of making the world a better place, or some shit like that, and they are convinced that if they fail the world will be destroyed soon."

"But what have I done to piss them off?"

"I don't know mate, but they seem to have a thing for City boys. A few have even joined them, but a bunch of others have disappeared and then turned up like you did."

"So, what, they're like anti-capitalists or something?"

"Sort of, I guess, but this lot take it to another level. They've decided traditional methods of protest and activism aren't getting the job done and trying to persuade people is futile anyway, so instead they just kidnap and brainwash them. From what I've heard they subject their victims to relentless psychological torture in order to completely erase their identity, then they try to replace it with a new one entirely given over to their ideology. The Chosen Ones seem to think a person is either cut out for enlightenment or they're not. If they come around to their way of thinking then great, but if the process breaks or kills them then that just proves they're beyond salvation."

"Fuck, that's hardcore. Have any of these pricks ever been caught?"

"Yeah, a few, but they haven't been around very long. I read they're made up of people who got kicked out of other activist groups for being too full-on. They don't seem to have a specific cause and they'll take anyone, commies, tree huggers, identitarians, anarchists, whoever, so long as they're prepared to do what it takes. The problem is there just aren't enough total nutcases around, so they had to start making them."

"But why, if they don't even have a cause?"

"I think they just hate the world and want to burn it down. They feel like losers at the game of life and want to flip the board over. I would call them nihilists, but I don't think that's how they perceive themselves. They reckon they're building something, but they just don't know what it is yet. What they do know is that things are shit and they wouldn't be if they were in charge, so they're building an army to mobilise once they've worked out what the fuck their grand plan is. Or maybe they're just miserable bastards trying to bring everyone down to their level. One of the biggest sources of pain and suffering in the world is pricks like them who haven't got the balls to take responsibility for their own lives."

"Yeah, there's a lot of that about. So you reckon they broke me, which is why I've been in a coma?"

"Seems the most likely explanation."

"But why don't I remember any of it, then?"

"Maybe your brain has shut it out to protect itself."

"I guess so, but then what about all the recent memories I do have?"

"Like this podcast you think you were on?"

"Yes, it feels like only yesterday."

"Maybe it was," said Amy, her head resting on his chest.

His parents shushed their granddaughter, but he intervened.

"No, let's hear her out," he said. "What do you mean, baby?"

"You know how when you have a dream you think it's real while it's happening? And sometimes even after you wake up it takes a little while before you realise it's not real. So maybe what you remember is what you were dreaming about just before you woke up."

The room went silent. All eyes were on Dalston as he stared into the middle distance, processing Amy's suggestion.

"Mel, have you ever heard of a bloke called Iain Tegritie?" he asked eventually.

"Integrity?" said Mel. "Not only have I not heard of a bloke called it, I don't know many who even have it."

"What about Ray Payshus or Sue Percilious?"

"What is this, Snow White and the seven dwarves?"

"OK then, Davina Jones and Dev Sharma. I must have mentioned them. Anyone?"

His assembled friends and relatives all shook their heads sombrely, with his Mum suggesting he should try to get some rest.

"Sounds like I've had plenty of rest, Mum," he said. "I feel fine and, anyway, I don't think I'm going to be able to rest until I've got to the bottom of what happened to me."

"Was I in your dreams Daddy?" said Amy.

"You certainly were, baby. In fact, now I come to think of it, you were a constant."

"I visited you every day after school and held your hand and talked to you. I knew you were just really fast asleep, so I tried to give you reasons to wake up. I even played music you like in case you could hear it."

Tears formed in Dalston's eyes at the love and devotion his daughter had shown him and they were soon matched by his entourage, with even his mates blinking furiously and looking around the room for suddenly-lost items.

"Come to think of it you all made an appearance," he said, laughing at the spectacle as he wiped his eyes with the back of his hand. "I remember chatting to you lads in the pub and having a row with Jack."

"That might be a real memory to be fair, mate," said Morrison.

"And I fell out with you too, Mum, but we also made up."

"I'm pleased to hear it Davey," she said, squeezing his hand.

"So do you reckon all those other people were just figments of my imagination then?"

"Sounds like it, man," said Al Blake. "Why don't you tell us what you remember?"

Dalston spent the next ten minutes narrating fragments of what he was increasingly coming to accept were his comatose dreams. As he described the Id Card it occurred to him there might be a structure and meaning to his unconscious experiences. If the aim of his captors was to dismantle his identity, then maybe the purpose of his imaginary adventures was to rebuild it. Did his psyche synthesise a scenario in which everyone was defined by their most fundamental drives in order to force him to draw upon his own?

But his recent experiences amounted to so much more and he was undoubtedly a different person as a result of them. Maybe the old Dave Dalston didn't have what it took to heal from the kind of psychological injuries he had sustained. Only by evolving and developing a much more robust self image could he undo the damage done and find the courage to return to a world that had previously inflicted so much suffering on him.

Morrison laughed as Dalston recounted memories of his turbulent time at Gold & Mackenzie, including their falling out, while all three of his friends were delighted to have featured so prominently. The regular appearances of Iain Tegritie and Jive Robin were a mystery until Blake suggested they stood for deception and honesty. Which led to speculation that all the mystery characters might be archetypes of concepts Dalston needed to resolve his relationship with. They also suggested the political scenarios he described represented his struggle to reassert his identity as an individual. His experiences with Whistleblower Hotline and Frank's Gym seemed to be further attempts to restore a sense of autonomy and individual agency, while the appearance of family members, especially Amy, probably represented a growing desire to get back to the real world

"It was like you appeared every time I started losing hope or going down the wrong path, baby," Dalston told Amy. "As if you were parachuted into my dreams to guide me."

"Maybe it was because I was here so much," said Amy. "Maybe you could sort of hear me and feel me holding your hand."

"Could be, but in addition I think you gave me the motivation to fight. Much as I love everyone in this room, you're extra special. I want to protect you and be the best Dad in the world for you. Maybe that's what gave me the courage to leave my coma and face the world again."

"Do you think that's why you woke up when you rescued me?"

"I'm sure you're right, you clever thing. I slayed the dragon and rescued the damsel in distress, didn't I?"

"Yes," said Amy, who threw her arms around his neck for their biggest hug yet.

"It sounds like you've been on a hell of a journey," said Georgiou.

"Just a bit, mate," said Dalston. "And do you what? I feel great. It's hard to describe, but everything just seems so much simpler now."

"Careful, everyone will be wanting to give comas a go if you keep bigging them up so much," said Blake.

"Good point Al, I'll be sure to tell everyone else what a nightmare it was. But there's no getting past the fact that I'm a changed man. Jack, I don't think I can go back to working at Gold & Mackenzie now I've realised what a load of bollocks it all is."

"If you had to go into a coma to work that out then you're even thicker than I thought," said Morrison. "Most of the people there see it for what it is, we just put up with it to pay the bills, innit."

"Well, that's just it, man. I don't think I'm prepared to anymore."

"Fair enough. So what are you going to do instead, once you're up and about?"

"Good question. I've got some cool ideas from my dreams, but all I really want to do is spend as much time with this little life-saver as I can and spoil her rotten. Apart from that I think I'll just take it one day at a time and see what life has in store for me. I might even start by writing about my experiences," said Dave Dalston.

Printed in Great Britain
by Amazon